Celebrations a

Francesca Capaldi has enjoyed writing since she was a child, largely influenced by a Welsh mother who was good at improvised story telling. She is a member of the RNA and the Society of Women Writers and Journalists. Francesca currently lives in Kent with her family and a cat called Lando Calrissian.

Also by Francesca Capaldi

Wartime in the Valleys

Heartbreak in the Valleys
War in the Valleys
Hope in the Valleys
Trouble in the Valleys

The Beach Hotel Series

A New Start at the Beach Hotel
All Change at the Beach Hotel
Dark Days at the Beach Hotel
Love and Loss at the Beach Hotel
Stormy Skies at the Beach Hotel
Celebrations at The Beach Hotel

Celebrations
at the
Beach Hotel

Francesca Capaldi

hera

Penguin
Random
House

First published in the United Kingdom in 2026 by

Hera Books, an imprint of
Canelo Digital Publishing Limited,
20 Vauxhall Bridge Road,
London SW1V 2SA
United Kingdom

A Penguin Random House Company
The authorised representative in the EEA is Dorling Kindersley Verlag GmbH.
Arnulfstr. 124, 80636 Munich, Germany

Copyright © Francesca Capaldi 2026

A CIP catalogue record for this book is available from the British Library.

Print ISBN 978 1 80436 849 7
Ebook ISBN 978 1 80436 850 3

Cover design by Diane Meacham

Cover images © Shutterstock.com; Dreamstime.com

Printed and bound in Great Britain by Clays Ltd, Elcograf S.p.A.

Look for more great books at
www.herabooks.com | www.dk.com

1

Dedicated to Lorenzo Capaldi, my paternal grandfather, killed in action in World War One in December 1915

Cast of Characters

Annie Twine: head scullery maid
Alice Twine: scullery maid
Lorcan Foley: Irish porter, returned from war
Jasper Jupp: porter, returned from war

Helen Bygrove: manageress of the Beach Hotel
Dorothy and Arthur Bygrove: Helen's children
Edie Moore: a baron's daughter, but now undermanageress
Charlie Cobbett: porter, returned from war, Edie's sweetheart
Mrs Imogen Leggett: housekeeper
Bridget Turnbull: storekeeper, from Tyneside
Gertie Green: head portress
Günther Schultz: German waiter
Lili Probert: Welsh head waitress
Fanny Bullen: head chambermaid

Rhodri Morgan: Lili's Welsh fiancé, returned from war
Walter Lehman: Fanny's American fiancé

DI Samuel Toshack: Helen Bygrove's fiancé
His staff at the police station:
Sergeant Barry Gardner, Alice and Annie's uncle
Constable Twort

PC Yates and PC Clampitt

Superintendent Harold Crooke, based at the police station in Arundel

Stanley and Leslie Morris: porters, returned from war

Peter Smith: waiter, returned from war
Johnny and Jerry Winborn: waiters, returned from war
Simon Lane and Dennis Ward: young waiters

Richard Watkins: head desk clerk
Stuart Coulter: desk clerk, returned from war

Mrs Nellie Norris: head cook
Joseph Norris: Nellie's son, head chef, returned from war
Will Fletcher: former chef who came out of retirement in the war
Jack Sinden: chef who was unable to fight due to flat feet

Phoebe Sweeton: head stillroom maid
Hetty Affleck: former head stillroom maid, engaged to Victor Perryman
Tilly and Milly: stillroom maids
Finn and Lucas: scullery lads

Vera Edge: nursemaid to the Bygrove children and Fanny's daughter Elsie
Amanda Lovelock: WPC during the war, returned to the hotel as bookkeeper
Major Thomas: long-term guest at the hotel

Killed in action:

Alex Tuppen, chef
James Wood, porter
Anton Martin, waiter
Alan Drew, head porter

Prologue

'Get a move on with that drying,' said Annie Twine, the head scullery maid at the Beach Hotel, pouring more hot water into the sink from a large copper kettle she'd heated on the small stove in the room.

'There must be loads of people in for dinner tonight,' said her younger sister Alice, clutching a tea towel and looking despairingly at the mound of crockery, cutlery and pans piled high on the long worktop, still needing to be washed and dried. There was barely any room for the dried items which were also piling up.

'The declaration of war ten days back ain't put people off dining out, that's for sure. Maybe they want to enjoy themselves while they can, before things start kicking off.'

'What d'ya mean, start kicking off? The battle with the Germans is taking place in Belgium, not here.'

'Dunno, but men are enlisting right, left and centre. Who knows what'll happen. I just 'ope our brothers don't feel they have to join the fray. They're daft enough.'

Alice tutted and looked heavenward. 'Everyone's daft to you.'

'Don't look like Lorcan got back for staff dinner. Ain't he taking over from Charlie in the foyer this evening?'

'Dunno,' said Alice. 'We'd 'ave seen him come through 'ere if he'd come this way. You keeping tabs on him or something? Or are you worried about him?' She raised her eyebrows and nudged her sister.

'No, course not. He's a grown man and can look out for himself.' She frowned at her sister as she rinsed a plate in the second sink. 'Just heard him say this morning that he 'ad a shift this evening.'

'The lady doth protest too much, methinks,' Alice chirped in an imitation of the posh accents often heard at the hotel.

'Do stop yapping and get drying a bit quicker.' Annie clattered the next plate onto the wooden draining board.

'I wouldn't blame you. He's good looking and very easy going.'

'Shh! He ain't my type.' She lowered her voice. 'And anyway, what's wrong with you? He's walking out with Hetty, ain't he.' She looked towards the small room next to the scullery, where the head stillroom maid worked.

'Is he? I didn't know that.'

'It only started recently.' Annie relived the painful twinge she'd felt when she'd first found out.

'Wouldn't 'ave thought he was Hetty's type… Since Lorcan ain't come in this way, I s'pose it's possible he's gone in the front way.'

'What, through the foyer? Mr Watkins would do his nut. I made that mistake only once.' She squeezed in her lips and looked sternly at Alice, doing an imitation of the head desk clerk while bobbing her head back and forth. 'Mr Foley, you know you are *not* allowed in the guest entrance. Now turn around and go back to the staff gate.'

Alice laughed. 'You do that *too* well.'

They went quiet and continued with their chores. Annie pictured Lorcan. He was good looking, as Alice had said, with his thick black hair and large blue eyes. He was tall and sturdy. She had to face it, even if he hadn't been walking out with Hetty Affleck, who was the head stillroom maid, he was more likely to be interested in Alice than her, with her long, dark blonde hair and bright blue eyes. She regarded her reflection briefly in a pan she picked up to wash. She was mousy haired with dull eyes, neither one colour nor another. Her mother always described her as having light brown hair with golden highlights and greenish-hazel eyes, but she was just being kind.

As she placed the pan in the water, ready to wash up, there was a clatter outside, and she leant forward to see what it was. She saw a figure lumbering through the yard. 'There's Lorcan. Blimey, he looks the worse for wear.'

A moment later, the door flew open and Lorcan almost fell in. He soon straightened himself. She could smell the alcohol from where she was standing.

'Ah, hello Lorcan, there you are,' said Annie, smiling. 'Why are you so late for dinner tonight? Have you been doing something—'

Lorcan ignored her, striding ahead to the stillroom. Alice laughed just before they heard Hetty's voice questioning him.

'What's so funny?' Annie's smile had gone. She felt hurt to be ignored so completely by Lorcan. 'He'll get into trouble with Mr Watkins. And gawd knows what Mr Bygrove'll say if he catches him. 'Specially as he seems to 'ave been drinking.'

'I know. It's just, you've gone the deepest shade of red I've ever seen anyone go.'

'Well, he was rude, ignoring me. He ain't normally rude. He's normally one of the politest of the men.'

'You've gone red because he ignored you? Don't seem likely. I reckon you've liked him for a while.'

'Oh, do be quiet, Alice in Wonderland!'

'Why 'ave you started calling me that?'

''Cos your mind is always wandering, making up stories, like you're in your own "Wonderland". And you're blonde with a blue ribbon, like Alice in the illustration in the book. You're eighteen now and it'd be more proper to wear your hair up.'

She hadn't meant to turn her explanation into a rant, but she was irritated with her sister for going on about Lorcan.

'Times are changing. Just 'cos you're an old lady at nineteen, don't mean I 'ave to be.'

Annie didn't reply to this immediately. Sometimes she did feel like an old lady, looking out for her brothers, who were all in their early twenties and older than her, along with her sister. It was like she was the oldest in the family.

'Sorry, Alice. There's just too much to do in 'ere this evening and it don't help that the scullery lad's off sick. We could do with someone to get this lot back to the various places they belong.' She surveyed the mound of dried crockery, glassware, cutlery and pans on the end of the worktop.

'I'll take the pans back to the kitchen, as they're taking up the most room.'

Alice held the handles of several in each hand, then struggled through the stillroom door on her way to the staff corridor. While she was gone, Annie stopped and dried a few things, since there was no room for anything else. When Alice returned, they carried on in silence.

Gertie Green entered twenty minutes later, with a pile of plates and crockery from the late staff dinner. 'You'll never guess what's just 'appened.'

Annie turned wearily towards the chambermaid, not in the mood for gossip. 'Mr Bygrove's employed more scullery staff to help us out?'

'No. Lorcan's only gone and enlisted.'

'He's what?'

'Maybe that's why he smelt of booze,' said Alice.

'Bygrove didn't 'alf give 'im some stick for turning up late, and threatened to throw 'im out, so he told 'im he could do what he liked 'cos he'd enlisted. He's off to training tomorrow.'

Annie's heart sank. That meant he'd be going away. He might even be killed. She felt sick at the thought. 'He's an idiot!' she declared, not wanting to give her real emotions away.

'Wouldn't mind betting he'll be the first of many to sign up, you wait and see,' said Gertie. 'The young porters, waiters and chefs, they'll all be gone.'

'Jasper wouldn't be daft enough to do something like that,' said Alice, sounding very sure of herself. 'He's always been the most sensible of them.'

'I wouldn't have 'ad money on Lorcan enlisting, but he 'as. I'd better get back as I'm on bed turndown.'

'And I'd better get some of this crockery back for storage.' Alice's mouth was turned down at the corners and she'd lost the cheerful manner she'd had before Gertie came in. She picked up a pile of dinner plates and left the room once more.

Annie was glad Alice hadn't carried on talking about the enlistments, and was relieved to be on her own for a while. She'd long suspected that Alice possessed a soft spot for Jasper, so that was maybe why her mood had dipped.

She plunged her hands back into the water and continued to wash up. She couldn't wait to get home later this evening and go straight to bed, to have a good weep, albeit a silent one, since she shared a room with Alice.

Chapter One

Alice led the way into the staff dining room at the late afternoon tea break on a wet, February afternoon, Annie dragging herself along just behind. She was glad to see the roaring flames in the substantial fireplace on the long side of the wall. The large window, situated to the left on the short wall, revealed the gloom of a day that had never really seemed to get light.

'Oh boy, I'll be glad to take the weight off me feet for a while,' said Alice, as she sat next to head waitress Lili Probert.

'Not been that busy today, it 'asn't,' said Lili in her Welsh lilt. 'Afternoon tea's been very quiet.'

Annie slumped down on the bench opposite them. 'We 'ad a whole load of new posh crockery to wash up, that Mrs Bygrove's just bought.'

'No point in moaning about it,' said the housekeeper, Imogen Leggett, sitting in her special chair at the end of the table opposite the window. She pressed her lips together and peered at them over the spectacles she hadn't long acquired for reading. 'At least she's been able to afford it. It wasn't that long ago we feared we'd have to close all together.'

'I s'pose you're right,' Annie conceded.

'Of course, there *is* still much to moan about, even with the war over, but it's taking place outside our walls.' Mrs Leggett lifted the newspaper she was reading. 'There are general strikes and riots all over the place, and no sooner do we finish a war with parts of Europe, then we embark on one with Ireland. Goodness knows what our men will be coming home to, when they're finally demobilised. It's certainly not the peaceful homecoming they'd wish for.'

Annie picked up the pot and poured herself a cup of tea. 'I wonder what Lorcan'll make of the war in Ireland.'

'I guess we'll find out when the government *finally* releases him from the army, along with all the other men.'

'You're quiet, Günther,' Alice said to the German waiter, sitting with his head in *The Weekly News*. He'd always been someone who'd said little, even before the war, but since he'd returned from Newbury internment camp, he'd not said a word unless spoken to. She always tried to include him in conversations, so he didn't feel left out or ignored.

'I am sorry to be rude. I was rather involved with an article here,' he said in his very precise accent.

'You weren't being rude, Mr Schultz,' said Mrs Leggett. 'We just want to make sure that you feel at home here, after what happened.'

Alice knew that the housekeeper was referring to the day, near the beginning of the war, when Günther was hauled away by the police after being reported by an anti-German guest, even though he'd been naturalised. He should have registered as an alien at the police station but hadn't got around to it, and had consequently been interned for the duration of the war.

'I am most grateful to Mrs Bygrove, and to you all, for accepting me back after they released me. I have been welcomed back also by the guests who remember me from before the war, though I fear not all the guests will feel the same. And when the men return to work here, as a couple are today, and a couple tomorrow, they may not welcome me after their experiences.'

'Then they're just being ignorant,' said Alice. 'You didn't do nothing to no one.'

'I agree with Miss Twine,' said the housekeeper. 'Though *I* would say that you didn't do *anything* to *anyone*. The male staff here had nothing but respect for you before you were taken away, and I'm sure that won't have changed. And just think, Miss Sweeton will be back in the stillroom tomorrow, after her stint with the Women's Land Army. You must be looking forward to that.'

Günther and Phoebe Sweeton had been walking out for a short while before he'd been taken away. Alice had felt sad for Phoebe when it had happened.

'Yes, I am very much looking forward to seeing Phoebe once more. Her letters over the years have kept me going, and I have been most grateful for them.' He closed the magazine and stood. 'Now, if you will excuse me, I am going to get started on laying up the dining room for dinner.' He bowed his head and left.

When he'd gone, Alice said, 'He's even more of a loner than before the war. Four-and-a-half years ago that was. Hardly seems possible.'

The housekeeper tutted loudly, several times. 'It was a disgrace, them marching him away that day, the way they did.'

'You said Phoebe's coming back to the stillroom, Mrs Leggett. She isn't going back to being a waitress then, as she was before she left?'

'No. She is one of the female staff who will go back to what they did originally.'

'Talking of the men returning,' said Annie, 'what's happening about Gertie? We 'aven't heard if she'll stay as head portress, or whether Charlie'll take that role back on.'

'I don't know if Mrs Bygrove has made a decision about that yet,' said the housekeeper. 'Though goodness knows when he and the other men in his battalion will be sent back.'

'Who's that?' said Edie Moore, the undermanageress, in her upper-class accent, as she entered the room with Mrs Norris, the head cook.

'I was referring to Mr Cobbett,' said the housekeeper. 'Along with the other men sent out to Russia.'

Edie's usually upright stance slumped a little. 'Charlie says in his letters that they're still having to sort things out there, whatever that means. I suppose it's the same for many of the men still in France and Belgium. I will be *immensely* glad when he returns though.'

Alice turned to her sister. 'Who are *you* looking forward to coming back?' she said, teasing.

Annie narrowed her eyes. 'No one in particular. All of 'em, 'cos they'll be safe. Especially our other two brothers, of course, what are also in Russia. As far as the hotel's concerned, let's face it, we've been doing fine without 'em.'

'I don't think we 'ave. We've been short staffed the whole time, even with replacing some of them with women.'

'So, who would *you* like to see return soon?' Annie gave her a look that told Alice she was getting her own back.

'Our brothers. And, like you said, all of 'em. Then things'll get back to normal.'

'I'm not sure what normal is any more,' said Edie, sitting on the bench next to Lili. 'Things have moved on for women, and I do wonder how the men will cope with that.'

'Well, I know who *I* wanta see back.' Mrs Norris crossed her arms under her bosom.

'Your Joseph?' said Alice.

'Yep. Though I might end up falling out with me son over who's in charge of the kitchen now. At least supplies are starting to get back to normal, even if nothing else is.'

Edie looked at her watch. 'Stanley and Leslie Morris should be in soon for their first shift in the foyer for nearly three years. And for the men returning tomorrow, it's been even longer – well over four years. It will probably be very strange for them all.'

'And for us,' said Alice.

'I dare say it will be better having the men back in stages,' said Mrs Leggett. 'All of them coming back at the same time would be quite overwhelming.'

'Either way, there'll be a lot of adjusting,' said the cook. 'And it'll take a while for everyone.'

The door opened a smidgeon, and two heads peeped around the doorway.

'Come on, come in,' said Edie, beckoning them.

The Morris brothers entered in porter's uniforms to a cheerful welcome from those sitting there. Although twins and sharing a likeness, with their high cheekbones and fair hair, they were not identical and were quite easy to tell apart.

'We're so grateful to Mrs Bygrove for 'aving us back,' said Stanley.

Leslie carried on with, 'We didn't know what'd happen to the hotel when we heard there'd been… um, bad news, about her husband.'

'That was nearly two years ago now,' said Helen, entering behind them. 'We've been through some difficult times, but we've all moved on.' She stood tall and straight, looking defiant. 'Everyone knew he was a bully and that our marriage was not a match made in heaven.'

Alice scanned the room, noting that they all looked as surprised as she felt. Everybody knew this was the case, but Mrs Bygrove had never voiced it this clearly before.

'Anyway,' said Helen, 'we are all glad to see you back, Stanley and Leslie. Get yourselves a cup of tea, and then I'll show you around and tell you what changes have occurred since you left. I will return shortly.' Having turned halfway in the opposite direction, she twisted back. 'Oh, yes, I forgot to tell you that Gertie Green is head portress now.'

'Until the others get home, I suppose,' said Stanley as he took a seat on the bench.

'No, for the foreseeable future, since we have lost poor Alan Drew.'

The two young men regarded each other with surprise.

'But Charlie took over as head porter when Alan enlisted. Isn't he coming back?' Leslie asked.

'As far as I am aware, yes. Now, I have something to do, but I will be back soon.' This time she did leave.

Leslie frowned at his brother, who shrugged and pulled a face, before they each took a seat.

Stanley took the cup and saucer offered to him by Mrs Leggett. 'To be honest, I'm glad to see the back of Bygrove. I know that sounds awful, and I wouldn't 'ave wanted to say it in front of his missus, but he did bully her something rotten, and the rest of us. Sorry if that's out of turn.'

'No, Mr Morris,' said the housekeeper. 'It's quite true and we all agree. But thank you for not saying it in front of Mrs Bygrove.'

'She's got a new sweetheart now,' said Alice. 'Detective Inspector Sam Toshack is a much nicer man, and a better match for her, I think.'

'He certainly is, Miss Twine. And jolly nice looking too.'

'Mrs Leggett!' said the sisters together. Alice added, 'That's not like you. We get told off if we say things like that.'

'I know. But it is true.'

'You're a dark horse, Mrs Leggett,' said Edie.

Everyone around the table laughed and the house-keeper looked a little embarrassed, but smiled, neverthe-less.

'And you'll not recognise Dorothy and Arthur now,' said Alice, referring to Helen's two children. 'They've grown so much. Dorothy's now ten.'

'Ten?' Leslie's face was a picture.

'Yes, and Arthur'll be nine at the end of the month.'

'There's going to be a lot to get used to,' said Stanley, looking a little concerned.

'Yes, I believe there will be,' Mrs Leggett confirmed.

–

Ten days later, there was an air of expectation in the staff dining room, as Annie entered for her morning break with Johnny Winborn in tow, who'd now returned to the hotel as a waiter with his older brother, Jerry. Phoebe Sweeton had also returned and was sitting at the end of the table with her arm through Günther's. Both looked content, making Annie feel a little envious, even though she was pleased for them.

'What's going on here?' said Johnny. 'You all seem a bit excited.'

Lili patted the bench space next to her, indicating he should sit down. She had a small child on her lap.

'And who's this?' said Johnny, pointing to the tot. 'Didn't know you'd 'ad a kid, Lili.'

'Elsie's not mine, she's Fanny's.'

'Oh yes, I 'eard about that. She's marrying some American bloke too.'

'That's right. Walter. Fanny went out early this morning to meet 'im at the station. He 'ad to go 'ome to the United States with the rest of the carpenters from the Rustington aerodrome when the war finished, but he wanted to come back and settle down with Fanny for good, here in Littlehampton. Isn't that romantic? They should be back any moment, I reckon.'

'*If* he arrived,' said Gertie, frowning.

'Of course he'll arrive, dead keen, he were, that were obvious from his letters.'

'And he was clearly thrilled to be back with Fanny the day war ended,' Annie added. 'When she brought him back 'ere after, I've never seen no one as excited as him to be with someone.'

Annie so wished that she had someone special she was meeting at the station today. Although she used the word 'someone' to herself, it was Lorcan she pictured, standing on the courtyard outside the station, that appealing smile of his in place. Her stomach flipped at the thought.

14

'I suppose I'm just worried for Fanny. I really don't want 'er to be disappointed again.'

Annie patted Gertie on the shoulder. 'She's ya best friend, so that's understandable.' She took a seat next to her, nodding her head towards Phoebe and Günther, where they were making eyes at each other, smiling.

Lili touched her heart and smiled, before pouring the newcomers a cup of tea each. 'I 'ope Fanny gets back soon so we can say 'ello to Walter. Nice it'll be, to make 'im feel welcome. And what better day to be meeting back up with your sweetheart than Valentine's Day.'

'Did you get a card from your Rhodri?' Annie asked.

'Ooh yes, a lovely one it is, with roses. I'll show you later.'

'Don't seem fair, somehow,' said Johnny. 'Foreign men getting to know the girls here while we was away. Walter, I mean, of course. Not Rhodri.'

'Not unless you count us Welsh as being foreign!' Lili chuckled.

'I'm sure the ladies'll be glad to see you all back now, lad,' said Bridget Turnbull, the storekeeper, looking up from her sewing. Annie had always loved her melodic Geordie accent. 'It's not like there were enough Americans came over for all the lasses here.'

'More's the pity,' Annie added.

'Someone in my battalion made some comment about us men being in demand now because there'd be such a shortage, what with some being lost.' Johnny fiddled with his lapel. 'Didn't think that was very, I dunno…'

'Tactful?' Mrs Turnbull suggested.

'Yes, tactful. That's the word. Like it's some kind of compensation for losing so many friends and colleagues.'

The atmosphere went sombre for a few moments, before the door opened and Helen Bygrove stepped in.

'Good morning. Has Fanny returned with Walter yet?'

'No, not yet,' said Gertie.

'Do let me know when they get back. In the meantime, I have some more good news.'

Annie was grateful for this, given the turn of mood.

'I have just had word that Jasper Jupp and Lorcan Foley will be back at the beginning of March.'

Annie felt another flutter in her belly, just stopping herself from grinning stupidly and clapping her hands like an overexcited child.

'That's great news, Mrs Bygrove,' said Johnny, cheering up. 'I'm really looking forward to them all being back. Well, them what survived.' He looked troubled once more, but soon pulled himself together to say, 'Is there any word of when them in the Eleventh Sussex Battalion will be back from Russia?'

'Not as yet, Johnny.'

He looked away, nodding forlornly.

'I will leave you all to your breaktime,' said Helen, who then left the room.

'I wonder what the "beginning of March" actually means,' said Mrs Turnbull.

'I'm wondering more what it'll be like having even more men back,' said Gertie. 'Don't think the men—' she glanced at Johnny, who was staring into the distance, 'I don't think all the changes will go down well with some.'

Annie half listened as they carried on, not wanting to offer an opinion in case her eager anticipation over Lorcan's return might show. But what was the point in looking forward to it? She'd never had a chance with Lorcan in the past because he'd always been interested in

Hetty, that much she'd been able to tell, even if they had only started walking out a short time before he'd enlisted. And now, even though Hetty was betrothed to Victor, she doubted he'd ever look twice at her, boring old Annie.

The door opened once again, and Fanny peeped around it.

'You're back!' cried Gertie, rising from the bench and hurrying to her. 'Where's, I mean, is, you know...?'

Fanny came into the room. 'Is Walter 'ere? Yes.' She stepped back into the corridor. 'Come on, they won't bite. You've met some of 'em before.'

Fanny returned, holding Walter's hand, her smile so wide it made Annie smile too.

'Hi, everyone.' He looked around at those at the table, his eyes resting on Phoebe and Günther.

'Come and 'ave a cup of tea and a biscuit, lad,' said Mrs Turnbull, beckoning him over.

'Thank you, ma'am.'

'Mummeee!' Elsie called, her arms outstretched. 'And Wa'ter!'

Fanny picked her up and sat with Walter at the middle of the table. 'That's right, sweetie. I told you he was coming. Say hello.'

' 'Ello, Wa'ter!'

'Hi, honey.'

'You've met most everyone else, but this is Johnny Winborn,' said Fanny. 'He's recently got back with his brother and is a waiter.'

'Hi, Johnny.' He held out his hand and the waiter took it, mumbling a reply.

'And at the end is Phoebe, from the stillroom, and Günther, who recently— returned.'

'It's nice to meet you at last,' said Phoebe, smiling warmly. 'I've heard a lot about you.'

Günther nodded his head once. 'Welcome back, sir.'

'Thank you. Fanny has told me about you both too. Where in Germany are you from, sir?'

The waiter pushed his hand through his sandy hair, looking a little alarmed. He didn't reply at first, maybe expecting some criticism, although Walter's enquiry had been polite. 'I am from Munich, in Bavaria.'

'Not so very far from where my Lehmann ancestors came from then. They were from Stuttgart.'

Günther smiled a little. 'No, not so very far, but in the next state of Baden-Württemberg.'

'That's the one.'

'Your family are from Germany too?' Johnny frowned.

'On my father's father's father's side.' Walter looked heavenward and moved his raised forefinger sideways, as if trying to work it out. 'Or there might be one more father involved there. Anyway, that part of the family came to the States well over one hundred years ago, but we still have some of their letters and documents. There are a lotta people in the States with German heritage. Well, we're all from places other than America, of course.' He laughed. 'Apart from the native Indian folk. I've met people whose families have come from all over the world, but 'specially Europe, particularly since I became a carpenter. And my mother's family have Norwegian and French ancestry.'

Günther slid along the bench to move closer to him. 'And you are from Kansas, Fanny tells us.'

'That's right. Originally. Ran away to work as a carpenter in some large northeastern cities in the States before I was sent here to help build the aerodrome in

Rustington.' He yawned. 'Sorry, it was a long day and night on that ship, coming across the Atlantic.'

'Did you have a good journey over?' Annie asked.

'It was okay, travelling on the packet ship, but I didn't sleep much as I had to share quarters with other people.'

'Well now, you can relax in here and have as much tea as you like, pet,' said Mrs Turnbull. 'And you're staying for lunch.'

'Then I'll take you over to see your lodgings,' said Fanny. She took his hand and squeezed it as they looked lovingly at each other.

Phoebe moved up to be next to Günther once again, leaning her head on his shoulder.

As pleased as she was for the two couples, their obvious love made Annie sad once more that she didn't have someone to be that cosy with. Her mother had pointed out to her a few days back that she'd soon be twenty-four and had never had a sweetheart. *It's high time you had a husband*, she'd added. *And about time I had some grandchildren.* Then her father had lent his support to her argument. Annie, in turn, had pointed out that the war hadn't helped matters, but still it had made her feel… unwanted. She didn't desire a sweetheart for her parents' sake but longed for one for herself.

It wasn't quite true anyway, that she hadn't had a sweetheart, if she could call him that. As an eighteen-year-old, she'd walked out for a couple of weeks with a boy she'd liked, but he'd soon moved on to another girl in the next street. Her mother hadn't known about any of that though. She'd only told Alice after it was all over.

Mrs Turnbull lifted her hand to look at her wristwatch. 'And that, folks, is the end of our break, I'm afraid. The next lot will be comin' in soon, so we'd better get cleared up. Except you three.' She pointed at Fanny, Elsie and Walter. 'You keep helpin' yourselves.'

The rest of them stood. Johnny left without a word. Mrs Turnbull went to pick up her cup and saucer.

'Don't worry about the china,' said Annie, 'I'll take it all back to the scullery with me.'

'Thank you, pet. Oh, I'd better let Mrs Bygrove know about Fanny and Walter's return.'

Getting back to work would help her escape the love-birds' happiness, and she knew that Alice would be keen to know that Fanny and Walter had returned. And she might be happy to know that Jasper was returning soon too.

'See you all later,' she said, as she picked up a tray from the dresser to load up with crockery.

—

Annie entered the staff dining room for early dinner to find the porters Leslie and Stanley sitting at one end of the table, engaged in lively conversation with waiters Johnny and Jerry, while Günther was sitting up the other end on his own, reading a book. She felt awkward, not knowing where to sit. The men might not welcome a female butting in on their conversation, and Günther might not want to be disturbed as he read. She compromised and sat in the middle, with neither group, knowing that other women would be in soon, but hoping she didn't look unfriendly.

Nobody had bothered to put the cutlery out, so Annie rose to collect it from the dresser, tutting to herself. As she laid it out, she realised that the conversation was more fervent than lively, as the four men discussed the parts they'd played in the war with some passion.

'It was awful, *awful*,' said Johnny, describing a particularly gruesome day during a battle.

Annie fetched the cruets and then the plates as they carried on talking. She knew such experiences must be hard to get over, but she wished they'd at least waited for a time when Günther wasn't around. No wonder he was as far away as possible, with his head in a book.

When she reached their end of the table, they ignored her initially, until Leslie looked up and smiled as he took a plate from her. The others took one each too, but didn't look at her and didn't thank her.

Annie was relieved when Alice entered, and behind her Jack Sinden, who was second chef in the absence of Joseph. He brought in a salver of pies, while a couple of other kitchen staff members brought in the vegetables. Soon other staff members were stepping in for dinner, among them Gertie, Lili and Hetty.

'The pies look delicious,' said Annie. 'What sort are they?'

'Steak and kidney. Or steak and kidley, as me little sister used to say.' Jack chuckled. 'We've done some mash today, and there's some leeks and carrots with 'em.'

'I 'ope you've got some leeks left for tomorrow,' said Lili, grinning.

'Why's that?'

' 'Cos it's St David's Day, of course. Though normally we'd wear 'em rather than eat 'em.'

'Not sure the guests would appreciate a waitress wearing a leek,' said Stanley. 'Don't you lot wear daffodils on March the first? I'm sure that's what I've seen you with in the past.'

'Us lot? You cheeky devil. I will certainly go out to pick a daffodil tomorrow.'

Everyone sat down and soon the food was being passed around. Annie ended up sitting next to Leslie, so was now near the men who'd been there when she'd entered.

'Are you sitting in Mrs Leggett's chair?' said Gertie, looking towards Johnny.

'Why is it *her* chair? Don't even remember it being here before we left.'

'No, she got it two or three years back. But she's the only one allowed to sit in it. And she always sits at that end.'

'Well, she's not here now, so unless you're gonna tell her, it doesn't matter. You're head portress, not head waiter, so you're not in charge of me. And anyway, we're not on duty.'

'No, *I'm* head waitress,' said Lili, 'and if Mrs Leggett catches you on it, she'll give you an earful, but that's up to you.'

'Yes, it is. We're not in the restaurant now.'

Annie had already heard some mutterings from the waiters who'd returned from the war about having a woman in charge of them, and she wondered if this was Johnny's resentment showing now.

'Whose pie is that, left on the tray?' said Hetty.

Jack looked up. 'Must be Mr Fletcher's. He just popped out to get an evening paper. He should be back soon.'

They settled down to eat, but it wasn't long before Johnny was calling up the table, 'I haven't had any salt yet. Where is it?'

Günther was sprinkling it liberally on his food. He'd always liked a good bit of salt. He looked up. 'I'll pass it down in a moment, Johnny.'

'That's Mr Winborn to you, and I don't want you emptying the thing before I've 'ad a chance to 'ave any.'

'There's plenty in the pot in the cupboard,' said Annie.

'Anyway, we should get first dibs, us men down here, after what we've been through. We 'aven't been locked up in a camp, twiddling our fingers.'

Annie told herself to be quiet, but she was incensed. She saw both Lili and Gertie about to open their mouths, but she got in first. 'Oh, you think you're the only ones to have suffered, do you? Well, you've got another think coming. It wasn't long ago we 'ad to close the hotel 'cos of Spanish flu—'

'It's still rattling round some parts of the country,' said Gertie. '*And* we've 'ad the river blown up, then it flooded all over the place...' She took a deep breath, in which time, Lili took over.

'Then there was all them libellous letters and Mrs Bygrove getting in bother then Bygrove returning 'ome causing all sorts of trouble, and then the murder.'

Gertie carried on, 'For most of the time we've been short staffed, but we've carried on, sometimes doing loads more shifts, and we got the 'otel through the war and all the troubles and scandals. You could say we've 'ad our own mini wars to contend with.'

'Maybe there wouldn't have been so much trouble if us men'd been here?' Stanley suggested.

'What, you would have stopped the flu would you?' said Gertie. 'And the Admiralty, and the river bursting its banks?'

'We'd have been able to stand up to Bygrove,' said Johnny.

'I doubt that *very* much,' said Annie. 'Especially after he got in with those crooked councillors.'

'*Mein Gott*, I cannot believe what you have all been through here,' said Günther. 'What I have been told sounds horrific.'

Johnny stood abruptly, pushing the bench seat back and causing those sitting nearest him to almost tumble off it. They all just managed to stay seated. 'What, more bloody horrific than what we went through in the war?'

'Of course not,' Günther replied, 'but nothing like that happened before the war. The ladies here have certainly been tested by the fates.'

'Unlike you, who've seen the war out in a cosy hut, away from it all. What a cushy number that was.' Johnny poked his finger in the German's direction as he said each word.

Jerry, Stanley and Leslie nodded vaguely and mumbled agreement at all he said but contributed nothing themselves. Annie thought Leslie looked slightly uncomfortable.

'Oh, come on Johnny,' said Jack. 'It wasn't nice the way the authorities dragged Günther away. And who wants to be locked up in what was basically a prison.'

'Says the boy with flat feet who got to stay at home.'

'That wasn't my fault. I was willing to go. I joined the Volunteer Training Corps and spent me time off training for invasion. And I'm not a boy, I'm twenty-two now, and a few months older than Leslie and Stanley here.'

'You still look like a boy to me. If you'd been in the army, you'd have looked like a man by now,' said Johnny, sneering.

Hetty rose and glared down the table. 'What a *stupid* thing to say. There were men at home here who worked hard, believe me.' Annie knew she was thinking of her fiancé, Victor, who had been in charge of building flying boats for the war. 'It's a good job Phoebe is out visiting her parents today, otherwise she would have given you a right talking to, having a go at Günther like that.'

'Can't he speak for himself?'

Günther patted her hand. 'It is all right, Hetty... Yes, *Mr* Winborn, I can speak for myself, but I do not see the point of arguing. We have all had enough of war, whatever part we have, or have not played, and we do not need to make more war here.'

The door opened suddenly and banged against the wall. Johnny let out a yell.

Old Will Fletcher, one of the chefs, stepped in, a newspaper under his arm, looking bemused. 'Sorry, didn't mean to enter quite so dramatically.'

'That was a bit of an *over*reaction, Johnny,' said Gertie.

He looked down, his face set hard. It seemed to Annie that he was breathing rapidly.

'Hope you've left some food for me,' said Will.

'There is plenty here, Mr Fletcher,' said Günther.

'Thank you, Mr Schultz.' Will took a seat next to him, opposite Hetty. 'Bad business going on in Germany, I'm afraid.' He showed Günther the front page. 'Lots of strikes have been called, and it looks like Berlin could be on its way to a famine.'

'*Oh nein!*' he exclaimed, closing his eyes and shaking his head.

'Serves them right,' Annie heard Johnny mutter. Jerry nudged him and widened his eyes.

'What was that, Mr Winborn?' Will asked, smiling. He clearly hadn't heard the content of the comment.

'What? Oh, nothing.'

The women sitting in the middle all looked in his direction, poker faced, before continuing with their meal.

Will now looked over at Hetty. 'So, it's your last day with us.'

'That's right.'

'Your last day?' said Jerry, looking confused.

'Yes. I'm getting married Saturday after next.'

'I didn't realise it was that soon.'

'Well, I hope you have a lovely day,' said Will.

There was a murmur of agreement around the table.

'I'll see some of you on the day,' she reminded them, 'as we're having the reception here.'

'We'll make sure the meal is perfection,' said Will.

'Thank you, Mr Fletcher.'

'To Hetty and Victor,' said Annie, raising her glass of water.

'To Hetty and Victor!' they all declared, with varying degrees of enthusiasm.

Chapter Two

Three days later, Alice and Annie were walking along South Terrace one afternoon, carrying baskets, ready to collect some fish from the fishermen on Pier Road. Edie, who had some time off, was walking with them. Usually, Alice enjoyed an errand that got her out of the hotel, but it was a dull, chilly day, and she would much rather have been in the warm scullery, with her hands in some nice hot water.

'I don't know why we always get this stinky job,' said Annie. 'Mrs Norris could have sent the scullery lads to do it. Finn and Lucas are in this morning.'

'I think she trusts you to look after the money and get the transaction right,' said Edie.

'Then she could have sent Alice with one of 'em. After all, I'm *head* scullery maid.' Annie made a *huh* sound through her nose.

Edie came to a stop outside one of the red brick houses that populated that end of the road, gazing up at the second floor and down to the basement, which had its own entrance and stairs leading to it. Alice wondered why for a few moments. Then she remembered. It was where Edie had boarded when she'd first moved to Little-hampton, escaping her previous life. It was also where her landlady had been murdered by her husband. She and Annie looked at each other, both raising their eyebrows.

'It's finally for sale again,' said Edie. 'It's been boarded up since Mrs Hadley's demise. It seems like a decade ago, but it's not even been quite five years since it happened.'

'It must have been horrible for you, finding Mrs Hadley dead like that.'

'Alice! I'm sure Edie don't wanna be reminded of the details.'

'It's all right, Annie, I'm always reminded of it every time I pass by. And of the day her husband, Gordon Hadley, tried to see me off too, on the promenade.'

'And Charlie saved you,' said Alice.

'He did. It's better to talk about it than lock it away.'

'That other poor woman what lived there too, wasn't she seen off by Hadley?'

'Pamela. Yes, that's right. It sounded like Hadley had been her "pimp", as they call them. She'd run away from him, but it seems he sent this Jim fellow to find her. I don't know the full story. Nobody does.'

'Jim was mentioned when Gertie told us about that bloke called Jimmy, what used to watch her playing football and then disappeared. Uncle Barry thought they might be the same person.'

'Uncle Barry? Oh, yes, of course, you mean Sergeant Gardner. There's no reason to believe they were one and the same, is there?'

'Except that they were both tall and blond. And they both disappeared. And both called Jim.'

'There is that. And it would be good to know what became of the first Jim. He was clearly involved in something shifty. He is probably far away now. Anyway, maybe, with the house having new owners and a new lease of life, I will finally be able to forget it…. You'd better get on and collect that fish.'

They got to The Nelson public house on the corner and turned onto Pier Road.

Alice looked up and down the river. 'The Arun seems so quiet since the war ended, and the Admiralty ships left. And when we walk by the beach, there are no sounds of guns from over the channel any more.'

'I for one am glad about that,' said Annie.

'I am also,' said Edie. 'Though I suppose it had become sort of normal, and it does seem overly quiet now. We don't even have as many sailing ships as we used to here… Anyway, I'm heading into town now, so I will see you both later.'

She walked away and they waved a farewell.

'Right,' said Annie. 'There are the fishermen we want, sitting on the bank. Let's get on with this and make sure they don't try to put the price up from the one they agreed with Mrs Bygrove. And let's hope they've got a decent catch.'

'I'll leave you in charge then.'

After paying the money and filling their baskets up, they headed back to South Terrace.

'Gawd, I'll be glad to be back,' said Annie. 'This is heavy. And it don't 'alf stink.'

'I thought that was you!'

'That's not funny, Alice in Blunderland.'

'Hey, I don't blunder around.'

'And *I* don't stink!'

'It was only a joke.'

'Hm!' Annie strode ahead a few steps before turning back abruptly. 'The pair of us'll stink after this!' She carried on, walking even faster, despite struggling with the basket.

Alice wondered what on earth was wrong with her sister. She seemed to have become even more bad-tempered recently.

The common ahead brightened and Alice realised that the sun had come out. She stopped to look at it hanging in the sky over the dunes of West Beach, across the river. She sighed. Spring was on its way and there were already signs of it with the flowering primroses and hellebores. And soon Lorcan and Jasper would be back. Just three days to go. *Jasper.* How she'd missed him. Not that she'd ever told anyone, *especially* not Annie. But would she still feel the same about him after all this time? She missed the person he'd been when he'd left. He might have changed.

'Stop daydreaming, Alice in Wonderland, and get a move on.'

She headed off once again, hoping her sister wasn't going to be in this mood for the rest of the day.

–

'Ooh, the princess looks so pretty,' said Phoebe, looking over Alice's shoulder at the magazine Edie had brought into the staff dining room to show them.

'Can't say I'd ever 'eard of Princess Patricia of Connaught before this wedding,' said Annie, already fed up with the 'oohing' and 'ahhing' over the royal marriage.

Phoebe tutted and looked heavenward. 'She's the daughter of Prince Arthur.'

'Who's one of Queen Victoria's sons,' added Alice, with an expression that suggested she couldn't believe her sister was so ignorant of such things.

'And it was the first royal wedding at Westminster Abbey since the fourteenth century,' Edie added.

Annie peered down at the photograph. 'Eight brides-maids? That's a bit excessive, 'specially after all the short-ages during the war. And a bit insensitive to ordinary folk, if you ask me.'

'Nobody was.' Alice shook her head. 'You're such a misery when it comes to romance.'

'What's bridesmaids got to do with romance?'

'Anyway,' said Phoebe, 'it's nice to have a happy story in the newspaper, after years of war and loss.'

'Just think, you're going to be Hetty's bridesmaid soon,' said Alice. 'And at a very prestigious wedding.'

Phoebe clutched her hands and grinned. 'I still can't believe it. If you'd told me a year ago that I'd even be *attending* a wedding involving the Perrymans, I'd have said you were mad, let alone being a bridesmaid!'

Annie glanced at the photo once again. The princess was in a long, white lacy dress, with a veil that reached her feet. If she ever got married, she'd never be able to afford any kind of wedding dress, let alone one so fancy. She'd have to make do with her Sunday best. Never mind the dress, she was even less likely to get a groom to marry in the first place.

The door opened, and in stepped Will Fletcher and Jack from the kitchen, both carrying trays of sandwiches.

'Grub's up,' said Jack placing his tray onto the table.

'What sandwiches 'ave we got today?' Annie asked.

'Ham or chicken, madame!' he replied, in a mock posh voice. 'And there's some chopped spring greens and grated beetroot to have on the side.'

Jack was fun and she'd always liked him. Could he be a possible sweetheart for her? He was over a year younger, but did that matter, now she was twenty-three? She sat at the table as he and Will placed the food down.

As they did so, several other staff members entered the room, including Mrs Leggett, Bridget Turnbull, Fanny, Gertie, Günther and another waiter, Simon, who'd been too young to go to war.

No, she concluded with regards to her question. Jack was a nice young man, but she didn't have *those* kinds of feelings for him.

'I presume that Mr Foley and Mr Jupp have not returned as yet,' said the housekeeper.

'You mean Lorcan and Jasper?' said Jack with a cheeky grin.

'You know who I mean, Mr Sinden.'

'We don't mind if you call us by our first names, Mrs L. You call Mrs Turnbull by her first name.'

'She's a close friend. And it's not how I was trained.' She pursed her lips and frowned as she looked over at Jack.

'Well, anyway,' said Edie, half smiling. 'To answer your question, Jack, Lorcan did say in his letter to Mrs Bygrove that they'd probably arrive late afternoon or early evening.'

'At least it has been a sunny day for their return. I presume their bedroom has been cleaned and tidied and prepared for their arrival, Miss Bullen.'

'Yes, Mrs Leggett,' said Fanny. 'I saw to it meself.'

'Good, good. They are the first live-in staff to return from the war, so we want to make sure they are comfortable in their accommodation.'

The housekeeper seemed to have forgotten that Günther was actually the first live-in to return, but Annie supposed she was referring to the men who'd been abroad.

They'd all just finished helping themselves when the door opened. Helen Bygrove entered. Her cheerful face gave Annie hope of some good news. But it was better than good, for behind her came Lorcan and Jasper. They were both in open army overcoats that revealed they were still in uniform, each carrying a large rucksack on their shoulders. Annie's immediate reaction was to smile broadly, but she quickly reined it in. If only she could have run to Lorcan and hugged him, like she'd seen other women do when their men returned. She'd played the scenario over in her mind many times. But he wasn't 'her' man and was never likely to be, not when he was attracted to beautiful, interesting women like Hetty.

She looked at her sister, surprised to find her staring at the table rather than at the newcomers, not taking any notice of Jasper, as she'd expected.

There was a chorus of 'Welcome back', causing both men to grin widely. Their sunny expressions were a contrast to Johnny and Jerry's when they'd returned, who had both seemed on edge despite a similar warm reception.

'Have you had your lunch yet, lads?' said Will, stepping over the bench to shake their hands.

'Not yet,' said Lorcan. 'Came straight from the train station, so we did.'

'That's right,' said Jasper, his soft, middle-class accent unchanged. 'I am rather famished. We haven't had anything since very early this morning. And we had a devil of a night sleeping over in the waiting room at Dover.'

'Then come and sit down. There's plenty left, so come and help yourselves.'

'I will see you later,' said Helen. 'I'm going up to have dinner with the children.'

After people had moved around to give them space on the bench seat, the pair of them ended up sitting opposite her and Alice. Annie came out in a warm sweat and hoped she hadn't gone red.

When the newcomers had got settled and served, Lorcan said, 'So, I hear that Hetty got engaged to Victor Perryman.'

Nobody spoke for a few moments, then Edie said, 'Yes, that's right. And they are, um, getting married this coming Saturday. The reception is going to be at the hotel.'

Lorcan looked down and pressed his lips together. Annie's heartfelt sadness for him clashed with her relief that he was free, confusing her even more. And his reaction suggested, as she'd feared, that he hadn't got over Hetty.

'So, she's not working here any more?'

'It was her last day over a week ago now,' said Edie. 'I believe you're down to be working a shift during the wedding, but it can be rearranged, if you would prefer.'

'Yes, sorry, that's my fault,' said Gertie. 'I weren't thinking when I did the rotas.'

Lorcan shook his head vigorously but continued to look down. 'No, what's the point? What's done is done. Anyway, I've had a while to get used to it.' He did now look up and smile. 'It's just grand to be back.'

He seemed cheerful now, though Annie suspected he was putting it on to hide his feelings. It was the kind of thing she would do.

'When are you two starting work?' Jack asked.

'I'm starting tomorrow,' said Lorcan. 'I never thought I'd look forward to a shift so much. But it'll be warm, safe and hopefully friendly, and what more could a man want?'

'I'm starting the day after next,' said Jasper. 'I'm going to visit my parents in Middleton tomorrow. Thought it only right, given I haven't seen them in seven months… How has everyone here been?'

People started relating the recent goings on in the hotel, nobody alluding to the floods and outbreak of Spanish influenza that had occurred only a few months back.

Eventually, Lorcan looked at the sisters. 'You two are very quiet, so you are. What have you been up to?'

'Nothing much,' said Annie, wishing she had a more exciting life to interest him with. 'We're stillroom maids, as we were when you left. Not like a lot of people who've shifted jobs.' She hoped that didn't sound resentful, as she didn't feel that way at all.

'On that note, I hear that Gertie has become a portress in our absence,' said Jasper, looking over at her. 'And I see you still have the uniform on. Are you going back to being a chambermaid once all the porters have returned?'

'Not all the porters are coming back. Alan Drew and James Wood aren't,' Gertie reminded him.

'Well, no, of course.' He looked uncomfortable. 'Sorry, I meant, of course, the ones who are returning.'

'Anyway, I'm remaining a portress, in fact, head portress. Mrs Bygrove has told me.'

'But what about Charlie? He took over from Alan when he enlisted early on, so won't he get that position back? It's not on if he doesn't.'

'Why is that?' said Alice, replying to Jasper. 'Some women have the vote now, and they've been doing a lot of the jobs during the war, even the *men's* jobs, so why shouldn't they be head porter, or head waiter, or anything they like? Lili is head waitress and *she's* staying in that position too.' She puckered her lips and glared at him for a couple of seconds, before lifting her sandwich to start eating again.

Jasper stared wide-eyed at her, with his mouth slightly open. 'I'm sorry,' he mumbled. 'I didn't mean to offend anyone.'

People started talking in small groups, with Lorcan and Jasper speaking to those either side of them.

It wasn't long before Gertie stood up. 'Anyway, I've finished, and I'll be off now.'

'That was rather quick, Miss Green,' said Mrs Leggett. 'You'll get indigestion.'

'I'll 'ave to risk it, Mrs L. I've got a football practice with me team and I don't wanna be late.'

Alice looked over at Jasper once more. 'I suppose you don't think women should play football neither.'

'No, I've nothing against it,' he replied. 'It's a good idea. And at least the men left behind in the war were still able to watch some matches.'

'Not *just* the men.'

'See ya later,' said Gertie, leaving hastily, as if she didn't want to get involved in an argument.

As she headed out of the door, Lili came in, immediately spotting the men who'd returned. 'Oh, you're back. Lovely to see you, it is.' She hurried over to where they were sitting, patting them both on the shoulder. 'Did you 'ave a good journey?'

'Not particularly,' said Lorcan, 'but it was worth it to get back here.'

'My Rhodri is due back today too.' Lili pressed her hands together and touched her chin with her fingers, as if she were praying. Her wide grin lifted her rosy cheeks.

'Aye, we ended up in the same carriage as him.'

'But you don't know 'im, do you?'

'No, but we got talking with a Welsh fellow who turned out to be your sweetheart,' said Jasper. 'He seems like a very nice chap.'

'Then he must be back now too. I've got the afternoon off, so I'm going straight to his house. Oh, I'm so excited!'

'We'd never have guessed,' said Jack, causing laughter around the table.

'Oh, you lot.' She giggled.

'Aren't you having any luncheon, Miss Probert?' said Mrs Leggett.

'I couldn't eat a thing, Mrs L. Byeee.' She hurried away.

People carried on with their conversations, but Annie, not being part of any of them, felt excluded. Alice, likewise, was talking to no one and looking glum. It wasn't like her at all; she was normally the happy, sunny one of them. She should think of something to say to or ask of Lorcan, but everything she thought of sounded silly to her. And goodness knows what the pair of them had made of Alice's outburst. They might think that she felt the same as her sister, but she didn't think Jasper had meant any harm. She'd longed to see Lorcan, but now she longed to hide away from him, back in the scullery. It wasn't like he'd miss her if she wasn't here.

She picked up her sandwich and started eating once more, but somehow it had lost all its appeal.

—

After the sisters returned to the scullery, Annie sent the two young lads there off for their lunch break. Alice wished they weren't going for she was sure Annie wasn't happy about what she'd said at the table and would give her a hard time over it. She had a face on her, as their mother often said, and she knew that expression well. It wasn't as if she hadn't already regretted her tone and words.

Sure enough, as Annie poured a pan of hot water into the sink to start a new batch of washing up, she said, 'Why were you being so mean to Jasper?'

Despite her own regret, she had her reply ready. 'Me being mean? He was the one being mean about Gertie. And about women.'

'He wasn't being mean about women, or about Gertie. He only said that Charlie should get back the job he 'ad before he left for the war. Seems fair enough. He wasn't saying that women shouldn't have them jobs at all.'

Alice picked up a drying-up cloth, ready to deal with the first glass. 'He kind of was, when he assumed Gertie would go back to being a chambermaid.'

'Not really. I'm sure if you'd questioned him politely about it, he'd 'ave explained it better. Remember, them men have been through a lot. I wouldn't 'ave wanted to be in a dirty, cold trench, being fired at. Would you? I'm surprised they're as cheerful as they are. Relieved to be 'ome, I suppose. Anyway, I thought you liked Jasper.'

Alice felt too confused to answer this question properly, as she wasn't sure of the answer herself. 'What d'ya mean, "liked"?'

'You know, had a crush on him. You used to say he was nice and good looking.'

My goodness he had been. He still was, but there was something even *more* about him now. More what, she wasn't sure. More grown up? She'd longed for his return, to see his cheerful, handsome face with his large, brown eyes, and golden-brown curly hair. It was shorter now, but you could still spot the waves. His shoulders seemed to have broadened in the war, yet he looked slimmer.

He'd only been twenty-one when he'd enlisted, and had still had that fresh, boyish look. Now he'd be twenty-six, and could definitely be called a man.

But she couldn't cope with these new emotions, which were even more confusing than those she'd had before he'd left. This bewilderment turned into the words, 'I thought he was all right. Nothing special.'

Her stomach clenched as she said it and she felt a little queasy. She'd always liked him and thought him one of the nicest men in the hotel – definitely someone special. Her regret at jumping in the way she had grew. What had possessed her? And now she was regretting saying he was nothing special, but what else could she say without looking silly? And hopefully it would shut Annie up.

'Nothing special? Why, you got someone more special in that wonderland of yours?'

'Let's get on with this, before the next lot of crockery, or pots and pans, comes in and we get behind.'

'I'm 'ead scullery maid, remember, so I give the instructions.'

She didn't normally emphasise this, but Alice guessed she was a little annoyed with her.

'There's no point talking about this all afternoon. I've said me piece. That's it. Maybe he'll think before he speaks next time.'

Annie shook her head but carried on in silence.

Hopefully she wouldn't encounter Jasper on a break for the rest of the day. Or did she secretly hope she would? She felt too confused to know what she wanted.

What had possessed her to talk to him like that? Fear. Yes, fear of liking someone that much, someone who was unlikely to look twice at her, silly old Alice in Wonderland.

She started drying the glasses. This could turn into a *very* long day.

–

Afternoon tea had just finished, and Annie had been asked to help clear up in the conservatory, as Jerry and Johnny had both been coughing by the end of their shift and complaining of headaches. They'd been sent home.

'I 'ope they 'aven't come down with the Spanish flu,' said Lili, placing empty tea things on a tray on the next table from Annie. 'Still going around a bit it is, from what the newspapers say.'

'Don't say that. Me and Alice never got it when you lot did, nor our family, and I don't want us getting it now.'

'They've probably just caught a cold.'

This didn't make Annie feel any better as she headed to the scullery with the tray of dirty dishes, followed by Lili. What if the men returning had brought the flu back with them? Then she'd likely already caught it and would know soon enough. A sliver of dread passed through her as she started unpacking the items to be washed, and she shivered.

'Are you all right?' Alice asked.

'Yes, I'm fine,' she replied in a curt manner, still annoyed with her sister for the way she'd spoken to Jasper.

She quickly finished unloading the tray and followed Lili back through the staff area to the conservatory.

Standing in the middle of the room when they reached it, were Lorcan and Jasper. They were sporting civilian trousers, shirts and jackets now. The clothes were out of date, but they still looked smart, as they always had done.

'What are you two doing here?' Lili asked.

'Just having a look around the hotel while it's quiet. Familiarising ourselves with it once again.' Lorcan did a complete turn to take in the conservatory. 'It's looking as grand as it ever did.'

'Well, there's only these coupla bits left,' said Lili, picking up a tea set and two cups from a table. 'So, looks like we're done with the clearing.'

She headed back out with the dirty dishes, but Annie didn't follow her this time. It wasn't often she got to stand in the conservatory, the abundant south-facing windows and glass ceiling ensuring it was the brightest room in the hotel. It looked pretty this afternoon, with the approaching sunset infusing the room with a pinky-orange tinge. And she did so love the large pot plants in here, which included a variety of palms.

'I suppose you two 'ave been unpacking this afternoon,' she said, amazed that she'd found something sensible to say.

'That's right,' said Jasper. 'Not that there was much to unpack as we couldn't take much with us in the first place. Most of our clothes and possessions were stored away by Mrs Turnbull, which we're very grateful for. It seems she thought to organise that before Bygrove had a chance to throw it all out, which had apparently been his intention.'

'She's the salt of the earth is Mrs Turnbull. She's always looking out for everyone.'

'We went for a walk afterwards,' said Lorcan. 'Not the best time of year for a stroll by the beach, but it's grand to see the sea again. And not to hear the guns no more. The last time I was on leave here, August 1917, I went for a walk on the prom with Hetty…' He stalled for a moment, taking a breath before he continued. 'Anyway, we could hear the guns from across the channel.'

'Yes, it's a relief to us all not to hear 'em any more,' said Annie, trying to think of a way to draw him away from his memories of Hetty. 'By the way, Jasper, I apologise for what Alice said earlier. I don't know what's up with her today.'

'I did wonder,' said Jasper. 'She's normally one of the most cheerful of people.'

Unlike me? thought Annie.

'Aye, she is.' Lorcan nodded. 'But it's bound to be a strain and rather awkward to begin with, so it is, what with the men coming home after so long. I dare say it'll be the same in people's homes with husbands and sons returning. There'll be a period of adjustment. That's what our sergeant reckoned.'

Annie was impressed with his understanding of what the women were going through, unlike some of the other men who only considered their own problems.

'And with brothers too,' she added. 'One of ours, Cecil, is home already, but the other two'll be coming back soon. It'll be mayhem to begin with, I've no doubt.'

'But you'll be glad to see them.' It was almost a question from Jasper, whose forehead was creased in query.

'Oh yes, of course. And relieved. But like Lorcan said, there'll be a period of adjustment.'

'How have Johnny, Jerry, Leslie and Stanley settled in?' Lorcan asked.

'Finding their feet, I think is the best way to put it. But Johnny...'

'What?'

She didn't want to talk out of turn, but now she'd started, she'd better finish. 'I think he's finding it the most difficult. He still seems very – cross, is the only way I can think to put it. And he's been taking it out on Günther.'

'Günther?' Lorcan frowned. 'Because he's German?'

Oh dear, she wished she'd kept her mouth shut now.

'I s'pose. He resents him having 'ad a "cushy number" as he called it, sitting the war out in an internment camp.'

'That's not his fault,' said Jasper. 'If any of us had been living in Germany at the start of the war, we'd probably have found ourselves in the same situation. And an internment camp is hardly a "cushy number".'

Lorcan shook his head slowly as he said, 'What an eejit Johnny is. He'd better not pick on Günther in my presence, or I'll give him what for. What do the other men think?'

'They 'aven't said much but seem to agree with Johnny, I think.'

She felt terrible now, as if she'd been telling tales out of school. She'd get herself into trouble if she wasn't careful. It might make her look untrustworthy.

'I'm glad you told us,' said Lorcan.

'Yes, me too.' Jasper nodded in agreement. 'We'll nip any of *that* nonsense in the bud. We've come home to have some peace, not for people to start new, pointless wars.'

Annie sighed with relief. She had done the right thing after all.

'Have you a few minutes to spare to walk around with us?' Jasper asked. 'You could tell us a bit more about what's been going on in our absence.'

'Um, yes, I don't see why not. Alice and the scullery lads can cope without me for a bit, since we're between meals.'

She hoped Lorcan wouldn't mind his friend's suggestion. He didn't seem put out by it though.

'For a start, when we had to close the 'otel 'cos of the flu, we were allowed to 'ave our breaks in 'ere.' She lifted her hand to indicate the conservatory.

'You lucky devils,' said Jasper. 'That must have made a change to the dark staff dining room.'

'It did. It was lovely. But of course, we were worried about people as they went down with the flu. Did you 'ave much flu in your battalion?'

'Quite a few went down with it,' said Lorcan. 'Not us, luckily, but several died. I heard that a couple of the guests here did too.'

'That's right.'

They headed to the guest dining room, which, like the conservatory, had a view of the back garden through the large windows and glass doors. A third of the room was also under a glass roof. The tables were very stylish with their white cloths, silver cruet sets and small pots of spring flowers, which gave the room a floral scent. The room had already been laid for dinner that evening.

'When the Admiralty blew the river up, and people thought first off that the Germans were bombing us, the guests and some staff hid under the tables in 'ere. Poor Hetty, she— that is…'

What an idiot she was, mentioning Lorcan's lost love!

'I don't mind you mentioning her,' said Lorcan. 'What happened?'

'When the explosion 'appened, she fell on some broken glass and cut 'er hand. The staff who'd been upstairs and in the staff area hid under the tables in our dining room and the kitchen.'

'You were very lucky not to be attacked either by aeroplanes or ships here on the southeast coast,' said Jasper.

'The east and northeast coasts and London were hit quite badly.'

'I know. We were all very grateful for that. We 'ad a lot of guests come to stay 'ere though, to get away from them attacks.'

She didn't want to tell them that on many days, it didn't feel like they were at war at all, not here, in Littlehampton, but it seemed the wrong thing to say. Besides, as Gertie had put it, they had been contending with a lot of their own mini 'wars'.

'Come on, come and see the ballroom,' said Annie, leading the way. She felt more comfortable in their company now than she had when she'd first arrived at the conservatory.

In the ballroom she smiled, having always loved this room with its arched mirrors, and embossed walls with pillars. The walnut and oak parquet flooring was in the shape of hexagons and stars.

'Ah yes, as elegant as ever,' said Jasper, looking up to admire the crystal chandeliers.

'Can't imagine there were many balls during the war,' said Lorcan.

'Not many traditional ones, no. We had a ragtime band at one party though.'

'How exciting!' said Jasper.

'There were a few weddings, but not many. The ballroom was mostly used for concerts, carol concerts, and children's and charity teas. We also 'ad a do for the injured men at Belgrave Hospital. Many of the events were to raise money for the men abroad. And the ordinary townsfolk were able to buy tickets for most of those.'

'How times have changed,' said Lorcan. 'I don't suppose that'll carry on no more, having ordinary towns-folk in.'

'Maybe not,' she conceded. 'Though now Mrs Bygrove's in charge, she might still do some things for 'em.'

Jasper smiled at her. 'It was admirable of her – of all of you – to raise money for the men abroad though.'

They came out of the ballroom into a short corridor and looked through the open entrance into the foyer.

'The private dining room is now a guest lounge,' said Annie. 'Wanna take a look?'

She headed towards the room, off the foyer, noticing that Mr Watkins, the head desk clerk, was peering at her above his spectacles. At this moment, she didn't care. She opened the door and, seeing only one guest inside, she stepped in and beckoned the other two.

'Hello Major Thomas,' the two men said together to the permanent guest who'd lived at the hotel since 1912.

The major stood up, a surprised grin on his face. 'My goodness, Lorcan and Jasper. You're back! How good to see you.'

They shook hands enthusiastically.

'How are you, Major?' said Lorcan.

'Fine, fine. Jolly glad that the war's over, as I'm certain you two young men are.'

'We are so. Annie here was just giving us a little tour and catching us up with some of the goings on.'

'This is where we gathered on the night of the storm, when the Arun broke its banks,' she said.

'Until the window broke and we had to evacuate to the foyer,' added the major.

46

They chatted for a while about the war and the men's time in France, until a young couple came through the door.

'Well, it was grand speaking to you, Major. I'm starting back tomorrow, and Jasper's starting the next day, so we'll see you again soon.'

They all left, standing on the edge of the foyer. Gertie was by the desk with Leslie, looking at a leaflet.

'This hasn't changed an iota,' said Jasper.

After another disparaging glare from Mr Watkins, they headed back towards the guest dining room.

'Mr Watkins certainly hasn't changed at all,' she said, when out of his earshot.

Lorcan and Jasper laughed, making her feel ten times better than when she'd first encountered them in the conservatory. She'd managed to talk to them – to Lorcan – like a normal person, not like a shrinking violet.

'I'd better get back to the scullery,' she said, feeling reluctant now to do so.

'Thanks for the tour,' said Jasper, raising his hand.

She simply smiled as she hurried back to the staff area.

Chapter Three

It was time for Lorcan to start a shift, on his second day back at work. He came down the stairs from the staff bedrooms, recalling the welcome he'd got the day before, from guests who remembered him. It had made the tiny bit of anxiety he'd had about starting back here after so many years vanish, and he soon felt like he'd never left. His duties, the persona he'd created to carry out his job, had come back instantly. He was glad to be back in a different uniform with its peaked cap, in mid blue instead of khaki. The jacket was shorter than he'd been wearing the last four years, with a high collar and three rows of metal studs. His trousers were neatly pressed with a crease down the middle. It was all lovely and clean, whereas his army uniform had often been caked in dirt. And he certainly wouldn't miss that uncomfortable steel helmet.

Coming out of the door, he encountered Annie rushing out of the stillroom with cutlery in her hand. He hadn't seen her to speak to since she'd given him and Jasper the little tour two days before. There was something a little different about the way she looked today, but he couldn't put his finger on it.

'Well, hello there. You heading for the late lunch?'

Her head went down as she mumbled, 'No, had mine already.'

'Just starting my shift for the wedding reception, so I am.'

She nodded dolefully, murmuring, 'Good, um, luck,' before hurrying off up the corridor in the direction of the kitchen.

He turned the other way, towards the foyer. How curious, the way she'd reacted to him. Maybe something had happened, or she'd been told off and wasn't in the best of moods. She'd never been the most talkative of people, not to him, anyway, though she had been with some of the other staff. It hadn't occurred to him before, but perhaps she'd never liked him for some reason. That made him feel a little sad and he wondered what he might have done to make her feel like that. She'd been fine with him two days ago, telling him and Jasper some of what had happened in their absence; really quite chirpy, in fact.

Jasper. He let out a brief huff of a laugh. Maybe her cheerfulness had been down to *his* presence. Might she have feelings for him? There was a thought.

He had reached the door to the foyer now and peeped around into it before entering. It was currently empty, apart from Mr Watkins and Gertie. He approached the side of the desk, where she was standing.

'No guests from the wedding yet?' he said.

'Nah, the wedding started at one, so the guests won't be here until at least two o'clock.' Gertie pointed at the grandfather clock, which stood between the cloakroom and the door to the guest lounge.

One-thirty. There was tension in his gut, at what was to come: Hetty Affleck, walking in with her husband. Or Hetty Perryman, as she would now be. Or even Henrietta Perryman, given her climb in social status. He'd told the others that he'd had time to get used to it. And he had, to an extent. But he still didn't know how he'd feel when he actually *saw* her.

'Have the lunch guests all gone?'

'Yep. Guest lunch was early today, 'cos of the wedding,' said Gertie, 'and only for residents.'

He nodded. 'I thought that's what I'd heard.'

'Did you hear about Jerry and Johnny?'

'That they might have the flu?'

'Dr Ferngrove apparently thinks it's not flu, just a cold. Their mum came and told Mrs Bygrove. But they can't come back for the next coupla days, so they're bringing in Annie and a part-timer to take their places, serving at the wedding. They would have had Phoebe doing it, but of course, she's one of the bridesmaids.'

'So I heard. She and Hetty always were the best of friends. Did Annie do any waitressing in the war?'

'Nope, never.'

That was what had been different about her: the uniform. She was normally in a black dress with a long white apron, but today she'd been wearing a grey dress with a shorter apron, which was the waiting staff uniform. That might explain her reaction when he'd encountered her. She would be nervous about doing a different job. He was nervous too, but for a different reason. She could have told him that, though.

'There's not going to be much to do until the wedding guests arrive then,' he said.

'No, unfortunately. I 'ate just standing around.'

'Me too.' Especially when it gave him time to worry.

It was daft, really, given what he'd been through the last four or so years, in the trenches and in various battles in France, but this thought didn't make him feel any better.

'That's enough chitchat.' The head desk clerk was standing straight and stiff behind the desk. 'You need to make yourselves ready for the guests arriving.'

'That might be a while yet, Mr Watkins,' said Gertie.

'It doesn't do for the guests to see you chatting.'

Gertie raised her eyes heavenward, only noticed by Lorcan, who half grinned.

There was the sound of people coming down the sweeping staircase and he looked up to see Lord and Lady Glanville, dressed in coats and scarves.

As they reached the foyer, Lorcan said, 'Are you heading out, my lord?'

'Yes, we are, Lorcan.'

'Do you need a motor taxi calling, or any information, my lord?'

'No, thank you. We've been invited to Arundel Castle, and Her Grace, the Dowager Duchess of Norfolk, is sending a motorcar to collect us.'

'Enjoy your visit there, my lord, my lady,' said Gertie.

'We will, Gertrude, thank you,' said Lady Glanville.

When they'd left, Gertie whispered from one side of her mouth towards Lorcan, 'Very nice, too, to have an invitation to Arundel Castle.'

He nodded to acknowledge the comment. It was now quiet again, and the three of them stood to attention, facing the front doors. Lorcan's gaze was fixed on the space outside, waiting for a moment he both dreaded and also wanted to get over and done with.

–

'Yes, yes, excellent,' said Mrs Leggett, as she inspected the last table in the dining room.

Annie sighed with relief. Having to rush to the scullery for extra cutlery had made her a little anxious, but they'd finished laying up the tables in the dining room in good time. They had been arranged in long rows, starting with the top table, which was in front of the doors that opened onto the garden. Each place had a name on a folded piece of card, so people knew where to sit. It was a shame it wasn't spring or summer, when the weather would have been better, and the wedding party could have wandered outside. At least it was sunny today, with the rays of sun shining onto the tables, but it was cold outside, and the recent rain meant that the lawn was wet.

'Please stand in a row so I may inspect you,' said Mrs Leggett, addressing the waiters and waitresses in the room. Lili was first in the row, and next to her, Günther, who took on the role of head waiter when she wasn't there. Next came young Simon and Dennis, then two live-out waitresses. Annie was right at the other end, anticipating some negative comment about her appearance.

As Mrs Leggett walked along the line, Annie thought about her encounter with Lorcan in the staff corridor. She'd been short with him. She hadn't meant to be, but she was overcome with that awkwardness again that she always felt in his presence. Two days ago, she'd found her voice and had done well, taking him and Jasper on the little tour, but today, she was back to boring old Annie again. How she regretted her missed opportunity. She could have told him that she was working as a waitress today, and how nervous she was. He'd have understood and probably offered some words of comfort.

Everyone seemed to be up to scratch so far. When the housekeeper reached her, she looked her up and down, her expression giving away nothing. She pulled out a tiny bit of lace on the bib of Annie's apron that had got tucked in, then smiled.

'You'll do very well, Miss Twine.'

'Thank you, Mrs Leggett.'

'Now everyone, please stand on the edges of the room, in different places, so you can help people find their seats, or help the older members, and those less capacitated, to sit down if necessary.'

'Yes, Mrs Leggett,' they all chanted in unison and started to move off in different directions.

'Let's give Miss Affleck the wedding reception she deserves.'

'Mrs Perryman, she'll be,' Lili pointed out, standing by the door. Annie stood close by.

'So she will, Miss Probert, so she will.'

Mrs Perryman. Annie still couldn't get her head around the idea of Hetty marrying the son of a shipbuilder. She doubted she'd ever be Mrs anything, unless she one day became the housekeeper here and had it as an honorary title, like Mrs Leggett did.

There was no point in thinking like that today. She was going to be part of a grand wedding, albeit as a waitress, and she was going to enjoy it.

–

Lorcan and Gertie were still standing up straight, staring at the doors, fifteen minutes later. The bride and groom would inevitably arrive first, especially as he'd heard that most of the guests would be walking from St Mary's, the parish church.

It reminded him of a dilemma he'd considered when he'd been walking out with Hetty, whether he'd have been happy getting married in the Church of England, or whether she'd have been willing to marry at St Catherine's, the Catholic church. Neither of them had been particularly religious, so they'd probably have opted for the registry office. His family would have been upset at either the first or third options, but then, they were back in Ireland, and they couldn't tell him what to do any more. It wasn't anything he'd ever discussed with her, it still being so early on in their courtship when he'd enlisted.

Why was he even thinking about the church dilemma? He couldn't see it ever playing any part in his life now. He wished *someone* would arrive so he could stop thinking about it.

Finally, he spotted a motorcar driving up to the front of the hotel. It was a black Rolls-Royce Silver Ghost, and he knew it would contain the bride and groom. He took a deep breath to still his nerves.

'I'll go and open the doors for them,' said Gertie, maybe thinking she was doing him a favour. It was good of her, but he wished people would just let him get on with it.

She went forward and pulled open the left door, bolting it onto the floor to keep it there. She then held open the right-hand door.

The chauffeur opened the motorcar door for Hetty and she stepped out. Even from where Lorcan was standing, he could tell that she looked stunning. She wore a white, silk dress, reaching just above her ankles. The wide, lacy sleeves were elbow-length, and her veil was as long as the dress. It occurred to him that she must be cold in this weather, but she looked a picture of happiness.

As she entered the hotel, he could see that the front of the dress was gathered in at the waist with a bow. Her shoes were silky and pointed, with a small heel. It was a long way from the overly long dress with its high neck and extensive sleeves that his sister had worn at her wedding in 1910.

Hetty stood near the door, presumably waiting for Victor. She turned and, noticing Lorcan, came forward, smiling.

'Lorcan, I'm so glad to see you're back safely. Phoebe tells me that Jasper has returned as well.'

'That's right, Mrs Perryman. Congratulations on your marriage, madam.'

'Oh Lorcan, I'm still Hetty to you. Please, if we come across each other anywhere, refer to me by my first name, the same as my other friends at the hotel.'

'As you wish, but in the hotel, while I'm serving you, it will have to be Mrs Perryman, so it will.'

'Quite right too,' said Mr Watkins, coming from behind the desk. 'Welcome, Mrs Perryman, and congratulations.'

'Thank you, Mr Watkins.'

Victor Perryman entered and was soon by Hetty's side. The way they looked at each other made Lorcan's insides squirm with envy.

'Congratulations, sir,' said the desk clerk.

Gertie was soon by their side. 'If you'd like to follow me, sir, madam, I'll show you to the dining room.'

As they walked away, Lorcan let out a long sigh. At least that was over and done with. What did he really feel for Hetty now? She was lovely, that was certain, and he had harboured strong hopes of returning to her after the war, to develop his growing affection for her. The damned war. If he hadn't enlisted so early on, and they'd got to know each other better, maybe they would have loved each other. He'd never know now. It was his own fault for being so impulsive. Though he suspected that his current dismay was not so much a case of being broken-hearted, as being intensely lonely.

It wasn't long before Victor's parents turned up in a motorcar. They were followed immediately by his sister, Hetty's sister and Phoebe, who had all been bridesmaids. More guests arrived, including Major Thomas in a smart, pinstripe suit with a row of medals along the left-hand side of his jacket. Edie, Mrs Bygrove and her sweetheart, Detective Inspector Toshack, were just behind him. Soon Mr Watkins was helping the porters direct the guests to the dining room.

It was going to be a long day, especially as the occasion was due to carry on into the evening with an orchestra and a band. He'd be glad when it was all over.

Chapter Four

Ten days later, several of the staff who'd been on their morning break were gathered in the staff corridor, having heard that Charlie Cobbett and head chef, Joseph Norris, had returned. Mrs Norris was beside herself with excitement to see her son once more, bouncing her ample body up and down in a little jig, as everyone greeted and shook hands with the returning employees.

Charlie was overwhelmed by the enthusiastic welcome back, making him even happier that he was home.

'D'ya know when they'll be sending Peter and Stuart back?' Gertie asked, referring to the waiter and desk clerk who'd enlisted in 1914 and 1915.

'Why, you got a fancy for one of 'em?' Alice asked, grinning.

Gertie glared at her. 'No I 'aven't. Just wondering, that's all.'

'Sorry, I was only joking. Two of me brothers are still in Russia too, Charlie. Cedric and Cyril. I don't suppose you know when they're coming back.'

'I know who ya mean, but I ain't got no idea when any of the rest of 'em are coming back, I'm afraid,' Charlie replied. 'There are still things going on along the border between Russia and Finland, so I reckon they'll keep a few men there for a while yet. They seem to be demobbing us from there bit by bit.'

'I dunno,' said Mrs Norris. 'Ya think the war's over, but it's still going on in places.'

'Makes me wonder if it'll ever be completely over,' said Joseph, as Lorcan made an appearance in the corridor.

'Well, would you look at that now, two more of the crew have returned,' said an Irish voice.

'Lorcan!' Charlie was soon shaking his hand enthusiastically at the same time as clapping him on the shoulder. 'Am I glad to see you, me old mucker.'

'The feeling's mutual, so it is. And it's grand to see you too, Joseph.'

'And 'ere's me other old mucker, Jasper.' Charlie went towards him and there was another round of hand shaking and shoulder clapping.

Just as they were finishing, Johnny and Leslie came in for their breaks, and the greetings started again.

'Am I glad to see you two,' Johnny said. 'It'll be good to have you back in the fold. And Charlie, I guess you'll be head porter again.'

'I dunno about that. Gertie 'ere's in charge now, I understand.' He looked around at where she was sitting nearby.

'Yep, as far as I'm aware,' she said. 'Mrs Bygrove ain't told me no different.'

'That's not on,' said Johnny. 'You can't take Charlie's job.'

Charlie tapped his shoulder. 'It's all right mate, I'm not bothered. It's not like it *was* me job in the first place. I was only stepping in for Alan, and now, sadly, he ain't coming back. Gertie filled in for a good deal longer than I did after I enlisted, so she's entitled to the job.'

'But it should go to a man. *We're* the breadwinners.'

'How'd ya mean?' said Gertie, glaring at him. 'It's not like none of you are married and keeping a family. And women do that too, nowadays, to make ends meet.'

'No, none of us are married yet. But, well, it's just not right, a woman being in charge, getting more money, when the other porters are men. You agree, don't you Leslie, being a porter too?'

The room had gone quiet, and it was a few seconds before Leslie replied.

'Maybe. I dunno. Gertie's doing a good job as far as I can see. Does it matter?' He shrugged, his face a little pink.

Johnny's eyes narrowed. 'I bet your brother Stanley would agree with me.'

'Times are changing,' said Lorcan. 'And we can't expect special privileges just 'cos we're men.'

'But *we're* the ones who've put our lives on the line these last years. Not the women.'

'I dunno about that mate,' said Charlie.

'Well *I* think—' Johnny started.

'*I* think that's enough of that talk,' said Mrs Norris. 'It's not up to us, anyway. It's Mrs Bygrove what decides them kinda things. Let's sit and have our break, and be glad that Charlie and my Joseph are back.'

There was an enthusiastic response to this, and those still standing found seats. Charlie, waiting to see where there'd be a space, noticed Johnny's face was puckered; he wasn't sure whether with annoyance or remorse.

Helen came into the room. 'Ah good, you two are settling in.'

'I've got a nice plate of biscuits to bring in,' said Mrs Norris. 'Won't be a tick. Come on now, Charlie, sit yourself down.'

'Actually, Charlie, I'd like a word with you in my office first, if you don't mind,' said Helen. 'It won't take long.'

Oh no, what was that about? Was she going to offer him back the job as head porter? As nice as that would have been, he'd feel a real hypocrite after what he'd just said.

He followed her around the corner to the small passageway that led to the front desk, a storeroom and her office. Inside, she sat down and invited him to do likewise. He felt nervous and hoped she'd get straight to the point.

'Don't look so worried, Charlie. I was only wondering whether you'd like to take on the job of running the hotel garage on Norfolk Place.'

'The garage? What's 'appened to George?'

'Mr Burgess would like to retire.'

'Well, it's kind of you to ask, Mrs Bygrove, but I'm not sure how much there'd be to do. I like to keep busy, me. The garage only looks after guests' cars and does small repairs.'

'At the moment, yes, but I would like it to do more, and offer a service to the people of Littlehampton, especially Beach Town. I understand you were a good motorcar mechanic before you, um…'

'Went to prison? Yep, me dad always reckoned I 'ad a talent for it. He weren't interested in taking me on after me spell away though. Thought it might reflect badly on 'is business.'

'You've made up with him since though, haven't you?'

'Oh yes, on one of me leaves from the army. Dead proud he was, that I'd enlisted.'

'I hope he won't think we're stepping on the toes of his business – if you agree.'

'Well, as it 'appens, he was talking about giving up the business to go to work for someone else. He struggled finding mechanics during the war and he's fed up with the business side of it, and he's not getting any younger. He just wants to play with motorcar engines and earn enough to keep 'em, as he put it.' Charlie chuckled.

'Well, if we're going to expand the business, we could do with at least one extra member of staff.'

'What, me dad?'

'Why not? My own motorcar went for repairs to his workshop when it broke down, and he got it going again and it's been fine since.'

'Yep, he is a good mechanic. Taught me everything I know, after all. I could certainly run it past 'im, see what he thinks.'

'So, you would consider doing that?'

'I loved me job as a porter, being sociable like, but I always fancied getting back to fixing motorcars at some point.'

'There's something else. As you probably know, there's a cottage that goes with that job. You can live there, make it your own. If you want. And should you get married at some point, you can both live there.'

He wondered whether Edie would want to live there, assuming they did end up getting married.

'Thanks, Mrs Bygrove. It would be nice to 'ave more than a room.'

'And you'd still be welcome here for your meals, after all, it's only down the road.'

'It's a lot to think about. When is George retiring?'

'In about four weeks' time, the thirteenth of April, when it'll be his seventieth birthday, so you have some time to consider it. It might be an idea though to start there before he goes, so you can get used to it.'

'I'll think about it over the next coupla days. I like the idea a lot, but I'd like to talk to Edie about it too.'

'Of course, that's only right. And if your father doesn't want the job, we can advertise for someone else.'

'Right. Thanks Mrs Bygrove. It's decent of you to consider me.'

She stood up and he did too.

'I am going out on a little trip to Worthing this afternoon, and Edie will be in charge.'

'I'm that proud of 'er, being made undermanageress.'

'And we're all proud of you, Charlie, winning a Distinguished Service Medal and being made a sergeant.' She nodded towards the medal and the three chevrons on his uniform sleeve.

'I'm just glad it's all over. Can't wait to get out of this uniform and into me own clothes. And I'm looking forward to some delicious food, after all the rubbish I've 'ad to eat over the last few years.'

'Well, you're not on duty until the day after tomorrow, so enjoy your days off.'

'I'll be with me parents some of that time, so I'll 'ave a word with me dad then… You spending the afternoon with Detective Inspector Toshack?'

'So you've heard then.'

'Course I 'ave. You can't keep a secret in this place. Well, mostly.' As they moved towards the door, he said, 'Will all the women be keeping their current jobs?' thinking once again about what Johnny had said.

'Only the permanent staff who've been replacing those who've been lost. I'm having to give less work to the part-time female staff now, unfortunately. I feel bad about that, but I can't afford to keep everyone on. The only woman going back to her previous job is Phoebe, and even she's had a promotion, what with Hetty getting married.' She stopped and looked him squarely in the eye. 'Do you have a problem with that?'

'No, course not. I ain't got no problem with the women keeping the jobs.' Should he mention Johnny's outburst? No. 'Got a lot of respect for the women, me. About time they got their due reward.'

'I'm glad to hear you're so enlightened. I believe there have been murmurings about it from some of the men. And about having a German working here.'

'What, Günther? The war's done and he ain't done nothing wrong. Got no time for that kinda thinking and I'll soon nip it in the bud if I come across it, Mrs B. And any talk against women.'

'I'm glad to hear it.'

He opened the door for her, just as Sam Toshack appeared in the corridor.

'Is this another one of your returnees?' he asked, limping a little as he entered.

'Yes, it is. Sam, this is Charlie Cobbett, one of the returning porters. Charlie, this is Detective Inspector Toshack.'

'Aye, I've heard all about you from Helen – Mrs Bygrove.'

Charlie grimaced. 'Oh dear.'

'Don't worry, lad, sounds to me like you've more than made up for any youthful misdeeds.' He pointed to the medal.

'I like to think so.'

'I'll see you later, Charlie. And do have a think about what I said.'

'I most certainly will, Mrs B.'

He walked away with a wave and started whistling.

—

Sam shut the office door after Charlie left. 'Mrs B? That's a little informal, isn't it?'

'Oh, I don't mind. It's affectionately respectful,' said Helen, 'and it's never said in front of the guests. I've heard Mrs Leggett and Mrs Turnbull be referred to as Mrs L and Mrs T, and they don't seem to mind either, and that's saying something for Mrs Leggett.'

'Sorry I'm a bit late. Come on, let's get on our way.'

'You're limping a little.' She pointed down at his left leg, where his artificial lower limb, below the knee, was hidden beneath his trousers and shoes.

'It's giving me a bit of trouble today, after all the *activity*.'

'Activity? You do seem a little put out. Is something up?' She took his hand.

'I'll tell you when we get out.'

They made their way through the stillroom and scullery, to exit through the staff entrance. Once they had passed through the outside gate, heading towards the road, he began to speak.

'I'm glad to get out, to be honest. I was delayed because we've had a big theft in River Road and reports of men being mugged and money stolen around Fisherman's Quay. No idea if they're related. It's not like there's been much trouble on the quay recently, well, not since I arrived.'

'Oh dear, I don't like the sound of that. Though I do recall something going on at the quay before, back in 1914, when someone lodging with Edie on South Terrace turned out to be involved. Pamela Brownlow, that was her name. It seems she may have been a, um, lady of the night.'

'Aye, I've read all the notes on that case, and Sergeant Gardner has filled me in too.'

'Then you know she was killed by Edie's landlady's estranged husband, Gordon Hadley. He killed his wife too and tried to kill Edie. He was executed. And there was some elusive man who'd been involved with Miss Brownlow, who was never caught.'

'Oh yes, "Jim". His name's come up a few times as a possibility when crimes have been committed. Anyway, no doubt this gang, or whatever they are, will move on elsewhere if they think they might get caught, but I'd like to get to the bottom of it. I don't want it escalating into murder again. I've placed Constable Twort on the beat there, to snoop around.'

They'd reached Sam's motorcar, an Austin Ten. He opened the door for Helen before getting in the driver's seat.

Once they'd set off, Helen said, 'I hope he does a better job this time.'

'Who's that?'

'Constable Twort. You remember three years ago, when he was sent to watch a pillar box because libellous letters were being sent, but he went home early…'

'Of course. He seems to have bucked his ideas up now. Though I do wonder if it's time to retire him once again… It would be good to solve the latest cases before Davis returns from the war.' He nodded, as if agreeing with himself.

Helen bit her bottom lip and fiddled with her fingers, anxious about the implication of his last sentence. 'Have you heard anything more about when DI Davis will be demobbed? And, well, what will happen to your job here?'

'He's not due to be demobbed until June, so I still have no idea.'

'Oh dear.'

Sam glanced briefly at her, frowning. 'What's wrong, Helen?'

'Well, they're unlikely to keep two detective inspectors in a small place like Littlehampton, so what will happen to us if they move you? I couldn't possibly leave the hotel.'

Her breathing became laboured as she felt the tears stinging her eyes. She'd thought about this many times, though had always brushed it aside as a worry for the future. But now, that time was coming ever closer. What if they moved Sam far away from here? She took a handkerchief from her handbag to dab her eyes.

He glanced at her once more, before taking the corner. 'Oh darling, don't cry. We'll worry about that, and sort something out, when we get to it.'

She nodded, knowing she'd still fret about it. But she did like being called 'darling'. Her late husband had never called her that, only 'dear', and that had often been said in a condescending way.

She'd try to leave her worries behind today, along with her memories of her less than adequate husband, and enjoy the trip to Worthing.

—

Back at morning break in the staff dining room, Alice was sitting at the middle section of the table, watching Mrs Norris making a fuss of Joseph, while Mrs Turnbull plied him with biscuits. Edie was pouring him a cup of tea.

Lorcan, meanwhile, was bombarding him with questions about what was going on at the Russian–Finland border. Many of those in the room were listening to the conversation. Apart from Johnny at the end of the table, who was looking down.

Sitting next to Alice was Jasper. She felt a contentment sitting there with him, yet mixed with it, was a curious resentment. She didn't *want* to feel this way about someone so out of her reach. He was above her in class, even if his family had fallen on hard times. He was better educated, better spoken, good looking. He could have anyone. He would never be interested in her.

As people slowly began their own conversations, Jasper turned to her. 'Would you pass the biscuits please? I haven't had one yet.'

She did so without comment and kept her expression neutral. Or so she thought.

'What's wrong with you, Alice?'

She did now look at him, a tingling sensation travelling around her body. It was nice yet embarrassing, all at the same time. 'What d'ya mean, what's wrong with me?'

'You're looking very miserable today. You used to be so cheerful. I haven't seen you smile since I returned.'

'There's nothing wrong with me.' She told herself to be pleasant, to just say that she'd been miles away or something, but ignored the good advice. 'Do I 'ave to go around all day smiling, just to keep other people happy?' came out rather petulantly.

'Well, no, but, I don't know. It's what you used to be like.'

'Well, I grew up a bit, didn't I?'

'You 'ave been a bit of a misery these past few days,' said Annie, sitting opposite.

'Must have caught it off you then.'

'Ha ha…How are your parents, Jasper?' said Annie. 'Did you have a good visit with them? I never did hear you say.'

'Yes, I did, thank you.'

He started telling her about his trip to Middleton-on-Sea. Alice turned away, pretending not to listen, but she was. Why had she been so rude? She'd thought of asking him the same question several days ago but hadn't plucked up the courage. It was plain daft. She'd have no problem asking any of the other men. She knew what it was really: she was protecting herself. If she persuaded him she wasn't interested, she might persuade herself too.

She'd thought, with him being away, that she'd get over these feelings for him, but if anything, they'd got stronger.

Charlie entered the dining room, looking confused.

'What's happened?' said Joseph. 'You look like you've had a shock.'

Edie went to him, her brow creased with worry. 'Are you all right, Charlie?'

'Yes, I think so. I've just 'ad Mrs Bygrove offer me a new job.'

'Doing what?' said Lorcan.

'Taking over the running of the 'otel garage from George Burgess. Except she wants me to do more repairs and whatnot. And I'd get to live in the cottage there.'

Edie took hold of his hands. 'That would be right up your street, Charlie.'

'It certainly would. I said I'd think about it and discuss it with you first though.'

'I definitely think you should take the offer.'

'Then I will. There, that's settled.'

'When are you two getting married?' Jack called up from the end of the table. 'Hetty hadn't even met Victor two years ago and they're already married. You two have known each other the best part of five years now.'

Edie's eyes widened and Charlie reddened a little. 'Well,' he said. 'All depends, don't it?'

'What on, lad?' said Mrs Turnbull.

'It depends on whether she wants to marry me.' He turned to Edie. 'Well, do ya?'

'It depends on whether you are actually asking,' she returned, half smiling.

He got down on one knee. 'Yes, I'm asking.'

'Oh Charlie, of course I will.'

He got up and they hugged each other, while everyone cheered. Alice joined in too, happy for them, but feeling a cavern of loneliness inside her at the same time.

'Will you stop being undermanageress?' Annie asked Edie.

'No, definitely not.'

Vera Edge, the children's nursemaid piped up, 'I'd be more than happy to have some more little children to look after.'

It was Edie's turn to go red and everyone laughed.

Alice wondered if there was anyone in this world who would be willing to go down on one knee for her. It was such a romantic gesture, and she did so love romance. And she did so love... No, she couldn't even say those words to herself. She glanced at Jasper who was still grinning widely at what had just occurred. If only.

-

Jasper returned to his shift after morning break and stood by the desk, waiting for a guest to help. He was still rather confused and, dare he think it, upset? Obviously, he'd been looking forward to returning home, but one of the reasons had been to see Alice again, even though he'd been reluctant to admit this to himself.

He had tried not to think about what might have happened while he was away, that she might have found a sweetheart. Not that it had been likely, with most young men at war, but then, other women had. But he was relieved to find out she was still single when he returned.

A few times, before enlisting, he'd thought of asking Alice to walk out with him but had never had the courage to do it. She was so pretty, but even better, she was a sweet, caring, sunny girl. Or she had been. Being in her cheerful company had always brought joy to his day. And she was still cheerful with other people, just not with him. Had he said something that had upset her? He thought back but couldn't recall anything untoward. They had got on very well together before he'd enlisted, having a similar sense of humour and always able to chat amiably.

It was a shame she'd changed. Or maybe she thought *he* had. Had he? It was certainly something to think about. He'd been through a lot in the war.

Major Thomas entered the foyer in his overcoat.

'Good morning, again, Major. I hope you enjoyed your coffee.'

'That and the wonderful palmiers were just the ticket. It's good to have some of the old favourites back on the menu after the shortages during the war. Now, despite the gloom, I'm going out for my daily constitutional.'

Jasper hurried towards the door, but was stalled by the major saying, 'It's all right, I can see myself out.'

'Enjoy your walk, Major.'

Jasper watched him as he lifted his arm in reply and left. He went to the doors and looked out. It certainly was gloomy, reflecting how he felt about his relationship, or lack of it, with Alice.

'Unless there's somebody about to enter, please return to your post,' the chief desk clerk called over.

'Yes, sir.'

Feeling like he did, and with Watkins in his usual overbearing mood, it was going to be a long shift.

–

'Just in time for a nice cuppa tea,' said Mrs Twine, as Alice and Annie walked through the front door that night, into the kitchen.

Alice revelled in the warmth of the room, after the chilly walk back, breathing in the fragrant scent of tobacco that always reminded her of home. She and Annie hung their coats on the wall hooks and joined their mother at the table.

Their father looked up from the armchair, where he was reading the paper and smoking his pipe. 'How did your day go?'

'Charlie asked Edie to marry him,' Alice said with enthusiasm, despite her feelings of despondency earlier. 'Right in the middle of the staff dining room, in front of everyone, at morning break.'

'Well, I never,' said their mother. 'That'll be another wedding then. Don't suppose it'll be as posh as Hetty's, from the way you described it. Unless Edie's dad, Lord Whatsisname, forgives her for marrying beneath her, and stumps up for one.'

'It's her mother what's the problem,' said Annie. 'And he's Lord Moreland, by the way. And Baron Moreland. Still can't work out when you use which title.'

'I reckon it'll be a simple wedding,' said Alice, picturing the two of them walking down the aisle. At least, she had started imagining Edie and Charlie, but somehow the vision had turned into her and Jasper. She coughed as if to clear her throat, but it was the disconcerting image she was trying to dislodge.

The sisters sat at the table, each taking the cups and saucers pushed towards them.

'Now the war's over, it's about time you two found yourself a couple of nice boys,' said their father. 'You'll be twenty-four next month, Annie, and you'll be twenty-three the month after, Alice.' He looked from one to the other, like a schoolteacher criticising a bad piece of work.

Annie tutted. 'We know how old we are, Dad. And don't you start on that again.'

'No, that's my job,' said their mother, chuckling. 'But he's right, ya know. You don't wanna be considered old maids.'

'Anyway,' her sister continued, 'they're not all back yet, the men. And since some won't be coming back, there'll be a shortage. And we're not *old*. *Old maid*. That's a label I'd put on someone like Mrs Leggett. Old maid indeed! Like we've got wrinkles or something.'

'Oh Annie, why do you always have to be so doleful?' said their mother. 'Why can't you be cheerful, like ya sister?'

'We can't all go through life pretending everything is lovely.'

'I do not!' Alice asserted. 'I just try to make the best of things, that's all. Not be sulky all the time.' Her good humour was starting to slip.

'I am not—'

'Arguing again?' said their brother, Cecil, as he walked in from the scullery. 'You two do that a lot these days.' He sat in the armchair opposite their father. 'It's not attractive, ya know. I could 'ear your conversation about marriage. Men don't like women who are silly, or are shrews.'

Alice couldn't keep up the good humour any longer. 'We're not silly!' came out in a much higher-pitched voice than she'd intended.

'And we're not shrews!' Annie crossed her arms as she pinched her lips in.

'That's enough now,' said their mother. 'Cecil, don't be so mean.'

'He's always been mean to us.' Alice poked her tongue out at him.

'See what I mean?' he said, triumphantly, as if she'd proved his point.

Their father slapped the newspaper down decisively on the small side table beside him. 'Let's talk about something else.'

'Any news when Cedric and Cyril'll be back?' said Alice.

'Not yet,' said Cecil.

'Charlie said the men from Russia are being demobbed bit by bit.'

'So it would seem,' he said, taking a packet of cigarettes from his trouser pocket. 'I wish they 'adn't split us up.'

'I don't suppose it'll be long now,' said their mother.

Cecil looked downcast, which rubbed off on Annie, who looked the same.

'I reckon Mum's right,' said Alice, hoping her two siblings would cheer up, but their expressions remained the same.

'The trouble in Russia could last a while yet,' said Cecil.

After that, they all sipped their tea in silence.

Chapter Five

Lorcan had been back just over two weeks now and still was not taking his wonderful surroundings for granted, as he had done before enlisting. Just standing around in the foyer had got boring to him at times back then, but now he wallowed in the comparable peace of it all. He doubted he would ever take it for granted again. The cream walls and beige marble floor and the dark oak reception desk were a far cry from the damp huts, draughty tents and the muddy trenches he'd been exposed to the last four-and-a-half years. He looked up behind the desk, at the wide, curving staircase with its black-and-gold railings, then shifted his gaze to the large crystal chandelier in the centre of the room. There was a painting on the wall he'd always admired, of a seaside scene.

When the end of the war had been announced, he'd thought they'd be sent home quickly, not imagining for a moment that they'd remain in northern France for another four months. And what a tedious four months it had been, walking from camp to camp, encountering destroyed bridges and roads that meant endless diversions. Everywhere had been wet and a mess. When they reached the various camps, they'd been subjected to pointless training and the practising of parades. They'd spent time salvaging that which was often barely salvageable. Recovering military equipment had been tedious and sometimes dangerous, never knowing whether some explosives might still be live. Gathering up the barbed wire hadn't been a pleasant job either. The worst bit, though, had been collecting items that had belonged to soldiers who had perished, like boots and paybooks.

Lorcan was pulled from his thoughts as Lord and Lady Raynolt entered and he surged forward to greet them.

'My lord, my lady, welcome.'

'Why, Lorcan, you're back,' said Lord Raynolt.

'That's right, my lord. A few of us have returned in the last few weeks.'

'That's good to hear,' said his wife. 'We haven't booked a table for luncheon, but we're hoping there might be one available.'

'I believe there are a few, my lady. Let me show you to the dining room.'

He led the way, past the desk and the stairs, to the small corridor that contained the doors to the ballroom and dining room. He opened the glass door to let them in. The room was around two thirds full, but he noticed that it was uncharacteristically quiet, apart from one raised voice.

Günther was standing at a table on the left of the room, his head bowed, while a man who Lorcan had showed in not five minutes ago was shouting at him.

'I didn't fight for four years in the war to be served lunch by the enemy.'

The gentleman, who looked to be in his forties, stood up. He had on a fashionable navy serge suit, the legs narrowing towards the ankles, the jacket single breasted and the lapels wide. Lorcan recognised quality when he saw it. He was very tall and towered above Günther.

'How many good British men did you kill, I wonder?'

Lili was soon by the waiter's side. 'Günther didn't even fight in the war, Mr Farnaby. He was put in an internment camp, despite having been naturalised.'

'And I have never agreed with the Kaiser's stance,' Günther added.

The man ignored him. 'So what. He's a dirty Hun and shouldn't even have a job here. He should be sent back to where he came from!'

Günther turned abruptly and ran from the room.

Lorcan, incensed by the outburst, went forward. 'The war's over now, and we have to forgive, so we do. What's the point otherwise?'

'Says the Irishman who, in all likelihood, didn't lift a finger in the war, like the rest of your sort.'

'My sort? I enlisted right at the beginning of the war, and there were plenty of my *sort* who did too, but I haven't been fighting for the last four years to have a war of some type go on indefinitely.'

'Tell that to your fellow countrymen, still causing trouble.'

'You don't want to get me started on the ins and outs of that history, so you don't. And anyways, it's got nothing to do with this.'

'I'm going to the police. They'll soon remove that devil.'

'What utter rot,' said Lord Raynolt, stepping towards them. 'I can quite assure you they will do no such thing, for he's done nothing but be a jolly good waiter. You're a disgrace, man. It's because of the attitude of *your* sort that wars happen in the first place.'

'Hear, hear!' shouted a voice that Lorcan recognised as Major Thomas's.

'You're all just cowards, sitting there keeping your mouths shut.' Mr Farnaby looked around at the guests.

'No, we're not, we just don't have your unwarranted prejudices,' said a woman on a table by the window, standing up. 'The war is over, and most of us want to move on from it.'

'That's easy for you to say. I lost my brother, killed by the Germans.'

'And *we* lost our son,' she said, with a laboured inhalation. She faltered for a moment before continuing with, 'But blaming people who had nothing to do with that is not going to bring him back.'

Major Thomas rose and joined Lorcan and Lili. 'May I suggest, if you have so much objection to the staff serving you, that you leave and do not return. I'm sure the rest of the guests here would be relieved to be rid of you.'

A murmur went around the room that suggested people agreed with him.

Helen Bygrove entered at this point, her expression concerned when she spotted what must have looked like a standoff. 'I am the manageress, and I understand there is some misunderstanding here.'

'No misunderstanding,' said the annoyed guest. '*I* am Mr Neville Farnaby, and I insist on speaking to the manager, or the owner. There's been a serious error of judgement, employing a German. And these *employees* have no business being rude to a guest. The customer is always right.'

'I am the manager, and I'm also the owner.'

He pulled his head back, forming a double chin, then looked her up and down with disapproval. 'No wonder there's no discipline then. I suggest to you, madam, that you put a *man* in charge.'

There were several loud boos from a table of young, fashionable women with straight-lined suits and bobbed hair.

'Mrs Bygrove is an outstanding manageress,' said Major Thomas. 'You'll find none better.'

'Then I have no more to say. Good day to you.'

'Good riddance to bad rubbish!' called one of the other guests.

He emitted a sharp, 'Huh!' before marching out as if he were still in the army.

'I am so sorry about the disturbance,' Helen announced. 'We will be open for luncheon a quarter of an hour later than usual, to make up for any lost time.'

The guests were soon chatting among themselves once more.

'Lorcan, could I speak to you in my office please?'

Although it was said quite casually, he guessed he might be in trouble. He wasn't sure how, as she hadn't even heard what he'd said.

'Yes, Mrs Bygrove.'

In the office she invited him to sit down.

'Johnny told me that Mr Farnaby was taking Günther to task over something he'd done wrong, and that you were rude to him.'

Johnny. Of course it was, the little snitch. He'd probably agreed with the guest and wanted to get anyone sticking up for Günther into trouble.

'He wasn't just *talking* to Günther, he was downright rude to him, Mrs Bygrove. I know that the customer is supposed to always be right, but most of the guests seemed to agree with me.'

'Yes, I could see he was a difficult customer, and I appreciate you supporting Günther, but I think if it happens again, it might be better if I was fetched *before* anything was said.'

'Yes, Mrs Bygrove.'

He could understand her point of view. It probably didn't look good for a luxury hotel if the staff argued with the guests. He wouldn't tell her that it was actually Lili who had first confronted Farnaby.

'If you could pass that on to any other staff members involved, I would appreciate it. You can return to your duties now.'

'Yes, Mrs Bygrove. Can I just ask, who exactly *is* Mr Neville Farnaby? He seemed to think I should know.'

Helen shrugged, with a hint of a smile. 'I have as much idea as you, Lorcan.'

–

Annie had heard whispers about an incident taking place in the dining room and was hoping to find out more during her afternoon break. The teacups were already placed in the middle of the table but nothing else had arrived yet.

'Phoebe,' she said, sitting next to her. 'Did something 'appen with Günther at lunch?'

'I heard something about a guest not wanting to be served by him because he's German, but he hasn't said anything to me. I haven't seen him since this morning. It's like that time when the war first started, and a guest reported him to the police, and they took him away.'

'They can't take 'im away again though – the war's over.'

Lorcan and Lili entered, both clearly still annoyed about the scene as they held forth with cross words.

'Is this about Günther?' Phoebe asked.

'That guest was out of order, so he was, insulting Günther like that.'

Annie could see that Lorcan wasn't only annoyed, but upset, which made her unhappy too. 'What happened?'

'A jumped up, pompous eejit called him some horrible names and implied he was the enemy. He referred to him as a "dirty Hun" and said he should be sent back to where he came from.'

'Oh no,' said Phoebe, her shoulders sagging as she pushed her bottom lip out. 'Poor Günther.'

'Me and Lili stuck up for him, as did Major Thomas and Lord Raynolt, and another guest. It seemed like most of the guests were on Günther's side.'

Lily took a seat opposite Annie and Phoebe. 'He said some mean things about the Irish too. Mrs Bygrove came in and he was rude to her as well, saying she should put a man in charge.'

'Bleedin' cheek!' said Annie. 'He does sound like an idiot.'

'Aye, reckoned he was gonna report Günther to the police.'

Phoebe put her hands out to the side. 'For what? It's not illegal to be German. And I can't imagine Detective Inspector Toshack taking him seriously.'

'Well, I don't know the man meself, but I hope you're right. You never know what web of lies a man like Farnaby might spin.' Lorcan sat down next to Lili, placing his chin on his hands as his elbows rested on the table. 'It was Johnny what went and got Mrs Bygrove, though I don't reckon it was to support Günther, but to get him into trouble. And me.'

'He does seem to have a bit of a problem with him,' said Annie.

Mrs Turnbull and Gertie came in with trays containing teapots, milk, hot water and a plate of biscuits.

'Did anybody hear about this incident with Günther?' Mrs Turnball asked.

Lorcan and Lili went over the story again, making Phoebe look even more miserable.

'Is Günther all right now?' Gertie asked.

'I dunno. He didn't have a shift this afternoon,' said Lili.

'I'll go and check his bedroom,' said Phoebe. 'He's probably there. I'll make sure he's all right.'

As she left, Johnny and Stanley entered the room.

'Biscuits, great,' said Johnny, rubbing his hands together. 'Just what I need.'

'Enjoyed snitching to Mrs Bygrove, did you now?' said Lorcan.

Annie flinched, not sure how this would end up. Johnny, a mild-mannered young man before he'd left for the war, now seemed constantly on edge, and jumped down people's throats at the least hint of criticism. Even when joking with people, he could suddenly turn on them.

'What d'ya mean?' said Johnny sharply, standing tall and straight, as if on parade.

Stanley, looking wary, took a seat.

'You implied to Mrs Bygrove that *I* started that argument with Farnaby.'

'Well, you did.'

'No, *I* did,' said Lili, 'and you know that.'

'He was picking on Günther in a very nasty way,' said Lorcan. 'If I hadn't stepped in, someone else would have done, I'm sure.'

'It would've been better for Mrs Bygrove to sort it—' Stanley started.

Johnny turned abruptly. 'I can speak for myself.'

Stanley held his arms up briefly, as if surrendering.

Lorcan pointed towards Johnny. 'But *he* told Mrs B that Mr Farnaby was taking Günther to task over something he'd done wrong and that it was *me* who was rude.'

'That's not true,' said Lili. 'Mr Farnaby was clearly being rude to Günther. Why did you lie, Johnny?'

'Because he was trying to get Günther into trouble, and me for sticking up for him,' said Lorcan. 'You've made it quite clear you think he shouldn't be here, so you agreed with that eejit guest.'

Phoebe rushed in. 'Günther's not in his room. Have you two seen him?' she asked Johnny and Stanley. 'I'm worried about him.'

Johnny brought his face too close to hers as he growled, 'With any luck he's gone back to Germany.'

Mrs Turnbull stood, her finger raised, presumably to admonish him, but Phoebe beat her to it as she swung her hand out and slapped his arm. 'You're *horrible*!'

He stepped back, as if stunned, letting out a long, tortured moan. He stumbled back, towards the wall, where he covered his head with his arms, groaning softly now.

Stanley stood and went to him. 'Hey, calm down now, pal.'

Johnny looked confused for a while, stumbling back to the seat, half helped by his friend, his eyes glassy as he mumbled something incomprehensible. Lorcan looked around the room at the others, baffled. He widened his eyes as they rested on Annie. She met his gaze and shrugged, clearly as dumbfounded as he was.

Phoebe burst into tears. Mrs Turnbull was the first to reach her, placing an arm around her shoulders. 'There, there, pet. I'm sure Günther will be fine. He's probably just gone for a walk.'

'He doesn't like going out as he gets the odd nasty comment from people when they hear his accent,' she sobbed. 'He's talked about going back to Germany. If he does, I'll go with him,' she said with conviction.

Annie got up and took her hand. 'As far as I'm concerned, Günther is welcome here and is part of our... family.' If a rather dysfunctional one at the moment, she thought, but didn't voice this. 'And any guest who says he ain't welcome is a nitwit.'

'Hear, hear,' said Lorcan.

Helen entered at this juncture, looking a little bewildered at what was going on. By this time, Johnny had his hands over his head once more, which was resting on his knees, and he was shaking.

'Oh my, is something wrong?'

'Phoebe's worried about Günther 'cos she can't find him,' said Annie.

'He's fine. He told me he was going to have a walk by the sea, to clear his head,' said Helen.

Phoebe let out a long sigh of relief, then took a handkerchief from her pocket and wiped her eyes.

'And, talking of Günther, I've just had a telephone call from Sam – Inspector Toshack – to say that Mr Farnaby did indeed report him to the police.'

'Oh no!' cried Phoebe.

Helen touched her arm lightly. 'It's all right, Sergeant Gardner told him he was aware of his employment at the Beach Hotel, knew him to be a decent sort, and sent Mr Farnaby away with a flea in his ear, as Sam put it.'

'That's a relief. Thank you for telling us, Mrs Bygrove.' Johnny stood up and hurried out of the room.

'Is he all right?' Helen asked.

When no one replied, Stanley rose from the bench. 'I'll go and make sure.'

'I'll leave you to your break,' said Helen, departing.

'I hope this resentment of Günther that Johnny has isn't goin' to last long,' said Mrs Turnbull.

'I've got a feeling there might be more to it than that,' said Lorcan.

'What exactly?' Annie asked him.

'Not sure,' he said, seeming reluctant to say more. 'Come on, let's have that tea and biscuits before this break's over.'

Annie regarded him briefly, wondering what he'd meant, but quickly looked away, not wanting people to think she was ogling him. She returned her attention to Phoebe.

'Come and sit down. Günther'll be back soon enough, I'm sure.'

Chapter Six

Late Monday evening, Mrs Bygrove had held a short memorial in the dining room for the staff members who had perished in the war: Alex Tuppen, Alan Drew, Anton Martin and James Wood. Most of the staff had attended, with some live-outs not on shifts turning up, and there had been standing room only. Photos had been located and put in frames on the mantelpiece. Mrs Leggett had said a prayer, and then Charlie said a few words about each of the men. Annie noticed some of the women dabbing their eyes as he spoke, including Alice. She felt tearful herself, faced with the reality that these young men would never return.

Afterwards, they shared their memories of the four men over a cup of tea.

'I'm glad Mrs Bygrove organised that,' said Lorcan, standing with Annie and Gertie. 'Only seems right to remember their time with us, so it does.'

Annie nodded. 'Yes, it's like a kind of, I dunno, closure. Like you get at a funeral, I s'pose.'

Gertie looked sombre. 'Not that their families'll get to give 'em funerals.'

'But hopefully they'll have some kind of service,' said Annie, trying to lift the mood once more.

'Aye, I should think so,' said Lorcan.

After this, the three of them drifted into other conversations. Those Annie joined echoed Lorcan's words, with further memories of the men shared.

Towards the end, Annie decided to take the empty cups and saucers back to the scullery, to wash up before she went home. She approached Alice, who was chatting to one of the live-out chambermaids about some new skirts they'd both spotted in a shop window.

'You gonna help me with these?'

'We're not even on duty. Finn'll do 'em when he's finished in here.'

'Let's just get 'em out of the way, then we can all go 'ome.'

'I'm in the middle of a conversation.' She turned back to talk to the chambermaid.

Annie headed off with the tray, huffing out her frustration as she went.

She washed the crockery with zeal, splashing more than normal, still annoyed at Alice's refusal to help.

As she was washing the spoons, Jasper entered the scullery, with a couple of teapots. 'My, you're keen.'

'Might as well get it over and done with.'

'I'll give you a hand.' He took one of the drying-up cloths down from where they were hung on hooks and picked up a cup.

'Thanks, Jasper.'

After a few seconds, he said, 'I've been meaning to ask you… um, whether I've done something to annoy Alice. She's been off with me several times now.'

'Like the time you asked her to pass you the biscuits?'

'Yes, that was one of them. But she's not been very friendly at all, and we used to get on so well. Doesn't she like me for some reason?'

'I don't know, really.' What had she said of him a while back? Oh yes, that was it. It would serve her right if she told him. Should she though? Alice would only have herself to blame. 'Except, um, I think she described you as "all right but nothing special" when you first came back. Something like that.'

Jasper looked rather taken aback, and she regretted saying it. What had possessed her? Only that Alice had been getting on her nerves a lot recently, being so damned happy, most of the time anyway. Even at home, her mother was always going on about how she wasn't as cheerful as her sister. And recently had implied that she'd never get a husband being so grumpy. That had really annoyed her. And now, Alice had ignored her instructions when *she* was head scullery maid.

'Oh, why did she word it like that?'

It did seem an odd thing to say for no good reason. 'Well, I thought at one time that she, you know, liked you in particular, so I asked her, and that's what she said.'

If he'd held out any hope of walking out with Alice, maybe it was just as well to tell him where he stood. Being cruel to be kind would be better in the long run.

'I see…' Jasper hung his head and his brow was creased. He looked a little like he was in pain. Annie felt sorry for him, wondering once more if she should have kept Alice's words to herself. Within a few seconds though, he lifted his head once more and the hint of a smile was back. 'It was a nice little memorial for the lost men this evening, wasn't it? That is, as nice as something like that can be.'

She was confused by the sudden change of subject but was glad that he'd recovered from what she'd told him.

They talked about the evening as she fetched another drying-up cloth and joined him.

When it was all done, Jasper hung the cloth back up. He turned towards her, pressing his lips together. 'Um, I was wondering, when is your afternoon off?'

It was a curious question. 'On Thursday. Why?'

'I thought it was. It's just, that's my afternoon off too. Would you like to go to the pictures? There's a western on called *The Narrow Trail*, and I wondered if you fancied seeing it.' He looked nervously hopeful.

She wasn't sure what she'd expected him to say, but it wasn't that. She was taken aback, ready to make an excuse about already having something to do, when she thought, why not? Alice had clearly gone off him so wouldn't mind. And Lorcan would never be interested in her. And they were surely only going as friends. Jasper was nice company, and she deserved a treat.

'Yes, I like a western. All right.'

He smiled. 'Good, yes good. We'll make arrangements during the week.'

'All right.' Was that all she could find to say? 'I'd better fetch Alice and get home if I'm going to be back here tomorrow bright and early.'

'And I'm also on an early shift tomorrow, so I'd better get to bed. Goodnight, Annie.'

'Goodnight, Jasper.'

He left first and she watched him go. He was handsome, that was for sure, and a nice person. She could certainly do a lot worse. And who knew, perhaps she'd grow fond of him. She hoped so.

Alice came into the room, grinning in her usual way, already in her coat and holding on to Annie's. 'Here you are. I wondered where you'd got to.'

'You know where I got to – doing the bleedin' washing up. We'd better get off home.'

'I just saw Jasper leave. What was he doing in here?'

'Bringing in some teapots and helping with the drying. That was nice of him, wasn't it?'

'S'pose.' She looked glum.

Her sister really did seem to have a problem with Jasper. Maybe she'd tell her why one day, but for now, it confirmed to her that she'd done the right thing in accepting his invitation.

Annie took her coat from Alice. 'Come on then, home time.'

–

'What are you doing this afternoon?' Alice asked Annie as she reappeared in the scullery after lunch on Thursday with her coat in her hand. She'd changed into her second-best dress.

'A trip to the pictures to see *The Narrow Trail*. It's a western.'

'What, on your own?'

She didn't have time to reply before the two young scullery lads, Finn and Lucas, entered from outside, chatting and laughing.

'Good, you're on time,' said Annie. 'Now go and hang your jackets up and come straight back as there's a pile of washing up still to do.'

They exited into the stillroom, which led to the staff corridor, just before Jasper entered.

'Ah, you're ready,' he said.

Alice glanced from one to the other. 'What's all this then?'

Her sister was looking down as she put her coat on and seemed rather embarrassed. 'I told you, it's a trip to the pictures.'

'A cousin of mine went to see *The Narrow Trail* a couple of days ago and reckoned it was very good,' said Jasper.

'So, you're going together?' Alice kept her face deadpan, displaying no emotion either way, as she picked up a plate to dry.

'That's right,' said Jasper. 'Oh, I nearly forgot my cap. Do excuse me while I fetch it. It's rather wet and blowy out there.'

As soon as he was out of earshot, Alice said, 'What on earth are you doing, going out with Jasper? I thought you liked Lorcan.'

'I've never said that. And you said you didn't like Jasper.'

'I never said that.'

'You said, and I quote, he was "all right, nothing special".'

'I didn't mean it like that.'

'Anyway, we're just going to the pictures as a couple of friends. All right by you?'

'Friends?' Alice put the plate down on the worktop. 'Since when have you been friends who do things together?'

'Since now. This is the first trip we've had out together. It's just for the afternoon.'

Alice picked up another plate, rubbing it roughly with the drying-up cloth. 'You'll be twenty-four next month, so you can do what you like. It's not like I'm the bossy big sister telling everyone what to do.'

'That's not very...'

'Here it is,' said Jasper, coming back in, flinging his cap onto his head.

Annie picked up her handbag and they headed out, as Finn and Lucas walked back in, still chatting merrily.

'Right, Finn, you carry on drying and Lucas, you finish the washing up,' said Alice. 'There'll be plenty more in soon, so I'm going to boil some more water.'

'Crikey, you sound like your bossy sister today. You're usually the cheery one, what makes us laugh.'

'That's enough of your cheek, Finn. When Annie's not here, I'm head scullery maid.'

She noticed the two lads pull faces at each other as if to ask what on earth had happened to her. What indeed? She picked up a metal bucket and filled it from the tap in the second sink. Surely, Annie spending time with Jasper, whatever the relationship, was as good a way as any for her to get over him. But she'd only wanted to do that because she'd thought he wouldn't look twice at her. What if it grew into something more than friendship, between Jasper and Annie? What if they ended up getting— No, she couldn't even consider it. But if he was prepared to spend time with Annie, then she might as well have set her own cap at him.

What a fool she'd been, taking this tactic. But even if she'd carried on being nice to him, he'd probably have preferred Annie, with her golden-brown hair and her big green eyes, not her, silly Alice in Wonderland. She probably seemed like a little girl next to Annie.

'Hey, the bucket's overflowing,' Finn called.

'What? Oh, yes, so it is.' She turned the tap off, then tipped a bit of the water out, so she could lift it without spilling any.

'You was miles away.'

'Yep, that's me.' *Silly old Alice in Wonderland*, she added to herself once again, as she lifted the bucket onto the stove.

When she'd first set off with Jasper, Annie had felt guilty about Alice finding out they were going to the pictures together. By the time they'd reached the Palladium, opposite St Mary's on Church Road, she'd talked herself out of it. Her sister had made it clear that she no longer had feelings for Jasper, or rather, her feelings had turned from a crush to disdain. She still couldn't fathom why.

During the film, Annie had wondered if Jasper might take hold of her hand, or even put his arm around her, but he'd done neither. She was relieved, wanting to keep it as a friendship, like she'd told Alice.

When they emerged into the daylight once more, there was a little bit of blue sky, although it was still breezy.

'At least it's not raining now,' he said. 'Do you fancy a walk somewhere?'

'Why not? We 'aven't got to get back until our early evening shifts. Where were you thinking?' Even as she said it, she wondered if it was a good idea, or whether he'd want to take her somewhere quiet to canoodle. She didn't want that. Not yet, at least.

'I was thinking maybe up Pier Road by the river, and then a walk on the promenade. I know it's a bit windy, but I do rather like the sea when it's rough. It has a lot more... character, for want of a better word.'

'Sounds good to me.'

That was a relief, as long as he didn't try to take her somewhere out of the way on their route there. She thought it unlikely; he'd always been quite a gentleman, had Jasper.

They headed through the town, peering into shop windows along the way, making comments about things they liked the look of. He was easy to get on with and quite entertaining. She wondered, once more, if she might get fond of him, given time.

Arriving finally in Pier Road, they walked close to the river's edge. Several fishing boats were moored there, and a couple of fishermen were sitting on the pebbles, mending nets.

'It's strange not to see the Admiralty's dazzle camouflage ships on the river any more,' said Annie.

'I only saw them once, when back on leave, as I spent most of the time at home in Middleton. Wasn't it strange, having such ships here?'

'It was to begin with. But then we got used to it, I s'pose. Like the noise of the guns. They were loudest on the promenade, but you could 'ear 'em in other places sometimes. It seems very quiet now... What am I thinking, it must've been far noisier for you?'

'Well, yes, I suppose it was... Do you fancy a cup of tea at the Harbour Tea Rooms?'

'I wouldn't mind.'

They crossed the road, only to find a sign up on the door.

'It's closed today. That's unusual,' said Annie.

'It says it's for "family reasons". I hope it's something nice, not a funeral or whatever.'

'Oh no, don't say that.'

'Sorry, I didn't mean to upset you.' He looked concerned.

'You haven't, don't worry.'

They crossed back over to walk by the river once more, and he took her hand. She wasn't sure at first, but it was harmless enough. Then again, the prom would be pretty empty on a day like this. Would he take advantage of that?

He's a decent man, remember.

Yes, of course he was. And if he did try something, and she said no, she was sure he'd respect that.

They walked past the pond and windmill, then reached the Casino Theatre.

'I'm glad to see that's still going,' he said. 'Has someone taken it over from Mr Janus? It used to be called the Kursaal.'

'No, it's still run by Mr Janus. He thought it sounded too German so changed it a couple of years into the war.'

'Looks like they've got some entertainments on, even at this time of year. Maybe we could go to one on another afternoon off?'

'I'd like that.'

They passed the coastguards' cottages and the old battery mound, turning the corner onto the promenade, past the pepper-pot lighthouse.

'You see what I mean?' He held his arm out, pointing to the sea about halfway up the beach. 'Look at those waves, tumbling onto the sand. Let's go and take a closer look.'

He jumped down onto the beach, then held his hand out to help her down. As they walked towards the water's edge, the crashing sound of the waves got louder.

'Isn't it marvellous?' he said. 'I've always preferred the sea on days like these. I know that sounds strange.'

'I don't think it does. I do prefer it when there are fewer people around.'

'I agree. Though it's not good for the hotel, of course.' He chuckled.

'I dunno, we get guests all times of the year, so clearly some just like being by the sea, whatever the weather's doing.'

'I suppose you're right.'

Jasper ran towards the waves as they receded, scampering backwards when a fresh wave chased him. Annie laughed, but didn't join in.

'I think the tide's going out,' he said. He looked at his watch. 'We could wander back to town and get some dinner, if you like. There'll be a couple of places open.'

'Um…'

'Or, we could go back to the hotel and have early dinner there.'

'Yes, that would be cheaper.'

'Oh, I wasn't meaning—'

'I didn't think you were, but it would be, and at least at the 'otel we wouldn't have to rush back.'

'No, that's true. Let's do that then.'

They trudged back up the sand, climbing some steps this time to reach the promenade. As they sauntered towards the hotel, she told him some more of the things that had happened while he'd been away. He didn't attempt to hold her hand this time, linking his hands behind his back instead. She felt relaxed in his company, able to talk to him naturally. Why couldn't she be like this with Lorcan?

'I can't, um, do anything on my afternoon off next week,' he said, 'as I'm visiting my parents in Middleton. And the week after, I'm seeing an old friend. But maybe we could do something the week after that? Always assuming you'll still have Thursdays off in April.'

'I do. All right. That'd be… the tenth.'

They were nearing the part of the prom closest to the Beach Hotel now. He tipped his head back. 'Looks like we've arrived just in time.'

She gazed at the sky and was soon squeezing her eyes shut as a few heavy drops fell onto her face.

They headed across the grass, towards the hotel, but it wasn't long before the drops became a downpour, and they ended up running the last third of the way.

–

Alice spotted Annie and Jasper as they rushed through the side gate of the hotel, through the pouring rain. A few seconds later, they were falling through the door, soaked and laughing. A wave of misery passed through her, giving her a brief desire to cry, but she breathed it back.

'Oh crikey!' said Annie, flapping her arms out at the side and shaking her head. Water sprayed out from her hat and coat.

'Hey, don't get that water everywhere. I'll 'ave to get a mop to wipe it up,' said Alice.

'Don't worry,' said Jasper. 'I'll get my coat off and do that for you.'

Alice looked heavenward, when what she should have done was say thank you. But she wasn't in the mood to be nice to either of them.

'I'll get me coat off too,' said Annie, following him.

'They looked like they was 'aving fun,' said Finn. 'Are they walking out?'

'Think they must 'ave just met on the way in,' said Alice, wanting to deny the reality of it.

Jasper was soon back. 'Where's the mop then? Ah, here it is.'

'You don't need to worry,' said Alice, harshly. 'We'll do it.'

'Nonsense. I'm partly responsible for it, so I'll clear it up.'

Why did he have to be so nice? If he'd snapped back at her, she'd have felt better about it.

Annie returned. 'Thanks Jasper, it's appreciated.'

'Any time. I'd better go and change into my porter's garb before dinner. I'll go and let Mrs Norris know we're back, so she can allow for two extras.'

'Good idea.'

'Right, you two, you'd better take these trays of crockery back to Mrs Turnbull,' said Alice.

'Righty ho,' said Finn.

The scullery lads left with a tray each, and Alice turned to her sister.

'How'd it go, then, the afternoon with Jasper?'

'Good. We enjoyed the film.'

'What else did you do?'

'Oh, ya know, this and that.'

'Right. You going out with him again sometime?'

'Perhaps. I'd better go and change too.'

Annie left the room, humming a happy tune, and Alice was left alone.

This and that. She got a squirmy sensation in her belly as she imagined them kissing. What else would her sister have meant by the vague comment? She'd been down-hearted all afternoon, picturing them together, and now she'd feel even worse this evening. She should have known better than to ask.

It was her own fault. She'd been cold to Jasper, and she'd made out to Annie that she didn't care about him. And now she had to live with the consequences of that.

Chapter Seven

Alice wasn't on the same tea break as Jasper the following morning, which she was glad about. Neither was Annie, which gave her a break from her sister, as well as the work.

The table was soon fully occupied, and chatter filled the room. Alice was in conversation with Phoebe, putting on her 'happy face', as she now thought of it. An expression that had always come naturally, until recently. Now it was becoming more of an effort. Lorcan was the opposite, telling a funny tale about an officer in the war to Jack, who had his head back and was laughing. Perhaps she should chat more to Lorcan, see if he might ask her out for the afternoon. She knew she didn't mean it. He was nice enough, but she just didn't have those kinds of feelings for him. But she did wonder how much Annie would mind if she walked out with him. She didn't hold with revenge though, as tempting as it was.

Edie and Charlie entered the room, clasping hands and looking excited.

'Come and sit down,' said Mrs Turnbull. 'We can shuffle around and make space.'

'No, it's all right,' said Edie. 'We've only come in to tell you our news.'

'What's that then, pet?'

Alice guessed what was coming.

'We've obtained a marriage licence and have been to see the vicar at St Mary's.'

'Have you set the date?' Phoebe called over.

'Yep, fourteenth of June,' said Charlie.

People rose from the table and surrounded them, offering hearty congratulations. Alice did likewise, and she was pleased for them, more than pleased, but at the same time it highlighted her lack of a sweetheart and reminded her that the man she was… fond of, was friendly with her sister, and that it might turn into more. And there was a possibility that maybe, sometime in the future, *they* would get married. Her heart plummeted.

Lorcan was shaking Charlie's hand vigorously. 'Well, that's just grand, so it is.'

'I'm glad you think so,' he replied, ' 'Cos I'm 'oping you'll be me best man.'

'It'd be a privilege.'

It wasn't long before those on the next break started filtering into the room, and, on hearing the news, added their good wishes.

Alice headed back to work, her break over, determined to be her usual happy self and not wallow in unwelcome thoughts.

'Charlie and Edie have actually set a date and are getting married in June,' were her opening words as she entered the scullery.

'Not before time,' said Annie. 'They've been courting for a few years, and I dare say they'd have been married a while ago if it 'adn't been for the war. Good for them.' It didn't really sound like she meant it, but she probably did. She was just back to being glum Annie again, after having been a lot cheerier yesterday.

'I think it's wonderful,' said Alice, determined not to be brought down by her sister, or her own gloomy thoughts.

–

Lorcan went into lunch with a letter Mrs Leggett had handed him in the corridor. He recognised the scruffy script. His brother had always struggled with handwriting and was still bad at spelling, so the fact he'd written the letter filled him with dread.

'Something up, mate?' said Jerry, already seated with several others. 'Looks like you've got the world on your shoulders.'

'Got a letter from home.'

'That's good, ain't it?' said Annie. 'You usually like hearing their news.'

'From me mammy, yes, but this is from me brother, Patrick. He never writes normally, and the fact he has this time tells me it's not good news.'

He stared at the envelope for a while.

'Just looking at it isn't gonna make whatever it is go away,' said Jerry.

'You're right, so you are.'

He turned it over and was about to open it when Mrs Leggett entered, followed by Mrs Turnbull and Fanny, carrying trays of sandwiches.

'Hasn't anyone set the plates yet?' said the housekeeper. 'Gertie, Lili, fetch them over please. Come on, chop chop, we haven't got all day.'

'Why is it always the women what have to lay the table?' said Gertie. 'The men should do it for a change. After all, some of 'em are waiters.'

'Not this again, Miss Green.'

'I've been serving and laying up all morning and could do with a break from it,' said Jerry.

Lili huffed. 'As 'ave I, look you.'

'Sit down, Lili,' said Lorcan. 'I'll do it.'

Mrs Leggett raised her eyes but didn't argue. He knew he was simply delaying the inevitable and, as Jerry had put it, whatever was in the letter wouldn't go away.

Once they were all seated again and had helped themselves to the sandwiches, Lorcan lifted the letter from the table and ripped open the seal, determined not to delay it any longer.

He hadn't got far into the short missive when he was sighing out a loud moan. It wasn't a death, as he'd feared, but it was unwelcome news all the same.

'You all right, mate?' Jerry asked.

'I'm sure Mr Foley will furnish us with the details if he wishes to.'

'No, it's fine, Mrs Leggett, I might as well tell ya.' He took a deep breath. 'Like I said, it's from Patrick. He says that the family needs me back in Limerick. Me father's been shot—'

Annie flung her hands to her mouth. 'Oh no!'

She sounded genuinely distressed, which surprised Lorcan. She didn't normally show that much emotion about anything.

'Don't worry, it didn't kill him, but he is in hospital with a nasty flesh wound in the leg.'

'Who shot him?' Jerry asked.

'The soldiers what are posted over there. He was protesting against Limerick city and part of the county being declared a "Special Military Area". Anyways, there's more. Me brother-in-law, who was also at the protest, is now in gaol. Patrick says me mammy and sister need my support, as he has his own family to look after.'

'I'm not sure that returning at this juncture is a good idea, Mr Foley,' said the housekeeper. 'There is a war for independence brewing.'

Will Fletcher, who always had his nose in a newspaper during the breaks, interrupted with, 'Indeed there is. Particularly in Limerick. It says in the papers that because the army has declared the city to be a Special Military Area, permits are required from the police for entering or leaving. You might not even get in.'

'Patrick hasn't mentioned that.'

'The last thing you need is to be involved in another war,' said Annie.

'Aye, that's the truth of it, but I've got to try to help. When I'm done here, I'll go and have a word with Mrs Bygrove.'

'Well, it's up to you, lad,' said Will. 'But I'd think very carefully before you make a decision.'

'They're my family and I've got to be there for them,' he said, decisively, even if he wasn't convinced by his own words. After all, what could he actually do? And Annie was right: he had no stomach to get involved in another war.

Having lost his appetite, he left the last quarter of his sandwich. He rose and left the room, calling, 'I'll be back in a bit.'

He made his way around the corner of the corridor to the narrow passage where the office was situated, knocking on the door, hoping the manageress was there. He was relieved when her voice invited him in.

'Lorcan. What can I do for you?'

He quickly repeated the contents of the letter. 'So ya see, Mrs Bygrove, I feel duty bound to go as quickly as I can. I'm really sorry if this is inconvenient, especially since I've only recently got back.'

'As inconvenient as it is, it is a family emergency, so I quite understand. Is it your intention to return here?'

'As quickly as I can, but I'll understand if you can't keep the job open for me.'

'No, you are one of the best porters I've ever employed, so I will certainly keep the position open for you.'

'That's very decent of you, Mrs Bygrove, and much appreciated. What will you do with a man down?'

'What we did during the war, Lorcan – get by.'

'Aye, I suppose you did. Thanks again. I'm going to go and organise meself now.'

'Very well. Have a safe journey, and I hope your family situation is sorted out soon. Now, I'd better sort out a replacement for you for this afternoon.'

He nodded and left, dreading what was ahead, the long, tedious journey to Ireland by train and boat, then who knew what? The quicker he could set off, the better.

–

Annie watched the door for a while after Lorcan left the dining room, willing him to return and say he'd changed his mind, that it was madness to head back to where there was yet another conflict brewing.

'I do hope the lad's doing the right thing,' said Mrs Turnbull. 'Should we try to talk him out of it?'

'I don't think we'd make any difference,' said Mrs Leggett. 'Just imagine you were in that situation, Bridget, with trouble brewing up on Tyneside, and your family needed you home.'

'Aye, I suppose you're right.'

The conversation moved on, to how food that had been scarce in the war was more readily available again, and how there seemed to be more in the shops now. Annie only half listened, not able to move beyond Lorcan's impending departure.

They'd all finished their sandwiches and were eating the parkin that Mrs Norris had brought in, when Lorcan re-entered the room, worry lines marring his usually smooth brow.

Perhaps Mrs Bygrove had not granted him leave, so he had no alternative but to stay? But that didn't seem like the sort of thing someone as understanding as Mrs Bygrove would do.

'Well, lad?' said Will.

'Aye, I'm off soon. I'll just have meself some of this, then I'll go and pack.' He picked up a slice of parkin and bit off a chunk.

'How long do you reckon it'll take you?' Will asked.

'I won't get there before tomorrow, for sure,' he said his mouth half full.

'Have you got the money for the fares?' Annie asked, wondering if this might be another flaw in his plan. 'It must be quite expensive to take several trains and a boat.'

'I have so. I saved most of me pay during the war as there was bugger— I mean, little to spend it on. And I was a good saver before the war.'

'So, when do you think you'll get back?' She tried to sound nonchalant, like she wasn't too worried, just curious. Always supposing he came back. She felt sick at the possibility that he might decide to stay.

'I've no idea. But Mrs Bygrove has said me job'll be here for me when I return.'

For a brief moment, Annie thought she was going to tear up, happy as she was at his apparent eagerness to come back, but she managed to hold it in.

He finished off the parkin, still standing, then licked his forefinger and thumb. 'Mm, delicious, as the cakes here always are. I'll certainly miss them while I'm away, having looked forward to coming back to them.'

I wish he'd miss me, she thought, feeling immediately guilty. After all, she and Jasper were heading out together again today, after he'd had lunch. But hopefully, only as friends once more.

'Well, that's me done. I'll go and pack now and see you all… sometime.'

Annie really wanted to say something to him, something positive and encouraging, but the words wouldn't come.

He was just near the door when Jasper entered, the first to appear for middle lunch. Lorcan quickly explained to him what was happening.

'Gosh, I don't know what to say, except, sorry this has happened to your family. Have a good journey, old friend.' They clapped each other on the back.

'And you behave yourself while I'm gone.'

'As if I wouldn't,' joked Jasper, after which, Lorcan left.

'That is our signal to clear up and make the room ready for middle lunch,' said Mrs Leggett.

Jasper went to the dresser. 'I'll fetch the clean plates.'

'You see,' Gertie said to Jerry. 'There are some men willing to help.'

He looked heavenward and tutted. 'All right, I'm helping to clear up, aren't I?'

Jasper brought some plates over to the table, where Annie was placing the cups and saucers onto a tray. 'I'll have my lunch quickly and then we can head off,' he said.

Jerry, stacking the side plates onto another tray, raised his eyebrows as he peered from one to the other. 'You two walking out then?'

'We're just, uh, going to the pictures together,' Jasper replied. He made it sound like they were just friends. And hopefully, that was the way he saw it. Or he felt it wasn't anybody else's business.

Either way, she no longer felt like going out, even though part of her had been looking forward to it this morning. She'd rather have been around to see Lorcan off. If he packed quickly and left, she might still be able to.

Lili entered the room, grinning from ear to ear.

'It's nice to see someone so happy,' said Mrs Turnbull. 'What's the occasion, lass?'

'I have news!' she said in a high-pitched voice, while bouncing up and down on her toes. 'Rhodri and I have organised our wedding for the seventeenth of July.'

'Another wedding! Well pet, that is good news, especially after hearing that Lorcan's leaving.'

Lili's face fell. 'He's leaving? He's only just got back.'

'Sorry lass, I should have said only temporarily, hopefully. His family back in Ireland have run into a spot of bother.'

'Supposed to be Charlie's best man in June, he is.'

'Oh yes, I'd forgotten that,' said Annie. 'I'm sure he'll be back by then.' She crossed her fingers, hiding her hand in her apron pocket.

As people congratulated Lili, Annie took a tray of dirty plates away, feeling guilty that she was in no mood to celebrate the good news.

In the scullery, Alice was washing up some pans, while Finn was drying.

'What's up with you?' her sister asked. 'You look even more miserable than usual.'

Finn chuckled, but ceased abruptly when Annie glared at him, looking at her apologetically.

'There's some good news—'

'What would you look like if it was bad then,' Alice joked.

'If you'd let me finish. Some *good* news, but also some not so good news.' She didn't want to say 'bad', for fear it might end up like that. 'Lili and Rhodri have set the date: July the seventeenth.'

'Oh, that's lovely. I'm so happy for them.'

'*But*, the not so good news—'

She didn't get a chance to finish before Lorcan entered the room, a rucksack on his shoulder.

'I'll be going now, so I will.'

'Going where?' said Finn.

'Annie can explain.' He carried on, out into the yard.

She went to the door, taking a step out to call, 'Take care.'

He turned briefly, smiling, if looking a little surprised, then waved and carried on out of the gate.

That smile gave her a brief exhilaration, before the misery of his departure was back. At least she had got to see him off.

She stepped back inside and told the other two briefly what had happened.

'Ain't it a bit dangerous out there at the moment?' said Finn. 'That's what Mr Fletcher was saying the other day.'

'The counter's rather full,' said Annie, not wanting to think about that again. 'Could you take the pans back to the kitchen, Finn?'

'Righty ho.'

After he'd gone, Annie said, 'Mrs Bygrove's keeping Lorcan's job open and he says he'll be back. But I do wonder if he will.'

'Well, at least you have Jasper,' said Alice, straight faced, though Annie detected a smidgeon of sarcasm in her voice.

About to retort, she was cut off by Jasper entering the scullery.

'Ah, the man himself,' said Alice. 'We was just talking about you.'

'Oh. Right. All good, I hope. Anyway, I said I'd be quick and here I am. Are you ready to go, Annie? The first picture starts at two.'

'What is it again?'

'Charlie Chaplin in *A Burlesque on Carmen*. It sounds like it might be fun.'

'Let me get me coat and hat.'

When she returned, Alice was washing up, ignoring Jasper, and he was in the middle of the room, whistling to himself.

'Let's go then,' she said. 'Bye Alice.'

'Bye,' came the abrupt reply.

Annie only hoped that Jasper wouldn't want to talk too much about Lorcan.

–

The following Monday, it was Alice's afternoon off. She was glad to get away from her sister, and the growing whisper around the staff that she was walking out with Jasper. At the same time, she felt lonely, wandering around the town on her own, her head filled with unwelcome thoughts from which there was little distraction. She'd asked an old school friend, who lived near them in Wick, whether she fancied a trip out, as they'd done on occasion. But her friend's day off from the grocery store was currently on a Wednesday.

Walking down High Street, she stopped to look in the window of Mann's, the draper's shop. Perhaps she should buy some fabric and make herself something, a dress maybe, like the straight-lined, mid-calf length ones she'd seen some young women wearing. It might do her good to have a little project like this to interest her. And it would be much cheaper to make it than to buy it. She unclipped the metal catch on her handbag and took out her purse to peer inside. There wasn't enough, and her savings were in a box at home, under her bed. She should have thought of it before.

She put the purse back in her handbag and was about to close the clip, when she was pushed forward, almost hitting the glass of the shop window. A young man had bumped into her, knocking her handbag off her wrist. With it still being open, her purse, comb and handkerchief spilled onto the pavement.

The young man crouched down quickly to pick the bag up, along with the items. At first, she panicked, afraid he was going to steal them, but he quickly stood up and handed the bag back to her, looking contrite.

'I am *so* sorry. How clumsy of me. I really should look where I'm going,' he said in a middle-class accent.

She was struck by his good looks and by how tall he was. His hair was very fair and a little longer than was fashionable. He had on a grey cap. His beard was fair too, with a hint of ginger, and he was wearing glasses. His neat, blue, three-piece suit, visible under a smart, open coat, was quite dapper.

'That's all right.' She smiled to make him feel better. 'No harm done.'

'I do feel guilty. I hope your bag and the other bits haven't got too dirty.'

'They'll survive.'

'Listen, to make up for my clumsiness, could I buy you a cup of tea somewhere?'

She faltered for a moment, not knowing how to react to this rather swift invitation.

'Sorry, where are my manners. I should have introduced myself first. I'm Jamie. Jamie… Sparks.'

She didn't know him from Adam, so would it be right to agree? Then again, there were plenty of people around, so it wasn't like she'd be in any danger.

She held out her hand and he shook it. 'And I'm Alice Twine.'

'Nice to meet you, Alice.'

'And nice to meet you, Jamie. Yes please, a cup of tea would be very welcome.'

For a moment she was hopeful that he'd suggest Read's Dining Rooms, as it was just around the corner on Surrey Street. She'd always fancied visiting it.

'There's a nice little tearoom at the end of High Street: Kimble's.' He pointed in the opposite direction.

'Yes, I know the one. All right.'

They said little as they made their way to Kimble's, and she wondered whether this would be a rather stilted affair.

She questioned her decision; she wasn't good at talking to strangers. But then how was she ever going to meet a future husband?

Future husband! She had no illusions that Mr Sparks was any such thing, but she had to start somewhere.

To her relief, once they were settled into the cafe, awaiting their order, he started chatting.

'It's my day off today and I wasn't looking forward to spending it alone, yet again, so I am glad I, um, "bumped" into you, though I wish it hadn't been quite so literally.'

'It's my afternoon off too. Where do you work?'

'I'm a reporter for the *Sussex Daily News*.'

'Isn't their office on Terminus Road, near the railway station?'

'That's right.'

'You must be well educated to do that job.'

'Oh, I don't know about that,' he said shyly. 'I'm just good with words. Where do you work?'

'I, um, work in the stillroom at the Beach Hotel, on the common.' It wasn't quite true, of course, but it sounded better than 'scullery maid', which might be considered the lowest job at the hotel.

'The Beach Hotel, eh? Very posh.'

He looked a little surprised – or was it even shocked? – at first. Didn't she look good enough to work there?

'It is very posh. I work with my sister mostly, which can get a bit much at times, as she's older and rather bossy.'

'What's it like, working there, apart from having a bossy sister?' He chuckled.

'It's a great place to work. The manageress, Mrs Bygrove, treats us all well. We're very lucky in that way. Of course, during the war, it was mainly women doing the jobs, even as porters. The male staff are starting to come back now... those what survived.'

He nodded. 'We lost a couple of the reporters I worked with too. I've always wanted to go for lunch or afternoon tea at the hotel, but I'm not classy enough.'

'I wouldn't say that.' It was out of her mouth before she'd had time to consider it. It might sound like she had a fancy for him. 'I mean, you talk very nicely.'

'That's kind of you to say, but when I've passed the hotel, walking down South Terrace, I've seen some of the people who frequent it going in and coming out. I recognised Mr James Perryman one time, who owns some of the shipyards. And I'm sure I saw Lord and Lady Raynolt arrive in a chauffeur-driven motorcar another time.'

'You probably did, as they're all regular guests. Not that I get to see 'em, being in the, um, stillroom.' She hoped this fib wasn't going to catch her out at some point. She really should have been honest with him. 'When did you return from the war? Sorry, always assuming you were in it. I know not everyone was. A couple of men at the 'otel were declared unfit for one reason or another.'

'No, I was in it. I started off in Kitchener's Seventh Special Service Battalion, back in 1914.'

'Really? A couple of porters at the hotel, Jasper Jupp and Lorcan Foley, were in that. Maybe you knew 'em?'

He looked thoughtful for a while. 'The names don't ring a bell, but of course there were a lot of us in that battalion.' He looked at his watch. 'Goodness gracious, is that the time? I hadn't realised it had got so late. I have an appointment I must get to.'

'Oh, I thought it was your day off.'

'And so it is, but I have a lead on a story for the newspaper, I can't say what as yet, but someone has agreed to talk to me about it. They could only make it today, and I couldn't say no.'

'That sounds intriguing.'

'I do hope it turns out to be.' He lifted his cup, tipping his head back to drain it. When he'd placed it back down, he said, 'Do you, by chance, have next Monday afternoon off too?'

'I would, if it weren't Easter Monday. I've got Tuesday off next week, but then Monday again after that.'

'Of course it's Easter Monday. I won't be working, but I could still do a swap to get Tuesday afternoon, if I do some overtime. I don't suppose… I hope you don't think me too forward, it's just, would you like to meet up again, maybe go to the Palladium or the Electric Picture Palace, to see some films?'

How funny that he should suggest the same outing that Annie and Jasper had now had twice. Jasper. This might be a good way to get over him, to see someone else. Jamie seemed like a good sort, and very polite. Not to mention rather good looking.

'Yes, I'd like that.'

'Perhaps I could meet you at quarter to two, in time for the two o'clock start? Would you be free by then?'

'Definitely.'

'We could meet in town. I know, outside Mann's, where we first met. That seems fitting.' He treated her to a wide grin.

'Yes, I suppose it would be.' He did seem like a lot of fun.

'Lovely.' Jamie lifted his hand to summon the waiter and paid.

Outside once more, he lifted his cap. 'It's been lovely meeting you, Alice. Until next week.'

'Bye bye, see you next time.'

He headed off down East Street and she watched him for a few seconds. She wondered what this secret story might be, and whether he'd be able to tell her next week.

She turned and started walking back up High Street, smiling, the melancholy she'd felt at the start of her afternoon now dispelled. Annie wasn't the only one who had someone to do things with. And, given time, she might develop an affection for Jamie.

She hoped so.

—

Alice was still in a good mood when she got back to the hotel, and was relieved to see Annie on her own. She'd soon convince her that she wasn't bothered about Jasper any more.

'Have a good afternoon off?'

'It turned out to be very enjoyable.'

'How come? Did you go to the pictures?'

'No. I went for a cup of tea with a very nice man.' Alice smiled, recalling the encounter.

'You what?' Annie's face was scrunched up with confusion. 'I didn't know you was walking out with someone.'

'I'm not, but I might be soon. He bumped into me outside Mann's and made me spill me handbag contents on the floor, and to make up for it, he took me for a cuppa tea. We 'ad a nice conversation, and he invited me to the pictures next week.'

'I don't like the sound of that. You only met him today and don't know nothing about him.'

'He's a reporter for the *Sussex Daily News*, so he's quite respectable.'

'That don't mean nothing. If he even is one. He might 'ave been lying.'

'Oh Annie, why do you always have to think the worst of everyone?'

'I don't. But he's a stranger. I'm going to tell our parents. They'll make you see sense.'

'But they're always going on about us meeting a man and getting married. They'd surely be pleased for me.'

'Not if it's some stranger no one knows nothing about.'

Alice was getting annoyed now. She'd expected some disapproval from her sister, but she wasn't going to let her interfere. 'You'd better not say nothing, or I'll knock your block off.'

'I'd like to see ya try.'

'I'll tell 'em about that time you broke Mum's vase what Dad gave her and blamed it on the dog. And anyway, who I go out with ain't none of your business, nor theirs. Have you told 'em about Jasper?'

'There ain't nothing to tell, and anyway, I've known him for years and know he's a decent sort.'

'And I can tell that Jamie is too.'

'Jamie who?'

'Jamie Sparks, he's called.' She wasn't sure if it had been wise to give his full name. What if Annie did tell their parents and they found him and had a word?

'Sparks? Like the big furniture shop in High Street. Is he related to the family?'

'I've no idea. Funny thing is, we were near Sparks when we met.'

'Sounds fishy to me. Too much of a coincidence.'

'It's a common enough surname.'

'Is it?' Annie looked doubtful.

'And he might 'ave been close by 'cos he'd popped in to see 'em, if they are family.'

'Wouldn't he 'ave mentioned it?'

'Why would he? This is ridiculous! Why shouldn't I walk out with someone? I don't care if you are older than me, you are *not* to tell Mum and Dad nothing. I will tell 'em when I'm good and ready – if I 'ave reason to. It may come to nothing.'

'You'd better watch out 'cos—'

'I don't 'ave to take orders from—'

The door from the stillroom swung open, and Jasper entered with a used tea set on a round tray.

'What on earth are you two arguing about?'

'Alice 'ad tea with a stranger and has agreed to meet him again.'

'Can't you keep your mouth shut for a second?' Alice was furious that she'd told Jasper, of all people.

He looked rather taken aback. 'Well, I suppose that's how a lot of people meet. After all, we're all strangers to each other until then, aren't we?'

'But she should be careful. She can be so dozy some-times, Alice in her own little Wonderland.'

'Don't start that again! I'm fed up with it. I'm gonna get changed back into me uniform, and when I get back, I don't wanna hear no more about it.' She humphed out loudly. 'Now I'm starting to sound like you, all bossy and self-righteous!'

She stomped off through the stillroom, eliciting looks of surprise from Phoebe and the young stillroom maids. No doubt Annie and Jasper would have a joke about her being silly old Alice while she was gone, but she didn't care. She was even more determined now to meet Jamie next week.

Chapter Eight

Edie was strolling along the promenade with Charlie a couple of days later, during the early afternoon, chatting about his new job running the Beach Hotel's garage, which he'd been doing for a few days now. She felt content with her hand in his, still revelling in the fact that he was home for good and wouldn't be leaving to return abroad. It was still hard to believe that the war was over, but the silence across the water helped to confirm it.

They passed the Beach Hotel, walking in the direction of Rustington. They soon reached a shelter that held a certain memory for Edie, one she wasn't sure she'd ever get rid of.

'So much has changed since that day we was walking along 'ere, back in August 1915.'

So, Charlie was thinking of it too.

'Annie, Alice and I were talking about it just recently,' said Edie, 'when we went past what used to be Mrs Hadley's house. It still feels strange, thinking of when I lodged there, before getting the job at the hotel, not knowing that my fellow boarder, Pamela, was involved with some very dodgy people, including Mrs Hadley's estranged husband.'

'The attack on you in that shelter by Gordon Hadley was going on four years ago now. Seems like yesterday. I would choose that moment to go to the lavatory and leave you alone!'

'But you still saved the day.' She let go of his hand and took hold of his arm.

'I just thank the Lord I wasn't no longer, otherwise gawd knows what would've 'appened… Talking of criminals… I could be wrong, and I 'ope I am—' He stalled.

'What is it, Charlie? You've got me worried now.'

'Like I said, I could be wrong, but I saw someone earlier today. I was under a motorcar at the time, so I could be mistaken.'

She stopped and turned him to face her. 'Who do you think it was?'

'He kinda looked like Frank Steel.'

'The thief who inveigled you into stealing from Billington's ironmonger's?'

'Yep. He 'ad the same thick bush of untidy grey hair and was haggard looking.'

'You should tell the police. After all, he was the one who got away with all the money when you were caught. He should be apprehended, and I'm sure the police would like the opportunity to get their hands on him. And he tried to get you involved in crime once more, before you enlisted. You don't need him around trying to spoil your life again.'

'Too bleedin' true. I didn't give 'im away before because of honour among thieves, and all that rubbish, and I was afraid of 'im, but I wouldn't 'esitate now. In a way, I suppose me getting caught and 'im scarpering saved me. It made me realise what a nasty piece of work he was. If I'd got away with it, gawd knows what I'd be doing now. Frank was a ruthless bleeder, so I dread to think what he'd've got me involved in. But what can I tell the police, that I might 'ave seen someone who was possibly up to no good, but I was looking at 'im upside down? That DI Toshack don't seem like the type to look into something so flimsy.'

'Maybe not, but he is a good policeman. Not like that Superintendent Crooke up at the Arundel police station, who has poked his nose into Littlehampton too many times and seems to be only too happy to let crooks get away with things.'

Charlie beamed and quipped, 'Because he is one?'

'Is one what?'

'A crook! Superintendent Crooke.'

'Oh Charlie!' She nudged him playfully and they both laughed. 'To be honest, nothing would surprise me about that man.'

'Nah, me neither,' he agreed, before they carried on walking.

–

Annie had been surprised when Mrs Leggett had told her she was the one who was going to be serving drinks this evening for the charity ball. It was Alice who'd been chosen before, and Annie had presumed it was because she was prettier and more presentable, so she was thrilled to be picked this time.

'Afraid the charity events might cease after the war, I was,' said Lili, showing Annie how to carry a tray full of glasses in the stillroom, where they were being filled up. 'I'm so glad they're continuing.'

'I wouldn't expect anything less with Mrs Bygrove in charge,' said Phoebe. 'This one's for children, isn't it?'

'Yes. Raising money for needy children in the town,' said Annie. 'Especially them what's lost fathers in the war.'

'Come on, now,' said Lili. 'Time for your debutante entry to the ball.'

'I wish!' said Annie. 'Can you still call it a ball when there's a whatsit band. What's it called?'

'The Original Louisiana Jazz Band,' said Lili. 'I dunno if you can still call it a ball. But it'll be fun, either way. More fun than an orchestra. Come on, now, we need to take over from Simon and Dennis.'

As they entered the ballroom, the band was playing a lively number. They stood near the back of the room and a couple of people came to collect a fresh glass while depositing those they'd finished with.

Annie looked ahead at the band that consisted of a pianist, two trombonists, a cornetist and a drummer. She wanted to tap her foot to the beat, but didn't know if that would be allowed in her position. There were several couples dancing, and some women on their own also. It was good to see dances where you didn't have to have a partner.

She leant towards Lili. 'Look, there are two coloured musicians. That's a novelty.'

'Not sure they'd want to be described like that,' said Lili. 'Remember being described like that myself, when I first came to Littlehampton and the 'otel, and someone 'eard my accent. Didn't appreciate it then, and I wouldn't now.'

'Sorry, I didn't mean no disrespect. It's just they're… different.'

'Different, but still people.'

'Yes, of course.'

'A few faces there are, from the past, what we ain't seen in a while. That's good.'

'Everyone seems to be having a good time,' said Annie.

Several other people came to swap empty glasses for full ones.

'I'd better give you the glasses left on my tray,' said Lili, 'and I'll go fetch some more.'

As Annie stood on her own, she watched a couple doing the steps to a modern dance. It was fairly simple, so she was soon imagining herself doing it. It wasn't long before Lorcan entered the fantasy, and she pictured the pair of them on the dance floor.

Lorcan, not Jasper. That was bad of her.

Lili returned, giving Annie an opportunity to swipe the image from her mind and concentrate on the people here.

–

Alice had been sad not to have been picked to serve drinks at the ball on Saturday, but she supposed it was only fair that Annie got a turn this time. She was pleased, however, to be chosen to help with the Easter egg hunt on the Monday, which was also taking place in the ballroom. She wouldn't get a chance to listen to the modern music and watch the dancers, but she always enjoyed working with the children. This time around, the helpers had been given a cardboard crown with rabbit ears to wear, made by Mrs Turnbull, so they could be the 'Easter bunnies'.

And there was a bonus: Jasper was also helping.

This ought to have made her feel guilty, what with him walking out with her sister, but it wasn't as if she was going to do anything untoward.

The afternoon had started with a few games, and presently there were several tables with Easter crafts. She was sitting at the table where children were painting the shells of boiled eggs, with food dyes that Mrs Norris had produced. Jasper was on the next table filled with Easter colouring sheets. She tried not to look in his direction but had found herself glancing over involuntarily several times. To compensate, she peered around at the other tables too.

The mothers, one father and a group of nannies were standing at one end of the room chatting, enjoying tea and biscuits.

'Well, children,' announced Edie, who had led the afternoon. 'It's time now for the event you've all been waiting for.'

'Easter egg hunt,' Elsie called out, from the table Jasper was looking after.

'That's right,' said Edie. 'Would my band of merry Easter bunnies like to take up their positions around the room and the garden, please? And children, please form a line for the first clue. Mothers and nannies, do come and help if your charge is quite young.'

Alice headed to the garden with a piece of card on which was written 'Clue 4'. It wasn't as warm outside as she'd have liked, but it was at least sunny. Seeing Jasper standing nearby with 'Clue 5', produced a weird edgy combination of delight and dread.

'It's been a, um, good afternoon, hasn't it?' he said, with a worried smile.

Was he afraid she'd bite his head off again? How many times had she regretted that? She'd do her utmost to be pleasant now.

'It's been lovely.'

His worried smile widened into a cheerful one. 'You're very good with the children.'

'Probably 'cos I 'ave young cousins. I don't s'pose this is your cup of tea.'

'On the contrary, it's been tremendous fun. Makes a change to opening doors and fetching things.'

'Makes a change from washing up, that's for sure.'

He chuckled. There was a pause, before he said, 'I'm sorry that Annie had a go at you, about Jamie. I imagine it was uncomfortable, having me there, witnessing it. But I think Annie only said it because she cares.'

'I suppose. But she'd better not go snitching to Mum and Dad like she's threatened.'

'I'll have a word with her. My older brother snitched on me when we were young. He'd caught me with some friends, pulling the flowers out of someone's decorative garden wall. But it did me good, because I never did it again.'

'Are you suggesting that Annie snitching on me might do me good?'

He looked worried once more. 'Oh, no, I didn't mean it like that. I was only eight at the time, and it was a naughty thing to do. Your situation is very different. And you're old enough to make your own decisions.'

He seemed to be over-explaining now, clearly concerned that he'd annoyed her.

'I wouldn't've had you down as doing something naughty like that.' She smiled so he wouldn't think she was reprimanding him.

'Like I said, I was only eight at the time. I was a good little boy after that.' He tipped his head to the side and grinned sweetly for effect.

She put her head back and laughed, causing him to laugh too. They were still giggling when a little lad approached her for the fourth clue.

'That was quick,' she said.

Edie came over. 'It might be better if you stand by the flowerbed, Jasper,' she called. 'So you're more evenly spaced out.'

He nodded and did as he was asked. At least, thought Alice, their conversation had been a little more civilised today. And they'd even shared a joke. Whether he and Annie continued to walk out or not, she'd have to bury whatever feelings she had for him and learn to be polite.

—

Alice was first outside Mann's the following Tuesday, but only by a few seconds. As she was looking in the window, she found Jamie beside her.

'Hello again, Alice. At least I didn't knock you over this time,' he said, merrily.

'Hello Jamie.' She smiled at him, relieved he'd arrived. She had been wondering as she'd walked here whether he'd turn up.

'So, are you still keen to go to the pictures?'

'I am. I believe *The Biggest Show on Earth* is playing at the Electric Picture Palace.'

'That's right, I was thinking we might see that one too. It's about a lion tamer in a circus who's sent to boarding school, so sounds rather intriguing. Let's go then.'

He bent his elbow, inviting her to put her arm through his. She didn't want to seem rude, so did so, though she wasn't sure about it. Would he get the wrong idea, and try to be over friendly in the picture house? Especially as it would be dark in there.

She decided not to worry about it unless it happened. If it did, she'd politely decline his advances. Hopefully he'd understand. They walked briskly to the picture house, which was opposite the railway station. He insisted on paying for her ticket, and she gave in quickly, not wanting to hold up the queue behind them.

The film had her engrossed, making her forget her worries. But about halfway through its fifty minutes, he took her hand. Moving her eyes sideways, wondering what might be coming next, she noticed him turn to smile at her, which she could see in the light from the film. He leant towards her, and she froze, expecting to feel his lips on her cheek, but he whispered, 'It's good, isn't it?', and moved away again.

She whispered, 'Yes,' back.

They stayed for the film afterwards, which was about the same length, but not quite as entertaining as the first, and after that, for part nine of a film neither of them had seen the first eight parts of.

Five minutes in, he whispered, 'There doesn't seem much point watching this when we've not seen the other parts. Shall we leave?'

She nodded and they rose, exiting quickly, back into the bright sun, though it was still a little chilly.

'I'm glad we decided on this picture house today,' he said. 'It's been an enjoyable afternoon.'

It sounded like he was bringing their time together to a close. She was disappointed. Did he have another meeting to go to? But she soon found out she'd misinterpreted his words.

'How about heading to Kimble's now, where we went last week? We could have some cake this time too. My treat.'

'But you paid for the picture house tickets.'

'And so I should. It's only right. I know ladies like to pay their way more these days, but I suppose I'm a bit old fashioned like that. Besides, I probably earn more at the newspaper than you do at the hotel. Please, let me treat you.' He looked at her, imploringly.

'All right. I must admit, I do fancy a bit of cake.'

They strolled back up to High Street, taking it easy this time. She felt more relaxed now in his company than she had earlier. He was clearly a gentleman.

'How was Easter at the hotel?' he asked.

'Really, really busy. All the rooms were booked, as were all the tables for meals, morning coffee and afternoon tea. It's the busiest Easter we've had since the war began.'

'Not surprising really, I suppose.'

'And that was on top of the party at the 'otel on the Saturday, and the Easter egg hunt on Easter Monday, which both raised money for a children's charity. I got to help, and I don't often leave the sc— er, stillroom.'

'That must have been exciting.'

'What was Easter like for you? I guess you had Good Friday and Easter Sunday and Monday off from the news-paper.'

'From the newspaper? Oh, yes, I see what you mean. I didn't have to go into the office. But I'm always working on something.'

'How did your meeting go, last week, about that story?'

'Oh, that. I'm not sure how much help the man I met was, but I'll follow it up and see where it goes.'

'You still can't tell me about it?' She looked at him hopefully.

'Not at the moment.'

They reached Kimble's and he opened the door for her. Inside it was busy, and they were lucky to find one table left.

'Perfect,' he said, and invited her to go ahead.

—

After their tea and cake, Jamie suggested they take a walk towards the river.

'How long have you got?' he asked. 'Have you got to get back to a shift?'

'Not until six forty-five, though I'd like to get back for some dinner first.'

Partway along Pier Road, they wandered onto Fisherman's Quay, past the Britannia public house, towards the workshops, and stopped at the water's edge.

'It's strange without all the military ships,' she said.

'I'm glad they've gone. They… well, spoilt the look of the area, especially with the Admiralty men around all the time.'

'I don't suppose you saw much of them, only when you was home on leave.'

'No. That's right. But what I did see gave me that impression. And other people said that to me too.'

'But it's mostly workshops, warehouses, lobsterpots and the public house.' She looked behind.

'And that's how I prefer it.'

'I suppose it is quieter. Do you live in this part of town? I've never thought to ask you before.'

'I live, um, on one of the streets behind the railway station, Maxwell Road, so not far. What about you? Do you live in at the hotel?'

'No, me sister Annie and me live at home with our parents, in Wick.'

'Now that *is* somewhere that's quiet.'

'Too blinking quiet sometimes.'

They laughed, and she saw his hand go towards hers. She liked the idea now of him holding her hand, but before he reached it, they heard voices, and he pulled away. Two fishermen walked onto the pebbles, chatting loudly, before heading into the public house.

She looked at her wristwatch, disappointed to see that it was now twenty to six.

'I'd better go if I'm gonna get some dinner before me shift.'

'So soon? Can we meet again?'

'Yes, all right. Me afternoon off'll be Monday again for the next few weeks. Though I do get the odd hour 'ere and there between shifts too.'

'Next Monday would be good for me. Let's meet in our usual place, outside Mann's, maybe a little earlier? Say one o'clock, if that suits you?'

'Yep, I can make that.'

Their usual place. That did make it sound like he was keen to keep on seeing her.

He touched her face briefly, running his finger down her cheek. 'You're so pretty, with your lovely fair hair and your big blue eyes.'

She felt embarrassed by the compliment but not displeased. 'Me sister says I look like the illustration of Alice, in *Alice's Adventures in Wonderland*. In fact, Alice in Wonderland's her nickname for me. It annoys me sometimes.'

'Oh, you're *far* prettier than the girl in those pictures.'

'Well, thank you,' she said, lowering her head a little as her eyes peered up at him. 'And you're really quite handsome with *your* fair hair and blue eyes.' She giggled, catching a glimpse of a possible future, with little flaxen-haired children. If they ever got that far.

He glanced towards the passageway on the other side, which led to River Road and more warehouses, then grabbed hold of her hand. 'Please, could you stay just a little longer. Tell me a bit more about yourself. About the hotel.'

It was all rather clumsy, but she guessed that he, like her, was feeling self-conscious.

'Maybe a coupla—'

There was the sound of whistling, and a policeman came around the corner. Jamie went red and let go of her hand.

'Looks like you might have a police escort back to the hotel,' he quipped, looking across the river.

'Oh, that's just Sergeant Gardner, and he would too, if he thought it necessary. His wife's me mum's second cousin, so he's a kind of uncle.'

'I see. I won't keep you now. I wouldn't want you to be late for your dinner. Until next week.'

He turned abruptly and crunched across the pebbles towards the passageway leading to River Road, and she headed towards the exit onto Pier Road.

As she approached the side of the public house, she called, ' 'Ello Uncle Barry.'

'That's Sergeant Gardner to you when I'm on duty. Who was that young man you was talking to then?'

'I dunno. He was just passing the time of day. He works in one of them workshops, I think.' She didn't want to own up to the real situation, in case he mentioned it to her parents.

'In a suit?'

'He might be clerical.'

'Did he say what his name was?'

'No. Why would he?'

'Anyway, what you doing on the quay?'

'It's me afternoon off and I like looking across the river. It's rather picturesque at the moment.' She looked up at where the sun was shining onto the white clouds, making them dazzle against the bright blue sky.

'I'd advise you not to come down to the quay by yourself, young lady.'

'Why?'

He glanced at the Britannia. 'Drunks. And there's been some trouble here recently. That's all I'll say.'

'The fair'll be coming in just over a month, so lots of people'll be 'ere then.'

'And it'll be fine for you to come here then, on your own or otherwise. Safety in numbers, and all that.'

'All right, Uncle Barry, sorry, Sergeant Gardner. I've got to get back to work now.'

'Take care and say hello to Annie.' He carried on, hands behind his back and whistling once more.

What a fusspot, she thought, as she walked on. She'd been on Fisherman's Quay loads of times and never come to any harm. Another week until she saw Jamie. It would give her something to look forward to.

–

The next day, Annie was on her afternoon tea break, pondering Alice's mysterious trip out the day before. This time, her sister wouldn't tell her anything. That could be bad, if there was something she wasn't admitting because she knew Annie would disapprove. Or, and this had occurred to her before too, maybe this 'Jamie' didn't exist at all, and she was making him up to get her own back on Annie for going out with Jasper.

She pulled the sugar bowl towards her and helped herself to a couple of spoonfuls. It was good to be able to do that again, having never got used to unsweetened tea during rationing. As she stirred it, she thought about her own romantic situation, if that's what you could call it. She and Jasper had been to the Palladium again last week, but he hadn't tried to kiss her, or even put his arm around her, only holding her hand for a short while. While she was still relieved about that, she also wondered if it was some fault on her part. Yet he'd asked to see her again tomorrow.

Vera, the nursemaid, entered the room with Lili. 'Have you been to have a look at the St George's Day event Mr Janus is holding behind the hotel?' she said. 'We just popped out for a quick peep and caught the end of a funny comic, and there was someone spinning plates when we left. The common's pretty busy.'

'You've missed five minutes of your break, Miss Edge and Miss Probert,' said Mrs Leggett.

'That's all right. Good to get some fresh air, it is,' said Lili.

'Can't be doing with the crowds,' said Johnny glumly, sitting at the other end of the table, next to Will Fletcher, mostly ignoring people, as he so often did these days. He used to be so sociable.

'What a shame the event wasn't tomorrow, on me day off,' said Annie. It would have given her and Jasper something different to do.

'I'm sure there'll be other events going on, now the busy season has started,' said the housekeeper.

The door opened, and two men in uniform stepped in. It was Peter Smith the waiter and Stuart Coulter the desk clerk, the last of the men to return from the war.

Will rose, dropping his newspaper on the seat and making a beeline for the newcomers, shaking their hands enthusiastically. 'It's good to see you lads back. We've only seen you once since you enlisted.'

'It was only right to spend our leave with our families,' said Peter.

'Quite right lad, quite right. So have the battalions in Russia all been sent home now?'

'No, there are still quite a few men left there. I reckon it'll be at least a coupla months before they're all sent back.'

Other staff members gathered round to greet them, apart from Johnny, who remained seated, staring into space. They were listening to Stuart's tale of the journey home from Russia, when Fanny entered with Gertie, who was carrying Elsie.

'I thought you two had a day off,' said Mrs Leggett. 'Look who's arri—' She frowned. 'Oh, what's the bouquet for, Miss Bullen? And you all look very well turned out, as if you've been somewhere special.'

'Well, you see...' Walter came in behind, in a smart suit, a small, white rose fixed to the lapel of his jacket. 'I'm actually Mrs Lehman now.' She blushed.

'Whaat?' said Annie.

'Walter and I got married at the registry office a few hours ago, and Gertie was one of our witnesses.'

Everyone was silent, with various degrees of shock on their faces, including the two newcomers. Only Lili seemed unfazed as she rushed forward to hug Fanny.

'Congratulations,' she hollered.

Johnny shrieked, but it wasn't to do with any kind of celebration. They all swung around to look at him, but he was soon rattling his cup and saucer onto the table. He rose unsteadily to his feet, brushing past Walter to vacate the room.

'What on earth's wrong with him?' said Peter.

There was no reply, before the housekeeper said, 'Why did you not tell anyone you were going to be married, Miss, I mean, Mrs Lehman?'

'We didn't want no fuss. And it's expensive, inviting lotsa people, so we thought, we'd just get on with it. Me dad was there, and 'is sister... Hello Peter and Stuart. It's good to see you back.' She shook their hands and introduced Walter.

'Nice to meet you guys.'

'You're American?' said Stuart.

'I sure am.'

'We met when he was helping to build the aerodrome in Rustington,' said Fanny.

'Blimey, has anyone else got married while we've been away?' Peter asked.

'Hetty married Victor Perryman last month,' said Annie. 'And she's left the hotel now.'

'Victor Perryman? What, of the shipbuilding family?'

'Yep. And Edie and Charlie are getting married in June.'

'And I'm marrying my Rhodri in July,' Lili added.

'Well, things have certainly been happening while we've been away,' said Stuart.

'Are you still going to be working at the hotel?' Lili asked Fanny.

'Course I am, though Elsie and me'll be moving into Walter's lodgings. We want to save up for somewhere a bit bigger.'

She looked up at Walter and he down at her, the love on their faces obvious.

'I've already spoken to Mrs Bygrove about it,' said Fanny. 'She knew about the wedding and has agreed to let Vera continue to look after Elsie when me and Walter are working.'

'I'm so glad,' said Vera. 'I'd be sad not to have sweet little Elsie to look after. To think she'll be three tomorrow. Maybe now other people at the hotel are getting married, I'll have some more children to look after.' She looked very happy at the prospect.

'You'll be running a nursery if you're not careful,' Mrs Leggett joked, as she did occasionally.

'Oh, that would be lovely!'

Helen Bygrove entered at this point, with Inspector Toshack in tow. 'Good, you're back, Fanny. Congratulations to you both.' She hugged her and shook Walter's hand. 'And I see you're settling back in, Peter and Stuart.'

'There's a lot to take in and get used to,' said Peter.

'Yes, things have changed quite a lot since you left, that's for certain.'

'And so many people are getting married. I hope there's some ladies left for us,' he said light-heartedly.

'There's plenty of single women left, don't you worry,' said Annie, who didn't like to add that it would be partly because so many men had died.

'Talking of weddings,' said Helen, 'Sam and I, that is, Inspector Toshack and I, have set our wedding date for the thirteenth of September.' She held her hand out briefly to show them her engagement ring.

Another set of congratulations and hand shaking did the rounds, making Annie wonder how much longer this could go on for. Would yet someone else come in with news? She was trying to be happy for everyone, she really was.

'The 'otel is certainly gonna be full of celebrations this year,' said Fanny. 'I wonder who'll announce their wedding next?' She looked briefly at Annie, raising her eyebrows twice.

Fanny surely didn't think she and Jasper were at that stage yet. They hadn't even been walking out a month, and they'd only been out together once a week. When they were together in the staff dining room, he often didn't even sit next to her. And she had to admit, despite her best efforts, she was still missing Lorcan. There'd been no word from him since he'd left for Ireland nearly two weeks ago.

Feeling a little apart from what was going on, despite being among the chatter, she wondered whether to head back to the scullery early. But that might make her look like the misery Alice was always making out she was.

The door creaked open, and she wondered what good news someone might be bringing now that she'd have to look happy about. When she realised who it was, she could hardly believe her eyes. Her tummy did a little flip as Lorcan entered, his expression amazed at the chaos and chatter. She seemed to be the only one who'd noticed him. How she'd have loved to have thrown her arms around him in greeting, but she imagined it instead.

'Well, what in the name of Mary and Joseph's going on here then?'

The noise stopped and Helen Bygrove cried, 'Lorcan, you're back!'

'I thought he was already back?' said Peter, looking confused.

'Had to go to Ireland to see me family, so I did. But, as Mr Fletcher said, I needed a permit from the police to get into Limerick, and I couldn't get it, especially when they found out I was the brother of Patrick Foley, because he's a member of the Trades and Labour Council. I had to stay with an aunt just outside the prohibited area. I found out me father's fine, just a flesh wound, and me brother-in-law's been released. There was no point staying any longer, and to be honest, there's so much trouble there, near enough war, and I've had me fill of war, so I have. Now, what on earth is all this commotion?'

'Oh boy, where to begin,' said Gertie.

Various people set about telling him the news so far, compelling him to start a new round of congratulations, along with hearty handshakes for his returning comrades, Peter and Stuart.

'So, you'll be Mrs Toshack,' Lorcan said to Helen. 'That'll take some getting used to.'

'For me too,' she laughed.

'I'm sorry to wind this all up,' said Mrs Leggett, 'but it will be time for the next staff break in a couple of minutes.'

'Of course,' said Helen. 'That will give Fanny and Walter a chance to tell others their news, and for Peter and Stuart to say hello to more of the staff.'

Annie thought this as good a time as any to vacate the room. There were plenty of others there to clear up. Lorcan hadn't seemed to notice her, so he certainly wouldn't miss her. And she ought to relay what had occurred to Alice, who'd missed a lot having gone to the first staff break.

She slipped out and made her way back to the scullery.

Sitting in the kitchen that evening, having just arrived home, Alice enjoyed telling her parents and brother all the good news from the hotel, even though she'd heard it second hand from Annie. She'd been disappointed not to have been on her break when it had all happened.

'It sounds like it was an exciting day,' said their mother. 'Fancy Fanny just going out and getting married and not telling no one. I hope neither of you two ever do that. I want to enjoy the celebrations.'

'It'd be cheaper for us,' joked their father.

'Oh, Colin, you don't mean that.'

'No, love, course I don't. I wanta see me girls married. Did Fanny's parents know she was getting married?'

'Her father was there to give her away, and her aunt was there too, but her mother died when she was a kid, remember. I told you – she was in the workhouse.'

'Yes, of course, you did tell us,' he said.

'With all the women getting married, we'll be lucky if there's any left for us men what's come 'ome,' said Cecil.

Annie humphed. 'That's more or less what our returning waiter, Peter, said. I told him there was plenty of ladies left, but didn't like to remind him why.'

'Oh, don't turn this into something miserable, Annie,' said her mother.

'I'm not. That's all I was gonna say.'

Mrs Twine turned towards Alice. 'And while we're talking about men and women, young lady, Uncle Barry called in earlier.'

Annie wondered where her mother was going with this conversation.

'He told us that you were seen talking to a man on the quay and that he advised you not to go there in future.'

'He was only some bloke from one of the offices of the workshops. A clerk or something, I guess.'

Was Alice actually *lying*? Had the man in question been Jamie?

'Barry said that the quay is a dodgy place to go, especially for young women.' Her father pointed the lip of his pipe at her.

'I dunno why,' said Alice. 'The workshops are respectable enough.'

'I dunno about that,' he replied. 'And the public house might not be, if it's full of drunks.'

'All right, I won't take a walk there again.' Alice rose and stretched. 'I'm tired and I'm on an early shift tomorrow, so I'd better get to bed.'

'Me too,' said Annie. 'G'night.'

Annie followed her sister up the curved staircase and they both entered the box room at the top, in which they shared a bunk bed.

'Were you on the quay with Jamie?' Annie asked.

'Yep.'

'So it weren't some clerk from a workshop.'

'No, but I don't wanna tell our parents about Jamie yet.'

'So you told a lie. Is there something wrong with him, that you don't want them to know?'

'No, but it might not last, so what's the point? And keep your voice down.'

'I think I should tell Mum and Dad, as why would Jamie take you to a dodgy place like the quay?'

'He didn't *take* me there. We was walking around and ended up there, that's all. It's where we parted, and Uncle Barry was coming round the corner as I was leaving. And you are *not* to tell Mum and Dad nothing.'

'I'll think about it.'

'I'm going back down. I need the lavvy.'

'Right.'

Alice left the room. Annie started undressing, wondering what she should do. She'd leave it for now, but she might tell their parents in the future if Alice didn't soon.

–

The following Monday, Alice was looking forward to meeting Jamie in the afternoon. What with Fanny and Hetty getting married, and at least three more weddings to follow, she at last had some hope of a happy ever after for herself, even if they were only at the early stages of their courtship, or whatever it was.

It occurred to her, as she dried dishes and stared out of the window into the yard, that Jamie had told her where he lived, but not if he still lived with his parents. The houses in that area were smallish, terraced houses, and tended to be filled with families, not used for renting individual rooms, so it seemed more likely. Then again, he might earn good money as a journalist and own a whole house by himself. That would be something, if their relationship did blossom.

'Did you hear me?' said Annie.

'What?'

'You daydreaming again about that "Jamie" whatsis-name?'

'Sparks.'

'Yeah, him, if he exists.'

'Not this again. Uncle Barry saw him, remember?'

'That person might've just been someone you'd come across on the quay, like you told Uncle Barry.'

'I'll bring him round to meet you today, if ya like.' She wasn't sure of the wisdom of this, but she'd said it now.

'Go on then.'

'Right. And I weren't daydreaming, I was looking out at the weather.' She didn't need to confess her real thoughts. 'It keeps going from sunny to cloudy, and I'm 'oping it'll decide on sunny by the time I go out.'

'So you'll bring him in when he arrives, to introduce him then?'

'He's not coming here. We're meeting at Mann's. We'll 'ave to come over later. If he wants to, of course.'

'That'll be your excuse for not bringing him, will it? Very convenient.'

'Oh do shut up, I'm fed—'

The door opened and Stuart Coulter entered. 'Alice, a young woman brought this letter to the front desk for you. It's a good job Mr Watkins wasn't on duty, as you know what a fuss he makes about things that should be delivered to the "tradesmen's entrance", as he calls it. I'm just off for me break, so thought I'd pop it in.'

'Thanks, Stuart.' She took the envelope off him and looked at her name, written in a neat, cursive script, on the front. She didn't recognise the writing.

'A young woman?' said Annie. 'Who could that be?'

'I've no idea.'

' 'Ere, you two, carry on with the washing and drying. We're going for our tea break,' Annie told the scullery lads.

Alice went outside to open the letter but soon found her sister beside her.

'Ain't you coming?'

'I wanted to read this first.'

'What is it?'

142

'I 'aven't taken it out yet, and I'd rather read it on me own, if ya don't mind.'

'Please yourself.' Annie stepped away, but didn't go back inside.

'You get along to tea break. I'll follow on.'

'I can spare a coupla minutes.'

Alice took the single sheet of paper out and read it. It was a short note only, no address at the top. It was from Jamie, and consisted of only two lines, telling her that he wouldn't be able to meet her because his boss had asked him to go out of town to do an extended reporting job, and that he'd send another letter when he returned. That was it.

She was swamped with disappointment. Had his boss really only just asked him today, or had Jamie been putting off telling her? And what if there was no job, but it was his way of letting her down gently? Either way, it meant she had no one to go out with today.

'So, what's it say?'

She might as well tell her sister. 'It's from Jamie saying he's got a job to go to, out of town, and he'll be a few days, so he can't meet today.'

'Then you definitely won't be bringing him to meet me.'

'Come on, let's get to the break.' Alice dragged herself back inside.

As they headed to the corridor, Annie said, 'So who was the young woman what brought the letter?'

That was a good point. 'I guess she was someone what works at the *Sussex Daily News* office. A secretary, or a clerk or whatnot.'

In the staff dining room, Peter Smith was standing at one end of the table, with everyone leaning towards him, listening to him speaking.

'When will you be leaving?' Mrs Leggett asked.

'You're leaving?' said Annie. 'You've only just got back.'

'I'm going to join Mr Janus's troupe. I had an audition yesterday, and he offered me a place.'

'You do have a good singing voice,' said Mrs Turnbull.

'But why now?' said Alice.

'It's something I've long wanted to do, but thought it better to do a regular, more steady job, like being a waiter in a prestigious hotel. Being in the war got me thinking. Life don't last long, and I really should have a go at something I've always dreamed of.'

'Well, good luck to you, lad,' said the storekeeper.

'It'll be my last day on Sunday. Then, next week, I'll be singing at the Casino Theatre, and sometimes on the common here.'

'Then we might see you,' said Alice. 'That's exciting.'

'I hope you do. I'll keep in touch, don't worry. Maybe, one day, I'll end up in a big theatre somewhere, like in Brighton, or London.' His face was a picture of hope. 'But for now, I'm gasping for a cuppa tea and a biscuit.'

He sat down, along with the sisters. A moment later, a face peered around the door. It was Amanda Lovelock, who'd once done the accounts at the hotel, until she joined the police force in 1916.

'Amanda!' exclaimed Mrs Turnbull. 'I heard you was coming back.'

'You've left the police force?' said Alice.

Amanda stepped in properly. 'No, I've been dismissed by Superintendent Crooke, who says that, since the men are returning, they won't need a *woman* any more.'

'That man is a menace, always poking his nose into what's going on at the police station in Littlehampton. Uncle Barry's always complaining about him.'

'I suppose that is his job,' said Mrs Leggett, 'but yes, he has interfered rather too much in the past, as we know firsthand.'

'I can't say I mind leaving there too much,' said Amanda. 'Mrs Bygrove has invited me back to do the accounts for the hotel once more. She reckons it'll take a weight off her and Edie's shoulders.'

'One in, one out,' said Annie.

'How do you mean?'

Peter had to start again, telling Amanda his news. Alice touched the letter in her apron pocket and was disappointed anew. What was she going to do by herself this afternoon? Have a walk around? Or she could get that fabric for the dress she wanted to make. And perhaps, by the time Jamie returned, she would have finished it and could wear it for him.

Chapter Nine

'So, are you seeing this Jamie this afternoon?' Annie asked Alice on her day off a couple of weeks later.

It reminded Alice, once again, that she had to find something to do on her own this afternoon. The fact it was misty and looked set to be so for the rest of the day, didn't help. It was tempting to just go home and carry on making the dress that she hadn't got very far with.

'No, he's still doing a job out of town.'

'But that was two weeks ago. Has he written to say he's still away?'

'No.'

'Then how do you know he is?'

'Because he said he'd contact me when he got back.'

'Unless he's changed his mind. Or doesn't exist.'

'Not that again, Annie. He *does* exist, and you know that, because Uncle Barry saw me with him.'

'He saw you talking to a man briefly. Could've been anyone.'

'And I had that letter from him.'

'You never showed it to me, so you might've written it yourself and got someone to bring it to the hotel.'

If Annie was trying to get her annoyed, she was doing a good job. But she wasn't going to rise to it. 'Maybe the story Jamie's working on is some big scandal, slowly unfolding. That would be exciting.'

Even as she said this, she wondered, once again, whether he was just trying to let her down gently. But why say he'd send another letter? He could have intended to, then changed his mind. Or he might have met someone else, someone more interesting than her, while he was away. That wouldn't be difficult, as everyone was more interesting than her.

Jasper came in, bringing a tray of staff crockery, deepening her feelings of being inadequate.

'Annie, could I have a word.' He was frowning as he placed the tray down.

'Course you can.'

'It's just, I can't make Thursday afternoon after all, as it's my younger brother's twenty-first birthday and my parents are holding a celebration for him. We're having a small party in the afternoon.'

'That'll be nice for him. Don't worry, it's fine. I quite understand.'

'Good, yes, thank you.' He pointed towards the inner door. 'I'd better get to my shift.'

When he was gone, Alice said, 'Why didn't he invite you along too?' even though the idea of it still made her stomach clench.

Annie looked horrified. 'I'm glad he didn't. It'll be a family thing, no doubt, and I'd only have felt left out.'

'Haven't you met his parents yet?'

'I'd've told you if I had. We've only been walking out, what, not even seven weeks. There's plenty of time for that kind of thing.'

She didn't seem bothered. Why was she walking out with him at all then? To make her feel bad? But maybe Annie was bothered and didn't want to show it, like her.

'Have you met Jamie's parents?' asked Annie.

'No. I don't even know if they live around 'ere, or if he lives with them or on his own.'

'You don't know much about him, do you? Is he secretive?'

'No. He told me he lived on Maxwell Road, but I didn't think to ask if it was with his parents or not.'

'Maxwell Road, eh? Perhaps I should go and invest-igate. I could get Gertie to come with me as she seems quite good at that kind of thing.'

'No, you will not! I'm a grown woman, Annie, not just your "little sister", so please, do not interfere. I don't interfere in your relationship with Jasper.'

'Hm. Well, here's Lucas, so I'm off for me break now.'

Annie vacated the room, leaving Alice feeling cross. If she did anything to interfere, she'd blow her top at her sister, then they'd see what silly old 'Alice in Wonderland' was capable of. But beneath the annoyance, she knew she had to take some responsibility. If only she hadn't been so dismissive about Jasper, if only…

'What d'ya want me to do?' said Lucas.

'You can start the staff washing up from break while I boil up some hot water for the next load. I dare say there'll be a flurry of crockery from morning coffee dumped on us soon.'

While telling him this, she'd made up her mind about her afternoon off – she would go home and carry on with that dress. Whether she'd ever get to wear it for Jamie was yet to be seen.

–

Helen Bygrove entered the police station on Gloucester Road, behind the railway station, hoping that Sam was ready. They were meant to be looking at wedding rings in Worthing this afternoon and the excitement of it all was overwhelming. The first time around, when she'd married Douglas, he'd taken her along to the jeweller's simply to have her finger measured for the ring he'd already picked, a plain band.

'Good morning, Mrs Bygrove,' said Sergeant Gardner, standing by the shelves to the side of the desk, sorting through some papers. 'Or is it afternoon?' He looked at his watch. 'Still morning, just.'

Constable Twort, who was at the desk, said nothing, simply glancing at her before returning to reading a piece of paper in front of him.

'Good morning, Sergeant. I presume that Inspector Toshack is in his office.'

'He's just finishing off some notes. I'll tell him you've arrived.'

He went to a door behind the desk and knocked. Helen heard a distant voice invite him in and he popped his head into the office.

A few moments later, he was out again. 'He says he'll be a couple of minutes and suggests you take a seat. Excuse me, I've just got to check on a drunk we brought in last night.'

'Oh dear.'

She took a seat at the end of a small row of chairs and had only just sat down when the outside door opened, admitting a rather annoyed-looking middle-aged gentleman in a smart suit and fedora hat.

'Excuse me,' he told the constable, 'I'd like to report a serious incident, down at Fisherman's Quay.'

'All right, sir, if you could give me some details, I'll take some notes.'

'I'd had a meeting at one of the workshops on the quay nearby and was walking down the alley onto River Road, when I was approached by a woman. She was in her twenties, I reckon, dark haired, in a dress that was far too short, and she, well, she…'

He looked round at Helen, before leaning forward and lowering his voice, but she could still hear him.

'She tried to solicit me. I told her to go away, but she kept on, and as I walked away, I was attacked from behind. Whoever it was, hit me on the head. I was disoriented for a time, and when I came to my senses, I realised that my wallet and watch had been stolen.'

'Are you sure that's what happened, sir?'

'Well, yes. I know I had a blow to the head, but it wasn't so bad I don't remember what happened.' He sounded offended.

Sergeant Gardner returned, standing nearby to listen in to the conversation.

'It's not just a case of you being angry because a young woman refused your advances, and you want to get her into trouble?' said Twort.

'No, no, it certainly is not,' the man blustered. He looked around at Helen once again and she could see he'd gone pink.

'I'll take over here,' said Gardner. 'You can take a mug of water to our guest in cell two, Constable.'

Twort pouted but did as he was told.

'Now, sir, I can see some notes have been written but can't make head nor tail of them. If you'd like to start again.'

The man huffed out an impatient sigh. 'Well, if I must.' He went over the story once more, even more quietly, so that Helen could only make out a few words.

'Thank you, sir, we will certainly look into this. I'm afraid I don't hold out much hope of returning your possessions, but we will do our best.'

'You're not going to suggest I brought it on myself, like the constable did.'

'Good gracious no, sir. I do apologise about that. Constable Twort has been around a long time and has seen a lot of, let's say, untrustworthy witnesses in his time, and it's made him somewhat cynical. Not always a bad thing in this line of work, but again, I apologise for any misunderstanding.'

'Thank you, Sergeant. He does seem a little long in the tooth to be working as a copper.'

'With age comes experience,' said Gardner. 'Now, write down your details here, and a description of the lost items, and we'll contact you if we manage to locate anything.'

Helen thought about Gardner's statement concerning Twort, convinced it was something to say to keep the complainant happy. *With age comes experience.* The man had been involved in trying to track down the libellous letter writer back in 1916 and had been useless. She was surprised he was still here, having only come out of retirement because of the war, but she guessed they were still short staffed, with some men having not yet returned. And some who never would.

Sam exited his office, smiling as soon as he spotted Helen. She stood and reciprocated the smile.

'Sir,' said Gardner, 'there's been another mugging reported on Fisherman's Quay. That's the fourth one, and three of them started with a woman approaching the man.'

'Not another one. Do you think this is connected with the soliciting that used to occur in that area?' said Sam.

'Maybe, but that was back in 1914. It sounds like it's only being used as an excuse to mug people now, though I suppose if a man were to agree to the proposal, they might not be mugged, so we wouldn't know.'

'Send a constable to have a walk around, Sergeant, maybe talk to a few people there, including in the workshops, to see if they've witnessed anything.'

'I'll send Twort, as he's not good with people on the desk.'

'Is he good at anything?' Sam muttered.

'He's a good beat cop now, sir, better than he was when he first started back.'

'Aye, perhaps.' He approached Helen and kissed her cheek. 'Sorry to keep you waiting, darling.'

'That's fine, my love. The motorcar's outside. Let's get to Worthing and have some lunch.'

–

Jasper was relieved to get out for his afternoon off after a busy morning in the hotel. Annie had said she had a couple of things to do first and would meet him by the side gate. It would be good to see the sun, which he'd noticed through the windows in the foyer.

As he stepped outside, he took a deep breath of the warm, fresh air, before he noticed Alice standing nearby. She was watching the small carriages being pulled by goats and carrying laughing children. This activity had long taken place in this spot in the summer season.

'It's not your afternoon off too, is it?' Jasper said, approaching her, hoping she didn't take offence at the comment as she had too often recently.

'No. I just had a peep outside the gate when I went to the pig bin and noticed the goats. I didn't think Finn and

Lucas would miss me if I went and watched them for a coupla minutes. I like goats.'

He was thankful that, once again, she was being civil to him, like she had at the Easter party for the children.

He stood next to her. 'Me too. They're sweet.'

'Did you ever have a go on those?' Alice asked, pointing to the carriages.

'Once or twice, when I was very young,' he said. 'I remember driving here in the motorcar from Bognor a couple of times.'

'Bognor? I thought you lived in Middleton.'

'My parents do now, but we lived on the outskirts of Bognor then. That's where they had three of their six grocery stores.'

'Six? And they had a motorcar?'

He thought back to the halcyon days of his childhood for a few moments before replying. 'Yes, before the businesses started to fail. They got to the point where they were all making a loss. My father got heavily into debt, so he went out of business. Luckily, he owned two of the buildings. He sold one to pay his debts off. The other he sold so that he and my mother could buy a house in Middleton. That was eight years ago, when I was eighteen, not long before I started at the hotel. My older brother was twenty-two. I'd started working in the shops as a sixteen-year-old, and my brother had already started four years before. Father had the idea that we, and our younger brother, would take over from him when he retired, but it was never to be.' He hoped he hadn't over-explained and bored her.

'What does your older brother do now?'

'He and my younger brother work at White and Thomson in Middleton, where they make the flying boats.'

'The hulls for those are made in Littlehampton, by Humphrey Wilmots, what's owned by the Perrymans.'

'That's right. But White and Thomson are going to be closing soon. I suppose they don't need the flying boats now the war's over. I've no idea what they'll do after that. I suppose it won't make much difference to the Perryman family, having a few other shipping businesses.'

'That's true enough. I knew your father used to have a coupla shops, but didn't realise he had six.'

'He does a bit of gardening for people now.'

Alice placed her head slightly to one side, concern in her pretty blue eyes. It filled him with a sensation he knew he shouldn't be feeling, when he was about to head off out with her sister.

'Were you disappointed, not to have the shops passed on to you and your brothers?'

'If I'm honest, not really. I'm not sure I ever wanted to be a shopkeeper, but it was part of my life and what I expected to go on doing. Still, that's life, I suppose.'

'Yes, that's life.' She looked away from him and back at the goat carriages.

If the businesses hadn't failed, he wouldn't have met her and Annie. But even that hadn't turned out as he'd expected, and who knew what the upshot would be.

Out of the corner of his eye he saw someone come out of the gate.

'Here's Annie now.'

'So, you're off out somewhere together then?' she asked, her eyes still turned towards the carriages.

'Yes, just a walk by the beach, I think.'

'Right. Nice.'

He turned to face the hotel, lifting his hand in greeting. 'Hello Annie.'

As she approached, she didn't greet him in return, but sounded a little annoyed as she said, 'What are you doing out here, Alice? You're not on a break.'

'Just watching the goats for a coupla minutes. I'm heading back now.'

As she turned and walked quickly towards the gate, he felt a twinge of regret at her leaving. But that wouldn't do, and he was sure he'd enjoy his afternoon out with Annie.

–

After their afternoon out being cancelled the week before, Annie was relieved to have someone to keep her company this week. Today it was warm and sunny, so Jasper had suggested a walk along the promenade, via the bandstand. She'd just needed to change and tidy herself up, and told him she'd meet him by the gate.

There, she was ready now.

She left the women's bathroom on the second floor and headed downstairs, then through the stillroom and scullery, hoping she hadn't left Jasper waiting too long. She opened the side gate, confused at first that he wasn't there, before spotting him a few yards away, talking to Alice.

Jasper turned and waved at her, calling, 'Hello Annie.'

A few steps away, she said, 'What are you doing out here, Alice? You're not on a break.' Was she spying on her and Jasper, to see which way they went?

'Just watching the goats for a coupla minutes. I'm heading back now.'

As she walked off, Annie said, 'Come on then, let's go... Honestly, she is a one. I suppose she was just standing there, daydreaming.'

'She said she likes the goats. Don't suppose it did any harm, just watching them for a couple of minutes.'

Was he sticking up for her? It might be better to change the subject. 'There's a band on; shall we have a look?'

'It wouldn't hurt.'

At the bandstand, they stood and watched for a while, as a military band played.

'Shall we pay tuppence for a deckchair to stay and listen?' he asked, not looking sure.

'I'd rather carry on to the prom,' she said.

'Yes, me too.'

It turned out there was now a lot happening there, confirming that the summer season had really got going.

Jasper bought them both a bottle of ginger beer, and they sat on the wall, their feet dangling over the top of the beach, watching the high tide roll in and out.

'There's a lot of nannies with children here today,' she said.

'I think there always are a few.'

She noticed one little boy in particular. He must have been six or seven, wrapped up in a large towel by a fussing nanny in a blue uniform, who was escorting him to the water's edge. Reaching the sea, she removed the towel and allowed him to go into the water up to his waist. He'd only been splashing around for a short while, when the nanny called him out and wrapped him up again.

'Did you ever have a nanny?' she asked Jasper.

'A nanny? No.' He laughed. 'We were middle-class, I suppose, and weren't badly off at one time, but my mother always looked after us. A nanny. Gosh, I can't even imagine having one of those.'

'I suppose Vera is a kind of nanny to Dorothy, Arthur and Elsie, even though she's called a nursemaid.'

'Yes, I suppose she is.'

'Your father's retired now, isn't he?'

He let out a small chuckle.

'Why is that funny?'

'It's just, I was talking about this to Alice before you arrived. Can't even remember how we got on the subject. Oh yes, she asked if I'd been on the goat carriages as a child, and it somehow led to that.'

'That sounds like an involved conversation. She is so nosy sometimes.' Again, was she fishing for information?

'I don't think she was being nosy, it was just how the conversation progressed. Anyway, as I told her, he works part time as a gardener now. He looks after a few people's gardens. He's never been one to do nothing. My mother's the same, and she makes clothes for people.'

'My mother does that too.'

'What a coincidence,' he said. 'What about your father? He's a farmer, isn't he?'

'A farm manager at Wick Farm. He doesn't own it, of course.'

'I'm sorry about last week and not inviting you to the party. Mother only wanted family in attendance, and since they'd never met you—'

'I understand. Would you like me to meet them?' She wasn't certain about this herself. Meeting his parents would make the whole relationship seem more… serious. Was that what she wanted?

'Would you like me to meet yours?' He didn't sound sure about it either.

'Well, it's not like either of our parents live far away, with yours in Middleton and mine in Wick, but… maybe it's not the right time yet.'

She hoped she hadn't hurt his feelings, so was relieved when he replied, 'No, you're probably right.'

They stopped for a while to watch the Punch and Judy show. He laughed, but she'd never enjoyed the aggression in it, not even as a child, seeing Mr Punch as a grotesque figure. He reminded her of a neighbour up the road from them, who used to beat his wife black and blue. She was relieved to move on to watch an organ grinder and his monkey.

A little further on was a tent at the top of the beach, with a fortune teller and reader of palms.

'Shall we have a laugh and see what "Madame Giovanna" has to say about our futures?' Jasper suggested.

Annie had never been to a fortune teller, not believing in such things, but she didn't want to look like a misery again. And, as Jasper had said, it might be a laugh. 'All right.'

Inside, they paid threepence each to a dramatic-looking young woman with wild, black hair and an exotic satin costume. On a small, round table in front of her was a crystal ball. Annie and Jasper sat on the other two chairs there.

She asked their names, then took Annie's hand, humming a strange tune, interrupting several times with an, 'Ah hah,' as if agreeing with herself. She then looked into the crystal ball, humming the tune once more.

'Yes, yes, this confirms it. You are hankering after something you think you cannot have, but you can have it if you make the effort. You undervalue yourself, but you are worth so much more. People will start to see that soon. Have faith.'

She moved onto Jasper, taking his hand and turning it over to examine his palm. 'Ah hah, ah hah. Of course, of course.' She followed it by looking into the crystal ball once more. 'Yes, yes, that is it. You are looking in the wrong direction, Jasper. Look the other way, and you will find your destiny. But do not wait too long, or it will be gone.' She looked from one to the other. 'Good luck to you both, for if you follow your destinies, you will find happiness. Good day.'

They both rose and left.

When they reached the promenade again, Jasper said, 'I think that might have been rather a waste of sixpence. What on earth was she talking about? It was all rather vague.'

'Which it's meant to be, I guess, so, whatever happens, it seems like her prediction has come true.'

'What are you hankering after that you can't have?' he asked.

'I dunno. A nice home of my own? More money? Everyone's hankering after something, aren't they?'

'It could apply to anyone. It's very generic.'

She knew that the answer for her was still Lorcan. Jasper was very nice and a lot of fun, but he wasn't that affectionate towards her. Nor did she want him to be. Her affections hadn't grown for him over the weeks, as she'd thought they might.

'Any idea why you might be looking in the wrong direction?' she asked.

'Goodness knows. Perhaps it's suggesting I need a new career, but I'm happy being a porter, for the time being.'

It occurred to Annie that *she* might be the cause of him looking in the wrong direction. Maybe he should be looking at Alice. 'I suppose that prediction could apply to a lot of things as well.'

'Look, there's Professor Seluph and his performing dogs. They're always entertaining.'

'I like them too.'

They set off down the promenade once more, and she for one was ready to have her thoughts directed away from Lorcan and Alice, and what could, or could not, have been.

—

After they'd exhausted the entertainments on the promenade, Jasper suggested a walk along the river, down to the bridge that crossed the Arun to the west bank. He'd decided it would be quieter there, so he and Annie might have a chance to be on their own.

On the bridge, they looked downriver, towards the mouth, where the Arun flowed into the sea. The fishermen's cottages on Pier Road, the windmill, battery mound and lighthouse could be spotted in the distance on the left. On the right could be seen the sand dunes of West Beach and closer to them, the golf club.

'It's not as busy here as it was before the war,' said Jasper. 'There don't seem to be nearly as many sailing ships and only a few steam ships. I used to enjoy watching them, especially the sailing ships.'

'Maybe more will start coming back later.'

'Maybe,' Jasper repeated, not convinced. Littlehampton seemed to have changed in so many ways since he'd left for the war, even if it looked the same on the surface. 'Is

Alice still walking out with this mysterious Jamie?' Even as he said it, he felt the disappointment once more. It would have been better not to ask.

'So it would seem.'

He waited for her to expand on the statement, but she said nothing more. Glancing around and seeing no one else about, he placed his arm around Annie's shoulders. She didn't object, but neither did she make any attempt to put her arm around him in return. Since they were alone, it might be a good time to kiss her.

He turned towards her and kissed her on the cheek. Again, she didn't object. She didn't really react at all. He didn't experience any of the thrill such an action should make him feel. Should he kiss her lips? She might think it odd if he didn't do so soon. The trouble was, he wasn't sure he wanted to. Despite what he'd said to Annie, that fortune teller had got him thinking. Had he been looking in the wrong direction? It was Alice he'd always liked. He'd often thought of her as he'd sat in the trenches, needing something to bring him out of his gloom. But she wasn't available any more. And she didn't seem to like him that much anyway. What if his hankering after Alice was him looking in the wrong direction, and he should appreciate Annie more? Then he needed to make the effort.

If he kissed Annie properly, he'd probably find he liked it and wanted more, and it might be the proper start to a romantic relationship.

He turned Annie to face him, leaning forward to kiss her, but he hadn't quite reached her lips when they heard the horn of an approaching motorcar. They parted and made sure they were out of its way as it passed by, but the moment was broken, and they went back to looking downriver.

A voice called from a small cabin, 'Off the bridge please, as we'll be opening it shortly for a ship.'

Jasper and Annie looked behind them to see a large ship in the distance, in full sail, coming towards the bridge.

'We'd better do as he says. How about a cup of tea somewhere?' Annie suggested.

'That's a good idea. I am rather parched.'

Coward, he reproached himself. It seemed fate was against him kissing Annie today, and if he was honest, he wasn't ready for it anyway.

Chapter Ten

It had been five weeks since Alice had last seen Jamie, and she'd not heard a word from him. As she emptied out a bucket of food scraps into the pig-swill bin in the yard, she decided it was safe to assume she'd seen the last of him. She was sad not to see him, as she had the afternoon off, but at least she had something to do today, and it was something she always enjoyed, even on her own. It was the twenty-sixth of May, on which day each year the fair came to Littlehampton. Her whole afternoon could be taken up by that.

'You gonna be emptying them scraps all day?' Annie called from the open scullery window.

'Nope. The bit at the bottom got stuck, that's all.'

She went back inside and glanced at the clock on the wall. 'I'll have to get going soon. I'm looking forward to the fair.'

'Lucky you, getting your day off on the day it's in town,' said Annie.

'I thought you were going this evening with Phoebe.'

'It's not the same as going in the day.'

'I wish we could go together, like we used to, when we was younger.' She took Annie's arm and hugged it briefly, thinking how much simpler life seemed before the war.

Annie's expression became glum. 'Well, we can't, 'cos we can't 'ave the same time off unless we ask for it well in advance.'

'We should bear it in mind for next year.'

Jasper entered, not carrying a tray but instead with a letter in his hand.

'This came for you, Alice. It was brought in by a young woman. Mr Watkins wasn't pleased, as you can imagine, and asked me to remind you to tell whoever sent it that it should be delivered to the scullery door in future.' Jasper seemed as put out as the chief desk clerk from his tone.

'If I knew who they were, I would.'

'I presume it's from that Jamie again,' he said. 'It was a woman who brought a letter for you last time.'

'Oh, Annie told you, did she?' Alice crossed her arms in front of her and frowned.

He glanced at Annie who said, 'Yep. Why shouldn't I?'

'Um, yes. Anyway,' said Jasper, 'you should have told him then to send messengers to the staff entrance.'

'I would if I'd seen him since then, but I 'aven't, so how could I?'

She glanced at the writing on the envelope. It did look the same as on the last letter he'd sent. She felt a little trepidation, not sure if she'd be disappointed or not if he wrote that he was unable to see her again.

Jasper stood there, unmoving, as if waiting for her to open it. She felt uncomfortable with him watching, having a fleeting thought that she wished it was from him. She pushed the silly idea away; he was walking out with her sister, so she mustn't think like that. She placed the letter down on the counter. With that, he left.

'Ain't you gonna open it?' said Annie.

'In me own good time. I've got to get changed now.' She picked up the letter and left.

She headed to Phoebe's room upstairs to retrieve her clothes, then went to the women's bathroom to get ready. First of all, she opened the envelope. She read the short note and was smiling by the time she'd finished it. Jamie had returned to Littlehampton and wished to meet her at one o'clock at the entrance to Fisherman's Quay, if she still had Mondays off and was available, so that they could enjoy the fair together. If she didn't turn up, he said, he'd understand that she couldn't make it.

If only he'd put an address, she could have replied if she hadn't been able to meet him. She could always have popped into the office of the *Sussex Daily News*, she supposed. But it didn't matter, because she *could* make it. And she had plenty of time to get there by one o'clock.

She changed quickly into the cornflower blue cotton poplin frock that she'd finally finished. It was the most modern item of clothing she owned, with its wide collar and turnback cuffs on long sleeves. It was straight, with a pleated skirt and a wide sash tied around the middle. Even their mum had been impressed with her needlework, adding that Annie should have a go at making something, which hadn't pleased her sister. It reached halfway down her calves, and was the shortest outfit she'd ever owned, which she'd feared her parents would comment on. But the only person who had was Annie.

Alice put on her straw hat and headed back downstairs. Deep inside, she hoped that Jasper would come back this way and see her in her new frock, but he'd made no appearance by the time she'd reached the scullery.

'Oh, you're wearing that short dress, are you?' said Annie.

'Yes. It's just the weather for it. See you later.' She wasn't going to engage in conversation about it now, especially with Finn and Lucas in the room, and she wasn't going to let her sister's mood spoil the day for her.

She enjoyed the sun on her face as she made her way to Pier Road, hoping there'd be a bit more to the fair on the quay and in Surrey Street than there had been during the war, when year on year it had depleted.

–

Alice was at the entrance to Fisherman's Quay a little early, feeling nervous about whether Jamie would turn up. The area was busy, with adults chatting and children shouting and squealing with joy, on top of which was the sound of the roundabout organ. It wasn't long before she spotted Jamie's tall, blond head with his gingery beard, coming through the crowd.

'Alice, I'm so glad you could come.' He was grinning with delight as he came to meet her, lifting her mood immediately. He was wearing a slimline navy-blue suit today, with a matching golf style cap, and looked very stylish. She was so glad she'd chosen to wear her new dress now.

'I got your letter not long before I headed out,' she said.

'I was afraid I might be too late. How are you?'

'I'm fine. How did your work trip away go?'

'It went. Not something I'd want to do again, but it revealed some interesting information. Again, I can't say much at this time.'

'While I remember, I've been told to ask you not to send someone to the front desk at the hotel. That's only for guests. Anything for staff must go to the side entrance.'

'Oh dear, I hope I didn't get you in trouble.'

She didn't want him to feel bad, so said, 'No, it's fine. Who was it brought the letter? They said it was a woman again, so I presume it was the same one as last time.'

'What? Oh, yes, um, Marta. She's a secretary at the office.'

'I thought she must be something like that.'

'My, it's busy today,' he said. 'I don't think I've ever seen it quite this crowded.'

'There seem to be more rides and things this year. There hasn't been so much during the war.'

'No… I, er, can imagine. I was never on leave when it was on. So, shall we have a go on something? And I'm going to say up front that this is my treat today, so no arguing.' He said it with a grin, persuading her to give in.

If it pleased him to treat her, then she'd let him do so. It wasn't like she had a huge amount of money to spend.

'All right. I was a bit early and had a go at the coconut shy but wasn't successful,' she said.

'I sometimes wonder if they're glued onto the stand. Oh look, there are the swingboats. Would you like a go on those?'

'I'd love to! I don't think they were 'ere last year.'

They joined the queue. She wanted to ask him more about his trip away, but he'd already seemed reluctant to tell her too much. Apart from which, there was such a din from everyone it was hard to speak.

Finally, they got on a swingboat, sitting opposite each other. It slowly rocked back and forth, getting higher and higher, creaking as it slowly swung out over the river. She giggled each time it went up, enjoying the view she got as it rose. He looked over at her, grinning, making her feel good about herself for a change.

She was disappointed when it started to lower and slow down, then finally came to a halt. Jamie helped her off onto the pebbles.

'Perhaps we could come back later for another go,' she said.

'Why not? What shall we have a go on now?'

'How about the gallopers?' She pointed to the large roundabout.

He nodded and they went to join that queue, passing a smaller roundabout for little children that had miniature motorcars on it. The big roundabout came to a halt after a few minutes. They managed to get a horse each, next to each other. As it started up, and the organ music played, she held on tightly to the horse's neck. As much as she loved the gallopers, she worried constantly about falling off, making her experience a cross between thrill and panic, but it never put her off going on them.

After the roundabout, they each had a go on the hoopla and the coconut shy, but neither was successful.

'Shall we go to Surrey Street now?' she said. 'To see what else there is? And I might spot some of my friends from the 'otel as I ain't seen any of 'em here.'

'I thought you wanted another go on the swingboats?'

'The queue's rather long at the moment. We could come back later.'

He seemed to think about it for a while, not looking sure. 'Come on then.' They made their way out by the Britannia public house, passing a gypsy caravan on the way, then headed around to Surrey Street.

As they went, he said, 'I suppose the Beach Hotel's a lot busier now the war's over.'

'It's been busier since Easter, and we've been full up most of that time, so yes, I suppose it is.'

'I'd love to see inside one day.'

'Fanny, our head chambermaid, gave her Walter a tour late one evening last year, so maybe I could do the same one night. It depends who's on duty.'

'I, yes, I'd like that. Late night sounds perfect. I'm sorry again for sending Marta to the wrong entrance. They must be real sticklers there. I'm sure she looked quite smart enough.'

'That wouldn't matter. Mr Watkins complained because the letter was for a staff member. If it had been for a guest, he wouldn't have worried.'

'I see. Do you get a lot of day guests in, for lunch and so forth? Or is it mainly those staying?'

'We get a fair few day guests. If you look smart enough and can pay, and there's a table available, anyone can have a meal or morning coffee or afternoon tea there.'

'You don't have to be a "sir" or a "Lord Someone" then?'

She laughed. 'No, course not. Most guests, including those what stay, don't 'ave any titles. Just the money to do so, I guess. We 'ave 'ad ordinary folk in, during the war, for the charity events. And we still hold them sometimes. You could always come to one of those.'

He nodded but said nothing.

They reached Surrey Street and Alice gasped. 'That's more like it. That's much better than the last coupla years.'

She looked around and up and down the street, at the cakewalk, chair-o-planes and another large roundabout. There were lots of side stalls, under pitched canopies with red and white stripes.

'What shall we go on first?' He indicated the whole street with his hand.

'Oh, the chair-o-planes, please. I do love 'em so.'

Again, there was a queue. Jamie took out a handkerchief to clean his glasses as he asked her about the hotel once more. They had to speak up above the noise to hear each other. She was glad he was so interested in her job, though wished he could tell her more about his.

'What kind of stories do you write when there ain't something secret going on?' she asked. 'Do you get to report on just ordinary things sometimes?'

'It varies. I might do the odd, you know, odd… big wedding or occasion, or an event like this.'

'Are you reporting on the fair? I'd love to see something of yours in the newspapers.'

'No, not this year. My editor wants me to concentrate on getting information for the big story I'm working on.'

Their turn on the chair-o-planes came. She squealed with joy as the seats on long chains swung around.

Walking away from the ride afterwards, Alice nearly bumped into Fanny, who had her arm through Walter's.

'Fanny! I hoped I'd see you two.'

'Wouldn't miss it for the world. I was lucky it was me day off.'

'Jamie, this is Fanny and Walter, who I told you about before. They got married just over a month ago.'

'Hello Jamie.' Fanny held her hand out and he shook it, then did the same with Walter. He looked a little awkward as he did this, with his head half down.

'We're gonna 'ave a go on the roundabout now,' Fanny said. 'Fancy coming to 'ave a go too?'

'We were going to go on the cakewalk first,' Jamie mumbled. 'Since we did the roundabout on the quay.'

Alice sensed there was something wrong, though couldn't work out what. 'We'll hopefully catch up with you afterwards.'

'Okay,' said Walter. The two of them waved as they headed off into the crowd.

When they'd gone, Alice said, 'They're very nice, Fanny and Walter. You seemed, I dunno, a bit awkward with 'em, like you didn't trust 'em.'

Jamie pushed his glasses up the bridge of his nose. 'I'm sorry, Alice. It's… not that I don't trust them, or there's anything wrong with them, it's just…' He looked like he was working something out. 'I'm just rather shy. Painfully shy, my… mother used to say. I find it hard to talk to strangers. I was amazed when I got talking to you, but that was probably because I felt so guilty, bumping into you like I did.'

'But you're a reporter. It's part of your job to talk to people.'

'Yes… exactly. I'm a reporter. It's my job, where I can pretend to be someone else. But when it's part of my private life, I struggle.'

'I'm shy too, so I sort of understand, but I don't think I'm quite as shy as you, which surprises me.'

'Look, why don't we have a go on the cakewalk, and then go and get something to eat. I didn't have any lunch before I met you.'

'Nor did I. Yes, let's do that. Though the cafes and tearooms are gonna be a bit busy.'

'Let's head down to Kimble's. Being the other end of High Street, it might be a bit quieter.'

'All right. Cakewalk then Kimble's.'

–

After returning from Kimble's, Jamie suggested they head back around to Fisherman's Quay to have another go on the swingboats. It was a little quieter now, so they got on more quickly.

At the end of the ride, he was helping her off as she spotted two other familiar faces in the crowd.

'There's Lili and Rhodri. Lili's the head waitress at the hotel.'

'Would you like another go on the swingboats as you like them so much?'

'Maybe later. And there's Fanny and Walter again. And they have Gertie with 'em now.' She lifted her hand to wave, but they hadn't noticed her.

'Oh, I wonder…' Jamie looked at his wristwatch. 'Goodness me, is that the time? I'm so sorry about this, Alice, but I do have a meeting with my boss. He wants an update as I only got back this morning. I asked for part of the afternoon off but promised to meet him later, and it's already half past four.'

'You have to go?'

'I'm afraid so.' He seemed agitated. 'I don't want him getting annoyed with me, as plenty of other people would like my job. I should have told you when we first met that I wouldn't be able to stay the whole afternoon.'

'I understand. I'll have to get back by about six anyway.'

'Is there a chance I could see you one evening? It'll be harder in the next couple of weeks to get the time off during the day.'

'I can't remember when my next evening off is, not until June I think, but those rotas ain't gone up yet.'

'What time do you finish this evening? I could come and meet you at the side of the hotel and walk you home.'

'I'm afraid I'll be walking home with Annie, as I normally do, and she might not appreciate you turning up.'

'Fair enough. By the way, I might have to go away again. And I'm going on holiday soon, to, um…'

'Have you forgotten?'

'The name of the actual place, yes. My, er, parents have organised it. It's in Hampshire though. I'll be in touch when I get back.'

He gave her a quick peck on the cheek, then disappeared into the crowd.

Was that it? Had he tired of her? But he'd given her a kiss, however cursory, and he hadn't done that before.

'Hello again,' said Fanny, coming up next to Alice. Walter and Gertie were just behind. 'Where's your friend gone?'

'He 'ad to get back to work for a meeting with his boss.'

'Is he the Jamie that Annie told us about?' Gertie asked.

Trust her sister to open her gob to all and sundry. 'Yes, that's right.'

'Then come join us,' said Walter. 'You don't wanna walk around all lonesome.'

'Thank you, I will.'

'To the swingboats!' Gertie declared.

She'd only just got off them, but Alice was more than happy to have another go. Hopefully, she wouldn't have to wait another five weeks before she saw Jamie again.

–

With a large number of people around, Alice and her friends were soon out of his sight. And more importantly, *he* was out of *their* sight. It had been bad enough meeting any of her friends, though, if he'd thought about it before, it was inevitable at an event like this. He'd just assumed the crowds would make him anonymous. And the last person he wanted to encounter was Gertie Green.

He was almost through the alley, on his way to River Road, when he felt someone grab his arm from behind.

He jumped around, about to punch the person responsible, but stopped dead still when he saw who it was.

'Bloody hell, Frank, I nearly gave you one then. Don't creep up on me like that.'

'So, what you found out then, Jim?'

'This and that. I'll tell you later, when we're not surrounded by people.'

'Let's walk onto River Road and find somewhere quiet.'

They did so in silence, walking halfway down the road, the houses on one side and the warehouses on the other.

'You managed to find a way of getting into the 'otel yet? And where the valuables are kept?' said Frank.

'I'm trying, but Alice has a sister who works there, and it's making it difficult as I don't want to be introduced to anyone else. And don't forget that Edie Moore, who was living at Hadley's wife's house when Pamela was there, might recognise me.'

'That was nearly five years ago now. And you said you'd kept a low profile.'

'I did, but I don't want to take any chances. I can't help thinking that I'm the wrong person for this job.'

'You're the only one with any class, so I ain't got a lotta choice. And you're the one what's good at taking on different personas. Huh. Should've gone on stage, you should've. D'ya think Alice'd give us information if we paid 'er?'

'No, not a chance. She's not the type. She seems very loyal to her boss. And she's got an uncle who's a police sergeant in Littlehampton.'

'What? You should've picked someone else, ya bloody numbskull.'

'I didn't know that when I picked her. It wouldn't look good for me now, to take an interest in someone else at the hotel.'

'It's a shame that little bitch Susie ran away, as we could 'ave got 'er to work at the 'otel, having some cleaning experience. If I ever catch that cow...'

Jim nodded, the tightness in his chest making him a little breathless. It was weird, his boss conjuring up that scenario, when going to work at the Beach Hotel was exactly what Susie had done. He'd found out through Marta, who'd seen her going in the staff entrance. Meeting Gertie at a football match and finding out she worked at the hotel had been a gift for finding out more about Susie's position there. Why the silly mare had stayed so close to Frank's operation after she ran away, he'd never know; she should have gone a lot, lot further. The last time he'd seen her the police were taking her away in a motorcar. She must have committed some other crime, and he had no idea where she was now, and didn't care. What he did care about, was Frank finding out that he'd known where Susie was and hadn't told him, and that he'd let her escape. If he did ever find out, heaven only knew what he'd do to him.

And now he had the worry of Gertie recognising him, as he was certain she would if she ever laid eyes on him, despite the longer hair, glasses and beard, and the fact that he'd discarded the large coat and hat he'd always worn in her company.

' 'Ere's a thought,' said Frank. 'Would this Alice make a good replacement for Susie? We still 'aven't replaced 'er, nor them two tarts what died of flu. Some men'd like a sweet little blonde like her, looking all innocent like.'

Jim was horrified at the idea but kept that emotion from his expression. 'No, I reckon she'd be useless. Our clients would be sure to complain.'

'Right. You just need to keep in touch with 'er to find out more. In the meantime, get back to 'eadquarters and get that ridiculous la-di-da suit off. You've got stuff to do before your trip to Portsmouth tomorrow. I'll see you in an hour or two.'

'Right, boss.'

He set off down River Road, towards the bridge and Frank went in the opposite direction. He wished he hadn't picked Alice for this now. He'd seen her, first off, coming out of the side entrance of the hotel and had followed her at a distance to the town, where he'd 'bumped' into her. But she was a sweet girl, and if things for him had been different, he would have been genuinely interested. That didn't happen very often to him, and it made him feel a good deal of regret about the situation he was in now. Still, there was little he could do about it.

When he got back from the job in Portsmouth, he'd tell Frank that he thought Alice was a dead end and they'd need to think of another way of finding out about the hotel. He'd be sad not to see her again, but he didn't want to involve her in this.

—

Annie had returned to the hotel with Phoebe after their trip to the fair that evening. She wanted to meet her sister, not wanting to do the thirty-minute walk home to Wick on her own. She also wanted to make sure that Alice didn't go off and meet Jamie again and end up alone with him at night.

As they walked up to Wick, her sister regaled her with tales of her afternoon with Jamie, then with Fanny, Walter and Gertie, every now and again her voice rising with excitement as they strolled along the roughly made road. It was a warm but moonless night, and with few streetlights now they'd left the main town, it meant they walked largely in the dark.

They approached the buildings of Wick Farm, where their father and brother Cecil worked, as had their other brothers before the war.

'What about your evening with Phoebe?' said Alice.

'It was fun, though some of the activities packed up before others, so we didn't get to do some of the rides and stalls we wanted to.'

'That's a shame.'

'You said Jamie left at half-past four. Did you know he was going to do that?'

'No, well, he'd forgotten to mention it when we met.'

'And he didn't mention it in the letter he sent you.'

'No.'

'Seems odd,' said Annie. 'And a bit selfish.'

'He couldn't 'elp it if he had a meeting with his editor.'

'As he did last time he met you. He could 'ave told you that at the beginning. Don't see how he could forget. He remembered when it got to that time. Seems like an excuse to me.'

'Oh, don't start and spoil my day. He's a busy man.'

'It's almost like he didn't wanna meet your friends, so scurried away.'

'He met Lili and Walter.'

'But you said he seemed embarrassed.'

'He was shy.'

'Or he didn't wanna meet them either. He's a reporter, isn't it his job to meet people?'

'He can do that 'cos it's his job, but it's different when it's his personal life. I think it's sweet, that he's so shy.'

'I think it's weird. I don't like the sound of him and I'm gonna tell Mum and Dad when we get in.'

'You'll do no such thing, Annie! There is nothing wrong or weird about Jamie. He's a nice man.'

'Who don't seem keen to meet anyone you know. Perhaps next time you meet him, do so at the 'otel and introduce him to me.'

'I will.'

'When are you meeting him again?'

'He's going on 'oliday with his parents, and then he might 'ave to be away for a job too.'

'How convenient.'

'You know, he offered to walk me 'ome tonight and I said no, 'cos I was walking 'ome with you, but I wish I'd said yes now if I'd known I was gonna get all this grief.'

'You *definitely* shouldn't walk out with him at night. Lord knows what he'd do. I'm definitely gonna tell Mum and Dad.'

They'd now reached their front door on the terrace of farm workers' houses they lived in.

'You bleedin' well won't!'

Annie opened the door into the front room, determined to carry out her threat, when their mother appeared, all smiles.

'You two can stop that arguing, whatever it's about. We've 'ad good news – Cedric and Cyril will be 'eading 'ome, end of July.'

Their father came through the door from the kitchen. ''Ave you told 'em, love, about Cedric and Cyril?'

'I 'ave love.'

'That's wonderful news,' said Alice, jumping up and down on the spot and clapping her hands.

'Yes, good news indeed,' said Annie, wishing Alice would keep still. Her leaping around was making her dizzy.

Now didn't seem the time to spoil the atmosphere by spilling her sister's secret. With this Jamie away for a while, Annie decided it could wait until another time. With any luck, he either wouldn't come back, or he wouldn't bother contacting Alice again.

Chapter Eleven

Edie couldn't believe that she'd married Charlie at last. All through the war, she'd feared it would never happen, because he'd be killed, or 'missing presumed dead', as she'd heard had happened to some men. But here she was, outside St Mary's Parish Church, in a white satin dress with a bouquet of pink peonies, surrounded by family and friends, though not many of either, admittedly. And she was now Mrs Cobbett. The Honourable Edith Cobbett. No, she'd never be using her old title ever again. 'Mrs' was good enough for her. She looked up at the brilliant blue sky of a gloriously sunny day and felt blessed several times over.

Lili and Edie's friend Julia, who were bridesmaids, were throwing rose petals over her and Charlie, who was pink in the face and smiling bashfully. The rest of the group from the hotel consisted of Helen, Mrs Turnbull, Mrs Leggett and Lorcan, who was Charlie's best man. She would have liked to have invited a good deal more, but they were needed at the hotel. At least they'd all be able to pop into the reception they were holding in the ballroom. Victoria Harrison, who'd been her tutor at home when she'd been between eleven and sixteen, was also there with her husband. Her only family members present were her father, her brother Freddie and his wife, Lucia, who was with child, around five months gone. Charlie's family consisted of his parents and an aunt and uncle.

Her father came up beside her as Charlie chatted with Julia and Lorcan, and the others had split into two groups to gossip together. 'That was a lovely ceremony, even if it was low key.'

'There was no point in making it anything else, Father, though I appreciate your offer to pay for a bigger affair. Who would there have been to invite? With Mother refusing to attend and having persuaded the rest of the family and friends that I've been taken in by a brigand, as I believe she referred to him, we could hardly have a society affair. Apart from which, I didn't want that, and I'm certain Charlie wouldn't have wanted it either.'

'I can't pretend that I didn't envisage a different life for you, but you know what, Edith? I admire you, I really do. You've been determined to make your own way in the world, and you've become an undermanageress in a prestigious hotel. And you picked someone who had a bad start in life, but has made the best of it, and now runs the hotel garage. And won a medal in the war for bravery. So many people I know had businesses and riches handed to them on a plate and have employed others to make a success of those businesses. Had you been a boy, I'd have been delighted to have had you in the timber business.' He lowered his voice. 'I'm not sure Freddie's heart is really in it. He'd rather be a novelist, or a poet. You've got the wherewithal to do well, Edie, and I am proud of you. I hope, one day, your mother comes to see it the same way.'

'Thank you, Father.' She doubted that her mother would ever change her mind, but having her father on her side meant the world to her, nonetheless.

Helen came over and Edie took her arm, saying, 'It's so kind of you to let us use the ballroom.'

'It's not as if it is being used much at the moment,' said Helen. 'I am quite happy for any of my staff who are getting married to use a vacant room. After the support you all gave me during the war, it seems only right and proper.'

'Despite what you say, Mrs Bygrove, I will be paying for the room hire at the going rate. It's a small enough affair as it is, so I can at least do this for my daughter.'

'Very well, Lord Moreland, as you wish... I suppose we'd better make our way back to the hotel. You have a photographer arriving soon.'

'Yes, you're right... Charlie?'

He turned away from where he was chatting to Mrs Turnbull and Mrs Leggett. 'Yes Mrs Cobbett?' he said cheerily.

She pointed up at the church clock. 'The photographer will be arriving at the hotel soon.'

'I 'ave to admit, I'm looking forward to that spread we chose. I'm famished, with us missing lunch.' Charlie patted the front of the waistcoat on the new grey suit he'd bought.

'And we want to be there by the time the afternoon breaks start, so staff can join in,' said Edie.

'Come along then, Mrs Cobbett.' He held out a bent arm, and she placed hers through it.

They led the party away, along the residential side of Beach Road, up to South Terrace and the hotel. Despite the absence of her mother, and a few other relatives who thought her marriage improper, Edie didn't regret her decision for a moment.

Annie had an hour free early evening, along with her sister, and had looked forward all day to Edie and Charlie's reception. Apart from being able to enjoy some delicacies normally reserved for the guests, she knew there was going to be a string quartet there, and she so loved the idea of joining in with a dance.

Then again, who would she dance with? Maybe only with Alice, or another female staff member, but it was better than nothing. It had been ages since she'd danced anyway, and she did so love to. She looked around for Lorcan, expecting him to be here as the best man, but she couldn't see him anywhere.

The room was decorated with peonies and lily of the valley in several large vases. She took a deep breath, inhaling the sweet floral fragrance.

Spotting the bride and groom, she went over to congratulate them. 'Did you say you was going away tomorrow for a few days?' Annie asked.

'Yes, down to Devon on the train for three days in a guest house in Torquay,' said Edie. 'Charlie's never been, and it is so picturesque there.'

'I've heard that. 'Ope you 'ave a lovely time.'

'Thank you, Annie. I'm so overwhelmed with everyone's good wishes.'

'You deserve it.' And she meant it. Being initially wary of Edie when they'd first found out she was titled, she'd proved herself a firm friend and ally over the years, not putting on any airs and graces like others who weren't nearly as privileged.

Annie walked away, allowing someone else to share their good wishes with the couple. At one end of the ball-room, which was much too large for the number of people present, there were canapés, savoury bites and sandwiches. Further along there were sweet treats. The staff who'd just entered, including Gertie and Fanny, helped themselves with eager delight.

'This is de*lic*ious,' said Alice, overstating everything as she often did, but she couldn't disagree.

'Try the lemon tarts,' said Gertie, reaching for a second one. 'Oh my.'

'You're supposed to start with the savouries,' said Annie.

'Don't care what order I eat 'em in.' She took a bite. 'Mm, mm, mmmm.'

'Very ladylike,' Fanny joked, elbowing her.

'That's me, Lady Gertrude Green,' she said, her mouth half full.

'Behave,' said Annie. 'Baron Howard Moreland is looking over.'

'Baron what? Oh, you mean Edie's dad. He's smiling.'

'Look, the band's setting up,' said Fanny. 'Walter should be 'ere soon. I'm looking forward to a dance, even if I'm not that good. Me and Walter danced in 'ere one night when we was walking out and I sneaked 'im in. We only 'ad the moonlight, and he hummed the tune, but it was *so* romantic.' She looked up at the ceiling, miles away, as if reliving the moment.

'So you've told us many times,' said Annie.

The door closest to them opened, and Lorcan walked in. Annie found it hard to breathe for a few moments. He was even more handsome than usual in his navy-blue suit, one she'd never seen him wear before. He must have had a haircut that morning, for it was shorter than it had been yesterday. Behind him came Jasper, but she couldn't take her eyes off Lorcan.

'Eyeing up your beau, are you?' joked Fanny, obviously mistaken about where exactly Annie's gaze was settled. 'Who knows, that might be you and Jasper soon.' She nodded her head towards Edie and Charlie.

'It's a bit soon for that,' said Annie, glancing at Alice, who looked rather serious.

'Me and Walter hadn't even known each other a year when we married.'

'We're all different.'

Having it suggested to her in such a direct manner, Annie was now sure she didn't want to go down that path with Jasper. Then why continue to walk out with him? It was something to do on her days off, she supposed. He was more of a friend than anything. She was sure he'd been going to kiss her on the bridge, but he hadn't tried again after they'd been disturbed.

As Alice, Gertie and Fanny moved towards where they were serving drinks, Johnny and Jerry entered the room, going first to talk to the couple before heading for the table, as everyone else had done. When they came to the food, Jerry looked delighted, but his brother seemed on edge, looking around at those there with an almost fearful expression.

'Gonna get some grub then?' Jerry asked him.

'It's really tasty,' said Annie.

'Haven't got much of an appetite at the moment, thanks.' He went to one of the open glazed doors, looking out at the garden.

'Is he all right?' Annie asked Jerry, coming closer so the others didn't hear. 'He's been a bit… distant, and jumpy since he returned, but it seems to 'ave got worse.'

Jerry sighed. 'To be honest, I'm a bit worried about him. He's been all right serving in the dining room and conservatory, but not friendly like he used to be with the guests. It has got worse and it's starting to feel like he's being, I dunno, not rude exactly. The least little noise makes him jump, which a couple of the guests have commented on. So far, he seems to have kept his temper while serving them but he's always complaining when we're collecting food or bringing dirty plates back.'

'I've noticed that in the scullery.'

'On our way home, he gets *so* angry about the guests, saying they're all privileged nobs and have no idea what we've been through, even those what were in the army, 'cos they were officers. He never used to talk about the guests like that.'

'A lot of officers died though, didn't they, leading their troops?'

'Yep. That's what I said, and you should've heard him having a go at me. I thought he'd hit me at one point. At home, he either doesn't say a word, or he argues with our parents and gets quite hostile. He's made our mum cry a coupla times, and it's got him into a heap of trouble with our dad. He seems to keep it under control when he's serving, but I wonder how long it'll be before he just, I dunno, explodes.'

Annie looked over at Johnny, who'd now stepped partly outside. 'I was reading a while ago, in the newspaper, about this thing they call shellshock.'

He let out a moan. 'We saw that with a couple of the men when we were in the war, though they were far worse than Johnny. But yes, it has occurred to me. I did suggest he saw the doctor, and he near enough bit me head off.'

'Oh dear, I am sorry.'

'Thanks for being so sympathetic, Annie. I haven't mentioned it to the other men here, as I'm not sure how understanding they'd be. Some of the men in our battalion saw those what had shellshock as weak. But I honestly think it'd scarred them, you know, up here.' He pointed to his head.

The quartet started on a gentle rendition of something Annie had heard before, but didn't know the name of. The next thing she knew, Johnny was charging back over to the food table.

'I'm going home, Jerry. I can't abide this noise.'

'It's only a few stringed instruments playing some tunes.'

'No, I can't be doing with it.'

'Do you want me to come back with you?'

'No, you've got a shift later. I'm not a child. I can find me way home.' He sounded angry with his brother.

'Right, if you're sure.'

Johnny said nothing but simply hurried out of the room.

'Where's he off to?' said Jasper, arriving at the table.

'Home,' said Jerry. 'He's not feeling well.'

'That's a shame. This food looks delicious.'

'It is,' Annie agreed, helping herself to another mini pork pie.

–

Alice was half listening to a conversation between Gertie, Fanny and Lili, looking over to where Annie and Jasper were standing together. Jerry, who'd been with them for a while, had just moved away, and the two of them were chatting. She wondered if they were discussing the possibility of their own wedding. How did she feel about that? Terrible.

The quartet began to play 'The Blue Danube' waltz. Edie and Charlie took to the floor, followed shortly by her brother, Freddie, and his wife, Lucia, despite her being pregnant. Alice was surprised to see Major Thomas, who'd been invited to the reception, dancing with Mrs Turnbull.

'Ooh, that would be a rather sweet romance,' said Lili, who'd also spotted them.

'It'd be nice for Mrs Turnbull to find a new husband, having been widowed so long,' said Fanny. 'And for the major to have a lady in his life.'

'They're only dancing for Pete's sake,' said Gertie, rolling her eyes.

Fanny's husband, Walter, entered the room the same time as Lili's fiancé, Rhodri, and the two women were soon whisked away to the dance floor by their men. Alice glanced around to see Jasper and Annie were also dancing, and she felt bereft once more.

'With any luck, Mr Watkins'll come in soon, and one of us can dance with 'im,' said Gertie.

Alice swung around, alarmed, only to see her smirking. 'Oh, you're joking.'

'Of course I am. It's a shame that Jamie of yours couldn't come. Gone away again, has he? That's what Annie said.'

'Did she now. Yes, he has. Maybe Joseph or Jack, or one of the other men'll pop in, and we could dance with them.'

'Can't say I'm bothered either way. I was never good at dancing at school. Were you?'

'I was all right. I enjoy dancing. Not that I get much opportunity.'

As she said this, she was aware of Lorcan heading towards them. It would be funny if he asked Gertie to dance, after what she'd just said. But it was her he stopped by.

'Hello there, Alice. Would you like to take a spin around the dance floor?'

'Yes, I'd love to. I was just telling Gertie how I enjoy dancing.'

'Aye, me too.'

He took her hand and led her to the middle. She felt nervous, hoping she wouldn't make a fool of herself. As she'd said to Gertie, she didn't get much opportunity to practise. Despite her doubts, the two of them were soon gliding in time to the waltz music.

'You're good at this, so you are,' he said.

'I'm glad I paid attention at school, though we used to have to dance with other girls there. I've only danced with me brothers and cousins at family parties since then.'

'Aye, me too. Love a party, do my family. Well, they did. Don't suppose they get much time for them now, things being as they are… So, how come we've never met this Jamie then?'

'Annie's been talking to you as well, has she?'

'No, well yes, but not to me directly. I overheard her telling Lili and Gertie. She doesn't sound too happy about him.'

'She's no need to worry. He's perfectly nice.'

'He couldn't come to the reception then? Edie said we could bring sweethearts and spouses.'

'He's out of town at the moment, working. I'm surprised you didn't hear that from Annie too.'

'No, didn't hear that. But I suppose it makes sense if he's a reporter… It's a shame there aren't more people here, but it does give us more room on the dance floor.'

The music came to an end, and the quartet struck up once more with a much livelier tune.

'Well, if it isn't Strauss's "Pizzicato Polka".'

'You're knowledgeable about music.'

'I've been to a concert or two in me time, and me parents have a gramophone and a few records. Can you do the polka?'

'I certainly can.'

'Come on with you then.'

They started dancing once more and she was soon giggling with delight as he swung her around.

–

Annie was enjoying a cheese bouchée in a world of her own when Jasper said, 'Well I never. Look at that. I thought she was walking out with that Jamie.'

'What's that?' He indicated the middle of the room, and she looked over. Her heart sank when she realised that Alice was waltzing with Lorcan.

'She is still walking out with Jamie, as far as I'm aware. Though he's not around at the moment. Unless she's decided…'

'Decided what?'

'I don't know. She don't tell me everything. I'm sure she's only dancing with Lorcan, nothing more.'

Maybe she had finished with Jamie, or he'd finished with her. Why hadn't she said anything then?

'Quite a few people are dancing now,' said Jasper. 'We should too. We've never danced before. If you'd like to. I presume you can dance, since Alice can.'

'Yes, I can, and I would like to,' she said, a little put out by even a tiny inference that Alice might have a skill that she didn't. She put her plate down on a side table and wiped her hands on a napkin. He did the same.

'It's a nice easy waltz, at least,' he said, leading her onto the dance floor.

Again, did he think her incapable of anything any harder? She had to stop taking everything the wrong way, she knew that, but always she felt she was lacking, especially in comparison to her sister.

Jasper was a good dancer, and she'd have enjoyed this little activity, if it hadn't been for Alice and Lorcan dancing nearby. Was her sister doing this to get her own back? But she'd stated categorically that she wasn't interested in Jasper. She was so annoying. She'd ignore her and make it obvious she was enjoying dancing with Jasper.

–

Jasper told himself to stop looking in Alice's direction and concentrate on dancing with Annie. He thought dancing would distract him, but it hadn't. It had been bad enough, discovering she was walking out with some stranger, but if she was now seeing someone at the hotel, and he had to witness the relationship, it would make it ten times as bad. Oh, why had he thought it a good idea to walk out with Annie in the first place? She was nice enough, but she wasn't Alice. He'd had a soft spot for her ever since she'd started working at the hotel, a month after him, in July 1911, when she was fifteen and he was eighteen. He remembered that first day she'd walked into the staff dining room.

That was eight years ago now. He'd felt she was too young to approach that first year or two. What an idiot he'd been leaving it all this time. It should have occurred to him that she'd find someone else, being as sweet natured and pretty as she was. If that someone else turned out to be Lorcan, it would make it hard working with him. Again, he remonstrated with himself over not talking to her directly about why she was grumpy with him all the time. They could have sorted it out and then, maybe then, he could have asked her out somewhere.

Yet she'd been all right at the Easter egg hunt, he recalled, and when he'd spoken to her as they watched the goat carriages. That might have been because he was seeing her sister and she'd been warned to keep the peace?

The waltz finished and the quartet started a lively polka.

'Are you up for this?' he asked.

'Yes, of course I am.'

As they whirled around the room, Jasper could see that Alice and Lorcan were still dancing. He really needed to find out what was going on, but how, without it sounding obvious he was put out? He'd have to play it by ear.

When the polka came to an end, Jasper bowed. 'Thank you madame, that was most entertaining.'

She chuckled. 'Yes it was. I'm gonna get another one of them bouchée things now, and talk to some of the other staff what 'ave come in.'

'I just need to use the, um, convenience. Excuse me.'

He wasn't that desperate, but it would give him time to think about things.

When he returned, Lorcan was helping himself to a glass of champagne from a tray held by one of the live-out waiters.

He'd make this sound easy-going, as if ribbing him.

'You walking out with Alice now then, are you?' He nudged him. 'Has she ditched that Jamie fellow?'

'Course I'm not, ya eejit,' he said light-heartedly. 'Just 'cos I'm dancing with her?'

'I was joking. Might be an idea to find someone though, to help you get over Hetty.' What was he saying? He didn't want to put the idea of walking out with Alice in his head.

'Aye, I suppose, and I will eventually. I'll have a dance here with several of the ladies this evening, take advantage of the occasion. I'm sure they'll all want to dance with the best man.' He winked.

Jasper clapped him on the arm. 'Good for you, chum, good for you.'

'Are you and Annie getting serious?'

'It's too early to say. She's fun to do things with, but I don't know if there's anything more to it than that.' He shrugged.

'Right, a couple of the housemaids have just come in, so I'm gonna ask one of them to dance, so I am.'

'Good luck!' Jasper called. What was he going to do next? He looked at his watch. He'd have to get to his next shift in the not-too-distant future, so he'd help himself to a bit more food before he went. And if there was time, he'd have another dance with Annie. If she wanted to. Maybe he could ask Alice to dance, just as a friend? No, it might cause trouble between the sisters, however innocent it was. And how innocent would it be if he enjoyed it too much? Then he'd only end up feeling guilty.

—

On their way home that evening, Alice had twittered on about the wedding, Edie's dress, Lady Lucia being with child, the lovely food, the tunes played by the quartet that she'd enjoyed the most… and so it went on. She'd required little input from Annie, and that had suited her fine.

It wasn't until they were turning from High Street onto Arundel Road, passing the Congregational Church and heading out of the main town, that there was a blissful lull in her sister's monologue. It didn't last long.

'You're very quiet,' said Alice. 'Didn't you enjoy the wedding reception?'

'We was only there an hour. It was nice enough. I liked the food.'

'Didn't you enjoy dancing?'

'I only took part in two of 'em.'

Unlike Alice, who'd had two more dances with Lorcan later on.

'Did you enjoy 'em though?' Alice persisted.

'Yes. I always enjoy dancing, you know that. What about you? Did you enjoy dancing with Lorcan?'

'Ah, is this why you've been so quiet?'

'I've been quiet 'cos I'm tired. It's been a long day. And it hasn't helped with you talking nonstop since we left the 'otel.'

'All right, there's no need to be like that. Talk about spoiling a nice day. And yes, I did enjoy dancing with Lorcan. He's light on his feet.'

'So, you given Jamie the heave-ho, 'ave you?'

'What? No. Oh, you think I'm walking out with Lorcan now? At least you'd approve of him.'

'Dunno if it's a good idea. I reckon he's still getting over *Hetty*,' Annie said with some emphasis.

'I'm not walking out with him, so it don't matter either way.'

'Good. It ain't wise seeing someone what hasn't got over someone else.'

'I agree. Talking of dancing with Lorcan, 'ave you been talking out of turn to people about me and Jamie? Lorcan asked about him, 'cos he over'eard you telling others you weren't happy about him.'

'You already know I feel like that.'

'But you don't 'ave to tell other people. It's my business. And you've got Jasper, so let me 'ave someone too.'

They walked along in silence after that. Annie felt guilty hearing Alice's last sentence. Despite her sister's negative reaction to Jasper, it was clear that she did still have feelings for him. What could she do about it, without upsetting Jasper? And would it make any difference if he wasn't keen on Alice anyway?

Annie was relieved when they reached their home in Wick, feeling weighed down by the silence between them. They'd bickered all their lives about little things, but they'd always been there for each other when it mattered. There had never been anything as big as this between them.

She opened the door, and the relief turned to joy, when she saw who was in the kitchen, flopped on the armchairs.

'Cyril, Cedric!' Alice cried, running towards them as they stood up. 'You're 'ome.'

Annie hugged Cyril, who was closest to her. At least this would take her mind off her current problems.

Chapter Twelve

Jasper was in the foyer a couple of weeks later, standing by the desk, waiting for something to do. His mind had wandered back two weeks, to Edie's wedding, and Lorcan dancing with Alice, even though he'd denied that anything was going on. He was still in two minds about what to do about Annie. He liked her, but not like that. He had no idea what exactly she felt for him. He didn't want to hurt her feelings. But he never had any romantic fantasies about her, not like he had about Alice. And as much as he tried not to have any about Alice now, they sometimes crept into his mind when he was falling asleep. He'd even dreamt a few nights back that it had been her on the bridge, and that he had kissed her, unlike in the real scenario with Annie. He'd felt so guilty when he'd woken up, though the pleasure of it had still surrounded him like a warm blanket.

He spotted someone coming towards the doors and hurried over to open them for him. In came a middle-aged man with a shock of neat, grey hair and a pinstriped suit. He was carrying two suitcases.

'Thank you, young man,' he said in an unsophisticated accent rarely heard among the guests of the hotel. He sounded like a couple of the lads in his battalion who'd come from East London.

'You're welcome, sir. Let me take your cases.'

'Ernie Brown's me name and I've got a reservation 'ere.'

'If you'd like to follow me to the desk, Mr Watkins will attend to you, and then one of us will show you to your room.'

He led Mr Brown over to the desk, where the man repeated what he'd said, eliciting a passing frown from the desk clerk.

'You're sure it's here you're staying, sir?' Watkins said in an even more haughty manner than usual, though Jasper had wondered the same.

'Beach Hotel, that's 'ere, init? Me secretary made the reservation last week. Got a recommendation from a client.'

Watkins ran his finger down a list in the book in front of him. 'Oh yes, here we are. Mr Ernest Brown.'

'That's me.'

'You're in room seven. You'll find a list of times for meals, morning coffee and afternoon tea in your room, along with other information. The porter will show you to your room and you can ask him for any other information you wish to know.'

He was dealing with him a lot quicker than he did most clients, who he normally took his time over, but it might have had something to do with the guests who'd just that moment walked through the door. Watkins would be a lot keener to welcome Lord and Lady Lane, who were regular guests. Lorcan, who'd just re-entered the foyer, hurried over to welcome them.

'Would you like to take the lift, sir?' Jasper asked Mr Brown. 'I'll convey your cases to the first floor and meet you there.'

'Nah, I can manage the stairs. Fit as a fiddle, me.' He looked up the sweeping staircase with its black-and-gold railings. 'Very nice.'

'Very well, sir. Follow me.'

—

After lunch, Jasper brought coffee to Mr Brown in the guest lounge, where he was sitting with Major Thomas. As he set down the tray, he listened to the conversation.

'I 'ad a factory before the war, just making machinery for gardens and whatnot, and it were doing all right,' he was telling the major. 'Then the war came so I started making munitions and that's when I really made me money. Done all right for meself I 'ave.' He took hold of his jacket lapel, running his fingers up and down to hint at its quality. 'Got a nice 'ouse in Highgate now. It was nonstop in the war, and then a coupla months back, I got the bleedin' flu. It nearly saw me off. After I recovered, me son and daughter suggested I take a break. I fancied some time away by the sea.'

'You sound like a very enterprising chap,' said the major. 'What do you make now the war's over?'

'The Great War might be over, but there's still wars going on, so we're still in business.'

'Excuse me, sir,' said Jasper. 'Will there be anything else?'

'Nah, that'll be all, ta. There ya go.' He handed him a couple of coins as a tip.

'Thank you, sir.' Jasper tilted his head forward and then left.

A tip for serving coffee. He didn't normally get that from guests. He'd already received a generous tip when he'd shown Mr Brown to his room.

It would soon be time for his own break, so he headed off to the staff dining room, armed with his story of the new guest. Alice was there and seemed quite amused by the account, which pleased him no end.

'He doesn't sound like the sort of person we should be getting at the hotel,' Mrs Leggett said dismissively, when he'd finished his tale.

'He seemed very pleasant, and a lot more polite than some of the guests we get.'

'Maybe because he knows what it's like to be in *our* shoes,' said Alice.

Jasper wondered whether this was a slight criticism of his own middle-class beginnings, before his family fortunes came crashing down. Was that why she'd had little time for him? Yet Annie didn't seem to feel like that, and he presumed they'd been brought up to have similar values.

'Mr Brown sounds like a breath of fresh air,' said Edie. 'In my experience, people who rise up through the classes are often the worst, as they don't want people to know about their backgrounds, and they overdo their privilege.'

Jasper suspected Edie was thinking of her own mother, whose beginnings had been humble and who had improved her fortunes by way of three advantageous marriages, the last being to Baron Moreland.

'If the other, more sophisticated, guests get wind of Mr Brown, it might put them off staying here,' said Mrs Leggett. 'People expect a certain standard, in their fellow guests as well as their surroundings.'

'Times are changing,' said Edie. 'We're going to have to accommodate the "nouveau riche", as they're called, if they're the ones who can afford to stay here, and—'

Edie was cut off by Lili's angry voice as she entered the room, followed by Günther.

'You must tell Mrs Bygrove. It's not on, what that guest said to you. He should be banned.'

'What on earth has happened?' said Mrs Leggett.

'Günther's had another anti-German comment from a new guest in the dining room,' said Lili.

'Please, I do not want to make a fuss,' said the waiter. 'And I would appreciate it if it was not mentioned to Phoebe. She is already worried enough.'

'But Lili's right,' said Jasper. 'The Treaty of Versailles has just been signed, so the war is formally over. There's no place in this new world of ours for this nonsense.'

'It's strange, isn't it?' said Alice. 'That there's a "formal" end, when it's been over for seven months now?'

After what felt like a criticism of him earlier, Alice had now reacted positively to his comment. He tried to brush away the glow it gave him, but he couldn't.

'It is,' Jasper agreed. 'And it's time to move on.'

'Well, I can't disagree with that at least,' said Mrs Leggett. 'Now come and sit down, Günther, and I'll pour you some tea.'

–

A few days later, Jasper was placing used crockery onto a tray in the guest lounge, half listening to a conversation between the Bunducks and the Balfours, two well-dressed young gentlemen and their wives, who'd arrived that morning for a week's stay. One couple were boasting about their new home, a manor house in Surrey. These exchanges between couples always amused him, as they invariably tried to outdo each other over what modern facilities, or decor or extensions they'd had.

'Oh yes,' said the blonde woman, to her husband's boast about their newly extended kitchen and scullery. 'We've turned the bedroom next to ours into an ensuite. Well, we have ten bedrooms you see, so we can spare a couple. We're going to attach one to another of the bedrooms next. And we're having the stables outside repaired and extended, so we can bring my horses from my father's estate and buy some of our own. I *do* miss riding since I married.'

'Sounds marvellous,' said the other husband. 'Our house already has an ensuite and three other bathrooms of course, so we're going to build a games room and extend the dining room to double its size. We might even add a small ballroom. And, as you know, we have a large stabling area where the horses are looked after very well by our staff.'

The door opened, and in strolled Ernie Brown, whistling. He'd proved to be quite a character, always having a cheery word for Jasper each time he came across him. And he'd proved to be a very generous tipper. Major Thomas had taken a liking to him, inviting him to join him at his table in the dining room a few times.

'Good afternoon, Jasper,' he started in his jocular cockney tone. 'I don't suppose there's a chance of a potta tea while I ponder me magazine.' He held up his copy of *John Bull*.

'I think you'll find that the tradesmen's entrance is around the side of the building,' called the moustached man sitting next to the blonde woman. The other three looked down their noses at the newcomer.

'A tradesman, in this whistle and flute?' said Ernie, smiling. He took hold of his jacket with both hands and opened it up to reveal his waistcoat. 'I don't fink so. I'm

Ernest Brown, Ernie to me friends, the owner of one of the biggest munitions factories in London which 'as made me a fortune. 'Ow'd you do? Self-made man, me, so I'll be sitting in 'ere with me pot of tea and me magazine. And maybe some biscuits?' He looked enquiringly at Jasper, who was pleased to hear his retort.

'Of course, sir.'

'My goodness, the standard of the hotel *has* gone down,' said the red-headed woman of the group in a low voice, which could still be heard quite clearly. 'Letting in the vulgar *nouveau riche.*'

Jasper kept his expression neutral, though he was furious with their attitude. He felt like telling them to leave if they were so bothered.

'*Nouveau riche?* I like that,' said Ernie. 'Sounds French, and very posh.'

'Really,' said the moustached gentleman, standing up. 'I think it might be better if we took that walk we were talking about.'

'Indeed so,' agreed his friend.

Ernie didn't seem bothered, taking one of the armchair seats close to a window.

After they'd departed, Jasper said, 'I'm sorry about that, sir. Some people are really very rude.'

'Ah, don't worry about it. I'm used to it now. What do I care? I've probably got more money than them, anyway.'

'I'll fetch your tea and biscuits.'

'Lovely. Thanks a bunch.'

'You're welcome.'

As Jasper left, he wondered whether his forefathers had harboured such attitudes. They'd long owned their own businesses, usually shops. His parents had never been like that, though his grandparents on both sides had been a little snooty.

As he passed through the foyer, Gertie came towards him. 'What's going on with them Bunducks and Balfours? They was complaining about rudeness from the lower classes when they came out of the lounge. You been rude to them? That's not like you.'

'No, not me. As soon as they got wind of Mr Brown's accent, they assumed he was a tradesman and were rude to him. He told them very politely who he was.'

'Ah, the self-made man speech, and all that.'

He laughed. 'That's the one. But they took umbrage anyway and left.'

She sucked in air through her mouth and shook her head vigorously. 'Like Edie said, they're gonna have to get used to the *nouveau riche*, as she called 'em.'

'That's funny, her using that expression, because that's how Mrs Bunduck referred to him, in a very unflattering manner.'

'Oh, by the way, that Miss Rosetta Stone was in here earlier, to make the final arrangements for her engagement party next Saturday. They're going to have that Original Louisiana Jazz Band, what was here at Easter. I'm really glad I'll be on duty that night.'

'Yes, me too. Anyway, I'd better get Mr Brown's tea.'

–

Alice had been beside herself when she'd heard she'd been picked to serve at Rosetta Stone's engagement party. She'd looked forward to the music and the fashions, and she hadn't been disappointed.

She, along with Johnny, Jasper and Lili, had been asked to take a tray of champagne each to the ballroom, where the jazz band were already playing some upbeat tunes. Once again, she imagined herself dancing with Jasper, despite the guilt she felt. It should be Jamie in her dreams, but then, he hadn't been in touch since May, over six weeks ago, so surely he really was out of her life this time.

Alice found herself swaying a little as she stood close to the door they'd entered by. Johnny had carried on and stopped near the outside doors, while the other two went further into the room.

'Enjoying the beat, young lady?' said a youth with fair hair and a centre parting, as he lifted one of the glasses with a wink. He only looked about sixteen.

She smiled in reply, having been warned against engaging guests in conversation.

He wandered off, humming along to the band. She watched the women there, who were all in the latest fashions in silks and crepes, with short, lacy sleeves, in greens, pinks and blues. Some of the dresses had ribbons tied into bows above the waist, and some had little beads sewn into patterns. They made the dress she'd sewn recently already look out of date. Many of the women had large, decorative slides or combs. She wondered what her mother would say if she had her hair cut into a bob, like some of the women here. But no, she liked her long hair. The men were equally dashing in their evening suits and bow ties.

She watched as some of the couples danced, hopping from leg to leg, then kicking them out and back and forth as they swung around the room. Rosetta Stone was among them, with her fiancé, clearly showing off her skill. The two of them jigged to the other end of the ballroom. Alice found herself tapping her foot and stopped, fearful that she'd spill the champagne.

A young woman in a pink dress came running into the room as if being chased. Alice went to step back but was too late as the woman slammed into her. The silver tray tipped up, before plummeting to the floor, with the eight remaining glasses, crashing to the ground with a terrific cacophony.

Immediately, she heard a man scream, the most blood-curdling sound she'd ever heard, and the clatter of another tray striking the floor. She looked around to see Johnny, cowering in the corner, whimpering. The band faded out and the room became silent, apart from Johnny's distressed moaning. Alice went towards him, afraid he'd been injured in some way.

Jasper was soon back up the room with Lily, both placing their trays on the small table there.

'What on earth?' said Jasper, going to Johnny and hunkering down. Lili and Alice stood nearby.

'What the bloody hell is going on?' Rosetta shouted, tip-tapping back up the room in black, pointed shoes. She stopped by the two men on the floor. 'What is all this? You're spoiling my party!'

My party, thought Alice. Not *our party*. It was typical of what she'd heard about the woman.

'I'll handle this, my dear,' said her fiancé, catching her up.

She turned towards him, stamping one foot. 'Then *do* something, Reginald, before it's all totally *ruined.*'

'What is going on?' said Reginald. 'Get this blubbering idiot out of here and clear up this mess.'

'We'll organise that now, sir,' said Jasper. 'Alice, would you go and find Mrs Bygrove please?'

'I'll fetch someone to clear up,' said Lili, hurrying out with her.

Alice turned towards her. 'I wonder where Mrs Bygrove is.'

'I'd try her office first, I would.'

Alice did so and was relieved to hear her reply when she entered. With her was Edie.

'Mrs Bygrove, someone bumped into me and made me drop me tray of glasses and it made a right noise and Johnny screamed and collapsed in the ballroom and the guests are distressed and there's champagne and glasses all over the floor and Lili's gone to fetch someone to clear it up and Jasper's trying to sort things out and Miss Stone is having a tantrum,' all came out in a rush.

'Oh my,' said Helen.

Both the women stood and followed Alice back to the ballroom, where the only sounds were Rosetta's complaining, Johnny's sobbing as Jasper attempted to drag him to the door, and the scraping of glass into dustpans by two of the housemaids.

Helen gasped as she saw the state Johnny was in.

'That idiot is ruining my party!' Rosetta screeched.

'Edie, ring for the doctor please,' said Helen. 'Jasper, take him to my office. Alice and Lili, please fetch more champagne and tell Mrs Leggett that I've asked her to help out here. She's in the staff dining room.'

As they left, they heard Helen apologising and asking them to continue with the party. They just caught Rosetta Stone yelling, 'I'll expect some money off for this inconvenience,' before they entered the foyer once more.

—

Lorcan went to his morning break the following day having heard all about the incident the night before, but none the wiser about what was wrong with Johnny. Edie had told them only that he'd been driven home, on Dr Ferngrove's instructions, along with Jerry to look after him.

'Anybody heard anything else about Johnny?' he asked, leaning his hands on the table.

'Not a dicky bird,' said Mrs Turnbull. 'Do you think he hurt himself on something?'

'I don't think so,' said Jasper, next to her. 'It sounded more like a kind of, well, a breakdown.'

'He has been very jumpy and nervous since he returned,' said Annie. 'He was in the scullery a coupla weeks back, when Alice was washing one of the oven trays. It banged against the sink, and he jumped and let out a cry.'

'I wouldn't mind betting…' Lorcan started. He halted for a moment.

'That he has shellshock?' Jasper finished.

'I don't wanna talk out of turn,' said Annie, her brow creased, 'but Jerry did say as much to me a few weeks back, at Edie and Charlie's wedding reception, when Johnny left early. Jerry had suggested to him that he see a doctor, but Jerry said he bit his 'ead off. Apparently, they had men in their battalion what thought them with shellshock were weak.'

'Jerry's never mentioned it to us,' said Jasper.

'He didn't know how sympathetic the men would be, so don't tell him I told ya.'

Lorcan sighed heavily. 'The eejit. We could have helped persuade him to see the doctor. I must admit, it had occurred to me. Wish I'd said something now, so I do. We had a couple in the battalion who were affected, didn't we?'

Jasper nodded. 'One of the men was very distressed and started shaking all the time. They were both sent home for treatment because our captain was sympathetic.'

'But you're right, Annie,' said Lorcan. 'Not all the soldiers in our battalion were understanding.'

'Poor lad, if that's what's wrong with him,' said Mrs Turnbull, looking mournfully at the table. 'It sounds like a terrible burden. Not surprising though, after what many of you young men went through. "The war to end all wars," it's been called by that author, H.G. Wells. Let's 'ope he's right.'

'Here's the man himself,' said Lorcan, as Jerry entered, looking like the woes of the world were on his shoulders. 'How's Johnny, chum?'

Jerry slumped onto the bench, facing away from the table. 'In a terrible state. He's had a complete breakdown. He's shouting all the time, and keeps talking about the awful things that happened in the battles we were in. The last few nights, he was calling out in his sleep, and I could tell he was having nightmares about it.' He faltered for a few seconds. 'Doctor Ferngrove is certain it's shellshock. He's going to try and get him admitted to a hospital, maybe Netley in Southampton.' He lowered his head and squeezed his eyes tight shut. 'I *told* him he needed to get help, but he wouldn't listen, and he warned me not to try to get help for him. I should have made him get help or got our mum to make him. She kept saying it was only natural to be a bit jumpy after what he'd been through. I should have tried harder.'

Annie rose and clutched his shoulder. 'It's not your fault, Jerry. You tried. You were only respecting his wishes.'

That was kind of her, thought Lorcan. He didn't often see her offering sympathy. She was showing a new side to her today, and he liked it.

'It's not like it only started when we returned here,' said Jerry. 'It began before we got back, but whenever he reacted to something badly, the sergeant just told him to pull himself together.'

Lorcan humphed. 'Typical bloody upstart sergeant.'

'I bet Charlie wasn't like that,' said Jerry. 'Shame we weren't in the thirteenth battalion with him.' He pulled himself up. 'Anyway, that's what's happened... Did the party carry on yesterday?'

'It carried on, all right,' said Jasper. 'But that Rosetta Stone insisted on having some of her money refunded. It's not like it disrupted it for more than five minutes. That woman is such a... no, I can't be that rude in front of the ladies.'

'Bitch?' Annie suggested as she retook her seat. She elicited several shocked looks, though Mrs Turnbull chuckled. She carried on. 'Sorry, but it's the impression I've got, from others what've come across her in the past. She likes to get her own way and acts like a great big cry-baby when she can't.' She pulled a face as if she was a toddler about to cry and pretended to rub her eyes, and a few more people laughed. Even Jerry managed to raise a small smile.

Lorcan watched with interest. Another side to Annie he didn't normally see, her being lively and entertaining. She was full of surprises today. 'I feel sorry for that fiancé of hers. What was his name?'

'Reginald Cavendish,' said Jasper. 'I wouldn't worry about him; he seemed to be able to stick up for himself. He was blunt too. She might have her work cut out there.'

'I do 'ope so,' said Annie. 'The way staff have described her, and after what Alice told me last night, she sounds *awful*.'

Mrs Turnbull lifted the teapot. 'Let's have our tea and biscuits before it's time for us to get back to our shifts. And let's all keep our fingers crossed for Johnny. I'm sure now his condition's been recognised, that they'll be able to help the poor lad.'

Jerry repositioned himself to face the table. Lorcan sat down, next to Annie, hoping this new livelier side to her might cheer him up some more.

'It'll be the National Peace Day next Saturday,' said Mrs Turnbull. 'There's goin' to be a parade in Littlehampton, I hear. Lots of people will get the day off, but I doubt many will here. We'll have guests to look after.'

'I'm lucky, as I just happen to have a free shift at the time,' said Lorcan.

'And me,' said Annie.

'Me too,' Jerry added, his hands linked tightly, resting on the table. 'But I'm not sure I'll feel like celebrating.'

'Your brother will be in good hands,' said Lorcan. 'Especially if they send him to Netley. You'll need something to cheer you up.'

' 'Spose so.'

'We'll see who else is free at that time, get a group together.'

'That's a good idea, Lorcan,' said Annie.

'The day before it, we'll have Lili and Rhodri's wedding,' said Mrs Turnbull. 'It's goin' to be a reet busy week.'

Chapter Thirteen

Annie had her Sunday best dress on, but still looked old fashioned compared to Alice next to her, who was wearing the dress she'd made a couple of months back. Still, at least they'd got to go to an actual wedding ceremony this time, not like with Hetty, Fanny and Edie's weddings. Today it was Lili and Rhodri's turn at the altar.

They were sitting in the second row in the Baptist Church, which was next to the library on Fitzalan Road, with Fanny and Gertie. Behind were Edie, Charlie and Helen, and in front were Lili's mother and her aunt Megan. On the other side of the aisle sat Rhodri's aunt and uncle, his brother and a few of his friends.

Lili was wearing a dark cream dress that she'd bought second hand, and that Annie knew she'd shortened and adapted herself to update it a little. She also had on a lace cap and short veil that she'd bought new.

As the couple faced each other and said their vows, Annie's mind wandered. *Yet another wedding.* It was lovely that her friends were now able to get married and be with their sweethearts after the awful war, and she was happy for them, she really was. But, as each wedding occurred, she felt a little lonelier.

Her days out with Jasper had become fewer, as one or other of them often had something else to do. Neither of them had been introduced to their families and he had come to feel more like a friend and nothing more. She was loath to break it off, whatever 'it' was, as he was at least good company. Was that enough in a relationship? No, not for her it wasn't. She needed to say something to him about it, but she hadn't built up the courage yet.

The couple were pronounced 'man and wife', a term that had always irked Annie. Why not 'husband and wife'? Either way, Lili was now Mrs Morgan, and they could get to the good bit of the wedding, in her opinion: the reception.

Out of the door of the church, they walked as a group behind the bride and groom, all the way up Fitzalan Road to South Terrace, where they turned left to walk back to the hotel. It was a warm day with a gentle breeze. The wispy, white clouds were skittering across the sun. They all chatted excitedly; Annie joined in, sounding more cheerful than she felt at this moment. What a misery she was, she thought. It was a friend's wedding, and all she could do was feel sorry for herself. If anybody else had said to her what she'd been thinking, she'd have given them an earful, and no mistake. No, this wouldn't do. She was determined to cheer up properly by the time they reached the hotel.

Entering the conservatory, reserved this afternoon for Lili and Rhodri's reception, she finally perked up. It looked as splendid as ever, with its glass walls and ceiling, the large pot plants in between the tables and its view of the garden, resplendent today with dahlias and hollyhocks. The room had been set up for a buffet afternoon tea and, as at other staff weddings, the hotel employees were invited to take part, according to their shifts. This had been made easier for some by the cancellation of the hotel's afternoon tea today.

'If I get married, I'd like my reception in this room too,' Alice said to her.

'You'd better find someone soon then,' said Annie. 'I daresay Mrs Bygrove has only been so generous in donating rooms for weddings because of the war and how we all helped keep the 'otel going. I'm sure there'll come a time when she won't feel obliged to be so generous any more.'

'Do you have to be such a misery?'

Was she? Already? It was only because Alice had said it. If anybody else had, she'd probably have agreed.

'I'm not. It's just common sense, really. Before the war, Mrs Bygrove didn't offer rooms to staff members when they got married.'

'That's because *Mr* Bygrove was in charge, the miserable old whatsit.'

'You're probably right.' Annie didn't want to go on disagreeing with her sister.

Mrs Turnbull entered with a tray of teapots, going over to congratulate Lili and Rhodri before setting it down on one of four tables positioned around the edge of the room, ready for the food.

'I'm gonna get a cuppa tea. You want one?' said Alice.

'I'll get one in a minute.' Annie walked over to the windows to look out on the garden.

'We should have the doors open on a day like this, so we should,' said a voice behind her, making her start a little. 'Sorry, didn't mean to make you jump,' said Lorcan.

Helen, overhearing him, called over, 'Yes, of course. It's lovely and warm today.'

He opened two of the several doors along that side. 'There, that's better. How was the wedding?'

'Very nice,' said Annie. 'Reverend Flatt made everyone feel welcome and was very cheerful as he took the ceremony. Not like some, what conducts them like a funeral.'

Lorcan laughed. 'Ain't that the truth. I've attended some dirgy weddings in me time, so I have. Me sister's, for instance.'

He started mimicking the priest, citing some lines from the marriage ceremony in a gloomy fashion. She chuckled as he did so, all the while aware that she was enjoying this little encounter with him a lot more than she'd ever enjoyed her days out with Jasper. She could never feel for him what she did for Lorcan – of that, she was sure.

'You should be a comedian on stage, Lorcan.'

'Not sure I could keep that up all day. Talking of which, I saw Peter Smith singing at the Casino Theatre on me last day off. He had a coupla numbers of his own, not just as a member of Nathaniel Janus's Entertainers.'

'I, um, saw him singing on the stage out the back one afternoon a while ago.' She had been going to say that she and Jasper had seen him, but didn't want to bring him into the conversation. 'I must go and see him at the theatre soon.'

It would be something to do on a day off, either with Jasper or, hopefully, if she had the courage to end it, without him.

'It's a shame there's no band today,' said Lorcan. 'I fancy a dance.'

What a shame indeed, since he was standing right here and might have asked her to partner him.

'I think it might be rather a challenge, dancing round the tables and pot plants,' she said.

He laughed and she couldn't help but do so too, which made her ridiculously happy.

Helen approached them. 'They'll be bringing out the food shortly but do help yourselves to tea. And… yes, here's Mrs Turnbull with some coffee too.'

'It's under two months now until your wedding, Mrs Bygrove,' said Annie.

'Oh yes, indeed. I am looking forward to being married to Sam. He should be here shortly.'

Helen looked round as the door from the dining room opened. 'More guests? Oh, they can't have seen the sign.' She headed over to the newcomers who were regulars in the conservatory. 'Good afternoon, Lady Blackmore, Miss Cecelia. I'm afraid we are not serving tea this afternoon.'

'We know,' said Lady Blackmore. 'We've just popped by to offer our congratulations to Lili, since she's always been marvellous to us when we've come to the hotel for meals.'

'Of course, Lady Blackmore. That is most kind,' said Helen. 'Do come in.'

As the two women spoke with Lili and Rhodri, Lorcan leant down towards Annie. 'Her ladyship's mellowed a bit since we first knew her, so she has,' he whispered.

'So have a lot of people. Mrs Leggett, for example.'

'You all went through a lot here, while we men were away,' he said.

'We did, but probably not 'alf as much as you lot went through.'

'We've become serious again. Let's paint those smiles back on.' He ran his finger across his lips in a curve and was beaming by the time he was finished. His large blue eyes were almost sparkling, giving her heart a jolt.

She chuckled again. 'Quite right.'

'I dunno about you, but I could do with a cuppa tea,' Lorcan said. 'Shall I fetch you one?'

'That'd be just the ticket, thank you.'

She watched him as he walked away, dressed in his smart porter's uniform, his black hair slicked neatly back with a parting on one side. Being with him always brought out the best in her, something she showed rarely to others, even Jasper. Oh, what a mistake that had been, one she needed to rectify. Not that she thought it would make any difference to her relationship with Lorcan. No, she'd better make the most of his company while she could, but she wasn't going to kid herself that there could be more to it than that.

–

Sam Toshack had got away from the police station a little later than he'd intended, but he was here now, at the hotel, to be with Helen as she celebrated yet another staff wedding. It was Lili today, he reminded himself, marrying Rhodri, whom she'd met when the man had been recuperating from a bullet to the thigh, at a hospital in the town. He could sympathise with that kind of injury, although Rhodri had not lost half a leg, like he had.

It was hard keeping up with everyone at the hotel and their stories, but he did quite well. Having a mind that had to hold lots of bits of information to solve cases probably helped.

These days he normally headed around to the staff entrance but today went through the foyer. He wanted to have a quick word with Mr Watkins at the desk, about his wallet that had gone missing yesterday while he was in town. On top of the attacks on the quay, they'd now had several cases of pickpocketing reported in the last few days. He still had no clue whether they were connected.

Constable Twort had taken the details and hadn't done a very good job of it, and since he was in the hotel, Sam decided he might as well talk to the man himself.

'Mr Watkins, good afternoon.'

'Good afternoon, Inspector Toshack.'

'I believe you reported the theft of your wallet yesterday. I was wondering if I could just take a couple of details from you.'

'Of course, sir, though the constable did take some notes.'

Not enough, thought Sam, but he couldn't tell him that. He got his own notebook out. 'His writing isn't always clear, I'm afraid. Where exactly were you when this theft happened?'

'I was in Surrey Street, looking in Gooch Brothers' window. Someone brushed past me and apologised, but I thought nothing of it until I went into the shop and tried to purchase a wristwatch.'

'I see. What did this man look like?'

'Tall, fair, I think, though it was hard to tell under the large hat. He sported a gingery beard. He had on a large overcoat, which was strange given how warm it was. I didn't really see his face properly, as he tipped his head down as he apologised and scuttled off. I presumed, in embarrassment, but I suppose it was so I didn't get a good look at him.'

'It seems likely. Of course, him bumping into you might be a coincidence, but I think it likely he was the perpetrator.'

'I had two ten-shilling notes in there, so not a fortune, but it's the principle.'

'Indeed, sir. It doesn't matter how much was in your wallet, it was a crime. Thank you, Mr Watkins. And if you can think of anything else, don't hesitate to contact me.'

'Thank you, Inspector Toshack. Now, I believe you're heading to the reception, which is, as you probably know, in the conservatory.'

'I do, thank you.' He lifted his hat.

About to walk away, he almost bumped into a man in his fifties, standing not far behind him. He was well turned out in a navy-blue pin-checked suit, his greying hair parted in the middle.

'Oh, excuse me,' said Sam. 'I didn't realise you were there.'

'That's all right. I should'n'a been standing so close meself.'

Sam was a little confused when he heard his accent, which didn't match the look of the man at all.

'So, you're an inspector I gather, eh?' said the man.

'That's right.'

'I'd better watch meself then.' He let out a raucous laugh, then put out his hand. 'Ernie Brown. I'm a guest 'ere.'

Sam took his hand, which was shaken enthusiastically. 'Welcome, Mr Brown.'

'I was only jokin' of course, about watchin' meself. I'm honest as the day is long, me, which'd make me very honest at the moment, it bein' summer.' He nudged Sam's arm and chuckled. 'Nah, jokin' again. I'm the owner of a munitions factory in London. Made me fortune during the war, I did. I fancied a few weeks by the seaside as I 'adn't 'ad a day off since the perishin' war started.'

'And, uh, I'm the detective inspector at the local police station,' Sam said, not knowing what else to say. 'Oh, and I'm, um, engaged to the good lady who owns this hotel.'

'Mrs Bygrove? A very nice lady she is too, the two times I've bumped into 'er. Seems to care a lot that the guests 'ave a lovely time 'ere.'

'She does indeed.'

'Well, I'm just off out since there's no afternoon tea 'ere today. I understand there's a wedding reception.'

'Aye, that's right, which I'm about to attend.'

'I'll leave ya to it, then. Nice to meet ya, and at least I'll know who to go to if I 'ave any bother.'

Ernie Brown marched away, singing a happy tune, and left the building.

'My, he's a character,' Sam said to Watkins.

'Indeed, he is, sir. Some of the guests like his forthrightness, but he hasn't been everyone's cup of tea.'

'Aye, I can imagine.'

Sam headed off now, taking the route to the conservatory through the guest dining room.

'Sam, you're here!' Helen was quickly beside him, kissing his cheek. After being so coy in front of the staff when they'd first started walking out, she was open about her affection now and he was glad of it.

'I've just met your guest, Ernie Brown.'

She smiled and raised her eyebrows. 'That must have been an experience. He seems very agreeable though.'

'I'll just go and speak to the happy couple.' He walked over to where Lili and Rhodri were sitting at a table. 'Congratulations to you both,' he enthused.

'Thank you, Inspector,' said Rhodri.

'How are you settling back in?' Sam asked him.

'A relief to get back, it was,' he said, in an accent similar to Lili's, both of them being from the Welsh Valleys. 'Dando's offered me my job back in their office straight away, so that was good.'

'How's the leg now?'

'Only a very slight limp I 'ave now, and I'm still doing them exercises they showed me at Belgrave Hospital.'

'I'm glad to hear it.'

'Do try some of the buffet, Inspector,' said Lili. 'It's *marvellous*.'

'I will, thank you.'

He went back to Helen, who was now sitting down at a table and patting the seat next to her.

'I'll get some food first. Could you pour me a cup of tea, darling?' he asked.

'Of course, my love.'

When he returned, Helen was looking thoughtful.

'Are you thinking about our wedding in September?'

'I was actually thinking about the very first time I sat in here, when Douglas and I came to look at the hotel, and Mr Edwards, the previous owner, invited us to have some tea here.' She lowered her voice now. 'It seems so long ago. I suppose it was nine years ago. And you know what, I can't summon up one single drop of emotion, even though Douglas and I got on well in those days. But only because I toed the line, I suppose. I realise now, in fact, I have done for a while, that I never really knew what love was until I met you, Sam.'

He felt himself redden. 'I do hope I turn out to be a better husband to you than he was.'

'I have not one single doubt about that, my love,' she said, running her fingers down his cheek and over his dimple.

'I've had some news, about DI Davis. He's about to be demobbed.'

Her hand went to her chest, and she looked anxious. 'Are they sending him back to Littlehampton? Will they send you somewhere else?'

'No, no, it's fine. He's being sent to Worthing. The detective inspector there is retiring.'

She closed her eyes and sighed. 'What a relief.'

'Are you talking about DI Davis?' said Edie, who'd been passing the table.

'That's right,' said Sam. 'Have you heard the same thing?'

'Yes, Julia told me this morning when I saw her. I was going to tell you later. Davis and Julia are getting married and moving to Worthing. She's already secured a teaching post there, starting in January.'

'So, there'll be yet another wedding,' said Helen.

'I believe they're talking about October for theirs.'

She walked away and Helen took Sam's hand. 'Are you going to the National Peace Day celebrations tomorrow?'

'You could say that. We're going to be busy in the town, making sure it *is* peaceful.'

'You don't expect any trouble, do you?'

'Not in the celebrations themselves. But, with the thefts we've had reported recently, we'll need to keep an eye out for scoundrels taking advantage of the crowds.'

The door opened to an excited kerfuffle as Dorothy and Arthur came rushing in, followed by their nursemaid, Vera.

'Mummy! School is over for the summer!' Dorothy called, heading straight for Helen. Arthur was just behind her.

'So it is, my darlings!' She hugged her children as they lunged at her.

'Hello Sam,' they said at the same time.

'Can we have some of the tea?' Arthur looked at the buffet, wide eyed.

'Of course you can. But do it daintily please. No rushing. That's particularly aimed at you, Arthur.' She half grinned, raising her eyebrows at him. 'And don't pile your plate up. But first of all, go and give your congratulations to Lili and Rhodri.'

They made a show of tiptoeing away and were soon chatting and laughing with the newlyweds.

'I can't believe Dorothy will be eleven in nine days' time,' said Helen. 'And I still haven't got used to Arthur being nine.'

'Are you still keen to have another baby? It would be a few years younger than them.'

'Oh, absolutely,' she said happily, before her face fell a little. 'Have you changed your mind?'

'No, not at all, darling, not at all.'

Chapter Fourteen

It was National Peace Day today, and Lorcan was looking forward to heading to the parade after lunch. He went up to the room he shared with Jasper, to change into his suit, so he was ready to leave as soon as he'd eaten his meal.

Back downstairs he was waylaid by the housekeeper, holding out a letter for him. *Not another one from home with bad news,* he hoped, but when he took it from her, it only had his name on it, no address.

'This was brought by a young lad earlier, Mr Foley.'

'Thank you, Mrs Leggett.' He took it, noting the neat, cursive script. It looked rather like Günther's writing.

When she walked away, towards the dining room, he opened it. There was a piece of paper and another envelope, addressed to Phoebe. He read the short note quickly.

'What in the name of Mary and Joseph—?'

'What's up?' said Annie, exiting the stillroom.

'It's a note from Günther. He's… he's gone back to Germany. Went early this morning. He says he can't live here with people always thinking he's the enemy. He's asked me to send his apologies to Mrs Bygrove, saying he won't be back. There's a letter for Phoebe too, but he wanted to let someone else know first so that we could support her when she read it.'

'Oh no! She's going to be devastated.'

'She will, that. I wonder if she'll be in this lunch break,' he said.

'She already is. I heard her from the scullery telling the stillroom maids she was going.'

Lorcan glanced at the letter once more. 'I wonder if the peace celebrations today hastened his decision.'

'I suppose it's possible. He might have thought they would make him feel even more unwelcome.'

'Aye. Are you still up for going, Annie?'

'Yes. It's not like there's a lot we can do about Günther. And we won't get another National Peace Day.'

'True. I guess we'd better get this over and done with.'

In the dining room, Phoebe was sitting near one end, next to Mrs Leggett. There were a few others in there, including Gertie, Fanny and Mrs Turnbull. Should he give her the letter, with everyone watching? But what else could he do?

He went around the table to stand next to her and leant down and spoke quietly. 'Phoebe, I've just received this note from Günther, and there was a letter for you in it.'

She looked alarmed, regarding the letter, not taking it immediately. When she did, she stared at her name on the front.

Mrs Leggett, who must have been able to hear what he'd said, leant towards them. 'What is it, Miss Sweeton?'

'Why has he written me a letter? We live in the same building.' She looked up at Lorcan. 'What did he say in your letter? Has he gone out for the day, or away for a few days?'

By this time, a whisper had run up the table, and everyone was looking in their direction. Annie, sitting opposite Phoebe, regarded Lorcan with a worried frown.

'I think you should open it, so you should,' he said. 'Read for yourself what he has to say. Would you rather do it on your own?'

'No, I wouldn't.' Phoebe pulled open the back of the envelope and took out the letter inside.

She made a few brief humming noises as she read it, and her face became ever more anguished. Reaching the end, she placed it back in the envelope, stared at her lap for a few moments, then looked around the table.

'Günther has gone back to Germany. He says, he says… that he can't live here any more, where too many people think of him as a traitor and call him names. He's apologised to me and told me to find someone who people will, will…' She sobbed out the word, 'respect,' before breaking down completely.

At that moment, Mrs Norris came through with a large tray of pork pies and pasties, followed by Will Fletcher carrying a bowl of tomatoes and lettuce.

''Ere we are, folks,' the cook said cheerily. 'Egg sandwiches and some—' She stopped suddenly. 'What's 'appened now?'

Annie turned to face the cook. 'Günther's left.'

'Oh. No.' She carried on to the table, placing the tray down, and Will did the same. He sat down, but Mrs Norris went back by the door. 'I'll get someone in the stillroom to fetch the tea in now.'

'As if that's gonna make it any better,' Gertie mumbled.

Phoebe's sobs became sniffles, and she blew her nose on a handkerchief she took out of her dress pocket. Everyone remained silent. Finally, she looked around at them all.

She stood and stepped over the bench seat. 'I'm going to my room as I'm not hungry now. This is my problem, not yours. Today is Peace Day, and I want whoever's going to attend to enjoy it. Hopefully, I will hear from Günther soon and we will sort this out. Please eat your lunch.'

With that she hurried from the room.

'Aw, poor lass,' said Mrs Turnbull.

Mrs Leggett rose. 'I had better inform Mrs Bygrove of this latest development.'

'He said in my note to give her his apologies,' said Lorcan.

'Was there anything else in your note I should tell her?'

Lorcan handed her the envelope. 'This is it, if she'd like to read it.'

The housekeeper nodded and headed out.

'I thought when the war ended, that things would get better. Be happier,' said Annie. 'But it's still one problem after another.'

'Should we still attend the Peace Day celebrations after lunch, those of us goin'?' said Mrs Turnbull.

'Yes, we should,' said Lorcan. 'Like Annie said to me before we came in here, it's not like we can do anything about Günther, and we won't get another Peace Day. And I think we need this celebration more than ever now.'

There was a murmur of agreement, before people started to help themselves to the lunch.

–

Alice so wished she could go to the National Peace Day celebrations in the town today, but it was Annie who had a break in her shifts at the right time, so that was that. At least she'd be able to get out a little later to see some of the events on the common. Mr Janus had set up a stage not far behind the hotel, and there would be a show there featuring Peter Smith, their former waiter.

As there was a lull in the washing up, and Finn and Lucas were getting on with what was there, she stepped outside into the yard and then took one step through the gate, which faced the eastern side of the common. South Terrace was already lined with hordes of people, waiting for the parade.

As she looked along the line, to see if there was anybody she recognised, a smartly dressed, middle-aged man approached her, whistling a tune.

' 'Ello there, by the looks of your uniform, I'm guessing you work at the 'otel, but somewhere I don't never get to see ya.'

The accent took her by surprise, being at odds with the way he was dressed. Could this be Ernie Brown, who Jasper had mentioned a few times?

'That's right, sir. I'm one of the scullery maids.'

'Responsible for all the spanking clean crockery and cutlery. And you do a good job, for it does shine.'

'Thank you.'

'Ernie Brown's the name.' He put out his hand.

It would be rude not to take it, so they shook hands. 'I'm Alice Twine.'

'It's good to meet those, I dare say, under-appreciated members of staff what 'elp make our stays so comfortable. I used to be one of those meself, as a lad, before I managed to rent a workshop, then a warehouse, and finally own me own factory. Made me money making munitions in the war, I did. I'm proof that even someone as lowly as me can make it big. People don't even realise how lowly I am till they 'ear me voice, when I'm wearing me expensive whistle.'

'Whistle?' She looked around the jacket area. He wasn't sporting a whistle.

He threw his head back and laughed. 'Sorry, forgot the East London lingo don't always translate down 'ere. Whistle and flute. Suit. That's what we call 'em where I come from.'

She chuckled. 'I see.' He certainly was a character, just as Jasper had said.

'That's a lovely tie pin,' she said, admiring the gold handicraft. In the centre was a not insubstantial pearl.

He looked down, lifting his tie between two fingers. 'Picked that up from a jeweller in the West End.'

'The West End?'

'Posh bitta London where the theatres and whatnot are. I'd never seen nuffing like this tie pin before, but it cost a pretty penny, so I says to meself, "Ernie, you've earned it. What else you gonna do with ya money, eh?" I'm in the 'abit of talking to meself, see. Early Victorian it is, antique.'

'It is very nice.'

'I'm off to see this parade now. Nice to see people so 'appy. Course, dunno what peace'll do for me trade, but I guess there's always wars somewhere.' He lifted his fedora. ' 'Ave a good afternoon.'

'You too, Mr Brown.'

He stuck his hands in his trouser pockets and headed off once more, whistling.

She stepped back into the yard as a group of people came out of the scullery. It was Lorcan, Annie, Jerry, Edie, Charlie and Mrs Turnbull. They didn't look particularly happy for people about to witness a celebration.

'Poor lass,' said the housekeeper. 'She was supposed to be comin' with us, too.'

'Who's that?' said Alice.

'Phoebe, pet. You won't have heard, but Günther left her a note, and Lorcan here, to say he's goin' back to Germany.'

'Oh dear.'

'She's gone to her room,' said Annie. 'If she comes down, could you keep an eye on her?'

'Yes, course. Poor Phoebe.'

'Thanks, Alice,' said Lorcan. 'It's appreciated, so it is.'

The four of them headed off into the crowd, and Alice returned to the scullery.

—

When Annie and the others exited the hotel's side gate, they were all surprised to see just how many people were lining the street on South Terrace.

'Shall we stay here or go into town?' said Annie.

'I imagine it'll be even busier there,' said Mrs Turnbull. 'Might be better to find somewhere along here.'

'Aye, I agree,' said Lorcan. 'Let's just walk up here a bit. It looks a little less crowded.'

They headed in the direction of Norfolk Road but soon found a suitable space on the pavement where they all had a good view. Annie was beyond pleased to find herself standing next to Lorcan, with Mrs Turnbull on her other side.

'I wonder how Phoebe's going to cope with losing Günther a second time,' said Edie.

'We'll worry about that when we get back inside,' said Mrs Turnbull. 'No point spoiling the afternoon, pet. There's nowt we can do at this moment in time.'

'I suppose not… I'd like to have seen the unveiling of the temporary Cenotaph in London yesterday, to commemorate the dead.'

'Aye lass, me too. Must have been quite something, though sad too.'

'Mr Fletcher was reading a piece about it from his newspaper this morning,' said Annie. 'They're talking about making a proper permanent one there.'

' 'Ere it comes,' called Charlie, pointing east, where a horse-drawn farm cart could be seen being driven along the road.

Cheering could be heard from further up the road, and it wasn't long before the noise, along with the cart, was getting closer. As the cart, decorated with flags, reached them, a mighty cheer went up among the crowds around them, and they all joined in. Annie felt an immense elation, what with the ecstatic reception of the parade and the fact she had Lorcan next to her. She wasn't going to let any thoughts of Jasper take that away from her just yet.

The cart passed, and behind came a group of people, waving as they walked. One of them, who she knew to be a well-known local businessman called Mr Robinson, was dressed as a Pierrot, in a dark clown costume with a huge white neck ruff.

Several other carts followed, all decorated one way or another, some with bunting or flags, or decorated poles, or a combination of all of them. Following on came a swathe of school children marching in line and grinning broadly. Then came a marching band, playing 'The British Grenadiers'. Behind them came a troupe of scouts, led by scoutmasters, and then a group of girl guides.

A few open-topped motorcars passed, with suited men waving.

'I wonder who they are?' said Annie.

'I believe they may be council officials,' said Edie.

'Ooh, there's a reet bobby dazzler,' said Mrs Turnbull, indicating a horse-drawn float decorated with rows upon rows of flowers.

'It's lovely!' Annie agreed, her joy rising several notches. She wished she could stand outside here all afternoon watching the parade, with Lorcan so close to her.

When a motor ambulance came up next, with a group of around a dozen nurses walking behind, the cheers became deafening.

As they subsided, Mrs Turnbull said, 'Isn't this wonderful?' She threw her arms around Annie and Edie, either side of her. Charlie then put his arms around Edie. Lorcan linked arms with Jerry, then put his arm around Annie. They all stood there together as the rest of the parade went past.

It had been a very long time since Annie had felt this happy.

Chapter Fifteen

It was now the fifth day of August, and Annie felt like the summer was rushing away. Before they knew it, it would be September. It didn't help that today was overcast and a little cooler than it had been.

'What are you doing today, on your afternoon off?' Alice asked, as they cleared up in the scullery. 'You 'aven't said.'

'I'm not sure yet.'

'You doing something with Jasper?' This question was always asked stiffly. Whether Alice realised it or not, Annie couldn't guess.

'I'm not sure. We 'aven't discussed it.'

'Right. Didn't you arrange it last week, when you went to the pictures?'

'No.' She didn't need to give any explanation. They'd said vaguely last week that they'd make a decision about what to do nearer the time, but they hadn't discussed it since.

'You'd better decide soon. You'll be going in five minutes.'

'I know,' said Annie, rather impatiently, wishing Alice would shut up about it.

'Wonder if it's as busy out there today as it was yesterday for the bank 'oliday.'

'I don't expect so.'

'It was quite busy when I 'ad a look after me break this morning,' said Finn, drying up a frying pan.

Annie wished Alice would keep her mouth shut about her private life when the scullery lads were in here. What business was it of theirs? Or Alice's, come to that?

Jasper came through the door a couple of minutes later. 'Could I have a word, Annie? Outside?'

'Course.' Had he decided on an activity? She really should have said something last week, to put him off, or to end it.

They headed out and were by the gate when Jasper said, 'Was there anything in particular you wanted to do today?'

This was her opportunity to say something. But what?

'The thing is, Jasper, I could really do with, well, doing some shopping in town for some bits and pieces, and I'm afraid you'll get bored.'

'That's all right. My mother did write to ask if I might help with a bit of painting today, so I'll take the omnibus over and spend a couple of hours there. Maybe we can do something next week?'

'Yes, maybe.'

What an idiot she was. She'd put him off today, but they hadn't broken up, as such.

Back in the scullery, Alice piped up, 'So what ya doing today?'

'Neither of us can make it today,' said Annie.

Alice looked confused. 'But—'

'I'd better get ready to go.'

'Me too,' said Jasper. He was about to leave when he halted. 'Have you heard from that Jamie recently, Alice? You haven't mentioned him at all for ages.'

'It's been nearly three months since you last saw him,' Annie added.

Alice, drying her hands, shrugged. 'It's summer, so it's probably a busy time for him.'

'Why would summer in particular be busier for a reporter?' Jasper didn't look convinced by the logic.

'Longer days. More happening. More sports to report on.'

'Does he report on sports?' Annie asked. 'I thought he worked on exclusive stories, the way you told it.'

'I dunno. He does a bit of everything, I guess.'

Jasper left, not commenting on this. Annie wanted to say more, but she was keen to get away. She was now looking forward to her hastily decided plan to go into town.

'I'll see ya later. You're in charge now, Alice, so make sure you keep everything tidy.'

'Oh, pipe down and just go, please.'

In the staff corridor, Annie went towards the hatstand to collect her jacket, then noticed Phoebe standing there, looking sad.

'You all right, Phoebe?'

She held up a letter. 'I was just coming for my lunch when Mrs Leggett gave me this. It's from Germany, from Günther. He says he has a job as a waiter in Stuttgart and not to worry about him.' Her head drooped. 'But I do.' She started crying.

Annie went to her, giving her a hug. 'I'm so sorry, Phoebe. It must be awful for you.'

'What's up?' came Lorcan's voice, as he came through the door from the foyer.

'Phoebe's had a letter from Günther.'

'Is he all right?'

Phoebe nodded forlornly.

'Isn't it your afternoon off?' said Lorcan, regarding Annie.

'It is.'

'Then off you go. I'll look after her... It's your lunch break now, isn't it?'

Phoebe nodded once more.

'Then come on with you, and you can tell us what he has to say for himself while we're eating. If you want to.'

'I do.' She went ahead of him, into the dining room.

'Have a good afternoon, Annie.'

'I'll try. Poor Phoebe.'

'Aye. I can sort of understand why the eejit ran off back to Germany, but it hasn't helped any.'

'No, it hasn't. I'll buy Phoebe some chocolate to cheer her up a bit. I know it's not much, but it's all I can think of.'

'That's a kind thought, Annie. I'll see you later.'

'See you later, Lorcan.'

She put her jacket on and left.

–

After agreeing with Annie that they had other things to do today, Jasper had headed upstairs to change out of his uniform. He felt a little guilty, making the excuse he had for not going out with her today, even though it was she who had postponed their day off first. He'd already had his piece about helping with the painting worked out.

His mother hadn't exactly asked him to pop over to help, only suggested that if he had nothing else to do, he might like to.

What to do, what to do? His mind always raced when he thought about this situation with Annie. They'd had

235

some entertaining afternoons out, but only as friends. After his failed attempt to kiss her on the bridge, he hadn't tried again, hadn't really had any inclination to. It could be that she felt the same way about their relationship. But what if she didn't? What if she really liked him but was happy to bide her time until he showed her some affection?

'You're an idiot,' he scolded himself. *Eejit*. That's how Lorcan would have put it. The way he pronounced it always gave it the emphasis it deserved. And it *was* all he deserved to be called.

He closed his eyes and huffed out his frustration. Despite their little falling-out a while back, Alice was still the perfect girl for him. If he'd had any chance with her, he certainly wouldn't have one now. Going out with her sister was the *worst* thing he could have done, whether Annie was fond of him or not.

He flung his cap on and left the room. He'd better get going if he was going to get to town in time to catch the omnibus he'd planned on taking.

Chapter Sixteen

Ernest Brown took a slow stroll by the riverside in Pier Road. It was a warm, sunny afternoon, not a patch of cloud in the sky. The river was rushing towards the sea and a couple of swans bobbed up and down as they floated in the same direction. Overhead, a flock of seagulls exclaimed optimistic cries. There was a whiff of fish and brine. Ernie stopped to chat to a couple of old fishermen. One was mending a net while the other was painting a boat with a dark stain.

'Nice day for it,' said Ernie, his thumbs stuck in his waistcoat pockets, his jacket wide open. 'Going out in a boat, fishing, I mean.'

The older of the two had haggard skin, darkened by the sun. His long, grey hair was coarse, and on top of it sat a wide, shabby hat. He looked up at Ernie with a puzzled expression. 'I'm a little long in the tooth for that now. I leave it to me son and grandson.'

'Thasright, me too,' said his companion, a thin cigarette bobbing up and down, hanging precariously from the side of his mouth as he spoke.

'I guess it comes to us all,' said Ernie. 'Must be nice though, sitting out in the sun, doing ya job.'

'It suits me fine,' said the older man. 'Bit of fresh air's good for the soul.'

'Better than sitting in a musty ol' fa'try all day, that's for sure,' said Ernie.

The men nodded but added nothing.

'Good day to you gentlemen.' He lifted his hat.

Again, they nodded, then carried on with their work.

He headed on down the road, past a timber mill on one side and warehouses on the other, whistling a happy rendition of 'Don't Dilly Dally on the Way'. He recalled hearing Marie Lloyd perform it at the Hackney Empire recently.

How long had he been here now? Nearly six weeks. The doctor had suggested he take some time off, but he'd better return home soon. He couldn't leave his son in charge indefinitely. What was the date now? *The Glorious Twelfth*, he thought. That's how some posh geezer he'd done business with had referred to the twelfth of August. The bloke had invited him to shoot grouse on his estate, but Ernie hadn't wanted any part in that. Shooting poor innocent birds for sport? *Nah*, he thought. It wasn't for him.

When he came to the opening that led onto Fisherman's Quay, he turned left onto it, crunching across the pebbles to get to the water's edge. It was the second time he'd wandered down here, and as he passed the Britannia public house, he pondered whether to go in for a pint. The last time he'd tried that, back in the East End, he hadn't been made to feel welcome, not like in his younger days, before his success. He suspected they didn't like the fact he looked like a nob and had done well for himself. Even the customers in his former local had become distant.

He had to admit that life had become lonely. His own class didn't want his company any more, thinking him a snob, and the upper classes, on the whole, looked down on him as someone who'd risen above his station.

It was quiet here today, with nobody working on the quay itself. He picked up several pebbles, hurling them into the river, as he used to as a boy, playing by the Thames.

There was an alleyway at the other end of the quay; it might lead to a road that would take him to the bridge. He hadn't had a walk on the west side of the river yet, and it looked rather pleasant.

Entering the alleyway, a youngish woman came up behind him. He wondered where she'd come from as he'd seen no one on the quay while he'd been there.

' 'Ello, sir.'

He noted the long, black hair that flowed over her shoulders, rather than being done up neatly, as was proper. She had on too much make-up in his opinion, the rouge and lipstick overdone.

'Good afternoon, Miss.' He lifted his hat.

Again, there was that surprised look he always got when someone first heard him speak, but she was soon smiling again. 'Would you like to spend some time with me? For a small consideration, of course.' She lifted her skirt to show a good portion of her thighs.

'Oh, I see. No, I wouldn't, so bugger off. I didn't get where I am today to pay money to some floozy.'

She narrowed her eyes and pouted, startling him with a brisk slap to the face.

'What the—' He was about to give her a piece of his mind when he felt something heavy thump against his head, and he slumped to the ground.

He was on all fours, clutching his forehead, a dizzy spell making him unable to move. He could feel someone rooting through his pockets. He was vaguely aware of a man's voice, saying, ' 'E might look posh, but he ain't got no manners, talking to a lady like that.'

His hands gave way, and he slumped onto his stomach, moaning. He heard footsteps as they walked away. For a moment, he managed to look up, and through a haze saw the woman strut off. There were two men ahead of her. The shorter of the two lifted his cap briefly to scratch his head, and he spotted a mop of thick, grey untidy hair. The other was very tall, with a scarf tied around his head, though he could see he was fair.

' 'E certainly got what 'e deserved, Frank,' said the woman.

'Don't use me name, ya silly mare.'

'Oh 'e can't 'ear me, 'e's spark out.'

At which point, Ernie felt a sharp pain run through his head and he lost consciousness.

–

Another Tuesday, and another afternoon off, thought Jasper, realising that these days had become ever more stressful as the weeks had gone by, when once he looked forward to them. Should he make another excuse to Annie today, or bite the bullet and go out with her somewhere?

It wasn't as if he could use bad weather as an excuse; the day was warm and bright and perfect for a walk around the beach activities, of which there'd be many. He fancied having a look around them, maybe dipping his feet in the sea. He didn't object to doing this with Annie, whose company was pleasant, but if he kept on spending days with her, she was likely to keep getting the wrong idea.

And how would it look when he did finally end it, as he knew he would have to, eventually? People would think him ungentlemanly at the very least, and who would blame them? No, he had to do the right thing.

He started walking towards the scullery, still not sure what he was going to say, or do. Perhaps he'd put off telling her today, and talk to her about it during the week. If she was going to be upset, he didn't want to spoil her afternoon off.

Excuses, excuses. What a coward he was. At this rate, he'd never get around to it.

Arriving there, he was at least relieved to see that Alice was not in the room, but the scullery lads were.

'Hello Annie, can we talk about today?'

'Where are you off to?' asked Lucas. 'There's loads going on outside here.'

'They'd probably rather be somewhere on their own,' Finn joked, with a mischievous grin.

Lucas laughed. 'Probably. Planning their future nuptials, like everyone else.'

Annie glared at them. 'Do shut up, you two.'

'Could we talk outside?' Jasper asked Annie, hastily. This had to stop.

'Course.' She looked wary, which made him feel even more awkward.

They reached the middle of the yard, and he started with, 'The thing is—' at the same time as she blurted out, 'I'm not sure this is going anywhere.'

'Oh,' he said. 'You mean, our relationship.'

'I'm sorry. Finn and Lucas going on made me realise I had to say something.'

'No, don't be sorry. I was about to say something very similar. I just hadn't really worked out what and hoped the words would… come.'

'You're not upset?' she said.

'No, I'm relieved, actually.'

'Good. So am I.'

'Not that I've anything against you,' said Jasper. 'Not at all. We've had fun, but it's been more as, you know…'

'Friends.'

'Yes, exactly.'

She nodded. 'I've enjoyed our days out, but to be honest, I don't think you and me, were, well…'

'Meant to be?'

'Yep. Not meant to be sweethearts, anyway, just meant to be friends.'

'And I will always cherish that friendship, Annie.'

'Me too, Jasper. And, if there's some other girl you're interested in, please, don't worry about me being upset. I won't be. I'll be pleased for ya. Whoever she is.'

He wasn't sure she would be, if she knew who was on his mind. 'The same goes for me… Well, what are you going to do this afternoon?'

'I'm gonna go 'ome and see if me mum would like to go shopping and for some tea somewhere. She always says she don't do much with me and Alice no more, and it makes her sad.'

'That's a nice thing to do. I'm going to enjoy the sun and have a walk along the prom. And I believe Gertie's playing a football match this afternoon, up at the sports field, so I'm going to go and watch for a while.'

'Sounds good. Alice'll be back from lunch in a minute, then I'll go and get ready to leave.'

'And I'd better change. Have a good afternoon, Annie.'

'You too, Jasper.'

He went back through the scullery and stillroom, pleasantly surprised at how that had gone. So, the feelings were mutual. What a relief. But that relief was edged with regret. Having walked out with her sister, it seemed likely he'd scuppered any remote chance he'd had with Alice.

Entering the corridor, he saw Alice leaving the staff dining room. A kind of grief washed over him, as he glanced at her. He turned quickly towards the staff stairs, to go up to his bedroom.

—

How odd, thought Alice, as Jasper disappeared upstairs. That cursory look he'd given her, with a frown on his face, as if she'd done something wrong. It looked like he'd just come from the stillroom, or the scullery, so had her sister said something about her?

As she entered the scullery, Annie was drying her hands.

'Good, ya back. I'll be going now.'

' 'Ave you said something to Jasper?'

'What? What d'ya mean?'

'Was he just in 'ere?'

'Yy… yes.'

'You don't sound sure.'

'You was talking outside with 'im, Annie,' said one of the scullery lads.

'I know that, Finn, and this ain't nothing to do with you, so pipe down.'

Alice stuck her hands on her hips. 'You was outside, talking about me be'ind me back?'

'No! You didn't even get a mention.'

'Well, someone's said something 'cos he looked at me like I'd done something really bad as he passed by.'

'Don't be daft. It's all up 'ere, in your imagination, Alice in Wonderland.' Annie poked her own head with a forefinger a few times.

'I'm fed up with you calling me that. I suppose you two'll go out this afternoon and talk about me be'ind me back too.'

'No, we won't, because, well, we just won't.'

'So *you* say.'

–

That was close, thought Annie. She'd nearly given away that she and Jasper had finished their relationship. She had been planning to tell Alice, when they were on their own, but now she could stew in her own juices.

'Why would I have any reason to tell Jasper bad things about you? I think you're just mad because I've been walking out with someone and your young man ain't even bothered to contact you.'

'It's not like that.'

'You don't even know where he lives.'

'Yes, I do. I told you. He lives on Maxwell Road.'

'But where on Maxwell Road? And you don't know if he lives with his parents, or on his own.'

'What does that matter?'

Finn and Lucas had stopped drying and were standing together, gawping at the two women.

'I'd say that he's been gone so long now, that you can't even claim to be walking out with someone.'

'He's gone on a job!' Alice yelled.

The door was pushed open roughly and Phoebe entered. 'I wish you two would pipe down. You're giving me and the stillroom maids a headache.'

'I'd be more than glad to,' said Annie. She stormed off towards the corridor, hoping she'd calm down before getting home so she could be in a good mood for her mum.

–

Alice watched Annie's retreating back, biting one side of her bottom lip. She must have said something for Jasper to have looked at her in that way. Or someone had. And since they were walking out, it was most likely Annie. Her stomach plunged again at the knowledge that her sister was close to the man she was so... fond of.

She distracted herself by setting to work, shifting three trays of teapots, cups, saucers and side plates to the stillroom, where the maids there unpacked them and placed the crockery on the shelves. As she was doing this, Annie came back through the rooms with her jacket on. She said not a word as she left the building.

At one of the sinks now, Alice started rinsing a stack of plates from the guest dining room, brooding. Did it matter if Annie told Jasper tales about her? It wasn't as if she'd ever had a chance with him. And there was always Jamie. But that hope was shrinking ever more rapidly as each week went by without his reappearance. He could, at least, have written to her. She felt herself welling up, but breathed the sensation back in, not wanting Finn and Lucas to see her cry.

Maybe Jamie, like everyone else, had tired of silly old Alice in Wonderland.

'How are you feeling, Mr Brown?' said Sam, as he approached the man sitting on the wall outside the Britannia public house, looking the worse for wear.

There was a cut above one eye, his face was grazed, and his suit was grubby with dust. Sergeant Gardner and young PC Yates were already standing with him. Outside the public house, several people had gathered to look on.

'Oh, it's you,' said Ernie. 'We met at the 'otel.'

'Aye, we did.'

'Gawd, I said I'd need to watch meself as a joke, but didn't 'ave this kinda thing in mind. Someone up in the 'eavens didn't like me little jest. Anyway, me 'ead's throbbing and I've got a lump the size of a golf ball.' He pointed to the top of his head.

'That does look nasty. Gardner, has the doctor been called?'

'The landlady's rung Dr Ferngrove.'

'Good. Can you tell me what happened, Mr Brown?'

'It's a bit 'azy now, but there was this woman greeted me, down that alleyway past the workshops. Long black 'air, she 'ad. She offered 'er, uh, *services*, for money. I turned down 'er offer. She slapped me face and the next thing I knew I was being set on. I felt a blow to me 'ead and I went down. I could feel someone 'aving a root round me pockets, and then I must've passed out. Next thing I know, there's a coupla blokes leaning over me, asking me what 'appened, and one says he'd get the public 'ouse to telephone the police. I've checked me pockets, and me wallet's gone, along with me rings and an expensive watch. Oh, and me lovely tie pin.' He moaned and clutched his head. 'It's bleedin' painful and I feel dizzy.'

A motorcar pulled up on the pebbles and Dr Ferngrove got out.

'Good, the doctor,' said Sam. 'I'll talk to you again when you're feeling a little better, in case there's anything else you can remember.'

Dr Ferngrove was apprised of the situation, then examined Mr Brown's wounds. Sam took a few steps away with Gardner.

'You and the constable have a look around, Sergeant, see if you can find the instrument he was struck with, or anything else suspicious. Have a word with the Britannia's customers, and people in the workshops too, in case they saw anybody loitering.'

'Righty ho, sir.'

Dr Ferngrove came towards them. 'I'm going to get the landlady to telephone for an ambulance. I don't like the look of that bump and want to get him to hospital. I'll stay with him until it arrives as I'm afraid he might have concussion.'

'Good idea,' said Sam. 'I'll head up to the hotel as he's a guest there and they'll wonder what's happened to him. I'll come back here afterwards to see if you've made any progress, Gardner.'

The three men headed off in different directions. Sam pondered this new case. If they didn't find out who was responsible for these assaults soon, someone might end up seriously hurt. Or worse.

Chapter Seventeen

'Has anyone heard how Mr Brown is now?' Annie asked at breakfast, a few days after the incident on the quay.

Everyone around the table shook their heads.

'He's not returned to the hotel to collect his things yet. We might get some news if DI Toshack calls by, as he's likely to,' said Lorcan.

'Perhaps now, Alice, you've realised why you shouldn't be on the quay by yourself, like Uncle Barry told you,' said Annie.

Jasper, cutting up a sausage, halted partway through. 'That does sound a little unwise. What were you doing there by yourself?'

'I wasn't by meself. I'd walked there with Jamie. You know that, Annie.'

'It's not what you told Uncle Barry though, is it? You told him you didn't know who he was and that you'd just been passing the time of day.'

' 'Cos it was none of his business and I didn't want him interfering or telling our parents.'

'You haven't told your parents that you're walking out with someone?' said Jasper.

'No, and neither has Annie told 'em about you, so what's the difference? Have you told your parents about Annie?'

'No, but, that is…'

'Jasper ain't a stranger, so I don't need to,' Annie interrupted, not wanting to give the game away just yet.

Jasper regarded her curiously, but didn't contradict her.

'You twos have done a lot of arguing recently, so you have,' said Lorcan, taking a piece of toast off a large plate on the table. 'What's wrong with you?'

'I'm just looking out for me little sister.'

Alice let out a noisy moan. 'I wish you'd stop this "little sister" lark. I'm only thirteen months younger than you. I'm twenty-three now.'

'Then you should act it.'

'It does sound a little suspicious,' said Jasper, 'this Jamie disappearing and not even contacting you by letter.'

'Annie been talking out of turn, has she?'

'Only because she was concerned. It's what siblings are for.'

'Aye,' said Lorcan. 'I'd have been concerned too, if me sister had some mysterious young man I'd never met. We weren't sure about her husband when we first met him, especially as she was only sixteen and he was twenty-five, so we made a few enquiries. Luckily, he turned out to be a good man.'

'I do wonder...' Jasper looked down at his plate, his mouth pinched in.

Annie leant forward. 'What?'

'Another theory?' Alice crossed her arms over her chest and frowned.

'Let's hear it then,' said Lili, leaning over with interest from her position at one end of the table.

'Well, it's just...' Jasper started. 'He told you he's a reporter, right? What if he was trying to get some information about the hotel. Befriending someone from here would be a good way to do it.'

Alice didn't look impressed. 'So, what you're saying is, he wouldn't be interested in me for any other reason.'

Annie noticed Jasper redden.

'No, no, I didn't mean that. It's just, you know, after some of the things that happened in the war – the libellous letters, the murder, and so on – perhaps he thought he could dig up some dirt.'

Alice twisted her body around to face him. 'Then why would he have told me he's a reporter? He'd 'ave kept that to himself, surely.'

Jasper nodded, not looking at her. 'That's a good point.'

'Anyway, none of you 'ave to worry 'cos, as you say, he ain't contacted me, so I guess that's that.'

'Good,' said Annie.

Mrs Leggett entered the room. By the expression on her face, Annie anticipated more bad news.

'It appears that Phoebe has left,' she announced.

'Left?' said Annie. 'What, the job?'

'The job, the hotel, the country. Though I doubt she's managed the latter yet.'

'Get to the point, Mrs L,' said Lorcan, eliciting a stern look from her.

'Phoebe has left a note saying that she's following Günther to Germany.'

'How on earth will she find him?' said Annie.

'Phoebe has an address from the letter he sent, so she's travelling to Dover to get a boat over. Some of her clothes seem to have gone, along with her suitcase, and she's placed other items in a box with a note asking us to pass them on to her parents.'

Jack had come in near the beginning of the explanation. With him were Mr Watkins, Mrs Turnbull, Jerry and Will Fletcher, and they all looked shocked.

'Does she even know how to get there?' said Alice. 'Stuttgart, wasn't it? Wherever that is.'

'And does she have a passport?' said Will. 'You need one now, to go abroad.'

'Maybe she got one without telling anyone,' said the housekeeper. 'She doesn't say. Do sit down before your breakfasts get cold.'

They sat down and placed their plates on the table. They all had bacon and eggs.

'I dunno,' said Mrs Turnbull. 'It seems we get through one predicament only for another to occur. How's your brother now, Jerry?'

'He seems to be getting better since being taken to Netley hospital. I'm gonna visit him on my day off.'

'It's a bit of a trek to Southampton,' said Annie.

'Under two hours on the train, pet,' said the store-keeper. 'Mrs Bygrove went a coupla times when her late husband were there, remember?'

Annie glanced heavenward. 'How could we forget, given he came back 'ere after to recuperate, and gave us all hell.'

'It's a shame we were away,' said Lorcan. 'He might have thought twice about that if the men had been here.'

'You forget, Mr Foley, that some of us *were* still here,' said Mr Watkins. 'He was no less bullying to the male staff than the female.' He held his knife aloft, as if to make a point.

Will and Jack muttered in agreement.

'I'm sorry to hear that,' said Jasper. 'But Lorcan may have a point.'

'Oh yes, 'cos you'd have all coped so much better than we did with him,' Alice said sarcastically. 'You big strong men.'

Not again, thought Annie. Why was Alice determined to argue with Jasper? It was Lorcan who'd originally made the point.

'Sorry, Alice, but I didn't mean it like that. I meant, safety in numbers and all that. It would have been easier for more of us regular staff to stand up to him together. You were short staffed and had a lot of temporary members as well.'

Alice was opening her mouth to reply, when the door opened once again, and Helen entered.

'I see Mrs Leggett is here, so you've no doubt heard about Phoebe.'

There was a chorus of glum affirmations.

'Then you'll realise that we are now yet another member of staff down, especially as Phoebe was in charge of the stillroom. If anybody is willing to do an extra shift there, with an increase in pay, of course, then I'd be grateful. It will hopefully only be for the short term.'

Jerry raised his hand. 'I presume that's aimed only at the women?'

'Well, of course,' said Alice. 'Because god forbid that any man would consider doing "women's" work, despite the fact that many of us took over men's work in the war.'

'There's no need to blaspheme,' said Mrs Leggett.

Helen's face was a picture of surprise and confusion. 'I, um, really don't mind who takes on a shift. Whoever thinks they can.'

Alice looked contrite. 'I'm sorry, Mrs Bygrove, my comment wasn't aimed at you.'

'Yes, I did realise that.'

'After what we've had to do in the war, I don't mind what I do,' said Jasper. 'I'm sure I could manage making beverages and drinks, but I wouldn't have a clue how to make jams and pickles, etcetera. They're very skilled at that in the stillroom, I must say.'

'Anybody who volunteers won't be expected to do that side of it,' said Helen. 'But everyone's capable of peeling and cutting up fruit and vegetables. The stillroom maids will do the cooking and storing part.'

'Count me in then,' said Jasper.

Lorcan lifted his hand. 'Aye, and me.'

'As willing as I'd be,' said Lili, 'we're already a waiter down in the dining room.'

'You are, but I do have a couple of people to inter-view as waitresses today, so hopefully that problem will be solved. Maybe one of them could work in the stillroom, but I am rather hoping that Phoebe will be back, so I'd like to keep the job open.'

'I 'ope you're right, Mrs Bygrove,' said Annie. 'I'd really miss her if she was gone forever.'

Everyone murmured in agreement. Helen nodded, then left the room, and the staff continued with their breakfasts.

Goodness knows what Jasper had made of Alice's outburst. Annie wondered if she'd been wrong about her sister liking him all along. Or maybe she was protecting herself against having any feelings for him because he'd been walking out with her. That twinge of guilt that she'd felt since her first trip out with Jasper grew a little bit bigger. She must get around to telling her the situation.

–

Four days later, Alice was washing up in the stillroom when the outside door opened and a familiar figure stepped in.

'Phoebe! You're back.'

The stillroom maid placed her small case on the ground. 'That remains to be seen. I don't suppose Mrs Bygrove will be very happy with me.'

'What happened? Did you get to Germany?'

'No, I wasn't even allowed out of the country. I didn't know that everyone needed a passport now.'

'So, you didn't have one. Mr Fletcher did wonder about that. But you've been gone four days.'

'I hung around Dover, trying to work out what the best thing to do was. I thought there might be a fishing boat willing to take me over, but I realised they don't go that far. And then how would I find Stuttgart from some unknown place once I got there, as they wouldn't be able to drop me at a station. I had to admit defeat in the end.'

'I am sure Mrs Bygrove will be relieved to see you. She—'

One of the scullery lads walked back through the door after having taken some pots and pans back to the kitchen.

'Phoebe!'

'Lucas, would you knock on the office door and see if Mrs Bygrove is there. And tell her the news,' said Alice.

He scampered off and they heard him calling the news to the stillroom staff. Soon the stillroom maids, Tilly and Milly, appeared in the scullery, surrounding the new arrival and welcoming her with enthusiasm. It wasn't long before Helen joined them, followed by Lucas.

'I'm *so* glad to see you back,' said the manageress. 'What happened?'

'I'm going to have to answer that question a few times, I guess,' said Phoebe. 'Lack of a passport and my ignorance about them.'

Helen hugged her. 'I'm so sorry that you didn't get to see Günther, and I can understand why you'd want to follow him.' She leant back. 'But I'm not sure it's the wisest course of action. You would know nobody but him there, you can't speak the language, and you'd probably have difficulty getting a job. I believe that the German nation is going through a hard time financially now.'

Phoebe's mouth dipped down at the corners. 'You're probably right. But, I… I so wanted to be with him.'

She looked so crestfallen that Alice felt a huge pang of sympathy for her, imagining what she'd feel like if she had a sweetheart who went a long way away. She'd felt bad enough when Jasper had enlisted.

'I know, Phoebe,' said Helen. 'And who knows, maybe Günther will be back?'

Phoebe straightened herself and seemed to pull herself together. 'So, how is Mr Brown now? Has anyone heard?'

'He's still at the hospital and apparently had a mild heart attack a couple of days ago,' said Helen.

'Oh no, poor man, after what he went through.'

'They think they might have caught the woman responsible, though not the men.'

'That's something. Maybe she'll tell them who they were.'

'I don't know. I think these poor women who find themselves in that line of work are probably under threat not to give away anything. But we'll see.'

'Phoebe!' said Annie, as she entered the scullery, and the welcome began all over again.

–

Detective Inspector Toshack drew up outside the hospital on Fitzalan Road. Ernie Brown had been in there over two weeks, latterly recovering from a minor heart problem, but he'd now been discharged. The hospital had rung Sam to tell him, and he'd agreed to come and pick him up and drive him to the hotel.

Ernie was limping down the path from the hospital entrance, accompanied by a nurse, when Sam got out of the car.

'Inspector, how good of you to collect me.'

'You're welcome, Mr Brown. I hope you're feeling better now?' He opened the passenger door for him and helped him in, before heading around to the driver's side once more.

'A lot better than I did. Good job I 'ad the money to stay in the 'ospital that long. Me old ticker obviously didn't appreciate me being assaulted the way I was, but the doctor reckoned the 'eart attack weren't too bad. I 'ope 'e's right. I've got a deal of living to do yet.'

'That's good to hear.'

As they drove off, Ernie said, 'Me daughter and her 'usband only got back from their trip to Scotland to see his family last night. They went the day before I was attacked so she didn't know anything about it until I telephoned from the 'ospital this morning.'

'It must have been a shock for her.'

'It was. She's arriving later this afternoon from Ealing to collect me and take me 'ome. Nice motorcar she's got, a Wolseley, which I bought 'er just before the war began. It was kind of the 'otel to keep me belongings safe for me while I was indisposed. I don't suppose there's been any developments in the case, or that me watch and whatnot 'ave been recovered?'

'I'm afraid they have not been recovered. However, another victim has identified a woman, who we did arrest.'

It had been reported four days before, by a Mr Foxworthy, who'd been very clear about who the protagonist was as he said he'd recognised her.

'Another attack since mine?' said Ernie.

'Yes. Much the same thing – attacked on the quay. But Mr Foxworthy managed to get away without any injury.'

'Lucky him. Could I take a look at this suspect to identify 'er?'

'We've had to let her go for now, due to lack of other evidence.' And the fact that something didn't seem quite right to him. 'Now, normally, I'd prefer to do a line-up, where you could pick out the person you thought it might be, but because we've let her go, I've brought an image.'

He pulled up outside the hotel, then removed a photograph from his suit pocket.

'Nah, I can tell ya straight away, that ain't 'er. I know I was knocked out, but I'd remember 'er anywhere. She was dark 'aired like this woman, but that's all.' He looked closely at the face. 'You can't really tell in this photograph, but this woman's eyes look dark. The girl what approached me had piercing blue eyes, stood out, they did.'

This was interesting, if Ernie was right. The woman they'd questioned was dark eyed. 'You didn't mention that at the time.'

'I was too confused before, but I've remembered a few things over the last few days. As they walked away, just before I conked out, she referred to one of 'em as "Frank". He 'ad an East London accent, I'd recognise it anywhere, and he told 'er off for using 'is name. He was short and dumpy, with a great unwieldy mop of grey hair. Looked in his late fifties, maybe. The other bloke was a lot taller, and I think, blond, younger, maybe late twenties, early thirties.'

'I'll make a note of that, thank you, Mr Brown. What did she speak like, this woman?'

'Common as they come. Like me!' he joked. 'She was a mouthy piece.'

The woman they'd brought in had been softly spoken and been anything but 'mouthy'. Sam got out and went around to open the door for Ernie.

'Thank you, Inspector.'

'Have a good journey home, sir. And if you remember anything else, you can telephone me at the station. Here are the details.' He reached into his other pocket to retrieve a business card.

'Cheerio Inspector. And good luck catching them scallywags.'

Scallywags, thought Sam. He guessed that Mr Brown was trying to be polite, but he could certainly think of several more suitable descriptions.

–

After dropping Ernie Brown off, Toshack parked on the left side of the hotel, in a small parking area set aside for guests. He entered the staff entrance and was greeted by the staff in the scullery and stillroom, who were now used to him coming in and out of the hotel. In the corridor, he met Helen, who was leaving the small passageway that led to her office.

'Sam, you're earlier than you said you'd be.'

'Aye, I've just dropped Mr Brown off, so I thought I may as well come now.'

'Good. Lorcan has been instructed to help Mr Brown pack and is going to offer him a free afternoon tea while he waits for his daughter to arrive. It's the very least I could do for the poor man. Now, I was about to have a cup of tea with whoever's currently in the staff dining room, as I like to do from time to time. Come and join us.'

He'd felt a little ill at ease in these situations when he'd first sat down with staff in this way but was now used to it. And they were an interesting group.

As soon as he entered the room of about a dozen people, there was a cry of, 'Inspector Toshack. I'm glad you're 'ere.' It was Annie, Sergeant Gardner's 'sort of niece', as he'd put it.

'And why is that, Miss Twine?'

'There's rumours going around Wick that the woman what you arrested in connection with them attacks was Rosie Barleycorn, what lives only around the corner from us, on West Terrace.'

He sat down, frowning. 'That got around pretty quickly. Where did you hear it from? Not Sergeant Gardner, I hope.'

'Nah, Uncle Barry won't tell us nothing about cases he's working on. Our next-door neighbour told me mum. Is it true?'

No point denying it. 'Aye, but we've released her because of the lack of other evidence. And, well, yes.' He was about to say that he'd shown a photo to Ernie Brown who'd denied it was her, but the man could have been mistaken, or there could be more than one woman involved. And it was confidential police business at this moment in time.

'Who on earth said it was her in the first place?' said Annie. 'She's always been really shy and polite and the sort to do as she's told.'

And maybe the sort to do what she's told by some thug controlling her, he thought.

'And that day what Mr Brown was attacked, she called round our 'ouse with some curtains what she'd repaired, me mum said.'

'When exactly?' said Sam, intrigued by this snippet of information.

'Sometime in the morning.'

'The attack was in the afternoon, so it doesn't stand as an alibi, I'm afraid.'

'What, so she was sewing curtains in the morning, and helping to assault a man in the afternoon?'

He couldn't fault Annie's logic, but it might be interesting to hear more about this young woman.

'So, you know Miss Barleycorn well?'

'She was in me class at Lyminster school, and we often played out in the street together. Like I said, she was the quiet one.'

'Don't they say it's the quiet ones you have to watch?' said Jack, before taking a gulp of tea.

'Not Rosie. She was the one what stayed at 'ome and helped her mum with her sewing business, after her siblings all left. I don't think she even goes out much these days, just sits at 'ome sewing. That's what our next-door neighbour said. It don't seem likely that she'd go around helping men to mug people.'

She had seemed the delicate sort when he'd interviewed her. The type not to say boo to a goose, as Gardner had described her. And she'd been adamant that it wasn't her, to the point of distressed tears that didn't seem put on.

'Like I said, there wasn't enough evidence to keep her, so, unless someone else comes forward to identify her, that'll be the end of the matter.'

'Good.'

He had to wonder, though, why anyone would point the finger at her if she had nothing to do with it. Mistaken identity?

Helen passed him a cup of tea and a biscuit, and the conversation moved on.

—

Sam was back at the police station by six o'clock, having taken a walk with Helen on the beach before he'd returned.

'Good evening, Inspector,' said Gardner, as he entered. 'You'll want to know the latest on the quay attacks.'

'There hasn't been another, has there?'

'No, sir, thank the Lord, but I called round earlier, to that address Mr Foxworthy gave us, the one who named Rosie Barleycorn as the woman what approached him.'

'And?'

'He doesn't live at that address, sir. There's a middle-aged couple living there with their three grandchildren. That's it.'

'Did Constable Twort get the details wrong?'

'Just what I was thinking, sir. Or, well…'

'Or this so-called victim wasn't a victim at all, and is trying to frame an innocent woman?'

'Yes, sir.'

'Interestingly, when I picked Mr Brown up, he remembered a few more details about that afternoon. It seems—'

'Hold on a moment, sir.' Gardner pulled a notebook from his breast pocket and picked up a pen from the front desk. 'Let me take this down.'

'Mr Brown said he remembered the woman having dark hair, like Miss Barleycorn, but that she had piercing blue eyes.'

'I don't remember Miss Barleycorn having eyes that stood out particularly.'

'She had dark brown eyes. I've always been good on the small details. And then I showed Mr Brown the photograph we took of Miss Barleycorn, and he was adamant it wasn't her.'

'That is interesting, sir, because I sent young Constable Yates out to show that photograph of Rosie Barleycorn to a couple of other victims, who also weren't convinced she was the one involved. I always thought it unlikely, and there's little other evidence that it could be her, only Mr Foxworthy's account. And her mother claims she was at home with her at the time of the attack.'

'Mr Brown also told me that one of the men was short and dumpy with unruly grey hair, and that the woman referred to him as "Frank". The other man was tall and blond.'

'That's a good lot of detail. He didn't tell us that at the time.'

'It's something he remembered while he was recovering.'

'Twort should be back soon,' said the sergeant, 'so I'll ask him about the address, in case he can throw any light on it. He might have misheard. And I'll tell the constables the new information, in case they come across any tall blond men or short ones with unruly grey hair looking suspicious.'

Toshack was about to go to his office but stopped. 'Actually, Gardner, would you just tell Constable Yates, and ask him not to tell anyone else.'

'Why's that, sir?'

'He's good at keeping things to himself. Twort isn't.'

'Very well, sir.'

Sam's reply to the sergeant wasn't the whole story, but he didn't want to divulge his vague feeling of discomfort at this stage.

Chapter Eighteen

Annie entered the staffroom at lunchtime a couple of days later to hear Charlie say, 'I see DI Toshack's here again.'

'He's here a lot, now,' said Gertie. 'It's just you don't see him, being at the garage. He is betrothed to Mrs Bygrove, after all.'

'It's a good job none of us is inclined to criminal tendencies then,' he said, winking.

The staff laughed, knowing he was referring to his less than honourable past.

'Does the inspector know about your… you know?' Stanley Morris asked, looking up from *The People's Friend* magazine he was flicking through.

'Oh, he knows, all right. Mrs B told 'im. And if she 'adn't, I'm sure Sergeant Gardner would have apprised 'im of the information. But she's also told 'im that it's way be'ind me. Eleven years ago, that was. And I left prison in Portsmouth in 1910.'

'Seems a lifetime ago, does 1910,' said Stanley, sighing heavily. 'The war's made it seem like the time before never even existed.'

'Well, it's over now, lad,' said Will Fletcher. 'And here's some good news for you – the Football League is being resumed. You like a bit of football, don't you, Stanley?'

'I do, Mr Fletcher. I suppose that means the women won't have to play any more.'

'Why is that?' said Gertie, scowling as she looked over.

' 'Cos people would rather see the faster game that men play.'

'Have you ever seen a women's match?' Annie asked, sensing that Gertie was getting cross.

'Well, a bit of one what Gertie was playing in, up on the sports field. Just five minutes.'

'Then you're in no position to judge, are you?'

'It's not just that. I read somewhere that they reckon it's not good for women's health to play.'

'This again!' said Gertie. 'And just who is "they"? *Men*, I suppose.'

'I, um, don't remember.'

'Or silly women what don't know any better! It's a load of old nonsense. If I hear one more time that—'

'All right, all right, Miss Green, you've made your point.' Mrs Leggett put her sewing down and held up her hand, to indicate silence. 'Now is not the time for men and women to turn against each other. We've just got over one war, we don't need another between the men and women here. It's not the first time I've heard similar arguments in this room, whether it's about sport or work, or just life.'

'I bet you agree though, don't you, Mrs L,' said Stanley.

'I do agree, Mr Morris, but I agree with Miss Green and Miss Twine, and the rest of the women who would like to see women's football continue. If the war proved anything, it is that women are equal to men in skills, even if they are still not equal in law.'

'But they have the vote now,' Stanley persisted.

'How many women around this table are able to vote yet? Hands up,' said the housekeeper. 'There you are: none. The only woman in the hotel who is able to vote is Mrs Bygrove, due to her being over thirty and owning property. All the men in the hotel can now vote. Is that fair? Do you consider women's brains to be inferior for the task of choosing a Member of Parliament?'

'Well, no, s'pose not.'

'Mr Fletcher?'

'Not me,' said the old chef.

'Mr Cobbett?'

'Me? Not bleedin' likely. Reckon some of 'em 'ave got a better idea than me. Edie certainly does.'

'Any of the men around this table disagree?' asked the housekeeper.

The rest of the men there shook their heads.

'No? Good. And I, for one, hope that the women's football goes from strength to strength.'

'Thanks, Mrs Leggett,' said Gertie, looking genuinely touched.

Annie gave Mrs Leggett a big smile, to show she approved of the housekeeper's words, and Mrs Leggett smiled back.

–

Sam was sitting next to Helen in her office, as they examined the menu for their wedding reception at the hotel.

'I think that's everything arranged now,' said Helen. 'Food, flowers, the band.'

'Two weeks today,' he said. 'I still can't believe it, nor how lucky I was, meeting you.' He bent forward and kissed her lips. As he pulled away, they grinned at each other.

'Nor I. I never expected a second chance at love.'

There was a knock at the door and the two of them leant back, putting on neutral expressions. Sam cleared his throat.

'Come in,' Helen called.

Lorcan entered, announcing, 'Superintendent Crooke to see you, Inspector.' He then mouthed, 'Sorry,' and pulled a face, before Crooke marched in, hands behind his back, with that smug look of self-importance that he invariably displayed.

'Thank you, Lorcan,' said Helen, before he nodded and left.

'You have an Irish fellow greeting guests in the foyer?' were Crooke's first words. 'Don't suppose that's very popular, with all the trouble they're causing out there at the moment.'

'Lorcan is *very* popular with the guests, Superintendent, and always has been,' said Helen.

'I'd send him back where he came from. At least that German fellow you had serving in the dining room has gone.'

Sam could feel Helen's body stiffening beside him, and he knew how she felt. Crooke had to have an opinion on everything, even when he knew nothing of a situation.

'Would you like to take a seat, sir, and tell us why you're here?'

'No, I would not, Toshack. I'm here to see *you*, not the two of you. I went to the station in Littlehampton, to find out that you're *here* yet again. Are there more crimes in the hotel to investigate? If so, it's about time the place was—'

'No, sir, no crimes here. And it is a Sunday. Helen – Mrs Bygrove and I are engaged, which is why I am often here, and we're getting married in a fortnight, which is why I'm here right now, to look at the final arrangements. And after we're married, I will be living here.'

'That's not convenient. Not convenient at all. What if you're needed when you're not on duty?'

'There are two telephones here already, sir, and a third is about to be installed in the quarters upstairs.'

'It's all a bit rushed and insensitive, don't you think? It's not long ago her husband *died*, and under suspicious circumstances.'

He was talking about Helen as if she wasn't in the room and, more worryingly, as if she were somehow responsible. He wasn't having that. 'It was over three years ago now, sir. And we know who the perpetrators were, so it's hardly *suspicious* any more.'

'I'm sorry, Superintendent, but is it any business of yours whom I marry? As Sam says, they found out who the perpetrators were, and you already know that my late husband was involved in extremely dodgy dealings, and was not the kindest of men to either me or our staff.' Crooke pressed his lips into a thin line but ignored Helen, not even looking at her as she spoke.

'Anyway, if you hadn't spent so much time away from the station, you would have found out that the girl you arrested for soliciting and being part of the criminal gang on the quay, and who *you* released, has been re-arrested by me. I know how to do the job properly.'

Sam stood up. 'But the only person who has identified her as the woman on the quay is Mr Foxworthy, and we can't even find him at the address he gave. A witness said she was delivering curtains that morning to a house around the corner from hers. And we showed a photograph of Miss Barleycorn to Ernest Brown, who said it definitely wasn't her, and two of the other victims were not convinced it was her either.'

'Photographs, pah! They're often not very clear, so the other two victims were just unsure. So she was somewhere else in the morning – so what? As for Ernest Brown, it might have been another woman helping the perpetrators that day. Or, and more likely, that knock on the head he got has just skewed his memory. Yes, that's likely.'

'But he was adam—'

Crooke put his hand up to stall him. 'I want to hear no more of your unfounded and frankly ludicrous deductions, Inspector. We have searched Miss Barleycorn's house and found a couple of items belonging to victims, so that, as they say, is that. Case closed.'

Sam took a deep breath to stem his rising anger. 'But we searched the house and found nothing.'

'Then you should have done a more thorough job.'

'I can assure you—'

'That's enough, Toshack! Now, I've had complaints of a constant police presence on the quay and wharf areas in recent days, from the warehouse and workshop owners there, and I am commanding you to stop harassing them.'

'There has been no harassment, sir, only a couple of constables doing extra beats there to ensure people's—'

'You're a disgrace to the force, Samuel Toshack, a disgrace. I wish Detective Inspector Davis was coming back here and that it was *you* being sent to Worthing. Or back to Hartlepool. Or better still, back to Edinburgh, where you came from. Now, for your information, Rosie Barleycorn is in the cells at Arundel and will stay there until she can be taken to Portsmouth to await her trial. Unless her parents can get a surety for bail, which I very much doubt they can afford. Do not, and I repeat, *do not* interfere in this case again. Good day to you, *Inspector.*'

With that, Crooke yanked the door open, letting it slam against the wall, and marched out without closing it.

'Of all the…' Sam started to rise, but Helen stayed him by clutching his arm.

'There's no point making a fuss, Sam.'

'I was only going to shut the door, darling.' He took her hands. 'I'm sorry he was so disrespectful towards you. I was rather surprised when you stood up to him, but good for you!'

'It's what I've come to expect from him.'

'It's still not right.'

'I'm more worried about the way he talked to *you*,' she said.

'Hold on.' He went over and shut the door, before coming back to Helen and taking her in his arms. 'Come on now, let's just have one more look at the arrangements, and remind ourselves that we have a happy event coming up.'

'Yes, all right.'

But as they looked at the menu once more, a few things went through his mind. How had Crooke found out as much information about the case as he had, and why had he got involved in the first place? How did he know that Sam came to the hotel a lot to see Helen? And, if the warehouse owners were so concerned about a police presence, why hadn't they come to the station in Littlehampton to complain?

Something here wasn't right.

Chapter Nineteen

Annie looked out of the staff dining room window, catching a glimpse of the blue sky above the wall in the yard. She puffed her lips out, emitting a popping sound, as Lorcan came into the room, and she felt daft for making a silly noise in front of him.

'What's the matter with ya?' He placed a newspaper down on the table and sat down.

'September, that's what's wrong with me. I can't believe it's 'ere already. Summer's nearly over.'

'You wouldn't think it to look at the weather. It's a nice day. I had a walk out for five minutes earlier. It's lovely and warm, so it is.'

She joined him at the table, picking up the cup of tea she'd already poured herself. 'I always feel like that about September. Have you taken over from Mr Fletcher, with your newspaper?'

'It's just a *Littlehampton Gazette* a guest left behind in the lounge.' He turned a page. 'Look, there's a piece about that woman you know, who was arrested and then released. It says they've rearrested her.'

'What!' She took the offered paper as others started filtering in. 'But that can't be right.'

'What's 'appened now?' said Alice, placing herself next to Annie.

'They've only gone and rearrested Rosie Barleycorn. It says 'ere that she's been identified as one of the perpetrators of the muggings on the quay.'

'That's just daft.'

'Ah, I wonder,' said Lorcan. 'You know I mentioned Superintendent Crooke coming in yesterday. Perhaps he has something to do with this.'

Edie entered as he was saying this. 'Are you talking about Miss Barleycorn being re-arrested?'

'Aye, there's a piece in the Gazette about it.'

'Helen told me about it. Crooke has taken the case off Inspector Toshack and says he's found some of the items stolen in a search of her house.'

'But Rosie's mum told our mum that they'd searched their 'ouse and found nothing,' said Annie. 'And Edie, you said that Ernie Brown told the inspector that it weren't her, when he saw 'er picture.'

'That's right,' Alice confirmed. 'And Rosie's mum said she was at 'ome when the mugging took place.'

'She might have been sticking up for her,' said Lorcan.

'*And* Rosie called on our mum a coupla hours before with the repaired curtains,' said Annie. 'And all this 'ere in the paper about her being known to the police as a troublemaker is a load of nonsense. She's the quietest little mouse I've ever known. And you know what else? That Constable Twort lives on her street, so he must know she's not like that.'

'It does all sound a little fishy,' Edie agreed.

Annie felt her anger heating up a little more. 'You know what? It's me afternoon off today, so I'm going to the police station to tell 'em they're wrong. They're not taking any notice of all the stuff that proves she can't be the woman involved.'

'But what about the things found in her house?' said Lorcan.

'I don't believe it for a minute. I reckon someone's put 'em there.'

' 'Aven't you got someone to go out with this afternoon?' Alice mumbled.

Annie felt guilty again. She *still* hadn't told Alice that it was over between her and Jasper. But now wasn't the time.

'Not today. You should come with me, Alice, 'cos you can vouch for Rosie's character too.'

'I ain't got the afternoon off, so I can't.'

'Then I'll go on me own.'

'Look,' said Lorcan, 'if you're sure about this, then I'll come along with ya, like, just as moral backup.'

Annie felt a little thrill in the pit of her stomach, but it was overwhelmed quickly by her current anger, so she wasn't able to enjoy it.

'All right. Thank you, Lorcan. They might take more notice if there's a man with me.'

'Uncle Barry'll take notice of you,' said Alice.

'He ain't so far.'

She doubted they'd take any notice of her, with or without Lorcan there, but she was sure Rosie wasn't the person they were looking for, so she had to try something.

–

Lorcan opened the door for Annie and they entered the reception of the police station on Gloucester Road, behind the railway station. She was relieved to see that it was Uncle Barry on the desk. Lorcan came in behind her.

'Annie, what are you doing here?' said Gardner.

'I read that piece in the *Gazette* this morning, about Rosie Barleycorn being rearrested, and I've come to say me piece because it ain't right and—'

'That's why we're here too,' said a woman standing to one side.

Annie turned to see a middle-aged couple, coming towards her. It was Rosie's parents.

'We've been waiting ten minutes to see Inspector Toshack,' said Mr Barleycorn. 'We didn't appreciate that Superintendent Crooke turning up and turning our 'ouse upside down. Left a right mess, he and 'is men did. And it had already been searched once.'

'You have told me this already,' said Gardner.

'Well now we're telling Annie,' said Rosie's mother.

A door behind the desk opened to reveal Inspector Toshack, who came towards the desk.

'Hello Mr Barleycorn, Mrs Barleycorn. And Miss Twine and Mr Foley?'

'And now we can tell *you* too,' Rosie's mother added, pointing towards the inspector. 'Those things Superintendent Crooke claimed they found, I don't believe it. They must've planted 'em, otherwise why didn't your men 'ere find 'em when they searched, eh? And I know my Rosie couldn't've been involved 'cos she was 'ome with me. And where's Constable Twort? He knows us. He'll vouch for Rosie's good character.'

'He's out on a beat,' said Toshack.

'Then ask 'im when he comes back. You should already have done.'

'And it's appalling, the newspapers making out our daughter's a wanton piece,' said Mr Barleycorn. 'She ain't no such thing. She 'ardly even goes out. They've made 'er out to be guilty when there ain't even been a court case.'

'I'm sorry about that,' said the inspector. 'It had nothing to do with anyone at this station, I can assure you.'

'Then it must've been that *horrible* superintendent,' said Mr Barleycorn. 'He has no evidence for the way me daughter's been described by the newspaper.'

'I agree,' said Annie. 'I dunno where the *Gazette* got its information, but it's wrong. She's a nice girl. I told you this already, Uncle Barry. And Alice would've come in to say 'er piece too, if she 'adn't been working.'

'Have you something to add, Mr Foley?' said Toshack.

'No, I've only come as moral support for Annie.'

She felt that little thrill again, even though he'd probably only made this decision because he didn't like the injustice either.

Toshack turned back to Mr and Mrs Barleycorn. 'I am sorry that you've been put through such an ordeal. The search and rearrest of your daughter had nothing to do with this station, and if you want to complain, you will have to go to Arundel, I'm afraid.'

'Can't we at least see our daughter?' said Mrs Barleycorn.

'She's also at Arundel. Like I said, we had no part in what happened.'

The woman slumped against the desk. 'What are we going to do?'

'Look,' said Toshack, 'I shouldn't be saying this, but I'm not happy with how this has been handled either. I will do what I can to make sure justice is done, but I'm... I'm not sure how easy it will be with Superintendent Crooke in charge. I'll do my best. I will also speak to the *Gazette*, and I suggest you do too, give them your side of the story.'

'We had someone down our street throw a jug of cold tea at us as we was heading out,' Mr Barleycorn said forlornly. 'Luckily, it only splashed us a bit, but she was calling us and our daughter all sorts.'

'That's not to be tolerated. Give Sergeant Gardner their name and address, and we'll send someone to speak with them.' Toshack returned to his office.

'I think your work's done here now, Annie,' said Gardner, widening his eyes at her.

She nodded and turned away. Lorcan was soon ahead of her, opening the door for her once again. He was such a gentleman. She wondered what they'd do now this little episode was over. She didn't want their time together to end.

'You did your best, so you did,' said Lorcan. 'I, um, I'll let you get on with the rest of your afternoon off.'

The disappointment overwhelmed her. Was there some way she could persuade him to stay a little longer? She plucked up her courage.

'Could I buy you a cup of tea to say thank you for coming along with me?'

'Well, yes, all right. What about going to Rota's near the railway station? But I'll pay. After all, that was a grand thing you did.'

'Oh, all right. Thanks.'

They headed down the street and around the corner, walking back to Terminus Road. In the cafe, she chose a table while he ordered two teas from the counter. She'd have liked a biscuit too and would have bought a couple for them both, if she'd been buying. She didn't want to push her luck since he was paying.

He'd only just sat down when the drinks arrived, and with them, a rock cake each.

'Oh, thank you,' she said. 'I didn't expect that.'

'Thought you deserved it, having the guts to go to the police station to right a wrong.'

'Don't know if I would've done it if Uncle Barry hadn't been there.'

'But you did.' He lifted his cup of tea. 'Here's to justice.' She lifted hers too and they touched cups lightly.

They chatted about the case and about Mrs Bygrove's impending wedding. There was a short lull in the conversation, where Annie wondered if she should ask about his family. He hadn't mentioned anything recently, not when she'd been around anyway, so maybe he didn't want to talk about it. But she didn't like the silence and needed to fill it.

'If you don't mind me asking, how are your family faring in Ireland at the moment?'

'Course I don't mind you asking. Me mammy doesn't say a lot in her letters about the situation there, but at least me brother-in-law's keeping out of trouble. How about your brothers? How are they settling back in?'

'Cecil's been back a while now and settled in very quickly. Too quickly! He was soon back to teasing me and Alice, as he always did.' She felt the usual irritation thinking about it.

'Guess that's what it's often like between siblings. Me brother Patrick could be the same. Used to get on me sister's nerves.' He chuckled.

'I can understand that! But Cedric and Cyril ain't never been like that with us. The two of 'em often mention the war, but Cecil says he don't wanna talk about it. They've all got their jobs back at the farm and seem to have settled back into that well enough. Probably takes their minds off the fighting.'

'Aye, I find me job as a porter useful for that. Though when it's slow, I do sometimes find meself thinking about some of the grimmer times.'

Annie's heart went out to him. 'I'm really sorry to hear that, Lorcan. If what I've overheard from conversations with Jerry, Leslie and Stanley are anything to go by, it sounds awful. And Johnny, before the doctor sent him to Netley.'

'Aye. I wish they wouldn't talk about it. But I suppose it's their way of coping with it.' He shrugged. 'I guess we all have our own ways. Not that it helped Johnny, by the looks of it. Dwelling on it *too* much isn't healthy either. I want to look ahead.'

'That's the best thing, I reckon.'

He lifted his cup once more. 'Here's to the future.'

They clicked their cups together and she added, 'I'll drink to that.'

If only her future could include him in some significant way.

They both finished their rock cakes, and she drained her cup just after he did, aware that their time together was running out.

'That was a nice break,' he said. 'I'll get going now, so I will. Got a few things to get in town.'

She hadn't decided what else she was doing today, so said on the spur of the moment, 'I'm going to have a look in W.H. Smith's at the railway station and get a magazine.'

They rose and left. Outside the door, he said, 'See you later at the hotel.'

'Bye.'

She watched him awhile as he strolled languidly away, hands in his jacket pockets. Finally, she crossed the road and headed for the station.

Having gathered that Miss Barleycorn's parents had left, along with Miss Twine and Mr Foley, Sam stuck his head out of the door to peer into the reception area.

'All clear, sir,' said Gardner, with a small chuckle.

He stepped out properly. 'Good. I don't appreciate our station taking the blame for Crooke's handiwork. Do you think it was him who went to the *Gazette*?'

'I'd lay good money on it, sir. You convince enough people that someone's guilty, and they might as well be.'

'Aye. I'm not happy, Sergeant, not happy at all. Crooke seems determined to interfere in every important case we have.'

'Yes, sir, even before you came here, he interfered in that attack on Gertie Green back in Inspector Davis's time. It would have been 1915. That time, I thought he was just trying to kowtow to the aristocracy. But the second time he interfered, with them libellous letters, I thought there was something funny going on.'

'That's all conjecture, Sergeant. And you shouldn't let anyone else hear you state it.' He said this, even though he'd had the same suspicions himself.

'Even so. And, I could be wrong, sir, but, I've been thinking, well…'

'Come on Gardner, spit it out.'

'You know, I've always thought Twort a bit of an idiot, even before he retired. But, when he returned during the war, I got to wondering whether he might, you know, have something to do with Crooke finding out about our cases.'

'I see.' Again, he'd had much the same thought.

'And it was him what said that the witness we now can't find had identified Miss Barleycorn as the girl on the quay. I am starting to have serious doubts about it being her.'

'You're right, Sergeant. And I have been thinking along the same lines. Keep an eye on him, would you? I'd dearly like to find out whether Miss Barleycorn was really involved, and, if not, why was *she* picked to take the blame? I'd like to wrap this all up before my wedding in, what?' He looked at the calendar on the wall. 'Thirteen days. But I don't think we have anything concrete to go on at the moment. Let's keep digging. It might be an idea to start at the *Gazette*, see where they got their information from.'

'Yes, sir!' Gardner said with some enthusiasm.

'And, I think it might be all right to involve young Constable Yates, but make it clear to him that he's not to tell anyone else.'

'Yes, sir. I think you're right: Yates doesn't have much time for Twort, so I think we can trust him.'

'Carry on, Sergeant.'

'Righty ho, sir!'

Chapter Twenty

Helen and Sam's wedding day had finally arrived, and she was now Mrs Toshack. The September weather, which so far had been as warm and bright as midsummer, was no different today. They were now standing on a small road at the back of St Mary's church, a photographer taking pictures of the two of them. They were then joined by Dorothy and Arthur, who were the bridesmaid and pageboy, along with Edie as chief bridesmaid, and Sergeant Gardner as Toshack's best man.

Helen hadn't been sure about closing the hotel for the day, and allowing no bookings over that weekend, but now she was glad she had done so, as it was a blessing to be surrounded by the staff who had supported her through the war, along with those who'd gone to fight. Major Thomas, who'd played a part in proving her innocence when she was arrested, was also there, along with Mr Janus and Sergeant Gardner's wife. She'd left the newer part-time staff to make ready the hotel for their return and to prepare the wedding breakfast.

'Let's have everybody in the next photograph,' she announced.

The staff shuffled into lines, sorting out who was shorter and who taller, making sure everybody's face would show up on the image.

'Come on, Major, you too,' she said, beckoning him.

'Oh, right, me too. Lovely.'

The photographer repositioned his camera stand, looking through it several times and indicating where people should move in.

After the photographer had finished, Charlie came towards Helen and Sam. 'Would sir and madam like to make their way to the motorcar,' he said, as if he were their chauffeur. Helen's Ford Model T had been decorated with ribbons from the roof to the front of the bonnet.

'Why, thank you, Cobbett,' Helen said, grinning and playing along. 'That would be most agreeable.' She turned towards her guests, calling, 'We will see you back at the hotel.'

The staff cheered as they got in. Dorothy and Arthur squeezed on the front passenger seat together and they headed off the short distance to the hotel.

'I do feel a bit silly, going in the motorcar,' she said. 'It's only a five-minute walk.'

'You gotta do it in style, Mrs B, I mean, Mrs T. Oh, that *is* gonna take a bit of getting used to.' Charlie chuckled. 'People on South Terrace would expect nothing less of the proprietress of the prestigious Beach Hotel.'

'He's right, you know,' said Sam.

'I suppose it is a *very* special day,' she said, kissing his cheek.

'Every day's very special with you, my darling.'

–

'This all looks wonderful,' said Helen, as she entered the guest dining room and surveyed the tables laden with a delicious buffet.

Helen had chosen a buffet rather than a sit-down meal, so not many staff would be needed to serve. She felt this more casual arrangement would also help the staff attending to feel at ease. Her wedding to Douglas had been a sit-down affair. And look what had happened to that marriage!

In the conservatory there were more tables laid for people to sit at. The exterior glass doors in both rooms were open. Helen had instructed the gardeners to lay out some croquet hoops and mallets on the lawn, to give the children something to do if they got bored.

'Mrs Norris and Joseph have done us proud,' said Sam.

'They certainly have.'

'Mummy, Mummy, can I have something to eat now?' said Arthur, looking smart in his waistcoat and bow tie.

'Let's wait until everyone arrives. And I'll want to say a few words to everyone first, as will Sam, of course.'

'And Sergeant Gardner also wants to make a very short speech as best man,' he said.

'Mummy, when is the band coming?' said Dorothy. 'Edie's going to teach me how to do a Turkey Trot.'

'Not until this evening, sweetheart. Mr Janus's entertainers will be putting on a show in the ballroom first.' It was to be his wedding present to them.

'Ohoo. But I suppose that'll be good too.'

'And there'll be a lot of lovely things to eat first,' said Sam. 'I believe there might even be some ice cream with the desserts.'

Dorothy jigged up and down, reminding Helen that although she was fast growing into a young lady, she was still a little girl at heart. She stopped suddenly, looking thoughtful, before going to Sam's side.

'Now you're married to our mummy, are we allowed to call you Daddy?'

This question took Helen by surprise, and by the look on Sam's face, it had come as a surprise to him too. Arthur looked on hopefully, his head tipped to one side.

'Well, um, aye, I don't see why not. If you really want to, I'd like that.'

'Yes please,' said Arthur.

'Our father's been gone two-and-a-half years now,' Dorothy said forlornly. 'To be honest, I hardly have any memories of being with him. He was always doing something else. Even when he was supposed to be taking us out somewhere, he'd often be too late because he'd been to the golf club, or playing tennis. You've been much more like a daddy to us already.'

Helen felt herself welling up and she could see that Sam was touched too. He put an arm around each of them and pulled them towards him. 'I'm sorry you don't have many memories with your dad, but I promise you I will do my very best to be a good father to you.' He kissed each in turn on their head.

Douglas had never shown that kind of affection for them, which had hurt her many times. A tear did now drip down from one eye as she watched them. The rest of the staff who were guests filtered into the room, chatting.

'Look, there's Elsie,' said Arthur. He scampered off with his sister, calling the little girl's name.

There were already waiters and waitresses in the room, handing out champagne and soft drinks.

Edie came over to the newlyweds, smiling, but was soon looking worried. 'Helen, whatever is the matter? You're crying.'

'Nothing's the matter, in fact, everything is wonderful, and this is a happy tear.' She dabbed it with her finger.

'Oh, Helen.' Sam put his arm around her and pulled her towards him, kissing her forehead.

Edie took her free arm. 'I'm glad to hear it, Mrs Toshack. You said you wanted to get the speeches over and done with first.'

'Yes. We might as well do them now, if everyone's arrived, especially as the drinks are being served, then we can get on with enjoying the buffet.'

'I'll get everyone to quieten down then.'

'Yes please.'

Edie had a commanding voice that carried, and she was good at organising people. 'Ladies and gentlemen, pray silence, please. The bride and groom would like to say a few words.'

Sam beckoned Sergeant Gardner over, who was chatting with his wife and Charlie. He held up a thumb and hurried over.

'You start,' Sam said to Helen.

'Are you sure?'

'Yes. It seems fitting as they're your staff.'

The last of the chatter ceased and Helen took a deep breath.

'Ladies and gentlemen, thank you so much for coming to our wedding. We'll be eating soon, but first of all, we would like to say a few words…'

—

Alice stood with Annie in the ballroom, tapping her foot to the band, which consisted of several brass instruments, violins, drums, a clarinet and guitars. She watched as Edie taught Dorothy the steps of the Turkey Trot, a dance she'd already more or less worked out by observing them.

She looked around the room, her eyes widening as she spotted Bridget Turnbull having a go at the steps with Major Thomas, both of whom were laughing at their efforts. There was a lovely atmosphere in the room, with everybody joining in with the spirit of the occasion.

' 'Ave you seen Mrs Turnbull and the major?' she asked Annie.

'They danced together at Edie and Charlie's wedding too.'

'I wouldn't mind 'aving a go at this.'

'We could 'ave a go together. It don't look too 'ard.'

'That'd look a bit sad,' Annie decided.

'Edie and Dorothy are dancing together. Look, even Arthur and Elsie are 'aving a go. Ah, they're so sweet. It's a wedding, don't be such a misery.'

'I'm not. Oh look, Mrs Leggett's dancing with Walter! I didn't think anybody'd get 'er on the dance floor.' She pointed to where the housekeeper was being led by Fanny's American husband.

A bit like you then, thought Alice, but didn't want to spoil the occasion by saying so.

Alice's heart fluttered as she saw Jasper and Lorcan approaching, clutching a glass of champagne each.

'It's a grand affair, don't you think?' said Lorcan stopping next to Annie. Jasper came to a halt on the other side of him.

Annie simply nodded, so Alice said, 'It's wonderful. Never been a guest at anything as lovely as this.'

'Are you ladies not dancing?'

'Not unless standing still is a new dance,' said Annie, chuckling. 'I wouldn't be at all surprised if it was.'

What had got into her all of a sudden, cheering up so quickly? thought Alice.

Lorcan laughed too, and Jasper grinned. It was normally her who made the jokes. Though, as always, with Jasper there, she felt rather lost for words. And if he and Annie went off to dance, she knew she wouldn't enjoy the occasion nearly as much. It was strange though, that they hadn't already taken to the dance floor, or even spoken much today.

'D'ya want to have a go?' Lorcan asked, holding out his free hand to Annie.

Alice was confused. Why would he do that when he knew she was walking out with Jasper? She fully expected her sister to decline, and was surprised when she said, 'Yes, I fancy a dance.'

Lorcan placed his glass on a nearby table and led Annie away.

This was awkward, being left with Jasper, especially after some of their recent encounters. She was in two minds whether to say anything, then ended up blurting it out.

'Don't you, um, mind?' He was still standing a couple of paces away.

He moved closer. 'Mind?'

'That Lorcan's dancing with your, er, sweetheart.' Even saying the word made her stomach squirm.

He pulled his head back a little and looked confused. 'We haven't been walking out for over a month. Didn't Annie tell you?'

'No, she didn't.' Alice felt a surge of irritation. Had her sister kept it to herself to punish her in some way? 'Did she break up with you?'

'No, it was mutual. We both decided that it wasn't going anywhere and that we'd only really been friends all along. I'm surprised she didn't mention it.'

Only friends all along? 'She can be secretive like that, sometimes.' It wasn't really true, as they'd always shared so much in the past, but recently their relationship had become a little strained.

He put his drink down. 'Do you, you know, fancy having a dance? I won't be offended if you say no, as I'm not sure if you like me much.'

Her heart sank. In her effort not to make it obvious how fond she was of him, she'd gone too much the other way. She'd suspected as much, but to have it confirmed troubled her.

'Why do you think that?' she asked, knowing full well what the answer was.

'Because you've been off with me quite a few times since I got back from the war. I wish I knew what it was I'd done. We used to get on quite well before I enlisted.'

'I thought that *you'd* got something against *me*. Especially after that *look* you gave me, about a month ago, when you passed me in the corridor. A real scowl, it was.'

He scrunched up his forehead as if thinking hard. 'If I was scowling, it wasn't anything you'd done... So, is that no to a dance then?'

What to do? If she danced with him, she might make a fool of herself and then— She stopped the thought right there.

'Yes, I would. Oh, the tune's finishing.'

'And another will start. Come on.' He put his glass down and held out his hand, which she took. The warmth of it made her tingle all over. This party had just got a little bit better.

—

Helen and Sam came to a halt at the end of a tune, deciding to have a rest for a while. They stepped into the garden for some air. The sun had disappeared behind the wall to the west, creating a red glow that became pink as it climbed higher in the sky. He stood behind her, his arms around her waist.

'The wedding and reception have all gone better than I even dreamed,' she said. 'It is so different to the starchy affair of… well, never mind.'

'Your first wedding?'

'Yes, sorry, Sam. I shouldn't even be thinking about it.'

'Don't apologise. I've been thinking about my first wedding too. That was also a starchy affair; Olive's parents made sure of that.'

'At least the marriage that followed was happy.'

'Aye, until she died.'

Helen turned to face him, stroking his cheek. What a fool she was, reminding him of that terrible time, when he lost Olive in the German naval attack on Hartlepool in 1914. 'I'm so sorry, Sam. I really shouldn't have started talking about this.'

'It's not as if I hadn't already thought about it. We're both bound to, aren't we?'

'I'm looking forward to going away tomorrow,' said Helen. 'A few days in Dorset will do us both good.'

'Aye, it will. I just wish I'd got to the bottom of the attacks on the quay. And we still haven't located the witness who Twort took the information from. I wish now that Gardner or one of the other constables had—'

She touched his arm. 'Sam, forget that for today. I know how keen you are to clear that girl's name, and to find out what's really going on, but you need some time away from it. And Sergeant Gardner is perfectly capable of running things while you're away for a few days.'

'Aye, I know. Sorry. I don't want to spoil our special day.'

'I just hope the children will be all right. I've never been away from them for more than a day. Well, apart from that time you arrested me.' Her attempt to conceal a smile failed.

He raised his eyebrows. 'It was only to keep you near,' he joked.

'And, of course, the time Inspector Crooke arrested me.'

'That man! Now he's someone I really *would* like to forget on our wedding day.'

'Sorry.' She placed her arms around his waist and pulled him to her.

'As for the children, Vera is very capable, and you know how the staff here will rally around.'

He always knew the right things to say to make her feel better. She kissed his cheek. 'I know. And they'll be at school for much of that time.'

Alone in the garden, they shared a long, lingering kiss, bathed in the golden light of the sunset.

–

Annie gazed out of the window, watching the silhouettes of Helen and Inspector Toshack against the glorious dusky sky. They were kissing and it made her envious.

She looked back into the room, to see Lorcan now doing a foxtrot with Phoebe. She had hoped that they'd have a few more dances, and, maybe, he'd have stayed by her side for the rest of the evening. What an idiot she was.

Of course he wouldn't. He was just being friendly, getting her to join in. With Günther gone, Phoebe was free now, so maybe he'd take an interest in her.

Jasper was still dancing with Alice, which she should have been glad of, but there was that voice in her head, and it belonged to their mother. She could just imagine what she'd say if Alice got married before she did. Some speech about being left on the shelf and how nobody would want her if she left it too long.

'What ya looking at?' said Jack, passing by, as one of the tunes came to an end.

'The happy couple,' she lied.

'I'm so glad for Mrs Bygrove. She deserves happiness.'

'Mrs Toshack,' Annie reminded him.

'Oh yes, her too!' he joked. 'Come and have a dance. I don't suppose we'll get many chances to attend a function like this.'

'Don't s'pose we'll get *any* more chances.'

'Nah, you're right.' A new tune started, and they could see people copying Edie and Charlie, who seemed to be doing well. 'How'd they get to learn these new dances?'

'Her brother and sister-in-law taught 'em, apparently,' she said.

'I've no idea how you do this one, but I'm willing to have a go.'

'Come on then. If Mrs Leggett can manage it, I'm sure we can.'

Chapter Twenty-One

Jim Marwood sat on a half-broken chair in one of the rooms they'd had fitted in the old warehouse Frank had rented on the west bank of the river. Marta handed him a cup of tea which he sipped. It was already lukewarm.

'I 'eard that manageress at the Beach 'otel got married yesterday, to that Inspector Tosh, or whatever 'is name is,' she said.

'Detective Inspector Toshack,' he replied. 'Yes, I knew it was in the pipeline.' Alice had told him as much.

Frank pushed the door open roughly, beckoning Marta. 'Get yourself dressed up and get into room four, gal. Sir Anthony Wilkins'll be 'ere soon.'

She strutted out, her expression suggesting she was bored. Frank pushed the door back in its place none too gently.

'I wanna word with you, Jim. You ain't managed to get me any good information about the Beach 'otel still.'

'You had me in Portsmouth for the last few months; I can't find out stuff here if I'm there, can I?'

'All right, enough of your lip. You've been back over a month. 'Ave you met up with that blonde bint again yet?'

'No. I haven't had time.'

'That Mrs Bygrove must be worth a bit and they'll likely have a pretty penny in a safe somewhere. I need to know 'ow to find it quickly, what're the best times to break in, and where. And some of them guest bedrooms'd hold a few valuables.'

'It sounds to me like there are always staff around, so I'm not sure how wise it'd be to try anything.' He didn't know if that was true at all, but he'd lost the heart to carry on with this little escapade.

'You won't know for sure until ya do a bit more digging. Get the gal to show you around one evening.'

'Too risky, Frank. There's a couple of people who live there who'd recognise me, I've no doubt.'

'What, Jim the Chameleon, what can turn into anyone 'e likes? Isn't that 'ow you described yourself when you first joined me operation?'

'Look, the girl's only a stillroom maid, not a chamber-maid, with access to the rooms, and even if she were, I told you she's not like that. And how would I find out anything from her without looking suspicious?'

'Why the 'ell did you pick 'er then? She sounds a right drip.'

'I didn't know what she did or what she was like when I picked her, only that she worked there. You told me to watch the staff who came out the side entrances, so that's what I did. And having not contacted her in several months, it'd look a bit odd if I turned up now. Why don't you just break into the hotel in the middle of the night, like you would anywhere else?'

He was about to take another sip of tea when Frank grabbed his collarless shirt around the neck and squeezed it tight, causing Jim to spill his tea all over himself. He dropped the cup as he tried to breathe, and it smashed onto the ground.

'You listen and you listen good. If you don't get some useful information from 'er, or find some way of getting into the 'otel without being spotted, you'll be the next one needing a pauper's funeral, like that silly cow Pamela when Gordon 'adley did for 'er. Except *your* pauper's funeral'd likely be a quick ditch in the river on a dark night. They might 'ave night porters or a security guard for all I know. That's the information you need to get, you useless piece of trash.' Frank pushed him away and he fell off the chair. 'Of course, *I* could always go there one night and look out for 'er coming off 'er shift and force the information out of 'er.'

'She always walks home with her sister,' he said, though he knew it wasn't always the case.

'I'll take Clegg with me and we'll choke the information out of the two of 'em.'

'No need to do that, Frank. I'll contact her.'

'Do it now, then. You can send young Bob over with a message.' He went to the door, calling, 'Bob? Bob! Come 'ere,' as Jim picked himself up off the floor.

A young lad scurried through the door. 'Yes Frank?'

'Jim's got an errand for ya. I've got somewhere else to be.' He left.

Bob looked over at him expectantly.

'I'm going to write a letter that I'd like you to take over to the Beach Hotel.'

'What, that posh one on the common?'

'That's the one. There's an entrance on the left, the staff entrance, that leads to the scullery. If you knock on the door, ask for Alice, and say you have a note for her. She works in the room next door to the scullery, so they should be able to fetch her if she's there. If she isn't there, you can leave it for her. If she is there, ask if she can send a reply straight away.'

'Right.'

'Hold on a moment, and I'll write it now.'

He went to a set of drawers where they kept all sorts of paper and took out a plain sheet and envelope. He quickly wrote an apology for not being in touch, saying that he'd been sent away on a few jobs recently by the newspaper. He added that his mum had been ill in Hampshire, and he'd had to visit her a few times too. That wasn't true either, but it would make his excuse for not contacting her look better. He asked her when she had some time off so that they could meet. If she couldn't send a reply straight away, or if she didn't receive the letter until later, he wrote that he'd send Bob back tomorrow for a reply.

He'd never had any qualms in the past, writing bogus letters, being part of conning people with false documents and the like, but now, it didn't feel so good. He'd picked Alice because he'd liked the look of her, and she'd turned out to be rather sweet. He'd left her alone after the fair for that reason, hoping Frank wouldn't pursue his project to steal from the hotel. But what else could he do now but try again to get some information? If he didn't, Frank might really do for him. You never knew with him which way he'd turn, and quite small failures could make him do unbelievably nasty things. And he might also carry out his threat against Alice and her sister.

He placed the sheet inside the envelope, then wrote 'Alice Twine' on the front.

'There you go, Bob. And if anyone asks, you're a runner for the *Sussex Daily News*, right?'

'Yes, Jim.'

'Oh, and I'm called Jamie as far as she's concerned, right?'

'Yes, Jim. Jamie.'

'Right, off you go now, and come straight back. I'll have a few coppers for you when you do.'

The boy beamed and hurried away, leaving Jim doubting the wisdom of what he was doing more than ever before.

Chapter Twenty-Two

'You're not seriously going out with that Jamie this evening, are you?' said Annie, who'd waited until Lucas had gone from the scullery for the middle dinner break.

She had not been happy since the note had arrived for Alice two days before, delivered by some scruffy little urchin who'd claimed to be a runner for the *Sussex Daily News.* He'd been back a couple of times as they'd exchanged notes and worked out when they were both free.

'Yes, I am going out with him,' Alice said defiantly, removing her apron. 'And me shift's over now, so I'm gonna go and get changed.'

'But you can't just go off with 'im on your own when you 'aven't seen 'im in four months.'

'I've got the evening off, so yes, I can. We're going to the Electric Picture Palace to see a film, so it's not like we'll be on our own.'

Annie leant forward, speaking in a low whisper, aware that those in the stillroom might get wind of an argument. 'You'll do no such thing, going out with a stranger without a chaperone.'

'A chaperone? What century do you live in?' Alice whispered. 'And he is *not* a stranger. Now stop this. I don't insist you have a chaperone when you go out with *Jasper.*'

The longer she'd left it, the more awkward it felt to tell her sister about the situation. 'No, well, I, that is… he's not a stranger. We've known 'im for years.'

'It don't make no difference. I *am* going and I do *not* need a chaperone. And frankly, it's none of your business.'

'If our parents and brothers weren't away at Grandma and Grandpa's, I'd tell 'em and they'd stop you.'

'I doubt it. You know how keen Mum and Dad are to get us married off.'

'Not to someone they don't know nothing about. And you going out means I 'ave to walk 'ome by meself at night.'

'You'd 'ave had to anyway tonight, as I'd've gone 'ome if I wasn't going out with Jamie. And you've done it plenty of times before, when we've been on different shifts. Anyway, if you're that worried, you could ask *Jasper* to walk you 'ome. Maybe he'd stay over too, with the rest of the family away.' She said this in a slightly higher voice, pulling a mocking face.

Annie gasped. 'Alice! How could you suggest such an improper thing? I would *never* allow that. And I 'ope you ain't thinking of staying over with Jamie.'

'No, I'm *definitely* not.'

'Anyway, as for Jasper…' Now was as good a time as any to tell her. '…It's just, well, it's not like, that is—'

'You're not walking out with him no more.'

'What? You knew?'

'Jasper mentioned it at the wedding. He was surprised you 'adn't told me. Why didn't you?'

'I dunno, didn't get around to it.' The guilt hung even more heavily on her now.

'You should've left him alone in the first place. You only went out with him 'cos you thought I liked him and you were being mean.'

'No, I thought you'd gone off him, the way you talked about him. You said he was all right, nothing special. And you had a go at him several times. So, you do still like him?'

Alice shrugged. 'He's all right. Quite a nice fella.'

'You 'ad a few dances with him at the wedding.'

'He's a good dancer. Anyway, I'm going to get ready now, or I'll be late.'

Alice headed into the stillroom as Lucas re-entered the scullery. Annie recognised that expression on her sister's face. She'd seen it many times over the years, like that time she tore her favourite dress and Mum had used it for a patchwork quilt. Alice had put on that false smile and pretended it was all right. Mum hadn't seemed to notice, but Annie could tell her sister wasn't happy. Had she put on that expression when they'd talked about Jasper before? If she had, she hadn't noticed it, or had been determined not to. What a terrible sister she'd been.

Five minutes later, Alice was back with her hat and undone overcoat, revealing the dress she'd made a few months back.

'Bye, Alice,' Lucas called.

'Bye. And Annie, don't bother waiting up for me. And I've got an earlier shift than you tomorrow, so I won't be walking in with you.'

'But—'

'Bye.'

Alice left the building. Annie went to the window and watched as she exited the gate in the twilight. Despite what her sister had said, she would wait up for her. She had the latest *Anne of Green Gables* book to read, which would while away the time.

–

Alice was waiting outside Read's Dining Rooms, gazing at the dark gold of the sky, willing Jamie to arrive. She looked at her wristwatch. He was already a couple of minutes late. Five minutes later, she spotted him coming from the direction of River Road.

'I am sorry to be a little tardy,' he said as he approached. 'I got out of the office late.'

He seemed a little awkward, as he had been when they'd first met. He'd told her he was shy with people he didn't know, but surely, even with the break, he didn't still feel like that in her company?

'Don't worry. There's still plenty of time.'

'It's so nice to see you again.' He smiled, which helped her relax a little.

'How come you was away on so many jobs?'

'Well, you know, that's how it happens sometimes. The editor found a couple of other possible big stories and wanted me to go undercover, pretend I was somebody else.'

'That seems a little… underhand.'

'Sometimes it's the only way to get to the bottom of something. And, uh, it's something I'm good at.'

'That's strange, isn't it, when you're so shy being your-self. You should have been an actor.' She nudged his elbow with hers, grinning.

'Maybe I should.'

'How is your mother now?'

'She's, yes, much better. Thank you… I am really sorry, Alice. I should have written to you before.'

'That's all right. You were obviously busy. We're going to the Electric Picture Palace, then?'

'If that's all right? There's a film called *Green Eyes*, which is meant to be quite good.'

'That's fine by me. I always like a good film.'

'Let's go then.'

She thought he might put his arm through hers as they went along, but he didn't.

'What have you been doing the last few months then?' he asked. 'What's been happening at the hotel?'

'I've been working as usual but there's been lots going on. We've 'ad a few wedding receptions, what with men coming 'ome and wanting to marry their sweethearts. And we've 'ad three weddings among the staff since I last saw you. Edie and Charlie got married in June, Lili and Rhodri in July, and Mrs Bygrove married Inspector Toshack only three days ago. They're away in Dorset at the moment, but the inspector's coming to live at the 'otel when they get back.'

'A policeman living at the hotel?'

'Yes.' She chuckled. 'That *will* be a little strange. I guess it could be handy, especially with what we've 'ad going on there the last few years.'

'Yes, I, er, suppose it will.'

'Did you 'ear about the attacks on the quay? You must've done as they've been reported in the local papers.'

'Someone did say something in the office earlier, though I was away when most of them happened.'

'One of the victims was Ernest Brown, what was staying at the 'otel. Poor bloke ended up in 'ospital and had an 'eart attack while he was there. Just a small one, but still. Rotten blighters they were, whoever was responsible. I talked to Mr Brown, just outside the 'otel, about three weeks before. On Peace Day, it was, and he seemed like a very nice fella. Came from nowhere by the sounds of it and made a fortune during the war with his munitions factory.'

'It would have been better if there hadn't been a situation in which he had the opportunity to make that much money,' he said, sounding very serious.

'Well, yes, of course. But that wasn't *his* fault?'

'I suppose not.'

They'd reached Terminus Road by this time, where the picture house sat almost opposite the railway station.

'So, when is Mrs Bygrove back with her new husband?' Jamie asked.

'Mrs Toshack now. And they're back tomorrow.'

'Not a long stay away then.'

'She don't wanta be away from the children too long, I think, and he's busy with the quay attacks. They've arrested someone, but I don't think the inspector's convinced she's guilty. And neither am I, 'cos I know her, but that Superintendent Crooke up at Arundel's convinced it is her. Both the *Littlehampton Gazette* and your newspaper wrote some horrible things about her, which I know for a fact ain't true.' She stopped and clutched his arm, halting him. 'Hey, you could maybe do a piece about it, showing how she couldn't be guilty. She's got an alibi and everything, and me mum even saw her only a coupla hours before she was meant to be involved in attacking Mr Brown.'

'Well, I don't think, that is, I'm given my assignments by the editor, I'm afraid. I can't poke my nose into someone else's story.'

'That's a shame.'

'Come on, there's a bit of a queue, and we want to get some good seats.'

He took her hand as they hurried to the entrance, and she wondered if he'd put his arm around her in the picture house.

—

When they emerged from the picture house it was not only dark, but a little chilly too. She was disappointed that Jamie hadn't put his arm around her as they'd watched the films. He hadn't even held her hand. Yet, at the same time, she didn't feel she was quite ready for that. The shadow of Jasper still hung over her and, although their relationship had improved, and she'd even danced with him, she didn't think he was any more interested in her than he had turned out to be in Annie.

'Did you enjoy the main feature?' Jamie asked.

'I'm not sure I did. The woman's 'usband seemed very jealous and flew into rages every time someone even looked at his wife. He didn't seem very nice. He reminded me too much of Mr Bygrove, what used to run the 'otel. Not that he got jealous of his wife, but he was mean to her and a real bully, as I told you before. I don't like bullies.'

'No, I know what you mean. Look, I'd really liked to have taken you for something to eat now, but it's too late. You could pop back to mine for a bit. I have got some nice coffee and some rather tasty biscuits from Groom's.'

'I'm not sure—'

'I'll walk you home afterwards, then I'll know you'll be safe. I won't try anything, honestly. I do get rather lonely of an evening.'

She had the feeling that he didn't make friends very easily, despite his job, so felt sorry for him. And she would appreciate being walked home at this time of night, despite what she'd said to Annie. On top of that, she was glad he wasn't scuttling away again, like he had the last couple of times.

'All right. I do like a nice biscuit.'

'We might as well head down the alley here then.'

'I thought you lived on Maxwell Road.' She pointed in the direction of the station, as that road was among the newer roads behind it.

'Yes, I, er, did have a room there, but I've just moved to River Road. I have a couple of rooms there, just past the King's Arms.'

They headed to the narrow alley known as Hampton Court, which led to River Road but, just as they entered, she realised her handbag was open.

'Hold on a mo,' she said, looking inside it to make sure she hadn't lost anything. Her purse and door key were there, along with her comb and some lip rouge. She couldn't think of anything else, so clicked the clip shut.

'Everything all right?'

'It is now, ta.'

Reaching the house he lived in, he let them in and led her into a room downstairs, close to the front door. On one side of the room was a short worktop upon which sat a small cast iron stove containing two rings. Next to that, was a small sink. The tiny table had two chairs. There was a door on the wall opposite, which she guessed led to his bedroom. Next to that was a bookcase with various things on. Was this all he could afford on a reporter's wage? Maybe they didn't get paid as much as she imagined.

He filled up the kettle from the tap and put it on the stove, then placed some coffee grains from a paper packet into a coffee pot.

'We'll have to wait for the kettle to boil.' He sat on the other chair, his head leaning against the wall. He lifted the centre of his glasses up with his forefinger and thumb and rubbed the bridge of his nose, before replacing them. 'So, how's the hotel doing? Got any interesting guests?'

'Not that I've heard about, and I would hear if there were any. They all seem very run of the mill at the moment.'

'It's coming to the end of the summer season now. What do your guests do with themselves during the day? Or evening.'

'The Casino Theatre's open all year and there are still some entertainments on nice days. But some of 'em 'ave motorcars, so they can go off for the day to Worthing or Brighton, where there are theatres and entertainments. And then there's Arundel with its castle. And we still put on the odd show or event for charity, though not as many as we did in the war. Of course, I don't normally get to talk to the guests, being in the scullery.'

'The scullery? I thought you were a stillroom maid.'

Darn it, she should have been honest in the first place. She didn't want to confess now, so she'd have to think of something. She did hate being dishonest. Why had she been so worried that he'd look down on a scullery maid?

'Yes, sorry, or the stillroom. I should've explained. I'm in the scullery sometimes if they're short, as I was today. Either way, it's just the same. I don't get to see the guests unless there's a big function and a buffet, and they want staff to serve drinks in the dining room or ballroom.'

'It must be strange, being confined in that space, with the same people, day after day.'

'Aren't most people? Workshops are the same. Even the waiters and porters at the 'otel are in the same spaces. I suppose you get out and about though, as a reporter.'

'Yes, I get out and about. What's it like, the staff area? You've only talked about the stillroom and scullery before, and a staff dining room? It's a big building.'

'It is, and even the staff area has a few other rooms. Apart from them three rooms, there's the kitchen, of course, and a few storerooms. And Mrs Toshack's office.'

'Her office? Does she spend a lot of time in there, or does she do other things around the hotel?'

'A bit of both, I suppose. In the war, she often filled in for other jobs when we were short, especially manning the desk.'

'What's it like at night? Are there night porters?'

'Just one. After the desk clerk goes home at ten, a porter sits on the desk.'

'That must be a boring job. What about—'

He was interrupted by a rapping on the front door.

Jamie looked confused. 'Who's that now? Might not be for me, of course, but I'd better go and answer it.'

While he was gone, she had a look around the small space. There were quite a few books on the shelves. She spotted a few by P.G. Wodehouse. Jamie must be a keen reader, but then he was a reporter so also wrote things, so it made sense. Maybe, one day, he'd write a book too.

On the other shelves, there were some copies of the *Littlehampton Gazette* and the *Sussex Daily News*. There was a chipped saucer with bits and pieces, including an old wedding ring. She wondered if it might have belonged to one of his grandmothers. There were also a couple of tie pins. One of them was silver with a fox's head. She'd seen him wear this. The other was gold, with what looked like a large pearl in the middle. It was probably a fake pearl, and maybe not real gold either.

Wait a moment.

She picked it up. She'd seen this tie pin before. Or one exactly like it. It was a dead ringer for the one Ernest Brown had been wearing that day she'd talked to him. And didn't someone say that it had been one of the items stolen from him when he was mugged on the quay? Did Jamie perhaps buy it from the thief, not knowing it had been stolen? It must have been sold cheaply then, because he'd never have been able to afford what it must be worth.

Maybe Jamie would have a description of the seller that he could give to Inspector Toshack, to help him catch the perpetrators. She'd ask him about it when he returned.

–

As Jamie headed for the front door, he recalled his conversation with Alice about not liking bullies. What a hypocrite he was, as he'd often acted like one himself. And 'acted' was the right word. It wasn't something he enjoyed but was often a case of self-preservation, and not getting on the wrong side of Frank.

He opened the front door, surprised to see his boss there.

'What do you want, Frank?' he whispered. 'I'm trying to get that information you want, from Alice.'

'She 'ere, is she? You trying to get something else out of 'er too?' He grinned lasciviously.

'No, I'm not. Just the information. Now, what do you want?'

'I've come for that silver tea set you was looking after.'

'It's a bit awkward with her here. It's in a box in my wardrobe.'

'Just bring it out in the box then and say it was a present you was looking after for a friend or something.'

'Right. Hang on a moment.'

He went back to the room, starting with, 'It's just a friend who wants to pick up a present I was—'

He stopped suddenly, his heart pounding. She was holding the tie pin they'd stolen from that bloke Frank had knocked out on the quay.

—

'Sorry, I didn't mean to go through your things. I was looking at the books on your shelves, when I saw this tie pin,' said Alice. 'I've seen it before. Mr Brown was wearing it when I spoke to 'im. Where did you get it? I reckon whoever sold this to you might be… what's wrong?'

There was a look of panic in his eyes that she couldn't quite fathom to begin with.

'It can't be the same one. That was—'

Another man appeared at the door. He was short with messy grey hair. She was assuming it was the friend Jamie had mentioned, when he leapt forward and grabbed her, muffling her mouth before she had a chance to scream. She struggled, but he gripped her even tighter. He smelled of something pungent that she couldn't name, but it made her feel sick.

'What the hell are you doing?' said Jamie.

'We can't 'ave this little bitch running to the police with this information.'

Was this awful man connected to the muggings? And, if so, did that mean that Jamie was, too?

'If you'd stayed at the front door, I could have handled it, Frank.'

'Nah, you've gone too soft. You're a bloody liability. Fancy 'aving the tie pin on display. You shoulda locked it away, with everything else.'

Oh lord, oh lord, she thought. He *was* involved. He must have been all along.

'I had a buyer for it.'

'Get some rope to tie 'er up. And something to gag 'er.'

'No, Frank, I can't—'

'Just bloody do it, or I'll do for you.'

She tried to struggle once more, but he placed his arm around her neck.

'You move again you little bitch, and I'll strangle you.'

Jamie went into the other room and returned with several slim pieces of rope and a long piece of fabric. Frank tied her arms behind her back, then tied up her legs. He pulled the rope far too tightly and it bit into her wrists and ankles, but she daren't even moan. Her breathing became rapid and her heart thumped as she felt a rising panic. She'd always been a little claustrophobic, and the thought of not being able to move her limbs frightened her.

Finally, he wrapped the fabric around her mouth and eyes several times, knotting it at the back. Not being able to see increased her anxiety, making her feel giddy. She was then pushed roughly off the chair and tumbled to the floor, unable to stop herself hitting it with a thud, and unable to prevent herself from whining. Her cheek and arm felt sore.

'Shut up!' Frank hollered, close to her head. 'We'll take 'er to the workshop and decide what to do with 'er there,' he said, now further away.

What to do with her? Would they try to silence her for good?

'Fetch a blanket, Jim, and wrap 'er up. There might be a few blokes 'anging around outside the pubs, so you can pretend you're carrying your sleeping little sister. People won't be able to see much in the dark.'

Jim?

'But I warn you, you little bitch,' Frank continued, 'that if you make as much as a peep, I'll see to you meself. You understand?'

She nodded.

Jim. It was just another shortening of James, after all, but something was bothering her that she couldn't quite work out at this moment. And the anxiety she was experiencing wasn't helping.

Chapter Twenty-Three

Annie awoke feeling bleary and uncomfortable. Her eyes fluttered open and she was confused at first. Then she realised she was still sitting in the armchair in the kitchen. There was light coming through the curtains, so it was morning already. She must have fallen asleep, reading. She pulled herself up, realising the book had slipped to one side.

Why on earth hadn't Alice woken her up when she'd got in?

She rose and went to the stairs, about to call up, when she realised that Alice would have already left for her early shift. She looked at the clock on the mantelpiece. It was nearly eight o'clock. Yes, she'd be long gone. And again, why hadn't she woken her?

Maybe she'd got in late and had overslept, in which case, she'd need waking up. She went to the stairs, dragging herself up to their shared room. Pushing the door open, she saw that Alice wasn't there.

About to go back downstairs, she decided that she might as well wash and get ready now, even though she wasn't due at the hotel for a couple of hours.

Alice must be really annoyed with her for having a go about Jamie; that would be why she hadn't bothered to wake her up. She'd give her a piece of her mind when she got to work.

Charlie Cobbett was enjoying his trip out in Mrs Toshack's Ford Model T on this sunny morning, heading up past the warehouses on River Road, whistling a merry tune. It was only a short trip to collect some motorcar parts, but it was good to be away from the garage for a while. And he'd always enjoyed driving, even if so far it had only ever been in other people's motorcars. Maybe, one day, he'd be able to afford one of his own.

He brought the vehicle to a halt, then bent down to pick up a piece of paper on which he'd written what he needed, as it had fallen on the floor. As he rose, he saw a familiar figure crossing the road. He ducked back down a little, peeping over the dashboard. He'd recognise that mop of grey hair and pale skin anywhere, and that short, chunky body that slumped as he walked.

It was Frank Steel, who'd got off scot-free with the robbery they'd committed all those years ago, while he'd spent two years in gaol. He'd thought he'd seen him a few months ago, walking past the garage on Norfolk Place, but he'd decided he must be mistaken. So, he *was* still around. And, knowing him, he'd still be up to no good.

As Frank disappeared down the road, Charlie pulled himself up properly again and watched him. What should he do? Edie had suggested going to the police when he thought he'd spotted him before, but it had seemed a flimsy reason to go. But this time…

Charlie got out and cranked up the motorcar to start it, then got in and reversed, before turning it around. The trip to the police station would only take a couple of minutes, and the parts would still be ready to collect when he got back.

He parked outside the station on Gloucester Road and got out, looking up at the brick building. It still didn't feel right, going voluntarily to the police after his experience before, but he was here as a responsible member of the public now. It was only right.

Inside, he was relieved to see Gardner at the desk. When the sergeant looked up, Charlie could see the surprise in his face.

'Hello there, Mr Cobbett. And what can I do for you?'

'This is gonna sound a bit strange, Sergeant.'

'I'm used to strange in my line of work. What's the problem?'

'You remember when you arrested me, all them years back?'

Gardner looked puzzled. 'I do. And?'

'I dunno if you remember this bit, but I told you there was some bloke called Frank Steel involved.'

'I do remember, as it happens. Never found him, we didn't.'

'No, but I might 'ave.'

Gardner leant on the desk, coming closer to Charlie. 'How'd ya mean?'

'I was in River Road, about to collect some motor parts, when I saw 'im. I'm dead sure it was 'im.'

'But it must be, what, a dozen years since you've seen him.'

'Eleven years since we did that job at the ironmonger's. But I actually saw 'im four years back, just before I enlisted. He approached me on the common while I was watching a performance, and tried to get me involved in one of 'is schemes again, and I said no. He said he'd been back a coupla months. Then I spotted him a coupla weeks later, on Norfolk Road, and I reckon he was looking for me.'

'You didn't tell us that at the time.'

'No, 'cos that was the day I enlisted. He was part of the reason I did. Didn't want 'im getting his dirty mitts on me again. Oh, and I thought I saw 'im back in April, near the hotel garage, but I wasn't sure then.'

'I'll certainly make a note of it. Could you give me a description?'

'He must be in his early forties now, but looks older, haggard. He's short, with a thatch of grey hair what reaches his neck. Pale skinned, freckly and thick set.'

'Thank you. Not sure what we can do with it at the moment unless we find him involved in something nefarious, but it could be useful.'

'What about the robbery I was arrested for?'

'A good point, but it was a fair few years ago now, so might just be your word against his.'

'Hmm. Not sure I wanta come up against him again anyway.'

'And I can't imagine Superintendent Crooke up at Arundel being impressed with us opening an old case.' He looked heavenward.

Charlie tutted. 'I 'eard a rumour that he's become involved with them attacks on the quay. Annie and Alice reckon he's arrested the wrong woman.'

'And don't I know it! I've heard nothing else from them.'

'And he caused a lotta trouble for Mrs Bygrove, as was.'

'But, anyway, I shouldn't be talking about a current case. Or about Crooke, come to that.'

'It won't go no further.' Charlie tapped the side of his nose twice.

'Right, let me get this down.' Gardner started to make notes on a piece of paper, asking Charlie to repeat some of the details. He was just finishing up when he said, 'Hang on. Frank Steel?'

'Yep, that's 'is name. Is it ringing a bell?'

'Not the Steel bit, but Frank. River Road, you say you saw him. That Ernie Brown what was staying at the hotel and was attacked on the quay...'

'What about 'im?'

'He said the woman involved referred to the "short, dumpy one", as he put it, as Frank. And he had, hang on.' Gardner went to a drawer and got out a file. 'Here we are. *Short and dumpy, with a great unwieldy mop of grey hair, looked in his late fifties, maybe.* That's what Mr Brown said. Late fifties though. You said early forties.'

'And like I also said, haggard. He's always looked a lot older than his years. And the rest of the description is spot on.'

'Oh, yes, and Mr Brown reckoned he had an East London accent.'

'Yep, that'd be right too. He came from a place called Poplar originally, in East London. Sounds like too much of a coincidence to me.'

'My thinking too,' said Gardner. 'I wish the inspector was back.'

'Isn't he due back today?'

'Yes, not till a bit later though.'

Through the front door walked a constable who looked like he should have retired years ago. With him was a young man, clearly inebriated.

'Morning, Twort.'

'Morning, Sergeant. Just giving this lad some time alone in a cell, till he sobers up.'

'Righty ho.' When Twort had gone, Gardner leant forward. 'Better keep this to yourself for now, Cobbett. And I definitely don't want *him* finding out.' He pointed towards the door to the cells.

'Constable Twort? Any particular reason?'

'Not anyone else's business, lad.'

'Gertie said he was a bit useless, keeping an eye on the post office a coupla years back, when the libellous letters were being sent.'

'He was, but don't go around telling people that. I think that's all, Mr Cobbett.'

'Cheerio then, Sergeant.'

Charlie was about to leave, when Gardner called, 'Hold on a moment.' He beckoned him back to the desk. 'You don't happen to know if Frank Steel had anything to do with Gordon Hadley, do you?'

'Him what killed Edie's old landlady? Nah, I'd never 'eard of Hadley before that happened.'

'What about a tall, blond young man called Jim?'

'Again, no. But that name's been raised before, so I've been told. Something to do with some young man Gertie met called Jimmy, what disappeared?'

'All speculation, but worth following up.'

'Sorry I can't 'elp. If they 'ad, or 'ave anything to do with Frank, it must have started after my time.'

Constable Twort re-entered the area.

'Anyway, thank you for the information, Mr Cobbett. We'll certainly look into it.'

'You're welcome.'

As Charlie left, he heard Twort say, 'What's all that about, then?'

'Just a report of someone looking suspicious on, er, Pier Road.'

Charlie smiled to himself. The sergeant really didn't want Twort to know about it. He felt a little better now, having reported the information. He'd head back to River Road but keep a look out for Frank. He didn't want to face him ever again – especially on his own.

–

Alice awoke feeling dizzy, and too tired to open her eyes properly. She'd had a terrifying nightmare, though she was hazy on the details. Then she noticed the musty smell, not like her bedroom at all. And she was cold.

She slowly opened her eyes, confused. Her room was white, but this was a light grey. Her wrist was aching so she tried to move it, then realised she couldn't. Had her hand gone to sleep? She looked at it, blinking. Then the night before came flooding back and she felt like she was drowning in the reality of what had happened. One of her wrists was handcuffed to a pipe on the wall. A salty bile filled her mouth, and she had the urge to be sick.

Under her was a thin mattress that had been placed next to the wall, and she was covered in a grubby blanket. She pulled herself up as far as she could and looked around the room. It was small and square, with a window high up on the wall where she was manacled. Her ankles and both her wrists were still sore from being tied up the night before. From outside, she could hear what sounded like a van's motor and then a motorcar horn. She must be near a road.

Where had they taken her? There'd been a blanket over her head as she'd been carried away from Jamie's rooms – *Jim's* rooms. She had no idea whether they'd turned right or left on River Road. She'd heard some noise from what was probably a couple of public houses, but that would have been the case whichever way they'd gone. And she wasn't at all sure how long they'd been walking. Five minutes, ten? Maybe even twenty. She'd been concentrating too much on not crying, in case this Frank had carried out his threat, and on the pain caused by the ropes. But it surely couldn't have been that far.

She'd been bundled into a dark room, which must have been this one. Yes, she remembered now, someone untying her and putting on the handcuffs. After which she'd cried herself to sleep.

Her tears fell once more, as she replayed what had happened. Had Jamie, Jim, planned this all along? It didn't sound like it from what he'd said, but she could be wrong. What *had* he wanted from her? Maybe he had only wanted to walk out with her. But whatever it was, she'd been wrong about him being a nice man.

Her sniffs became sobs, and she leant her head against the wall. What a fool she'd been. Annie had been right all along.

Annie! She knew she'd gone out with Jamie. When she realised she hadn't come home, she could tell the police. But she'd told her sister that Jamie lived on Maxwell Road, so how would they find her, wherever she was?

Jamie. Jim. Something had niggled at her the night before, but as they'd carted her away and she'd panicked, she hadn't been able to work out what it was. And that nightmare she'd had, there was something in it, some connection she'd made. But what?

Jamie, Jim… Jimmy.

That was it!

There'd been a Jim who Edie had said had been involved with her fellow boarder, Pamela. He'd

318

disappeared when she'd been found dead, and they'd wondered if he'd been involved.

And then there'd been a Jimmy, who had turned up at Gertie's football matches. He'd been curious about someone at the hotel who'd turned out to be a nasty piece of work. And then he'd disappeared. A connection had been made at the time, but no one had taken it seriously.

The two men both had something in common, which, in turn, they had in common with Jamie. They were all described as tall and blond.

She felt a cold dread creep over her, and she started shivering. What was going to happen to her? Even if she was wrong about the connection, she still knew too much, had seen too much.

She heard the door on the opposite side of the room being unlocked and was only mildly relieved to see it was Jamie, not Frank. His brow was creased, and he looked sad. He wasn't wearing glasses today.

'I've brought you a cup of tea.'

'You're *horrible*.' She forced out the words but didn't speak too loudly. 'I thought you was really nice, but you're, you're… a nasty piece of work.'

He looked down, still clutching the tea. 'I'm sorry. I do like you, but this is business.'

'Business? What are you going to do, sell me?'

He looked up, horrified. 'No! I mean, you found something that's to do with the business I'm involved in. I'd have found some excuse as to why I had the tie pin. I wouldn't have got you involved. It was unfortunate that Frank turned up at that moment.'

'So why *did* you pick me to walk out with?'

He looked down once more, pressing his lips together. 'You work at the hotel, and Frank wanted information about it. I'd decided not to pursue it after the May Fair, and I was sent to Portsmouth for a while anyway. But he insisted I carry on when I got back. He's not a man to cross.'

'So, you're not a reporter at all.'

'No.'

'And you're actually called Jim, not Jamie.'

'I'm called James. People call me Jim now, but my parents used to call me Jamie.'

She wanted to carry on, accusing him of being a crook, but she didn't want to turn him against her. He might be an ally against Frank if he decided to do something bad to her. Should she mention the connections she'd made? No, best to keep that to herself.

'Here, have this tea while it's warm,' he said, placing it in her free hand.

She sipped at it awkwardly, realising she was thirsty. Outside the door, she could hear a woman complaining, and a deeper voice that she suspected was Frank's. Her heart thumped as she willed him not to come into the room. Jim crossed his arms and leant against the opposite wall, looking forlorn.

–

'You gotta cuppa tea for me in that pot?' said Charlie, as he entered the staff dining room. Edie was there with Gertie and Lili.

'You took a while to pick up those motorcar parts,' said Edie, pouring him a cup.

He sat down opposite the women. 'I, um, went to the police station to, er, report something.'

Gertie lunged forward, eyes wide. 'What's happened?'

'If I tell you, you have to keep it to yourselves for now, right?'

They nodded, all looking eager for his news.

'I'd just parked up in River Road, when I spotted Frank, you know, the bloke what got me robbing the ironmonger's all them years back.'

'Frank Steel?' said Edie. 'You thought you saw him a few months back.'

'Yep. Looks like I might've been right. I wasn't sure then, but I sure as 'eck am now. I kept a low profile, 'cos I didn't want him spotting me. Once he'd disappeared, I drove around to the police station and reported it to Sergeant Gardner. I'm glad it was 'im on the desk and not one of the others. Particularly that Twort.'

'Oh, he's useless,' said Gertie, flicking her hand as if dismissing the man.

'I have to say, Gardner don't seem too keen on 'im neither. He didn't want 'im to 'ear what I was saying, for a start. Anyway, the sergeant realised that my description was exactly like the one that Ernie Brown gave, when he was mugged on the quay. He said the woman called the short, dumpy man, Frank, and that he 'ad an unwieldy mop of grey hair. Just like the Frank I knew.'

'You think it could be the same person, then?' said Lili.

'Sergeant Gardner certainly seems to think so. He also asked me if I knew whether he had a connection with Gordon Hadley, or with a young blond man called Jim.'

'Who were connected to my landlady's and Pamela's demises,' said Edie. 'Well, Hadley definitely was, and Jim had a connection to Pamela, who they think was a, you know, *lady of the night*.' She whispered the last bit.

'Yep. So, I think he's looking forward to Inspector Toshack getting back so they can investigate it. And, like I said, let's keep it to ourselves for now.'

'By the way,' said Lili. 'You 'aven't seen Alice on your travels, 'ave you? Mrs Leggett says she 'asn't come in for her shift and she was on an early one.'

'No, I ain't seen 'er. Isn't Annie here?'

'Not due in till ten-thirty she isn't. That's not long now. Maybe Alice isn't well.'

'That's probably it,' said Charlie, as others came to join them for the break.

Chapter Twenty-Four

Annie pushed the door open into the scullery, to be greeted by both Lucas and Finn exclaiming, 'Annie!'

'That's me. I'm not late, am I?'

'What's up with Alice?' said Finn. 'Is she ill?'

'Ill? What are you talking about?'

'She didn't come in for her shift first thing,' said Lucas. 'It's just been us all morning. Luckily it ain't been too busy.'

'What do you mean, she didn't come in? She must 'ave. She's not at 'ome.'

'Honestly, Annie, she ain't here,' said Finn.

Annie stopped dead still. Had she stayed over at Jamie's last night? In which case, was she still there? Or, or...

'I've gotta see Mrs Toshack.'

She was about to rush off when Finn called, 'But she ain't here neither. She's still away.'

Annie stopped dead. 'Of course she is. Then I'll 'ave to find Edie.'

She ran through the stillroom into the corridor, to see the undermanageress coming out of the dining room.

'Edie! Finn and Lucas said Alice never showed up.'

'No, we assumed she was ill.'

'She ain't ill. I checked the bedroom this morning and I assumed she'd gone to work. I fell asleep in the sitting room, 'cos she went out with that Jamie last night, and when I woke up, I assumed I 'adn't heard her come in and she'd just left me there.'

'You think she might not have come home at all?' said Edie.

'I do. Which means she's missing.' Annie felt the rising panic, finding it hard to breathe.

Mrs Leggett came out next, with Charlie, who said, 'Alice is missing?'

Annie told them the story again, noting their increasingly worried expressions. 'I told her not to go, that it wasn't a good idea to go out with him at night, but she wouldn't listen. She 'ardly knows the bloke.'

'Where does he live, this Jamie Sparks?' said Charlie.

'He told her Maxwell Road a few months back. But I don't know where. And that he works as a reporter at the *Sussex Daily News*.'

'I think we should call the police,' said Edie.

–

'I'd better go,' said Jim, when the argument between Frank and a woman ceased. 'I'll bring you some food soon.'

He opened the door but moved back several steps as Frank entered. What did he want now?

'What you doing in 'ere?' He looked over at Alice. 'Bringing 'er tea? Don't be so bloody soft.'

Behind Frank stood another man, recently employed, who Jim had taken an instant dislike to. He didn't know his first name, as he was always referred to as 'Clegg'. He was tall, though not as tall as him, but he was broad in the shoulders, his rolled-up shirt sleeves displaying a large mass of muscle.

Jim glanced at Alice to see her cowering.

'I wanna talk to you in me office,' said Frank. 'And don't come in 'ere again without asking.'

He led the way to what he called his office, at the front of the warehouse. Clegg followed on, standing behind Frank when they reached their destination, his arms folded across his ample chest.

Frank leant his hands on a very untidy desk. 'We've gotta work out what to do with 'er.'

'Her?' said Jim.

'Bloody Alice. If push comes to shove...'

'No, Frank. She's done nothing. Maybe it's time we closed the operation in Littlehampton. It's a small place, and sooner or later someone's going to recognise one of us. We could disappear.'

'And do what with madam?'

'Um, tie her up and leave her somewhere remote to be found, like, oh, West Beach. We could leave her there one night, do a flit, and be gone by the time someone found her in the morning.'

'Don't be bloody stupid. I've spent a lotta money fitting out this warehouse, making it look like we're up to something legit. I ain't giving it up now. And we've a thriving business 'ere, among them what want it and can afford it.'

Thriving for you, thought Jim, who had never made as much from it as his boss had originally promised.

'I suppose we could take 'er to the operation in Portsmouth,' said Frank. 'They'd like 'er there. Especially the sailors.'

Jim wanted to avoid that at all costs. 'For pity's sake no, she'd be no good at that.'

There was a knock at the door and Marta came in. She was wearing a low-cut dress in the modern, straight style, a little shorter than was fashionable.

'You asked to see me, Frank?'

'I've just 'ad a telephone call from Mr Berringer. He'll be 'ere soon, so get one of the girls into room five. And tell Bob to put some other bit of woodwork out the front, so it looks like we're working.'

'Whatever you say, Frank. By the way, Harold's 'ere, saying he's not 'appy with 'is share this month and wants to speak to you.'

'Tell 'im I'm busy for the moment, and you can keep him 'appy for an hour or so, can't you?' He raised his eyebrows.

'Never 'ad any trouble doing so before,' she said, grinning to one side.

She left and Frank took a seat. 'Sit down, both of ya. I wanna discuss our plans for the next week. And maybe we'll come up with a solution for *sweet* little Alice.'

He said this mockingly. Jim's dislike of Frank had been growing over the years, but now he hated him more than ever before.

–

Sergeant Gardner arrived with young Constable Yates twenty minutes after Edie telephoned the station, and now several of them were sitting and standing around the staff dining room.

'So that young man I saw her with on the quay that day, she was walking out with him?'

'Yes, Uncle Barry,' Annie admitted. 'She didn't want you to go telling our parents, which is why she said she didn't know him. I didn't like the sound of him from the start.'

'And his surname is Sparks,' said Gardner.

Annie nodded. 'Jamie Sparks. He claimed to be a reporter at the *Sussex Daily News*.'

'You've met him?'

Annie shook her head.

'I did, briefly,' said Fanny. 'He seemed a bit *too* shy, like he didn't really want to meet us. He couldn't even look at us. Walter thought 'im a little odd too. A bit later that day, we saw 'em on the quay and went to say 'ello again, but he'd gone by the time we'd walked over. Alice said he'd remembered he 'ad to be somewhere.'

Gardner got his notebook out. 'Could you describe him?'

'He was very tall,' said Fanny. 'It was the first thing I noticed about 'im. And very blond, with a small gingery beard and glasses.'

' 'Ang on a moment,' said Charlie, coming forward. 'A tall, blond bloke called Jamie? Remember our conversation earlier, Sergeant?'

'I certainly do, Mr Cobbett, and I think I know where you're going with this.'

'Oh, my gawd!' Gertie's hands flew to her cheeks. 'You're not thinking what I think you're thinking, are you?'

'Probably,' said Charlie. 'Tall, blond, mysterious, disappears suddenly and called something short for James.'

'What, you think he might be that fella, Jimmy, what Gertie met by the sports field last year?' said Fanny.

'And the same as the Jim I saw with Pamela at the guest house?' Edie added.

'You said he was tall, skinny and blond, as I recall,' said Gardner.

'He was,' Edie confirmed.

'But Jimmy didn't 'ave a gingery beard,' said Gertie. 'Or glasses.'

'He could have grown the beard quickly enough,' said Gardner. 'And glasses would be easy enough to get hold of.'

'There must be more than one tall, blond man in Little-hampton called James.' Lili didn't sound convinced by her own argument.

'We might be completely on the wrong track,' said Gardner. 'But, I dunno. Like you said earlier at the station, Charlie, it's too much of a coincidence.'

'What were you at the station for?' Annie asked.

'I, um. Look, I saw that bloke what got me involved in that robbery all those years back. Frank. I went to report it, that's all.'

'Do you think he's involved with this Jamie fella too then?' Annie felt even more frightened now. What if Alice had somehow got involved with someone from a gang?

She noticed Uncle Barry and Charlie glance at each other and knew she must be right. A terror gripped her heart.

'I'm sure he ain't got nothing to do with it,' said Charlie. 'Just a coincidence that I saw 'im this morning, that's all.'

This didn't make Annie feel any better.

At this moment, Mrs Toshack and her new husband entered the room.

'Hello everyone,' said Helen, smiling. 'How has everything been going? Oh, Sergeant Gardner.'

Annie's tears came suddenly, not giving her any time to stifle them. Helen's smile slipped instantly.

'What on earth has happened?' said Toshack.

'Alice has gone missing,' Gardner replied.

Chapter Twenty-Five

Sam had listened to Annie's story, then Sergeant Gardner's and Charlie Cobbett's theory about the three men who might be the same one.

'Aye, I remember that coming up last year, when we dealt with that maid who caused a lot of trouble here, Susie Shorn.'

'It's time people went back to their shifts, or whatever else it is they have to do,' said Mrs Leggett, standing.

'We'd like to help though,' said Lili.

'I'm not sure how you can at the moment,' said Sam. 'Unless anyone else has any information?'

The was a mumble of 'no' and most headed for the door.

'Let us know if we can help though,' said Lili. 'Going out to look for her, or whatever.'

Gertie went over to Annie. 'I 'aven't got a shift now, so would you like me to stay with you?'

Annie nodded and Gertie sat next to her. Helen took a seat on the other side of her.

'I'll go and help in the scullery as they'll be a bit short-handed like,' said Mrs Turnbull.

'And I shall bring some more tea in,' said the house-keeper.

Sam was always impressed by the way they rallied around to help each other here. It had certainly got them through some sticky times in the past few years.

Charlie, still in the room, approached Sam with Gardner, who had his helmet clutched under his arm. 'Inspector, could we have a word in private?'

'Aye.'

They went to the corridor and waited for a couple of stragglers to leave.

'What is it, Gardner?'

'This morning, Mr Cobbett here reported seeing a man called Frank Steel in River Road. Steel is the man who was involved in the robbery with Charlie back in 1908, but he disappeared and was never brought to justice.'

'Aye, I remember you telling me about the case. What's it got to do with this?'

'Frank Steel fits the description of the short stocky man that was involved in the attack on Ernest Brown.'

'Yep,' said Charlie. '"Dumpy", the sergeant said he was described as, which would fit. And with a bush of grey, untidy hair and an East London accent. That's Steel to a tee. And I did see him on the Common, four years or so back, when he tried to get me involved in something again.'

'And you saw him today on River Road?' said Sam.

'Yep. Kept me 'ead down as I was in your wife's motorcar, collecting some parts, but it was 'im all right.'

'And the man on the quay with the short, dumpy fellow, whether it was Steel or not, was described as tall and blond,' said Gardner.

Sam looked up and blew out a long breath. 'Aye, he was, you're right. Just like this Jim, Jimmy, Jamie, or whoever he is. Or they are. Right. Thank you for reporting the sighting, Mr Cobbett. There may or may not be a connection, but it's somewhere to start.'

'I'd better check back at the garage as I've left me assistant in charge this morning. If you need any help looking for Alice, though, you know where I am.' He sauntered off towards the stillroom.

When he'd disappeared through the door, Sam said, 'If there is a connection, we're going to have to get involved in the quay attacks again.'

'Didn't Crooke tell us to stay out of it?' said Gardner.

'Aye, but I've never been inclined to take orders from him. If I'd obeyed him three years ago, when Helen's first husband was killed, I'd never have got to the bottom of that, or all those thefts taking place.'

'It's like we said before, sir, it's as if there are selected crimes he doesn't want us involved in.'

'Aye. But we'll keep that theory under wraps for now, Gardner.'

'Of course, sir.'

'Now, I must get back to the station to brief the rest of the team. Gardner, you go with Yates to the *Sussex Daily News* office on Terminus Road. Ask if this Jamie Sparks does indeed work there. If so, and he's there, ask him to come to the station. If he's not there, find out where he might be, or what his address is, and see if you can locate him so we can interview him as soon as possible. It's possible that this Jamie is genuine and that she stayed with him last night. She might even still be with him now.'

'Don't think me niece would do that, sir. Always been a decent girl.'

'I've no doubt, Sergeant, but we've got to ask. It's also possible that she went missing after they parted company. If we could find out where that took place, it might help.'

'And if we can't locate him?'

'Just come back to the station.'

It might not be good for her reputation, but he hoped that Alice Twine was still with this Jamie and hadn't really gone missing, for her sake and that of her family. Especially if those two thugs from the quay were involved.

–

Lorcan came into the dining room for lunch with Jasper, having just been relieved of their shifts.

'Has something happened? A guest said they saw a coupla policemen leaving the—'

Jasper nudged him, and he saw that Annie was sitting at the table, crying, with Gertie holding her hand on one side and Mrs Leggett the other.

'What in the name of Mary and Joseph has happened?'

'Oh, Lorcan,' she sobbed, unable, it seemed, to get any other words out.

'It's Alice,' said Gertie. 'She's gone missing.'

'Missing!' exclaimed Jasper. 'What do you mean?'

Gertie told them the story, as other people trickled in and were soon listening intently themselves.

As the story unfolded, Lorcan felt ever more miserable for Annie. He wasn't sure why he felt quite this bad; he guessed it was the idea of a sibling being lost. But he also felt sorry to his heart for Annie, who was clearly heartbroken.

'I told 'er, told 'er, *not* to go,' she sobbed. 'I just had a bad feeling about the whole thing. And… and something's going on, 'cos… 'cos Charlie reported something this morning, about a bloke called Frank Steel and… and I dunno, I've got a feeling that they think there might be a connection.'

'Where does this Jamie live?' said Jasper, sounding riled and concerned at the same time. 'We should go around there, see if Alice is there. He might be holding her against her will or something.'

'She… she told me Maxwell Road. I told the police.'

'The police will go there, I'm sure,' said Mrs Leggett. 'Inspector Toshack implied before he left that they were going to look for her.'

While other people expressed their worry and sympathy to Annie, Lorcan stepped to one side with Jasper and nudged him. 'You're not walking out with Annie any more, are you?'

'No. Haven't been for a while. But I still feel… wretched for her. And I'm worried sick about Alice.'

'I always thought you had a soft spot for her, so I did. That's why I thought it a bit odd when you started walking out with Annie.'

'I did have a soft spot for Alice. I still do. And we used to get on so well before the war. But she seemed to have something against me when I got back. Yet we got on again at the wedding reception. What can I do? I've got to do something.'

Lorcan patted his friend on the shoulder. 'Inspector Toshack's a good policeman, from what we've heard. I'm sure he'll do all he can. And Sergeant Gardner's part of Alice's family, so he definitely will.'

'Their family!' Jasper turned and headed to the table, through the throng of people who'd gathered there. 'Annie, have you contacted your family in Hampshire?'

'I… I can't. There's no telephone at my grandparents' home. And they're not due back until Sunday.'

'Everybody, sit down,' said Mrs Leggett. 'Lunch should be here now. I'll go and see what's happened to it.'

She got up, and Lorcan soon sat in her place. He took Annie's hand as the housekeeper had done. 'It must be a huge worry for you. I know how I'd feel if me brother or sister went missing.'

'It's all my fault. If I hadn't... I hadn't... ohhh!'

He put his arm around her, and she leant against his chest, letting go of Gertie's hand. He liked the feeling of it, which made him feel bad under these awful circumstances.

'Of course it's not your fault. You warned her it was foolish. What else could you have done? She's a grown-up. You could hardly stop her by force.'

'But if I hadn't... hadn't... She wouldn't have gone out with Jamie in the first place.'

If she hadn't *what*? Maybe they'd had an argument that day and Alice had decided to go out with Jamie to spite her. Or... another possibility occurred to him. Maybe Alice had liked Jasper too, as he liked her. If Annie hadn't walked out with him, maybe Alice wouldn't have ended up with Jamie? It didn't pay to speculate, but Annie was clearly blaming herself for something.

Lorcan glanced over at Jasper, who looked a picture of misery.

Will Fletcher and Jack came into the dining room, each carrying a tray of bread rolls with ham and cheese. The housekeeper followed on.

'I know a lot of us will feel too worried to eat,' said Mrs Leggett, 'but we need to keep our strength up. Maybe we will be able to do something to help when we find out more.'

The staff there slowly picked the rolls off the trays and started nibbling, looking glum. Jasper sat at the end of the bench but ate nothing.

'Come on, Annie,' said Lorcan. 'Like Mrs Leggett said, we need to keep our strength up, in case Alice needs our help.'

Annie picked a cheese roll off the tray and took the tiniest of bites. Lorcan took one too, eating with a little more enthusiasm to encourage her, though he'd lost his appetite now.

The door opened and everyone looked up to see Sergeant Gardner in the doorway. He came over towards Annie, stopping a foot from the table.

'I've just called at the *Sussex Daily News*. They say that there is no staff member, reporter or otherwise, named Jamie Sparks. Nor has there been in the past. Are you sure you got the surname correct?'

Annie dropped the roll onto the plate, her face pale. 'Yes, Uncle Barry. It was definitely Sparks, because I remember asking if he was related to the people what own the big furniture shop.'

'All right. The inspector is organising things, so we'll get onto the other information we have. I'd better get back.'

After he left, Annie said, 'What other information, though? There's nothing else much to go on.'

'They might have information we don't know about,' said Lorcan, though he didn't feel very hopeful himself.

—

Sergeant Gardner's news had Jasper's insides twisting and turning with unease. This Jamie Sparks, or whatever he was called, was a bad sort; he must be, otherwise why would he lie about being a reporter? He should have tried to sort things out with Alice before, not just assumed that she'd taken against him. He couldn't just sit here, waiting for more bad news.

He stood suddenly, making Lili, next to him, jump.

'I'm sorry,' he said, 'but I can't just sit here. We've got to do something. *I've* got to do something. I'm not on duty again until later this afternoon.'

'Neither am I,' said Gertie, turning on the end of the bench and getting off.

Annie was soon following her. 'You're right! There's no point just sitting here.'

'But it could be dangerous,' said Mrs Leggett. 'And where would you even start?'

'Well, well…' Annie's brow creased, and she seemed to be thinking. 'The Electric Picture Palace! Of course. I should have told the inspector about that. It's where they were going last night. I completely forgot.'

'Or it's where Alice *thought* they were going,' said Gertie.

'Either way, it's a start,' said Jasper, a little more optimistic now a plan was forming.

'I'll come too,' said Lorcan. 'The more of us there are, the better chance we'll have.'

Charlie rose. 'I'll give an 'and too. It might be better if I went to the beach and 'ad a look along there. Me dad's at the garage this afternoon and he can cope without me for a coupla hours.'

The beach. Jasper shuddered inside, remembering that it was where they'd found Mr Bygrove's body a couple of years back. No, he couldn't think like that.

'I'll come with you,' said Lili. 'Jerry, Simon and Dennis'll have to cope without me. It's not like we're full up at the moment.' She got up and hurried from the room.

'Count me in,' said Jack. 'I'm not on again until after two. I'll scour the beach area with Charlie.'

'I will walk up to Wick to make sure she hasn't gone home in the meantime,' said Mrs Leggett. 'You're right – it's better to be doing something than just sitting here waiting for news. Though I'd better go and tell Mrs Toshack what's happening.'

'I'll come with you, pet,' said Mrs Turnbull. 'The store cupboards can wait a few hours longer.'

Jasper looked around at them with appreciation as they all went to fetch their jackets or coats.

'Thank you, Jasper,' said Annie, passing him, 'for encouraging people to do something. I appreciate it. And I'm sure Alice would too. Especially as I believe she has a soft spot for you.'

'She does? But I thought—'

'I'll explain later.'

'Yes, yes, we should go now,' he said, and followed the others to the corridor.

Chapter Twenty-Six

'Good afternoon, madam,' said Jasper, through the gap in the window at the box office in the foyer of the Electric Picture Palace. 'I was wondering if you remember a young lady and gentleman who might have come here yesterday evening. If you were working here then, of course.'

'I was, but I serve a lot of people every day, lovey. You're going to have to be a bit more specific than that.'

'She would have looked quite a lot like this lady here.'

Annie walked forward. 'She's my sister. Her hair's a bit lighter than mine, but people always say we look quite similar.'

'Hmm, can't say I do really.'

'What about a very tall man, very blond. Slim.'

'Ah, now that rings a bell. There was indeed a man like that, 'cos I remember thinking he was quite handsome and a bit unusual. I wondered if he was maybe Scandinavian, but he sounded English. He had a small gingery beard too, and glasses.'

'Yes, that could be him,' said Annie, sounding excited.

'So, he was here last night?' Jasper asked.

'If it is the same one, yes. He was a bit shy and didn't seem to want to make eye contact. Are you the police? Has he done something wrong?'

'No, I'm not the police. We just need to track... that is, to talk to him about something important.'

'Come to think of it, there was a young lady with him, but I didn't get a good look at her.'

'Thank you for your help.'

'There's a good film on today, if you want to see it.'

'Maybe another time.' Jasper smiled to show his appreciation.

'Are you two wanting tickets?' she asked Lorcan and Gertie behind.

'No thanks,' Gertie called. 'But again, thank you for your help.'

The woman looked curiously at them as they left.

'At least we know she was probably here with him,' said Lorcan, once they were outside. 'It looks like he did take her to the picture house, as she said he would, Annie.'

'You think that he might have been genuine, then?' she asked. 'And that something happened after she left him?'

'No, I'm not saying that. The fact that no one at the *Sussex Daily News* has heard of him tells us he's still a fraud, so it does. But we know at least that she was here. Where next?'

'We could go up to Maxwell Road and knock on doors, see if anyone knows him,' said Jasper.

Lorcan shook his head. 'If he's not even called Jamie Sparks, it seems unlikely anyone would have heard of him. And if we ask if they know a Jim or Jimmy or Jamie, that's much too broad a question. For all we know, he's not even called James and the whole thing is a deception.'

They walked along a few yards. When they reached the alleyway known as Hampton Court, Jasper stopped. 'Charlie said he saw that Frank Steel character on River Road. Why don't we have a look there? Although "Jamie Sparks" is probably an alias, he might have used the name for other things. We could ask at the warehouses there, see if anyone's heard of him. Or if they've seen a tall, blond man with a ginger beard.'

'We need to be careful,' said Gertie. 'If Frank Steel 'as associates on River Road, and he might do since Charlie spotted 'im there, we don't wanna alert them to us snooping around.'

'True,' said Lorcan. 'But it wouldn't hurt to take a look.'

They all agreed and set off down the alleyway.

They'd only gone a few steps when Jasper spotted something on one side. 'Hold on,' he said, bending down to pick it up.

'What is it?' said Gertie.

'It's an 'andkerchief.' Annie gasped. 'It's Alice's 'andkerchief! Look, it has 'er name on it and a rose. I embroidered it meself. She must have come down 'ere. We should tell the police.'

Jasper felt the despair wash over him once more. 'Let's have a look further down first, in case we see something else. We need to give the police as many clues as possible.'

They started down the alleyway once more.

On River Road, Lorcan asked, 'Which direction?'

Jasper looked both ways. 'Let's head towards the bridge. That's the way Charlie said he saw Frank Steel go. If they're connected, they might have a place around there.'

They started off, but Lorcan halted them. 'Maybe you ladies should stay behind. It might not be safe.'

'I'm going nowhere,' said Annie defiantly.

'Nor me,' said Gertie. 'We weathered a helluva lot in the war. I'm not gonna be a chicken and run away.'

'All right, but let's be careful, like.'

On River Road they headed down the pavement next to the houses, peering over at the side with warehouses, in case they should spot anything. They were just passing the

King's Arms when they spotted a tall, blond man coming out of a front door, a couple of houses on, carrying a cotton bag with something in it. Jasper, who was leading, pushed them all back so that they were standing by the side of the public house, peering around, hidden from the man's view. They watched him walk in the direction of the bridge.

'Is that him, Gertie?' Jasper asked. 'The fellow who called himself Jimmy?'

She peered around a bit more, then stepped out a little. Jasper went with her. They saw the man look up at the windows of the house, then walk on. Gertie and Jasper joined the other two once more.

'I'm pretty sure it is. He don't 'ave that heavy overcoat on, nor the hat, but, yes. When he turned to the side, it did look like 'im.'

'I'll wring his blasted neck,' said Jasper, stepping out once more. 'I'll find out what he's done with her.'

Lorcan pulled him back. 'Don't be an eejit. He might be violent, or have a weapon, or both.'

Jasper took a deep breath to calm himself down. 'Then let's tail him from a distance. See where he goes. Gertie, you walk behind us, so he doesn't see you. He won't know the rest of us from Adam.'

They stayed on the side with the houses, trying to keep him the same distance ahead as they went along. At the end of the street, where it continued to the wharf, he turned left and started heading over the bridge. They held back a few seconds until he was partway across, then followed on again, passing a motorcar paying the toll. They were halfway over the bridge when it drove past them, hooting its horn. They all turned away from the direction the blond man was going, in case he looked back and spotted them.

With the motorcar gone, they carried on, Gertie still behind them. They chatted, as if on a day out together, making light talk. At the corner of his eye, Jasper could see that the man was heading towards a large metal warehouse with a curved roof, on the right-hand side of the road. There seemed to be no company name on the premises.

'Right, Annie and Gertie, you go to the police station and tell them we've found him, Jimmy, Jamie, whatever,' said Jasper.

'I'm not going nowhere. If there's a chance that Alice is 'ere,' said Annie. 'I wanta make sure she's all right.'

'I'll go on me own,' said Gertie. 'I'm a good runner so will get there quicker anyway.' She set off immediately at quite a speed.

'You and I should approach the warehouse and find out what's happening,' said Jasper.

Lorcan nodded. 'Agreed. Annie, you stay here. If the police arrive, you can tell them where we are or get help if needed, so you can.'

'But there might be violent criminals there.'

'If there are, and Alice is there, the quicker we rescue her the better.'

'Don't do anything stupid,' she said.

Lorcan laughed mirthlessly. 'We faced worse in the war, I've no doubt. Keep your distance, Annie, so they don't realise you're with us if anything happens. If you stay here, looking upriver, you can keep an eye on the warehouse. If anything is amiss, or we don't reappear in the next five minutes, you can get help. Hopefully, it won't be too long before the police get here.'

'Be careful.'

Coming off the bridge, and approaching the warehouse, Lorcan spotted a few bits of abandoned narrow lead piping on the side of the road, by a bush. He bent down and picked up a couple of pieces, gesturing to Jasper to hide behind the bush with him.

'Here, stick that up your jacket.'

Jasper looked down at the piping for a few moments before taking the offered piece. He wanted Alice to be here, for them to find her, but at the same time feared that she'd been taken by people who'd need to be handled with this kind of thing.

Hidden from the road and the warehouse by the bush, they peeped around it and saw the blond man light a thin cigarette and smoke for a few minutes. After he'd stubbed it out with his foot, he started a conversation with a man in a suit who'd come in the opposite direction. The discussion seemed to turn into a disagreement, before the suited man nodded and looked around as if checking whether anyone was around. He handed Jimmy what looked like some money, then entered through a door on the flat frontage of the warehouse.

'Wonder what that was about,' said Lorcan.

'It all looked rather… surreptitious.'

'I'd put good money on there being something fishy going on there.'

Jimmy lit up another cigarette, looking up and down the road, and over at the large shipbuilding yard opposite.

'Should we go and question him?' Jasper asked. 'There's two of us and only one of him.'

'No, he might run away if he sees us approaching, and we want to make sure he's connected to this warehouse. Alice might be in there.'

Finally, Jimmy stubbed out the second cigarette and entered the door to the warehouse.

'Come on,' said Lorcan.

They hurried to the door and let themselves in quietly. Inside, they saw Jimmy entering a room. He hadn't noticed them, so they crept along and peeped in through the open door.

There, handcuffed to a pipe, was Alice. Jasper felt sick. He went to put his finger to his mouth to indicate for her to say nothing, but her look of amazement when she spotted them must have alerted the blond man, for he turned and spotted them.

Before they could do anything, the man, Jim, or whoever he was, screeched, 'Frank!' at the top of his voice.

Chapter Twenty-Seven

Gertie reached the police station out of breath. She pushed the door open roughly and rushed to the desk, where Inspector Toshack seemed to be addressing several uniformed policemen. Some of them she'd never seen on the beat around here.

'What on earth…?' Gardner started, but she didn't give him time to finish.

'I'm pretty sure we've found 'im, the tall blond bloke. He looked like the same one what talked to me last year. Jimmy,' she panted urgently.

'What do you mean?' said Toshack. 'How have you found him?'

'We – me, Annie, Lorcan and Jasper – went to the picture 'ouse to find out if they'd really gone there last night and it looks like they did 'cos the woman saw a tall blond bloke with a gingery beard so we 'eaded to River Road 'cos that's where Charlie'd seen that Frank bloke and found Alice's hankie in the Hampton Court alley and on River Road we saw Jimmy or whoever he is and followed 'im and he went over the bridge and 'eaded to a ware'ouse on the right and the others stayed to watch 'im and I ran 'ere to tell ya.'

She took a deep breath and let out a long sigh.

'All right, all right, calm down now,' said Gardner.

Toshack took two steps towards her, frowning. 'Why didn't you just come and tell us when you found the handkerchief? It's our job to follow possible felons. You'd no idea what you might come up against.'

'Never mind that! Come on, if ya want to catch 'im.'

Toshack shook his head vigorously, turning to his men. 'Right, you've heard where our suspect is. I think it wise if we go there in force since we've no idea what's going on there.'

'It's probably just a wild goose chase,' said Constable Twort. 'And we might be wasting our time when we could follow other leads.'

'This is the best lead we have, Constable,' said Toshack, 'and if Miss Green here says she recognised him, I believe her. We need someone to stay and man the station, though.'

'I'll do that,' said Twort.

'No, you come with us. PC Clampitt, you stay here.' The inspector pointed to a young, lean constable who looked about fifteen, but presumably was a little older.

Clampitt looked more capable of such an operation than the aged Twort, and Gertie wondered whether the inspector didn't trust him to be left alone for some reason. He wasn't very efficient by all accounts.

'Gardner, you drive the police van,' said Toshack, leading the way out. He stopped just before he reached the door, calling, 'You stay put, Miss Green, or go back to the hotel. I just hope that Mr Foley, Mr Jupp and Miss Twine don't do anything rash.'

There's no way I'm staying put, thought Gertie. But she'd better give them a tiny bit of a head start before she ran back to the warehouse.

With this Jimmy chap shouting blue murder, Jasper realised that they had no choice now but to defend themselves, and Alice, and get her out of there.

Jasper surged forward, pipe aloft, delivering a blow to Jim's head that had him reeling and falling to his knees, moaning. Jasper had always hated fighting; he'd loathed having to shoot at people he had no personal quarrel with during the war. He'd had no choice then, and he had no choice now if he wanted to get Alice out of here.

A short, thick-set man ran in, who Jasper guessed was Frank Steel, and behind him came a brute of a bloke. This could be tricky. If only Charlie and Jack had come with them, instead of searching the beach. When the two men produced knives, Jasper stood in front of Alice and Lorcan stepped back.

At that moment, Annie ran in, and spotting Alice on the floor, flew to her. It was enough to distract the two thugs. Lorcan lunged at the bigger of the two men, rapping him across the head with the pipe and kicking him in the stomach, winding him. Jasper delivered a swift blow with his foot to Frank's groin, which had him bent double, shrieking an unintelligible oath, before he stumbled backwards and fell onto his back. All that training they'd done, and the continuing practice in the field when not fighting, had paid off.

The big thug, who had blood running down from his forehead now, righted himself and lunged forward once more, but this time he had both Lorcan and Jasper to contend with. He might be large and strong, but he wasn't very agile. They soon had him on the floor again, moaning, while Frank attempted to scramble away on his hands and knees. Jim was on his side groaning. Lorcan grabbed both knives, which had fallen out of the hands of the other two men, and gave one to Jasper.

'Let's get her out of here,' Jasper said, running back to Alice.

'I can't get these handcuffs off her,' said Annie. 'And Lorcan, you're bleeding.'

Jasper turned to his friend to see he had a cut across his cheek. The big thug's knife must have caught him.

'I'll survive.' Lorcan started tugging at the pipe Alice was tethered to.

Jasper was about to kick it to dislodge it and free her when the door opened once more. He and Lorcan lifted their knives, but it was Inspector Toshack who came running in, with the limp he still displayed on occasion. There were three other policemen with him, including Gardner and Twort. The newcomers looked around at the chaos, mouths open in astonishment.

'Well, I'll be—' Toshack started, but didn't finish before another voice was heard.

A man in rolled-up shirt sleeves, the buttons half undone and his braces off his shoulders, strolled in.

'Steel, what the hell is going on? Oh.'

'Superintendent Crooke?' Toshack and Gardner said at the same time.

Crooke looked accusingly at Twort. 'Why the hell didn't you tell me about this operation?'

' 'Cos I didn't know till just now, sir.'

'So you *are* a snitch?' Gardner glared at Twort, his voice heavy with contempt. 'I thought you might be.'

'Not a snitch,' said Crooke. 'Just keeping an eye on mavericks. I'm in the middle of an operation myself, until you lot intruded.'

'So that's your reason for being half undressed, is it? I don't think so, sir,' the inspector said firmly, and with scorn, as Frank Steel sat up and slumped against the wall, moaning.

'Don't you talk to me like that, Toshack,' said Crooke. 'I'll have you out of your job before the end of the week. I told you not to interfere with the quay attacks inquiry.'

'So, this operation here is connected then, is it?'

'Shut up and mind your own business.'

The door was pushed open again, and Gertie entered. 'Oh my gawd, what's 'appened here? Alice, you're safe.' She hurried over to her.

'What the hell!' said Crooke. 'I'm going now, Toshack, and god help you if—'

The inspector rushed to the door, barring his way. 'I don't think so. Crooke by name, crook by nature.'

'How dare you, you bungling, incompetent idiot. Get out of my way.'

Crooke went to push him, but the sergeant grabbed his arm. 'I don't think so, *sir*.'

Jasper watched all this with fascination, as did Lorcan, Annie, Alice and Gertie. Police against police. This was a first in his experience.

Jim sat up, clutching his head. 'It's Frank Steel who's in charge. I never wanted to kidnap Alice in the first place. I just did as I was told, for fear of being killed.'

'You shut up with ya lies, Jim Marwood. I'm only the middleman,' Frank said in a rasping tone, as if he had a sore throat. 'It's Crooke what's in charge. Has been ever since Gordon Hadley met his maker.'

'I doubt he met his maker,' said Gardner. 'More likely to have gone the other way.'

'Too right,' said Jim. 'He was an evil *bastard*.'

'And you're not, after kidnapping an innocent girl?' Jasper felt compelled to point out.

'I told you, I didn't want to. I liked Alice. I was only trying to get some information about the hotel out of her.'

'You strung 'er along, making out you was a reporter and told her great big fibs,' said Annie. 'I think that makes you an evil… person too.'

'It's lies, all lies, about me being in charge,' said Crooke. 'They're just trying to get me to take the blame. You'll be sorry if you believe them, Toshack.'

'Don't give me that,' said the inspector. 'You're as guilty as hell, you and Twort. This isn't the first time I've had my doubts about you.'

'And you think you're going to arrest me and the others with these few nincompoops?'

'Nope. I've got a few others waiting outside for instructions. Borrowed them from Rustington and East Preston. Seems we're not the only ones who don't trust you, *Crooke*. Yates, ask the other coppers to come in.'

'Yes, sir!' the young constable saluted and marched out, soon returning with the six other policemen.

Toshack turned to the tall blond fellow, still sitting on the ground. 'I presume that you're not only Jamie Sparks and the Jimmy who watched Miss Green play football, but also the Jim who was seen with Pamela Brownlow by Edie.'

Jim looked up. 'I didn't kill Pamela, if that's what you think. That was all Hadley. I didn't even know he'd done it till the day after.'

'Aye, I've no doubt. But now we know that we don't have to look for anyone else called James. If that's your actual name.'

'It is.'

'Do you have the key to unlock these handcuffs on Alice?'

Jim dipped his hand in his pocket and handed Toshack a key.

'Do the honours, Mr Jupp,' said the inspector.

Jasper took the key and hunkered down to release Alice. 'Are you all right?' He felt his heart swell with love as he looked into her big blue eyes, which were brimming with tears. She looked scared and grateful, all at the same time.

'I am now. Thank you.' She flung her arms around him for a brief moment, before releasing him. 'How did you find me?'

'That's a story for later,' said Jasper, helping her up. She wobbled as she stood, so he kept his arm around her waist.

Meanwhile, the suspects were rounded up, including Twort. The big thug was now trying to sit up; his efforts were rewarded with handcuffs.

As this was taking place, a woman entered the room, looking fashionable but scantily dressed. She emitted a little scream and attempted to run away, but Toshack caught her and passed her to Yates to handcuff.

'Long dark hair, worn down, and piercing blue eyes,' said the inspector. 'I think we may have caught our third Fisherman's Quay assailant.' He pointed to a couple of the constables. 'You two, check who else is in here. I suspect there might be others. And Gardner, you stay here with them to have a look around, find evidence. Some of us will be back to assist, as soon as we've processed this lot.'

The constables led the felons out, Superintendent Crooke still throwing threats at them.

'It's lies, all lies. You'll be sorry, Inspector.'

'Don't give me that,' said Toshack. 'You're a disgrace to the police force, Harold Crooke, a disgrace.' After Crooke had been removed, he turned to Sergeant Gardner. 'We will have to reopen the case of Rosie Barleycorn. It seems likely that she was framed. And since Twort lives a few doors away from her, I'm guessing he picked her because she had a likeness to the woman who was responsible.'

'Rosie will go free then?' Annie asked.

'I certainly hope so, Miss Twine. Now, you wait here, and I'll return soon with my motorcar, to drive you and your sister back to the hotel. Then Nurse Bolton can have a look at you, Alice.'

'And Lorcan,' said Annie. 'He's got a cut on his forehead.'

Toshack looked at the porter. 'Aye, you'd better come with us too, Mr Foley. In fact, I'll try to squeeze you all in.'

'Thank you for coming so promptly, Inspector,' Jasper called as they left.

Toshack twisted his head briefly to nod, then was gone.

'Now, maybe you can tell us what happened last night, Alice,' said Jasper.

–

Alice gave a faltering account of what had occurred the night before. It felt like she was relating the plot of a film she had seen, not something that had happened to her. Jasper was still holding onto her, for which she was grateful. She still felt rather wobbly.

Afterwards, Annie gave Alice a quick rundown of what had happened in the last couple of hours.

'I hope they lock them all away for a very long time, so I do,' said Lorcan.

'Especially Crooke,' Jasper added. 'It's even worse when it's someone who's meant to be upholding the law.'

Sergeant Gardner came back in. 'How are you now, Alice? Oh, look at the state of you. Those rotten devils.'

'I feel a lot better now you've all rescued me.' Despite saying this, a few tears fell, which she tried to sniff back. Jasper pulled her in a little closer and rubbed her arm.

'I'll have a word with Mrs Toshack, but I think she'll agree that you and Annie should stay at the hotel until your parents get back,' said the sergeant. 'They're going to be in for a shock when they hear what's happened. What were those rascals planning to do with you, do you know?'

'I don't think they'd decided.'

'Anyway, it looks like we might be here a while, me and the constables, that is. I reckon there's a fair bit of evidence here.'

'Don't suppose you want a hand?' Gertie asked, looking hopeful.

'No thank you, Miss Green… I'll come and see you at the hotel later, Alice, and bring your aunty Mabel. She'll want to make sure you're all right.'

'Thanks, Uncle Barry.'

After he left, she looked around at her fellow workers and her sister. 'Thank you, all of you. Thank you for being so brave and coming to rescue me. Especially you, Jasper and Lorcan.' On an impulse, she kissed Jasper on the cheek.

He put his other arm around her and gave her a hug. 'I was so worried,' he whispered into her ear.

Alice noticed her sister looking over with a small grin and felt her face heat up.

Annie's attention moved to Lorcan. 'That cut looks quite bad. Come 'ere, I've got a clean hankie in me pocket.'

He did as he was told, leaning down a little as she stretched up on her tiptoes and dabbed the still wet drip of blood from the wound. She held the other side of his head, her hand on his black hair, as she did so. 'Like I said, you'll need to get Nurse Bolton to look at that too. She'll likely put some antiseptic on it.'

'It's only a flesh wound, so it is, but it wouldn't hurt, I suppose.'

'You don't want it going septic.'

It was Alice's turn to look on with a little wry amusement, which lifted her a tiny bit from her anxiety. But she was also exhausted and ached all over from sleeping in such an uncomfortable position. She knew there were spare staff bedrooms at the hotel, now some of them had married, and she hoped Mrs Bygrove would let her go straight to bed. She felt like sleeping for a week.

It wasn't long before Inspector Toshack returned.

'Mr Jupp, would you help Alice to the motorcar?'

'Of course, sir.'

Jasper was guiding her slowly along, when she stumbled.

'Right, come on,' he said, placing one arm under her knees and lifting her up.

'Oh, I can walk,' she said, though not displeased by the idea of being carried by him.

'No, I'm not having you falling over.'

Inspector Toshack opened the front door, and Jasper placed her gently on the passenger seat.

'Thank you,' said Alice.

'You're welcome. Any time.' He looked a little abashed and withdrew.

The other four squeezed into the back and the doors were clicked shut.

Annie, sitting behind her, leant forward. 'I'm so glad you're all right.'

'Thank you for coming to find me.'

'Jasper was the leader there, really. He encouraged the others.'

'Thank you, anyway.'

Inspector Toshack got into the driver's seat, and they set off back to the Beach Hotel.

Chapter Twenty-Eight

Annie walked into the staff bedroom that Mrs Bygrove had allocated them back at the hotel and saw that her sister was already lying on one of the beds.

'How are you now?'

'Really tired,' said Alice. 'I know it's not long past three o'clock, but I'm going to have a nap.'

'I don't blame you. Perhaps you'll feel better at dinner time and can come down for something to eat.'

'I 'ope so. What about my shifts though?'

'Mrs Toshack has sorted out covering both of ours for today. She says that she'll see how you feel tomorrow before she decides what to do then. And we can stay till our family returns on Sunday. At least Nurse Bolton's given you the all-clear. How do your wrists and ankles feel now?'

'Still a bit sore, especially where I 'ad the handcuffs. But she said the marks were superficial and gave me some cream to soothe them.'

'Alice, I'm sorry.'

'What for?'

'Walking out with Jasper for a start.'

'That's my fault too,' Alice admitted. 'I did make out that I didn't like him much. I s'pose I was afraid that he wouldn't like me the way I liked him.'

'I should have guessed that. We need to put that right. *I* need to put things right. And I'm sorry I didn't take enough care of you, when you started walking out with Jamie, Jim, whatever.'

'In all fairness, Annie, you did try. I'm sorry for not taking any notice of your wise words. I honestly thought he was quite nice. He could certainly act it.'

'And he acted like a different character for Gertie too. I wonder how many other characters he took on, to take advantage of people.'

Alice tipped her head to the side and said, 'I don't think he was as evil as Frank and Inspector Crooke. He really didn't seem to want to see me hurt. I 'ope the other two get a more severe sentence than him.'

'I certainly 'ope Crooke does.' She stood up. 'I'll leave you to sleep and come up later to see how you are.'

Downstairs, she found Lorcan on his own in the staff-room, slumped in Mrs Leggett's chair at the end of the table, his feet up on one of the benches. He was drinking tea while reading a newspaper.

'Nurse Bolton sorted you out then,' she said, indicating the bandage around his head.

Lorcan placed his feet down and sat up, putting the cup back on the saucer. 'She did so. Just a flesh wound, she said. That carbolic acid don't half sting, though. How's Alice now?'

She sat on a bench next to him. 'A lot better, but tired. She's going to have a sleep.'

'Best thing for her.'

'Thank you for helping to rescue her, Lorcan.'

'Like you said, it was Jasper who led the way.'

'But you didn't 'ave to join in. I'm really grateful you did.' On an impulse, she rose and leant over to kiss him on the cheek, before sitting back down.

What on earth had induced her to do that?

'Sorry, just wanted to show my appreciation,' she said, looking down at the table. She rose once more, feeling she had to do something to relieve the awkwardness. 'I'll just go and let the scullery staff know how Alice is. And Inspector Toshack said he'd take me up to our house at half-past two, so I could collect some clothes and bits.'

As she was about to move off, he leant forward and took her hand. She looked at his face now, to find he was smiling at her.

'You played your part today too, Annie. I knew you were a strong woman, but today showed just how brave you are too. Don't think I've ever really appreciated just how, well, impressive you are. And how caring. I think you hide your soft-hearted side too well sometimes.'

She couldn't quite make eye contact with him, feeling a little overwhelmed by the touch of his hand and his words.

'Well, it don't always pay to show your feelings. But I do care.' She did now summon the courage to look at him. 'I care a lot.'

They locked eyes for a few moments, before he said, 'I was wondering whether we could get a day off together sometime. If you want to.'

Now *that* she hadn't expected. 'Are you over Hetty?'

'Hetty? Who's Hetty?' he said, the smile becoming wider still as he raised his eyebrows.

She chuckled. 'All right, why not?'

He leant back once more. 'That's grand, so it is.'

She headed to the door, grinning and flushed. Despite the drama of earlier, she couldn't help feeling a little bit thrilled. No, a lot thrilled.

Now, what could she do for Alice and Jasper?

–

Alice awoke just before five o'clock in the afternoon. She'd only slept about two hours, but it had been enough to refresh her. And, having eaten little when they'd arrived back earlier, she was now famished and ready for the early dinner.

She spotted the suitcase of clothes on the opposite bed, open, and was relieved she'd have something else to wear. The skirt and blouse she'd been wearing earlier was in a heap on the floor, stained and dusty. She got up and had a wash in the staff bathroom, then got dressed, feeling better still.

She was just putting her hair back up in a bun, after having combed it, when there was a knock at the door.

'Come in,' she called, expecting it to be Annie.

But it was Jasper who peeped around the door.

'Hello, sorry if I've disturbed you. I won't come in, I've just come to ask— Oh, you're up. Good.'

'Yes, and ready for something to eat.'

He opened the door a little wider. 'Annie sent me up to ask you if you were coming down for dinner.'

Why had she sent Jasper and not come herself? Ah, of course. Their earlier conversation. She'd said she needed to put things right. Was this part of it?

'Come in, Jasper. I'm nearly ready.'

He came in cautiously, only a few steps, probably thinking it not quite proper, but she had something she wanted to say to him.

She finished pinning her hair up and then went a few steps towards him. 'I want to apologise, Jasper, for being mean to you in recent months. Especially when you first came home from the war.'

'Well, I suppose I did wonder what I'd done to upset you.'

'You didn't do anything. It was all me. Before you left, I was, you know...' *Go on, just say it!* 'I was very fond of you.'

'And the feeling was mutual,' he said, looking towards the window.

'I thought, with you being gone so long, that I'd maybe not feel like that when you returned, but I did.'

He looked at her now, his mouth slightly open. 'I don't understand.'

'I know it sounds silly, but I was afraid that you wouldn't like me, silly old Alice in Wonderland, always daydreaming.'

He came forward, stopping just short of her. 'But I did. I *do*. I've always liked you. And you're not silly. I know Annie's long had that nickname for you, but I found it endearing. And, well, when I'm near you, I always feel like I'm in some kind of wonderland.'

Alice felt herself welling up. 'You do?'

He took her hands. 'Yes, of course. You being annoyed with me really upset me.'

'I am *so* sorry I was so daft about it. I know we did get on before you left, but I didn't think that someone like you, who speaks so nicely and is more educated than me would, well, like me in that way, or think I was interesting.'

'Someone like me? I'm nothing special, Alice. So, my family had a few shops, which they lost. In a way, I'm glad they did, otherwise I would have ended up helping to run the family business and would never have come here to work. Then I would never have met you.'

'Oh Jasper.'

'I'm surprised you still think like that, with Hetty having married the son of a shipping magnate.'

'I s'pose. But that's clever Hetty, not me. And then, when you went out with Annie, I, well, I dreaded you ending up together forever, knowing how upsetting that would be for me. I didn't know you were only friends really.'

He took her in his arms. She revelled in the feeling of warmth and affection, which she could appreciate more now than this morning, when they'd been so close to danger.

'To me, you're everything. Not silly Alice in Wonderland, but my *lovely*, wonderful Alice. Earlier today, when we realised something had happened to you, it tore at my heart. I couldn't bear the thought of you being hurt.'

He moved back a little, then moved in again, to kiss her lips briefly. It made her feel giddy, but in a good way now.

They gazed into each other's eyes for a few moments before Jasper said, 'Come on, you must be starving.'

'I am. Are you having dinner now too?'

'Yes. We can sit together and maybe plan an afternoon out, for when you're feeling better.'

'Yes, I'd like that.'

Chapter Twenty-Nine

By five to eleven on the morning of the first Remembrance Day, staff at the Beach Hotel were keeping an eye on the clocks around the building. The few guests in the conservatory, enjoying morning coffee, and those in the guest lounge, were also aware of the time.

As the minute hand crept towards its destination, the chatter and activity quietened, and the guests in the lounge came out into the foyer, where male staff members were already standing to attention. In the conservatory, the guests who were sitting, stood, ready for the moment.

Several second hands reached twelve, all at slightly different times, then all around the hotel downstairs the various chimes were heard, particularly that of the grandfather clock that stood between the lounge and the cloakroom in the foyer.

In the conservatory, Jerry Winborn, and his brother Johnny, who had returned to work in October, stood together by the dresser, both of them staring out of the windows.

In the foyer, porters Leslie and Stanley Morris, along with Jasper Jupp and Lorcan Foley, stood in a line in front of the desk, with desk clerk Stuart Coulter. Charlie Cobbett, who'd once been a porter and had come over from the garage for the occasion, stood at the end, his Distinguished Conduct Medal proudly displayed on his jacket. Peter Smith, although now a singer, had also dropped in for the occasion, and was standing next to Charlie.

In the kitchen, Joseph Norris stood to attention, his hands behind his back.

The rest of the staff, whether on a shift or not, stood in the various rooms downstairs.

All was still as they silently recalled family, friends and fellow soldiers, no longer with them because of the war.

They remembered waiter Anton Martin, second chef Alex Tuppen and porter James Wood, all killed at the Battle of the Boar's Head in June 1916. They remembered Alan Drew, the head porter, killed at the Battle of Kemmel in April 1918.

Major Thomas, who had his eye on the time, had borrowed a bugle from one of Mr Janus's musicians. When the two minutes were up, he played the 'Last Post', to signify the end, as he had on some occasions as a young soldier.

When it was over, those assembled carried on with their day, though all were subdued for a while after, and only slowly did the chatter start up once more.

Epilogue

'Well, that's the evening buffet all served up for the guests,' said Lili, as she entered the conservatory, where the staff Christmas buffet was already laid out. 'Jerry and Johnny can take care of it now. And they'll come along afterwards.'

'It's a good job there are only half-a-dozen rooms occupied today and tomorrow,' said Bridget Turnbull.

'Yep, but we're filling up again on the twenty-seventh,' said Gertie. 'So, we'd better take advantage of the next coupla days.'

Some tables had been laid out in a long line, to accommodate all the staff members. Annie and Alice were already sitting down next to each other, with Lorcan and Jasper either side of them. The hotel was closed to non-residents today, so staff members working all over the hotel would be joining them. Several porters were taking short turns in the foyer in case of an emergency, or guest request.

'It's good of Mrs Toshack to organise this Christmas do for us,' said Lorcan.

'We've had 'em before,' Annie pointed out. 'Even before you went to war.'

'Not like this. And not in the conservatory.'

'Things have changed since Mr Bygrove passed on,' she said.

'They certainly have.'

While Lorcan and Jasper chatted to the people on the other side of each of them, Annie leant towards her sister. 'It's been a lovely Christmas this year.'

'The best,' said Alice. 'What time are Mum and Dad doing dinner tomorrow?'

'Three o'clock. We'll be back from our shift by then. It'll be really special this year, our Boxing Day with them, being able to take Lorcan and Jasper with us.'

'I'm so 'appy that our family's taken such a shine to 'em both.'

Annie wrapped her arm around Alice's. 'I think that Lorcan and Jasper being so nice *might* 'ave something to do with that.'

Alice chuckled. 'Yep! Are you going to tell people our news today?'

'We 'adn't decided, 'ad we?'

Alice tapped Jasper's arm to get his attention, and her sister did the same to Lorcan.

'Well,' said Annie. 'Shall we?'

They both knew what she was talking about.

'Aye,' said Lorcan. 'It seems the right time.'

Jasper nodded enthusiastically. 'It's finding the right moment.'

–

Helen and Sam Toshack entered the conservatory with Dorothy, a very excited Arthur and the nursemaid, Vera.

'This all looks lovely,' said Helen, turning on the spot as she regarded first the decoration, then the food laid out on tables by the inside wall.

'You've got Mrs Turnbull, Mrs Leggett, Gertie and Nurse Bolton to thank for that,' Phoebe called over from one end of the table.

'And Mrs Norris, Joseph, Will and Jack to thank for the food,' Mrs Turnbull added.

'Well, it's *all* wonderful,' said Helen.

'Here's Fanny, Walter and Elsie,' Jack called, as the three of them came through the door.

'Gee, this looks swell,' said Walter, as an excited Elsie ran to join Dorothy and Arthur.

'Are you feeling better now, Fanny?' Phoebe called over.

'Yes, the morning sickness doesn't last all day any more. 'Opefully it'll be gone altogether soon.' She patted her tummy, where a bump was just beginning to show.

They joined Gertie, who had saved seats for them.

Just behind them, came Edie and Charlie.

'Did you have a good time with your parents?' Lorcan called.

'Yep,' said Charlie. 'Good old goose and plum pudding, like they 'ave every year. Can't beat it.'

Some of the people still standing found seats, while others remained standing to chat.

Through the door now came Lili and Rhodri, who'd spent the afternoon with his brother and his aunt and uncle.

Finally, Hetty and Victor Perryman entered, bearing several boxes of chocolates, each tied with a red bow. Helen went to greet them.

'I'm so glad Mrs Toshack invited Hetty,' Annie told Alice. 'Even though she don't work here no more.'

'It's great to see her. I miss her not being in the room next door.'

'We've brought chocolates for everyone to share,' Hetty called, eliciting a chorus of 'oohs' and cheers from the gathering.

'Everyone, please, do come and help yourselves to a glass of wine or cordial,' Helen announced. 'Whichever you fancy.'

People rose to help themselves to the glasses set out on trays on two tables, chatting happily as they did so.

'Mummy, can I try a glass of wine?' asked Dorothy.

Helen glanced at Sam, who widened his eyes and grinned. 'No, I'm sorry, you're too young as yet,' she told her daughter. 'And there are some very nice cordials there. Especially the elderflower.'

Dorothy stuck her bottom lip out and flounced off.

'Oh dear, she's getting to that age,' said Sam.

After a few minutes, when everyone seemed to be holding a glass, Helen went to stand by the outer doors and coughed loudly to get their attention.

'This is the first Christmas since 1914 that we've all been together.' She stalled for a moment, as if composing herself. Sam placed his arm around her, and she continued. 'So much has happened since then.'

'Like Nancy Astor being the first woman to take her seat in the House of Commons,' Gertie called out.

'Indeed. One of the many, many things that have occurred.' Helen stalled again, trying to find the words.

Edie joined her, putting her arm through Helen's. 'I know so much has certainly changed since I got off the train in Littlehampton in June 1914. And the way things are going, it looks like the nineteen-twenties could be an exciting decade.'

Annie and Alice looked at each other, grinning.

Annie stood up. 'I think the nineteen-twenties will be a very exciting time for us.' She looked at her sister and their sweethearts, who all rose from their seats.

'We have some news,' said Lorcan. 'Yesterday, me and Annie got engaged.'

'And so did Alice and I,' Jasper added.

The two couples snuggled up and beamed, as the room broke out in raucous cheering, myriad good wishes and much hand shaking and hugging.

When the congratulations had died down, Edie coughed to get their attention. 'Let's raise our glasses to the Beach Hotel, and whatever the future brings.'

'To the Beach Hotel,' they all echoed enthusiastically.

A Letter from Francesca

Dear Reader,

11 November 1918 would have marked the end of an era for many people, not least for the characters of the Beach Hotel, as well as marking the fast approach of the end of a decade.

It was the conclusion to a period of history that the men returning from war would be grateful to see the back of. Some, of course, never returned, like my paternal great grandfather, Lorenzo Capaldi, killed in January 1915, when my father was only eleven months old. Many who survived would long be haunted by their experiences, like Johnny Winborn in this book.

I'm sure the women would have been tremendously relieved to have the men home. Despite this, there would have been a good deal of re-adjusting to do, especially for those who'd taken on men's jobs. Even though the men returned in dribs and drabs, it must have taken some time for the men and women alike to get back into the rhythm of life together. I hope that the real staff at the Beach Hotel were able to celebrate as many happy occasions as my characters.

It's not surprising that the next decade became known as the 'Roaring Twenties', when life got livelier, maybe in an effort to forget the past, and there was certainly a rapid cultural and social change.

Thank you to all the readers who've sent me messages and supported me on social media. I'm always happy to chat. If you'd like to contact me to discuss the novels, or discover more about them, you can find me here:

Website and blog: www.francesca-capaldi.com/
Facebook: www.facebook.com/FrancescaCapaldiAuthor
Twitter: @FCapaldiBurgess
Instagram: francesca.capaldi.burgess
TikTok: @francesca.capaldi.author

Acknowledgements

A big thank you to Eilidh Beaton, the voice actor who does a wonderful job for the audio versions of my Beach Hotel books.

Much appreciation to Mike and Lucy at Pier Road Coffee & Art in Littlehampton, where I do book launch signings, and where I'm now an honorary patron.

Thank you to all the bloggers who've taken part in my blog tours, particularly Rachel Gilbey of Rachel's Random Resources, who organises them.

I'm very grateful to the Library of Wales for its historical newspapers, the Library of Scotland for its old maps, to the Ancestry website for all the relevant information it provides and to the Met Office for its historical weather records. Also, the museum and library in Littlehampton, for the information I've discovered within them. Thank you to the Facebook group Bygone Littlehampton, an excellent community history page with wonderfully evocative old photos.

Big thanks to The Romantic Novelists' Association and The Society of Women Writers and Journalists, for their parts in my writing career.

Cheers to all my writing friends, especially Elaine Roberts, Angela Johnson, Karen Aldous, Sarah Stephenson, Natalie Kleinman and Vivien Brown. Thank you to the late Elaine Everest for starting me off on my publishing journey.

Thank you to my dad, Giuseppe, and my history teacher, Miss English, for sparking my love of history, and to my mum, Maureen, for all the off-the-cuff storytelling that encouraged me to make up my own stories. All gone but never forgotten.

Finally, a big thank you to Jennie and Keshini and everyone at Hera Books.